MODERN HUMANITIES RESEARCH ASSOCIATION
CRITICAL TEXTS
VOLUME 59

ELIZA HAYWOOD, *THE FORTUNATE FOUNDLINGS*

Eliza Haywood,
The Fortunate Foundlings

Edited by Carol Stewart

Modern Humanities Research Association
Critical Texts 59
2018

Published by

The Modern Humanities Research Association
Salisbury House
Station Road
Cambridge CB1 2LA
United Kingdom

© Modern Humanities Research Association 2018

Copy-Editor: Anna Davies

First published 2018

ISBN 978-1-78188-267-2

CONTENTS

ACKNOWLEDGEMENTS

First, I would like to thank Gerard Lowe, editor at the Modern Humanities Research Association, for his patience with this project. I am particularly grateful to Ian Campbell Ross for his ongoing support and advice. Thanks are due to Murray Pittock and Daniel Szeci, as well as the staff at the British Library, who helped me to locate some elusive Jacobites.

C.S., January 2018

INTRODUCTION

The last thirty years have seen a remarkable recovery from obscurity for Eliza Haywood, one of the eighteenth century's most prolific authors. Few writers have benefitted more from the recognition of women's contribution to the emergence of the novel as a genre, a recognition central to such studies as Dale Spender's *Mothers of the Novel* (1986) and Ros Ballaster's *Seductive Forms* (1992).[1] Some twenty-five titles, out of seventy-two works attributed to Haywood, have appeared in scholarly editions since the 1980s. Haywood's longest and arguably most technically accomplished novel, *The History of Miss Betsy Thoughtless* (1751), has been in print since 1986, and the reader can now also access many of the early, racier novellas that made the author's name in the 1720s, or such inventive, hard-to-categorize works as *Adventures of Eovaai, Princess of Ijaveo* (1736), a mixture of political satire and oriental fable.[2] A major step forward, in terms of making a range of Haywood's writing more accessible, came in 2000–2001 with the publication of *Selected Works of Eliza Haywood I* and *II*.[3] Six volumes included her periodicals *The Female Spectator* (1744–46) and *The Parrot* (1746); the series of fictional letters entitled *Epistles for the Ladies* (1748); conduct-books *The Wife* (1756) and *The Husband* (1756); *The Dramatic Historiographer* (1735), her guide to popular plays of the period; and miscellaneous writing from 1729–43. The territory was opened up further by Patrick Spedding's comprehensive *Bibliography of Eliza Haywood* (2004).[4] Kathryn R. King's pioneering *Political Biography of Eliza Haywood* (2012) brought detailed research and scholarship to bear on Haywood's literary career, and showed that from the mid-1740s the author was

---

[1] Dale Spender, *Mothers of the Novel: 100 Good Women Writers before Jane Austen* (London: Pandora, 1986); Ros Ballaster, *Seductive Forms: Women's Amatory Fiction from 1684–1740* (Oxford: Oxford University Press, 1992).
[2] Eliza Haywood, *The History of Miss Betsy Thoughtless*, introd. by Dale Spender (London: Pandora, 1986); Eliza Haywood, *Adventures of Eovaai, Princess of Ijaveo: A Pre-Adamitical History*, ed. by Earla Wilputte (Peterborough, Ont.: Broadview, 1999).
[3] Eliza Haywood, *Selected Works of Eliza Haywood I*, ed. by Alexander Pettit, 3 vols (London: Pickering & Chatto, 2000), I: *Miscellaneous Writings, 1725–43*, ed. by Alexander Pettit; II: Epistles for the Ladies, ed. by Alexander Pettit and Christine Blouch; III: *The Wife, The Husband and The Young Lady*, ed. by Alexander Pettit and Margo Collins. Eliza Haywood, *Selected Works of Eliza Haywood II*, 3 vols, ed. by Alexander Pettit (London: Pickering & Chatto, 2001): I, *The Dramatic Historiographer* and *The Parrot*, ed. by Christine Blouch, Alexander Pettit, and Rebecca Sayers Hanson; II–III: *The Female Spectator*, ed. by Kathryn R. King and Alexander Pettit..
[4] Patrick Spedding, *A Bibliography of Eliza Haywood* (London: Pickering & Chatto, 2004).

increasingly involved in writing for the Patriot Opposition.[5] A recent addition
is an edition of *The Invisible Spy* (1755), Haywood's substantial contribution to
Opposition propaganda.[6] Haywood scholarship has gone hand in hand with
the publication of new editions, and we are now, perhaps, beginning to gain
some perspective on a woman who was professional, politically engaged, and
innovative, and who gave the female situation in her own time repeated and
searching attention. Yet there are still many gaps — around two-thirds of her
published output — and much that remains to be discovered. This volume
brings together *The Fortunate Foundlings*, a novel that has received little critical
attention, and *A Letter from H — G — g, Esq.*, the pamphlet for which Haywood
was arrested in 1750.[7] The first of these is a mix of military history and romance,
an implied critique of the codes that governed women's behaviour, and a work
of teasing political allusion. The latter is another political intervention, though,
again, less straightforward in its intentions than is at first apparent.

As is almost always the case with Haywood, we know little about her personal
circumstances at the time of writing or publishing *The Fortunate Foundlings*.
After the prolific 1720s, acting at the Little Theatre in the Haymarket in the
1730s, and *Eovaai*, she falls silent for five years, reappearing in the world of print
in 1741 with *Anti-Pamela: or, Feigned Innocence Detected*, a satiric response to
Samuel Richardson's *Pamela* (1740). Critics have speculated about the reason
for that silence, with a period abroad, or feeling crushed by Alexander Pope's
satirical portrait of her in the *Dunciad*, or going into prostitution, all being
offered as explanations, though without proof. Haywood's reference to a 'severe
Indisposition' that interrupted her translation of Charles de Fieux, chevalier de
Mouhy's *La Paysanne Parvenue* (1735–36) before 1740 is the closest we have to
an account of the missing years.[8] Her version was published as *The Virtuous
Villager* in 1742. Other publications from the early 1740s are *The Sopha* (1743),
a translation of Claude-Prosper Jolyot de Crébillon's erotic novel *Le Sopha,
Conte Moral* (1742); all or part of the three-volume *Memoirs of an Unfortunate
Young Nobleman* (1743), an account of the sensational life and disinheritance of
James Annesley, heir to the title of Lord Altham; the conduct-book *A Present*

---

[5]   Kathryn R. King, *A Political Biography of Eliza Haywood* (London: Pickering & Chatto,
2012).
[6]   Eliza Haywood, *The Invisible Spy*, ed. by Carol Stewart (London: Pickering & Chatto,
2014).
[7]   Critical articles on *The Fortunate Foundlings* are Earla Wilputte, ' "Room to Fable Upon":
The History of Charles XII of Sweden in Eliza Haywood's *The Fortunate Foundlings*',
The Eighteenth-Century Novel, 2 (2002), pp. 23–44; and Carol Stewart, 'Eliza Haywood's
The Fortunate Foundlings: A Jacobite Novel', *ECL*, 37.1 (2013), pp. 51–71. The novel is also
discussed by Rachel Carnell in *Partisan Politics, Narrative Realism and the Rise of the British
Novel* (Basingstoke: Palgrave Macmillan, 2006), pp. 143–52.
[8]   Patrick Spedding, *A Bibliography of Eliza Haywood* (London: Pickering & Chatto, 2004),
pp. 355–56.

for a Servant-Maid (1743); and possibly *The Lady's Drawing Room* (1743), which bears striking similarities to her earlier work, *The Tea-Table* (1725).[9] Between 1741 and 1744 she was also what the eighteenth century called a bookseller — in modern terms, more like a publisher — at the Sign of Fame in the Piazza of Covent Garden, selling pamphlets and longer works attacking Prime Minister Sir Robert Walpole, who finally resigned in 1742; romances translated from the French; and some pornographic wares. A possible indication of Haywood's prosperity at this time is the fact that she occupied a substantial four-storey residence: who might have shared the house with her is unknown. From an advertisement for the sale of her household goods from April 1744 we know that she owned a four-poster bed lined with satin, along with a number of feather beds, chests of drawers, card-tables, a grandfather clock, and other furniture indicative of genteel status. The shop itself was well appointed and occupied a commercially desirable site at the corner of Russell Street and the Great Piazza.[10] Again, we don't know why she ceased business, though the date of the sale could suggest that she wasn't able to pay the quarterly instalment of rent due in April. She must have begun work on *The Female Spectator* (1744–46), her ambitious periodical, while still trading.

The Fortunate Foundlings, published in January 1744, begins fifty-six years earlier in the 'ever memorable' year of 1688: the year of Prince William of Orange's assumption of the English throne and James II's flight to France. Dorilaus, a gentleman living in retirement in the country, finds a baby boy and girl left in a basket in his garden, with only a note to assure him they are of good family, and that they are brother and sister. He takes them in and raises them as his own. The boy, Horatio, reaches an age when he is expected to go to university, but chooses to become a soldier, and leaves to join the armies of John Churchill, first Duke of Marlborough (1650–1722) in Flanders. After Horatio has left, Dorilaus becomes enamoured of Louisa, Horatio's sister, and asks her to marry him. Horrified, Louisa flees and takes up employment as a seamstress in London, next becoming a companion to a lady, Melanthe, who wishes to travel in Europe. Meanwhile, Horatio is taken prisoner by the French at the Battle of Blenheim in 1704. He becomes a gentleman of the bedchamber to James Francis Edward Stuart (1688–1766), son of James II, in exile at his court at Saint-Germain-en-Laye. Here he falls in love with (the fictional) Charlotta de Palfoy, maid of honour to Princess Louisa, daughter of the late king. When Charlotta's father discovers their relationship, Horatio leaves to join the army of Charles XII of Sweden (1682–1718) in the campaigns of the Great Northern War, and follows the Swedish monarch as he installs Stanislaus Leszczyński

---

[9]   The first three titles are listed in Spedding's *Bibliography*, while the last is an attribution suggested by King, p. 109.
[10]   King, pp. 100–02.

(1677–1766) as king of Poland. After Charles XII's defeat at the Battle of Poltava in 1709, Horatio is taken prisoner by Russians under Tsar Peter, and spends months incarcerated in St Petersburg. Louisa, meanwhile, moves from the court at Vienna to that of Venice. She and a M. du Plessis fall in love but, conscious of her low social status, she initially rejects his offer of marriage. Pursued by a would-be seducer, Louisa is placed in a convent, becomes a virtual prisoner thanks to the machinations of the nuns, escapes, and makes her way to Paris. In the end both Horatio and Louisa are reunited with their true loves and find out the secret of their parentage. Dorilaus, as we may have expected, is their real father, and the foundlings are his illegitimate children by Matilda, a Roman Catholic woman now married, and near death, in Ireland.

In outline, then, the story is a conventional one in terms of eighteenth-century fiction, though the familiarity of the plot only underlines its appeal for contemporary readers. Abandoned, orphaned, and illegitimate children abound, and eponymous foundlings or bastards include Daniel Defoe's Colonel Jack, Henry Fielding's Tom Jones, Fanny Burney's Evelina, Tobias Smollett's Humphry Clinker and Charlotte Smith's Emmeline. The trope has been seen as indicative of the middle-class quest to detach virtue from birth: we might also read it as symptomatic of the long shift from collective to individualist values. Horatio proves his worth as a man on the battlefields of Europe while Louisa proves hers by establishing her moral superiority to her mistress. Both siblings profess to attach great importance to duty, gratitude and obedience even as Louisa rejects her benefactor's offer of marriage and Horatio defies his summons home. Their individual choices prove to be compatible, in the end, and as is so often the case, with acceptance by authority and social respectability. The challenge posed to authority is any case never very great: we are not likely to feel that Horatio does anything wrong by remaining loyal to the king he serves, or that Louisa errs by rejecting Dorilaus's sudden advances. The reader coming to *The Fortunate Foundlings* acquainted with Haywood's more obviously provocative novellas from the 1720s may well feel that something has been lost. Neither Horatio nor Louisa shows any signs of giving way to the passions that drove Haywood's earlier protagonists. There are no 'warm' scenes. The novel seems true to its prefatory claim to present exemplary characters who should serve as enticements to virtue.

For the names of the French nobility whom Haywood has frequenting the court at Saint-Germain-en-Laye, it seems likely that she drew on scandalous memoirs such as Roger de Rabutin, comte de Bussy's *Histoire Amoureuse des Gaules* (1665), Marie Catherine La Mothe, comtesse d'Aulnoy's *Mémoires des Aventures singulières de la cour de France* (1692), and Marie-Madeleine Pioche de la Vergne, comtesse de Lafayette's *Histoire de Madame Henriette d'Angleterre* (1720), all of which were available in English, the first often in the form of selections.[11] From these sources, Haywood borrowed names only: the intrigues they recount play little part in her novel. David Baker, Haywood's earliest biographer, placed *The Fortunate Foundlings* among Haywood's 'reformed' writing, and Mary Anne Schofield, writing in the 1980s, found the characters 'sanctimonious'.[12] We might now see the novel as cannily marketed for the new 'polite' taste, a taste fostered by Samuel Richardson's *Pamela* (1740). Haywood was undoubtedly careful about packaging, presenting the work for publication without her name on the title page. While the novellas of the 1720s typically did bear Haywood's name, the works published after 1740 did not. Possibly the author decided that her name, and her reputation as a scandalous writer, could deter buyers. Haywood's perceived moralism has no doubt contributed to the novel's critical neglect, yet in its own way *The Fortunate Foundlings* questions the *status quo*, offering alternative models of behaviour and different political choices.

Placing the narrative outside England allows Haywood to explore the scope and influence allowed to women elsewhere, primarily in the French salon. In the salon, or the *ruelle*, men and women mix and converse, with women's refined and delicate manners working, it was thought, to create the *honnête homme*. The idea that women's company would have a softening and refining effect on an otherwise rough and boorish masculinity had been popularised by Joseph Addison in the *Spectator*, but in early eighteenth-century England there were no salons, no distinctively feminine spaces for mixed company: possible domestic equivalents might be the tea-table, or the dining room. Salon culture in Britain and Ireland virtually disappeared between 1660 and 1740.[13] Once she is at court abroad, though, Louisa learns how to receive 'a multiplicity of company', male and female, without compromising her reputation. Out in the 'great world', she enjoys showing her skills in dancing, singing and music, and receiving admirers. Her position as the companion of the pleasure-seeking Melanthe legitimises a female equivalent of the Grand Tour: Louisa has 'a great desire to see foreign parts'. When the season of carnival approaches Melanthe heads for Venice, where Louisa is courted by the perfidious Count de Bellfleur

---

[11] Anonymous translations of and selections from *Histoire Amoureuse des Gaules* appeared as *The Amorous History of the Gauls: Written in French by Roger de Rabutin, Count de Bussy, And now translated into English* (London, 1725); and *The History of the Amours of the French Court, viz. of Madam de la Valliere, Madam de Olonne, Madam de Chastillion, Madam de Sevigny, With the Intrigues of Several Other Persons of Great Quality in the Palace-Royal* (London, 1684). A translation of d'Aulnoy by 'Mr. A. B.' was published as *Memoires of the Court of France* (London, 1697), and Lafayette's *Histoire* was translated as *Fatal Gallantry: or, The Secret History of Henrietta Princess of England* (London, 1722).
[12] David Erskine Baker, *The Companion to the Play-House* (1764), n.p.; Mary Anne Schofield, *Eliza Haywood* (Boston: Twayne, 1985), pp. 86–87.
[13] See Amy Prendergast, *Literary Salons across Britain and Ireland in the Long Eighteenth Century* (Basingstoke: Palgrave Macmillan, 2015), p. 45.

and, subsequently, the honourable du Plessis. Like so many of Haywood's works, *The Fortunate Foundlings* makes an implicit case for female experience, female education and the right to choose. Louisa's lone, adventurous journey across Italy and France symbolizes her independence. Even though the narrative seems equally weighted between Horatio and Louisa, male and female, the balance favours women. Horatio is a feminized man, awed by the moral discriminations of Charlotta: in true salon style, the woman educates the man. In a sign of the power of love — the woman's realm — he is stricken and confined to his bed when Charlotta's father sends her away. When Horatio is held in a dungeon in St Petersburg it is a woman, the Russian Prince Menzikoff's mistress Edella, who has him released and contrives better treatment for the prisoners. Even Charles XII, whom Voltaire, in his very popular *Histoire de Charles XII* (1731), portrayed as an iron martial hero, is feminized in Haywood's account. He carries a picture of James II's daughter, Princess Louisa, next to his heart, snatching his eyes away from it 'as fearing to be too much softened'. It is significant, also, that Louisa, the female foundling, is still illegitimate at the novel's close. As Lisa Zunshine has noted, the female bastard is a rarity in eighteenth-century fiction.[14] Lost male children were allowed to stay illegitimate, but a girl's sexual virtue was predicated on the known chastity of her female ancestors. In *The Fortunate Foundlings*, then, Louisa's moral character is autonomous; and Haywood is at pains to show, at the end of the novel, that Matilda's sexual lapse is compatible, later, with wifely fidelity and charitable works.

The code of manners Haywood represents is a different kind of 'politeness', an alternative to the domesticated virtue and the idealisation of marriage more commonly promoted in the Whig tradition, primarily by Addison and Steele in *The Spectator*, and later in the novels of Samuel Richardson and Henry Fielding. Haywood's novel draws on the salon romance convention that men should not freely make declarations of love, and nor should women encourage them — both Louisa and Charlotta adhere to this rule. As Theanor explains in Madeleine de Scudéry's *Clélie* (translated into English as *Clelia*, and attributed to Georges de Scudéry): 'the best way or course to prove one's love, is by a thousand cares, and a thousand services, sighs, glances, and a thousand other ways more effectual than words, without offending a fair person, who will not have the respect due to her, lost'.[15] Women must be treated with deference. The potential power in matters of love and courtship this code might give women would be explored again in Charlotte Lennox's *The Female Quixote* (1752). Male suitors might expect to wait years for a show of affection. Moreover, for Haywood,

---

[14] Lisa Zunshine, *Bastards and Foundlings: Illegitimacy in Eighteenth-Century England* (Columbus: Ohio State University Press, 2005), p. 13.
[15] *Clelia, An Excellent Romance: The Whole Work in Five Parts ... Written in* French *by the Exquisite Pen of* Monsieur de Scudery, *Governour of Nostredame de la Garde* (1678), Part IV, Book III, p. 576.

women at the French court are apparently allowed 'innocent liberties which the French ladies, above those of any other nation in the world, enjoy'. Haywood would expand on this theme in Book V of *The Female Spectator*, published in September 1744, where she advises the mother of an erring daughter to send her to France. Haywood's ideals are not at home in England. Horatio, taken prisoner by the French after the Battle of Blenheim, is less than eager to return to his native country, being charmed by the 'politeness and gallantry' of his captors. At the Stuart court, he learns a 'manly way of thinking'. He is inspired by a love of *la gloire* and military heroism. Again, one thinks of the contrast with Richard Steele's very different idea of the character of a military man in *The Christian Hero*, which was itself written to draw a contrast between Louis XIV and William III. Steele's ideals are temperance and moderation: 'to assault without Fear, Pursue without Cruelty, and Stab without Hatred'.[16] The French tradition — or her idea of it — seems far more congenial for Haywood. Siting the action in continental Europe allowed Haywood to suggest that there were other ways of doing things.

For eighteenth-century writers the past, sometimes even the past of a hundred years previously, was always available as a context for current political speculation and argument. European locations, people and events Haywood pictures in her novel are extraordinarily resonant and can be related to political choices in the 1740s. The siblings' travels and adventures take in the chief dynastic rivals — Bourbon and Habsburg — whose interests and ambitions shaped much of seventeenth- and eighteenth-century political life. In 1744, Britain was involved in another war of succession, that following the death of the last male Habsburg, the Holy Roman Emperor Charles VI (1685–1740). Britain supported the cause of the Archduchess Maria Theresa (1717–1780), his daughter, against France, Prussia and Bavaria. The Battle of Blenheim was one episode in the War of the Spanish Succession (1701–1714), a war triggered by the death of the last Habsburg king of Spain. When Carlos II of Spain died childless, he bequeathed the throne to Philippe, duc d'Anjou, grandson of Louis XIV. Fears that Bourbon domination would disrupt the much-treasured 'balance of power' in Europe brought the Netherlands, France, Spain, Bavaria, Austria, Portugal and Savoy into a long war. That war ended in a compromise — or as Whigs tended to see it, a defeat — when Philip was recognized as king of Spain as long as he renounced the French throne. The twenty-one year conflict in which Charles XII of Sweden played a leading role involved Poland-Lithuania, Denmark, Saxony, Sweden and Muscovy in a contest for control of the Baltic regions, but Haywood is particularly focussed on the rivalry for the monarchy of Poland-Lithuania. From early modern times comparisons were

---

[16] Richard Steele, *The Christian Hero*, ed. by Rae Blanchard (London: Oxford University Press, 1932), p. 10.

made between Poland-Lithuania and Britain as both had 'mixed' constitutions in which neither the monarch nor parliament had complete control.[17] Following the death of John III Sobieski in 1696, and with the male line extinct, Frederick Augustus, Elector of Saxony was one candidate while François-Louis, prince de Conti (1664–1709), was favoured by his cousin Louis XIV. Conti was elected, but not crowned, while Augustus, thanks mainly to his bribery of the *szlachta* — the class of legally privileged nobility who had the right to vote for a king — achieved election and coronation. Augustus subsequently allied himself with Tsar Peter I and Frederick IV of Denmark to attack Charles XII, but after a series of military defeats he was deposed and the Swedish king installed Stanislaus in his place in 1704. The choice of (an entirely unparticularized) Venice as a location for Louisa's adventures is not accidental. As a republic, Venice enjoyed a reputation for openness and tolerance of foreigners, as well as stable government combining monarchy, aristocracy and democracy. It is as if Haywood canvassed every possible method of succession and governance: hereditary, by conquest, by election, with and without a monarch.

In the 1740s there were, depending on one's politics, one, two, or possibly three potential heirs to the British throne, each of whom offered an alternative to the unpopular Hanoverian incumbent, George II. One was James Francis Edward Stuart, pictured very sympathetically in *The Fortunate Foundlings*, though hardly as an active contender for the monarchy, even though he would only have been a young man between 1704 and 1709. At the time of the novel's publication, rather than its setting, he was fifty-six years old. The second was his son, Charles Edward Stuart (1720–1788), pictured as a military leader in armour, and with the star and garter indicating his entitlement to the throne, in portraits dating from the mid-1730s. Such portraits were part of a very conscious propaganda exercise by his father, and were circulated as prints.[18] Charles's presence at the Siege of Gaeta in 1734, during the War of the Polish Succession, was used to underline his identity as a warrior. In the late 1730s another candidate emerged in the shape of Frederick, Prince of Wales (1707–1751). The Prince was effectively estranged from his mother and father, breaking with them openly in 1737, and decisively separated from the current, unpopular Hanoverian monarchy. Frederick became the somewhat unlikely figurehead of the Patriot Opposition to Prime Minister Sir Robert Walpole. In *The Craftsman* (1726–1731), *A Letter on the Spirit of Patriotism* (1736), and *The Idea of a Patriot King*, circulated in manuscript in 1738, Henry St John, Viscount

---

[17] See Benedict Wagner-Rundell, 'Liberty, Virtue and the Chosen People: British and Polish Republicanism in the Early Eighteenth Century', in *Britain and Poland–Lithuania: Contact and Comparison from the Middle Ages to 1795*, ed. by Richard Unger (Leiden: Brill, 2008), pp. 197–214.

[18] Robin Nicholson, *Bonnie Prince Charlie and the Making of a Myth: A Study in Portraiture, 1720–1792* (Lewisburg: Bucknell University Press, 2002), p. 42.

Bolingbroke, the chief architect of 'Patriotism', argued that distinctions of Whig and Tory should be set aside, and the country united under a king who would stand for an ideal of selfless public activity. Haywood's own *Eovaai* was one of the earliest works to promote Frederick as the 'people's prince'.[19] He appears as the heroic rescuer of the eponymous princess, embodying a spirit of national renewal. In *The Fortunate Foundlings* Charles XII of Sweden draws together something of both Stuart and Hanoverian claimants. In his own time, Charles XII had been 'the valiant Swede' in Jacobite songs, and, as a Protestant king who might support the Stuart cause, a desirable ally. In 1715, prominent Tories approached the Swedish ambassador and offered loans to aid the Swedish war effort in the Baltic on the understanding that Charles would invade England when he could spare the resources.[20] He was a formidable warrior-king who, in the novel, could stand as a proxy for the Stuart Charles. On the other hand, Haywood underlines the disinterestedness of his conquests, pointing up the necessary qualification for a Patriot king.

It could be said that the issue of entitlement to the throne never really receded in England until after Charles Edward Stuart's death in 1788.[21] In the 1740s, before the defeat at Culloden, forces seemed to be aligning in the Jacobites' favour. If Britain were involved in a war with a European power, as it was in 1744, there was always the hope that its enemies might support the Stuart cause while the British themselves were weakened. For foreign powers, domestic rebellions were themselves a tool of state. Deteriorating Anglo-Spanish relations in the 1730s gave Jacobites cause for optimism. In 1739 Britain went to war with Spain, and since diplomatic relations between Britain and France had cooled in the 1730s, there was a real danger that France would intervene to support Philip V. By 1740 British forces were engaged in the War of the Austrian Succession. Even though France did not formally declare war against Britain until 1744, the armies of both countries were engaged in hostilities by 1741. In January 1742 an alliance of Whigs and Tories succeeded in getting the Prime Minister Robert Walpole to resign, but when the one time Patriot Whigs William Pulteney (1684–1764) and John Carteret, earl of Granville (1690–1763) put their own ambitions first, and there was no sign of an end to nearly thirty years of proscription from office, many Tories began to think again about the exiled king. Just before Walpole's resignation, James, the 'Old Pretender', had sent a letter to Tories and Opposition Whigs declaring his willingness to support the Church of England and grant toleration to Dissenters. At the same time the son of the exiled king picked up characteristically Oppositional language

---

[19] King, p. 73.

[20] Daniel Szechi, *1715: The Great Jacobite Rebellion* (New Haven: Yale, 2006), p. 48.

[21] See Paul Kléber Monod, *Jacobitism and the English People, 1688–1788* (Cambridge: Cambridge University Press, 1989), pp. 344–45.

and themes as he declared an aversion to 'arbitrary power at the expense of the liberty and property of the subject'.[22] Cardinal André de Fleury, who had always been an obstacle to French support for the Jacobites, died in 1743. In the spring of that year, five leading Tories wrote to Francis, Jacobite Lord Sempill (d. 1748), who had assumed the role of Jacobite agent in the French court, asking him to issue an invitation to France to invade England. Between August and October 1743, Louis XV's equerry toured southern England assessing the extent of support for the Stuart cause, and reported that at least fifty per cent of the gentry and aristocracy were crypto-Jacobites. In November 1743 Louis XV gave the order to prepare a surprise attack. By February 1744 the French navy was assembled at Brest for that very purpose. *The Fortunate Foundlings* was published in January: the timing of a work that is full of pro-French sentiment was impeccable.

If *The Fortunate Foundlings* dates from a time when the Jacobite cause seemed hopeful, *A Letter from H — G — g, Esq.* (1749) also republished here for the first time, marks a downward shift in its fortunes. The Jacobite army had been decisively defeated at Culloden in April 1746 and Charles Edward Stuart had fled to France. There was an upsurge of sympathy for the rebels as they were brought to trial and executed in the summer and autumn of 1746: entries in Haywood's own journal *The Parrot* are instances of it. A borough election in Lichfield provoked pro-Jacobite riots, with other demonstrations at Newton races and Oxford in 1748.[23] Portraits of Prince Charles were on public display in central London.[24] Even Prince Frederick courted popular support by walking around in plaid at an election of 1750. The covert movements and disguises of a charismatic and romantic prince exercised a hold on the public imagination, catered for by works such as *A Letter*, Ralph Griffiths's *Ascanius; or, The Young Adventurer* (1746), the anonymous *Alexis; or, The Young Adventurer* (1746) and M. Michell's 'translation', *Young Juba, or, the History of the Young Chevalier* (1748). *A Letter from H — G — g*, purportedly written by Charles's real-life aide Henry Goring (d. ca. 1754), provides the secret, inside story of the prince's movements around the continent. Far from being haphazard his journey is part of a greater plan, a plan that will, it seems, astonish all Europe, but cannot now be divulged. The epigraph to the title page — *Victrix fortunæ sapientia* (Wisdom is the conqueror of fortune) — sets the tone for what follows. Charles is shown to be brave, wise, just and, above all, kingly. *A Letter* seems like one of the most straightforward expressions of Haywood's Jacobitism. However, as Kathryn King has argued, the prince of *A Letter* resembles Prince Frederick

---

[22]   Cited by Eveline Cruickshanks, *Political Untouchables The Tories and the '45* (London: Duckworth and Co., 1979), pp. 28–29.
[23]   See Cruickshanks, pp. 108–10.
[24]   Nicholson, p. 83.

at least as much as he does Prince Charles.[25] In January 1737 the Hanoverian prince had spent a day helping to put out a fire that broke out at the Temple in London, and the event was commemorated in a painting by Richard Wilson. The painting showed Frederick wearing the ribbon of the Garter and being acclaimed by spectators. The episode where the hero of *A Letter* rescues a woman from a burning building might have reminded readers of Frederick's courage and public spirit. The would-be king sounds the Patriot themes of disinterestedness, liberty, the constitution of England and government by consent of the people. There is nothing here about the claims of heredity and legitimate succession.

Attention to the political resonances of locations and allusions in the pamphlet serves to point up the fluidity of Haywood's allegiances. The anonymous *Alexis* ceases abruptly with the defeat at Culloden. *Young Juba* concludes with Charles escaping from Scotland, and Griffiths's *Ascanius* ends with the prince falling gratefully to his knees on the French shore. Haywood, in contrast, begins with Charles's flight from the papal enclave of Avignon. In reality, that move came after pressure from France, Britain and the papacy. Under the terms of the Peace (or Treaty) of Aix-la-Chapelle (1748) that ended the War of the Austrian Succession — a Treaty Haywood mentions in passing — Louis XV was to recognize the right of the House of Hanover and repudiate the Pretender. Charles furiously resisted attempts to remove him from Paris and the whole, faintly absurd struggle was rehearsed in the pages of English newspapers.[26] In the end the French king had Charles arrested, and he was allowed to move into the Apostolic Palace. The flight from Avignon, and the reminder of the treaty, could serve to underline the fact that the Stuart prince no longer enjoyed French support. *A Letter* draws to a conclusion with the Stuart prince in the commonwealth (in Polish the *rzeczpospolita*) of Poland-Lithuania, so-called because the *szlachta* had the right to elect the king. There was a family connection here, by way of the prince's Polish mother Maria Clementina Sobieska (1702–1735), but Haywood seems at pains to bring in an old nobleman who served under the Polish king John (or Jan) Sobieski III of Poland (1629–1696) to greet the Stuart prince. For more republican-minded thinkers, the election of a king provided a perfect example of civic virtue in action, with the state achieving a perfect balance of monarchical, aristocratic and popular elements. Arbitrary power would be held in check and the liberty of the people preserved. The enthusiasm with which the old nobleman greets the prince might serve to suggest that such liberties would be preserved by the incumbent to the British throne — whoever he was.

In January 1750, Haywood was arrested for her part in the writing or

---

[25] King, pp. 184–86.
[26] McLynn, p. 355.

distribution of *A Letter* as part of the government's investigation into the 'Scandalous Seditious and Treasonable Pamphlet'. Depositions taken at the time show that Haywood had taken delivery of around 800 copies of the pamphlet at her house in Durham Yard, off Fleet Street, around the middle of November 1749. After the copies were seized in mid-December, booksellers Charles Corbett and John Barnes named Haywood as the possible author, but she denied the charge.[27] There was no subsequent prosecution. Ralph Griffiths, writing in the *Monthly Review* at the time of Haywood's arrest, identified her as the author, albeit with ellipses: 'The noted Mrs *H — d*, ... is the reputed author of this pretended letter', and the attribution to Haywood is now widely accepted. The seized copies of *A Letter* seem to have been returned to Haywood and then found their way on to the market, to be followed by a second edition and a French translation in 1756. Much later, *A Letter* formed the basis of an unfinished novel by Robert Louis Stevenson. Andrew Lang, journalist, author, and specialist in Jacobite history, had a transcript made of the work in the early 1890s and sent it to Stevenson who was then living in Samoa.[28] Stevenson's piece was to be entitled 'The Young Chevalier', and it was to begin in a wine-shop in Avignon with two Jacobite gentlemen, one dark, one fair, with nothing left to them but 'exile and the bottle'. Charles Edward Stuart was sketched out as a 'young man in distress of mind'. Stevenson's fiction was shaped by his knowledge of the demise of Jacobitism, while Haywood's might aim at its eventual success, but *A Letter* still provided him with what Lesley Graham has called a 'rich imaginative space'.[29]

The Fortunate Foundlings also enjoyed an extended afterlife. It was translated into French and freely adapted as *Les Heureux Orphelins* (1754) by Claude-Prosper Jolyot de Crébillon (Crébillon *fils*). *Les Heureux Orphelins* follows Haywood's novel up to the point where Louisa (now Lucie) meets Melanthe (now Lady Suffolck). Thereafter, the narrative is taken up by the latter's affair with the deceitful Lord Durham, and, finally, letters from Lord Durham detailing his plots to seduce women. The story of Horatio — here Édouard — and his military exploits disappears altogether. In *The Happy Orphans* (1759), novelist Edward Kimber, apparently unaware of Haywood's original, took Crébillon's version as his starting point, following it up to the point where Lady Suffolck (now Suffolk) tells of her unhappy love for Lord Durham (now l'Anglai). In the embedded narrative, we hear how Lady Suffolk discovered L'Anglai's infidelity to a now pregnant former mistress, Mlle St Hermione. Lady Suffolk tricks him

---

[27] See Catherine Ingrassia, 'Additional Information about Eliza Haywood's 1749 Arrest for Seditious Libel', *N&Q,* 44.2 (June 1997), p. 203.
[28] Lesley Graham, 'Robert Louis Stevenson's "The Young Chevalier": Unimagined Space', in *Living with Jacobitism, 1690–1788: The Three Kingdoms and Beyond*, ed. by Allan I. Macinnes, Kieran Graham, and Lesley Graham (London: Pickering & Chatto, 2014), p. 200.
[29] Graham, p. 201.

into marrying her, but he leaves, only to be killed in a duel. Lucy and Edward, it turns out, are the babies whom he fathered and are thus legitimate after all. Other episodes include the abduction of Lucy by the libertine Lord Chester. It is quite possible that the opening of Haywood's novel also inspired the most famous 'foundling' novel of the century, Henry Fielding's *Tom Jones, or, The History of a Foundling* (1748–49), which itself mirrors the equal weight given to male and female histories by Haywood's novel.

The Fortunate Foundlings was commercially successful in its own time, being published three times in London and once in Dublin. For a record of its contemporary reception, there is only an unfavourable comparison of its 'farrago of adventures' with Kimber's more moralistic *The Happy Orphans* in the *Critical Review* of February 1759. We can now move beyond the issue of Haywood's morality. For those interested in the role of translation in eighteenth-century writing, or taking an international perspective on the 'rise of the novel', *The Fortunate Foundlings* has provided a valuable test case.[30] Consideration of the popularity and significance of the 'secret history' intersects with discussion of Haywood's novel, and *A Letter from H — G — g*.[31] The nature and extent of Haywood's influence on other writers also deserves further research, research that goes beyond thinking of her as a supplier of erotic material that Samuel Richardson exploited, and then tamed. Taking Eliza Haywood seriously is still an unfinished project.

---

[30] Antoinette Sol, 'Lost in Translation: Crébillon-fils' *Les Heureux Orphelins* and Haywood's *The Fortunate Foundlings*', in *Altered Narratives. Female Eighteenth-Century French Authors Reinterpreted*, ed. by Servanne Woodward (London: Mestengo Press, 1997), pp. 16–40.

[31] Rachel Carnell, 'Eliza Haywood and the Narratological Tropes of Secret History', *JEMCS*, 14.4 (Fall 2014), pp. 101–21; 'Slipping from Secret History to Novel', *ECF*, 28.1 (Fall 2015), pp. 1–24.

SELECT BIBLIOGRAPHY

Primary Sources

ADLERFELD, GUSTAVUS, *The Military History of Charles XII, King of Sweden*, 3 vols, trans. into English (London, 1740)

ANON., *Alexis; or the Young Adventurer: A Novel* (London, 1746)

ANON., *Clelia, An Excellent Romance: The Whole Work in Five Parts... Written in French by the Exquisite Pen of* Monsieur de Scudery, *Governour of Nostredame de la Garde* (London, 1678)

ANON., *Fatal Gallantry: or, The Secret History of Henrietta Princess of England* (London, 1722)

ANON., *The Amorous History of the Gauls: Written in French by Roger de Rabutin, Count de Bussy, And Now Translated into English* (London, 1725)

ANON., *The History of the Amours of the French Court, viz. of Madam de la Valliere, Madam de Olonne, Madam de Chastillion, Madam de Sevigny, With the Intrigues of Several Other Persons of Great Quality in the Palace-Royal* (London, 1684)

B. A., *Memoires of the Court of France* (London, 1697)

BAKER, DAVID ERSKINE, *The Companion to the Play-House* (London, 1764)

BUSSY, ROGER DE RABUTIN, COMTE DE, *Histoire amoureuse des Gaules* (1665), 5 vols (London, 1777)

DEFOE, DANIEL, *The History of the Wars, of His Present Majesty Charles XII, King of Sweden; from His First Landing in Denmark, to His Return from Turkey to Pomerania* (London, 1715)

GRIFFITHS, RALPH, *Ascanius; or, the Young Adventurer* (London, 1746)

HAYWOOD, ELIZA, *Selected Works of Eliza Haywood I* and *II*, ed. by Alexander Pettit, 6 vols (London: Pickering & Chatto, 2000–2001)

JONES, DAVID, *The Life of James II, Late King of England* (London, 1702)

KIMBER, EDWARD, *The Happy Orphans*, ed. by Jan Herman and Beatrijs Vanacker, MHRA Critical Texts, XXIX (Cambridge: MHRA, 2015)

LAFAYETTE, MARIE-MADELEINE PIOCHE DE LA VERGNE, COMTESSE DE, *Œuvres complètes*, ed. by Camille Esmein-Sarrazin (Paris: Gallimard, 2014)

MICHELL, M., *Young Juba: or, the History of the Young Chevalier, from his Birth, to his Escape from Scotland, after the Battle of Culloden* (London, 1748)

STEELE, RICHARD, *The Christian Hero*, ed. by Rae Blanchard (London: Oxford University Press, 1932)

VOLTAIRE [FRANÇOIS-MARIE AROUET], *Lion of the North: Charles XII of Sweden*, trans. by M. F. O. Jenkins (London: Associated University Presses, 1981)

WALPOLE, HORACE, *Horace Walpole's Correspondence*, ed. by W. S. Lewis and others, 48 vols (New Haven: Yale University Press, 1937–1983)

Secondary Sources

CARNELL, RACHEL, 'Eliza Haywood and the Narratological Tropes of Secret History', *JEMCS*, 14.4 (Fall 2014), 101–21

——*Partisan Politics, Narrative Realism, and the Rise of the British Novel* (Basingstoke: Palgrave Macmillan, 2006)

——'Slipping from Secret History to Novel', *ECF*, 28.1 (Fall 2015), 1–24

CORP, EDWARD, *A Court in Exile: The Stuarts in France, 1689–1718* (Cambridge: Cambridge University Press, 2004)

CRUICKSHANKS, EVELINE, *Political Untouchables. The Tories and the '45* (London: Duckworth, 1979)

GENET-ROUFFIAC, NATHALIE, 'Jacobites in Paris and Saint-Germain-en-Laye', in *The Stuart Court in Exile and the Jacobites*, ed. by Eveline Cruickshanks and Edward Corp (London: Hambledon Press, 1995), pp. 15–38

GRAHAM, LESLEY, 'Robert Louis Stevenson's "The Young Chevalier": Unimagined Space', in *Living with Jacobitism, 1690–1788: The Three Kingdoms and Beyond*, ed. by Allan I. Macinnes, Kieran Graham, and Lesley Graham (London: Pickering & Chatto, 2014), pp. 197–207

HATTON, R. M., *Charles XII of Sweden* (London: Weidenfeld & Nicolson, 1968)

HATTENDORF, JOHN, *England in the War of the Spanish Succession: A Study of the Grand Strategy, 1702–1712* (New York: Garland, 1987)

HIBBERT, CHRISTOPHER, *The Marlboroughs: John and Sarah Churchill 1650–1744* (London: Penguin, 2001)

INGAMELLS, JOHN, *A Dictionary of British and Irish Travellers in Italy* (New Haven: Yale University Press, 1997)

KEENAN, P., *St Petersburg and the Russian Court, 1703–1761* (Basingstoke: Palgrave Macmillan, 2013)

KING, KATHRYN R., *A Political Biography of Eliza Haywood* (London: Pickering & Chatto, 2012)

LANG, ANDREW, *Prince Charles Edward Stuart: The Young Chevalier* (London: Longmans, Green, 1903)

McLYNN, FRANK, *Charles Edward Stuart: A Tragedy in Many Acts* (London: Routledge, 1988)

MONOD, PAUL KLÉBER, *Jacobitism and the English People, 1688–1788* (Cambridge: Cambridge University Press, 1989)

NICHOLSON, ROBIN, *Bonnie Prince Charlie and the Making of a Myth: A Study in Portraiture, 1720–1792* (Lewisburg: Bucknell University Press, 2002)

NOLAN, CATHAL J., *Wars of the Age of Louis XIV 1650–1715: An Encyclopedia of Global Warfare and Civilization* (Westport, CT: Greenwood Press, 2008)

PRENDERGAST, AMY, *Literary Salons across Britain and Ireland in the Long Eighteenth Century* (Basingstoke: Palgrave Macmillan, 2015)

SOL, ANTOINETTE, 'Lost in Translation: Crébillon-fils' *Les Heureux Orphelins* and Haywood's *The Fortunate Foundlings*', in *Altered Narratives: Female Eighteenth-Century French Authors Reinterpreted*, ed. by Servanne Woodward (London: Mestengo Press, 1997), 16–40

SPEDDING, PATRICK, *A Bibliography of Eliza Haywood* (London: Pickering & Chatto, 2004)

STEWART, CAROL, 'Eliza Haywood's *The Fortunate Foundlings*: A Jacobite Novel', *ECL*, 37.1 (2013): 51–71

SZECHI, DANIEL, *1715: The Great Jacobite Rebellion* (New Haven: Yale, 2006)

WAGNER-RUNDELL, BENEDICT, 'Liberty, Virtue and the Chosen People: British and Polish Republicanism in the Early Eighteenth Century', in *Britain and Poland-Lithuania: Contact and Comparison from the Middle Ages to 1795*, ed. by Richard Unger (Leiden: Brill, 2008), 197–214

WILPUTTE, EARLA, ' "Room to Fable Upon": The History of Charles XII of Sweden in Eliza Haywood's *The Fortunate Foundlings*', *The Eighteenth-Century Novel*, 2 (2002): 23–44

ZUNSHINE, LISA, *Bastards and Foundlings: Illegitimacy in Eighteenth-Century England* (Columbus: Ohio State University Press, 2005)

PART I

The Fortunate Foundlings

NOTE ON THE TEXT

The Fortunate Foundlings was published three times in London, in 1744, 1748 and 1762, and once in Dublin, in 1745. A 'second edition' of 1746 was in fact a re-issue of the first edition. The first edition of 1744, BL 12614.eee.16, has been chosen as the copy-text, and checked against the second edition of 1748, the only other edition published in Eliza Haywood's lifetime. Corrections to spelling and typographical errors from the second edition, such as the spelling of 'monastery' and 'fierce', have been followed, and the spelling of proper names has been regularized to avoid confusion. Otherwise Haywood's sometimes variable spelling has been retained. The long eighteenth-century 's' (ſ) has been replaced with 's'.

THE

FORTUNATE FOUNDLINGS:

BEING THE

GENUINE HISTORY

OF

Colonel M——rs, *and his Sister, Madam* Du P——y, *the Issue of the Hon.* Ch——es M——rs, *Son of the late Duke of* R——l——d.

CONTAINING

Many wonderful ACCIDENTS that befel them in their TRAVELS, and interspersed with the CHARACTERS and ADVENTURES of SEVERAL PERSONS of *Condition*, in the most polite Courts of *Europe*.

The Whole calculated for the Entertainment and Improvement of the Youth of both Sexes.

LONDON:
Printed and published by T. GARDNER at *Cowley's Head*, opposite *St Clement's* Church in the *Strand*.

————

M, DCC, XLIV.

The Fortunate Foundlings offers to give readers the 'genuine history' of 'colonel M——rs, and his sister, Madam du P——y, the issue of the Hon. Ch——es M——rs, son of the late Duke of R—l—d', but no scholar has been able to find a Charles Manners born either to John Manners, first duke of Rutland (1638–1711), or to his son John Manners, second duke of Rutland (1676–1721). It may be that Haywood simply intended to slur a Whig family by stirring up memories of a scandal involving the first duke of Rutland, known as Lord Roos. In 1658 Roos married Lady Anne Pierrepoint (bap. 1631, d. 1697), but following Anne's adultery he was granted a separation in the ecclesiastical court. He then obtained private acts bastardizing children Anne had borne since 1659, and another allowing him to marry again. The revelations about Anne's sexual promiscuity attracted public attention, and issues raised by the Manners case were debated in parliament. (See Jean Morrin, 'Manners, John, first duke of Rutland (1638–1711)', *Oxford Dictionary of National Biography*, Oxford University Press, 2004 [http://www.oxforddnb.com/view/article/17957, accessed 31 August 2017].) Despite Haywood's spelling (with ellipses) on the title-page, 'du P[less]y' is 'du Plessis' throughout the novel.

THE
PREFACE.

THE many Fictions which have lately been imposed upon the World, under the specious Titles of Secret Histories, Memoirs, &c. &c. *have given but too much room to question the Veracity of every Thing that has the least Tendency that way: We therefore think it highly necessary to assure the Reader, that he will find nothing in the following Sheets, but what has been collected from* Original Letters, Private Memorandums, *and the* Accounts *we have been favoured with from the Mouths of Persons too deeply concerned in many of the* chief Transactions *not to be perfectly acquainted with the Truth, and of too much Honour and Integrity to put any false Colours upon it.*

The Adventures are not so long passed as to be wholly forgotten by many Living Witnesses, *nor yet so recent as to give any Reason to suspect us of Flattery in the Relation given of them, the Motive of their Publication being only to* encourage Virtue *in both Sexes, by shewing the Amiableness of it in* real Characters. *And if it be true (as certainly it is) that* Example *has more Efficacy than* Precept, *we may be bold to say there are few fairer, or more worthy Imitation.—— The Sons and Daughters of the greatest Families may give additional Lustre to their Nobility, by forming themselves by the Model here presented to them; and those of lower Extraction, attain Qualities to attone for what they want in Birth:—— So that we flatter ourselves this Undertaking will not fail of receiving the Approbation of all who wish well to a Reformation of Manners, and more especially those who have Youth under their Care.—— As for such who may take it up merely as an Amusement, it is possible they will find something, which, by interesting their Affections, may make them better without designing to be so. — Either way will fully recompence the Pains taken in the Compiling by*

The EDITORS.

THE
CONTENTS.

CHAP. I.

Contains the manner in which a gentleman found two children: his benevolence towards them, and what kind of affection he bore to them as they grew up. With the departure of one of them to the army.

IT was in the ever memorable year 1688,[1] that a gentleman, whose real name we think proper to conceal under that of Dorilaus, returned from visiting most of the polite courts of Europe, in which he had passed some time divided between pleasure and improvement. The important question if the throne were vacated or not, by the sudden departure of the unfortunate king James,[2] was then upon the tapis:[3] on which, to avoid interesting himself on either side, he forbore coming to London, and crossed the country to a fine seat he had about some forty miles distant, where he resolved to stay as privately as he could, till the great decision should be made, and the public affairs settled in such a manner as not to lay him under a necessity of declaring his sentiments upon them.

He was young and gay, loved magnificence and the pomp of courts, and was far from being insensible of those joys which the conversation of the fair sex affords; but had never so much enslaved his reason to any one pleasure, as not to be able to restrain it. Hunting and reading were very favourite amusements with him, so that the solitude he now was in was not at all disagreeable or tedious to him, tho' he continued in it some months.

---

[1]   *the ever memorable year 1688*: In 1688 English politicians invited Prince William of Orange (1650–1702), nephew and brother-in-law of the reigning monarch, to take the throne. He landed at Torbay in Devon in November 1688, and James II (1633–1701) fled to France in December.

[2]   *if the throne were vacated or not, by the sudden departure of the unfortunate king James*: The question of whether James II's flight to France constituted an abdication that left the throne 'vacant' was contentious. In January 1689, the House of Commons put forward a resolution stating that the king had, by his actions, broken the original compact between monarch and people, and that the throne was indeed vacant. The House of Lords, not wanting to endanger the principle of hereditary succession, preferred 'deserted' to 'abdicated', and wanted to omit any reference to a vacant throne. In February 1689, the Commons' motion was passed. (For a comprehensive, contemporary account see David Jones, *The Life of James II, Late King of England* (1702), pp. 230–58).

[3]   *upon the tapis*: literally, on the carpet; under discussion.

A little time before his departure an accident happened, which gave him an opportunity of exercising the benevolence of his disposition; and tho' it then seemed trivial to him, proved of the utmost consequence to his future life, as well as furnished matter for the following pages.

As he was walking pretty early one morning in his garden, very intent on a book he had in his hand, his meditations were interrupted by an unusual cry, which seemed at some distance; but as he approached a little arbour, where he was sometimes accustomed to sit, he heard more plain and distinct, and on his entrance was soon convinced whence it proceeded.

Just at the foot of a large tree, the extensive boughs of which greatly contributed to form the arbour, was placed a basket closely covered on the one side, and partly open on the other to let in the air. Tho' the sounds which still continued to issue from it left Dorilaus no room to doubt what it contained; he stooped down to look, and saw two beautiful babes dressed in swadling cloaths: between them and the pillow they were laid upon was pinned a paper, which he hastily taking off, found in it these words.

To the generous DORILAUS:

> IRRESISTIBLE destiny abandons these helpless infants to your care. — They are twins, begot by the same father, and born of the same mother, and of a blood not unworthy the protection they stand in need of; which if you vouchsafe to afford, they will have no cause to regret the misfortune of their birth, or accuse the authors of their being. — Why they seek it of you in particular, you may possibly be hereafter made sensible. — In the mean time content yourself with knowing they are already baptized by the names of Horatio and Louisa.

The astonishment he was in at so unexpected a present being made him, may more easily be imagined than expressed; but he had then no time to form any conjectures by whom or by what means it was left there: the children wanted immediate succour, and he hesitated not a moment whether it would become him to bestow it: he took the basket up himself, and running as fast as he could with it into the house, called his maid-servants about him, and commanded them to give these little strangers what assistance was in their power, while a man was sent among the tenants in search of nurses proper to attend them. To what person soever, said he, I am indebted for this confidence, it must not be abused. — Besides, whatever stands in need of protection, merits protection from those who have the power to give it.

This was his way of thinking, and in pursuance of these generous sentiments he always acted. The report of what happened in his house being soon spread thro' the country, there were not wanting several who came to offer their service to the children, out of which he selected two of whom he heard the best character, and were most likely to be faithful to the trust reposed in them, giving as great a charge, and as handsome an allowance with them, as could have been expected from a father. Indeed he doubtless had passed for being so in the opinion of every body, had he arrived sooner in the kingdom, but the shortness of the time not permitting any such suggestion, he was looked upon as a prodigy of charity and goodness.

Having in this handsome manner disposed of his new guests, he began to examine all his servants, thinking it impossible they should be brought here without the privity[4] of some one of them: but all his endeavours could get him no satisfaction in this point. He read the letter over and over, yet still his curiosity was as far to seek as ever. — The hand he was entirely unacquainted with, but thought there was something in the stile that shewed it wrote by no mean person: the hint contained in it, that there was some latent reason for addressing him in particular on this account, was very puzzling to him: he could not conceive why he, any more than any other gentleman of the county, should have an interest in the welfare of these children: he had no near relations, and those distant ones who claimed an almost forgotten kindred were not in a condition to abandon their progeny. — The thing appeared strange to him; but all his endeavours to give him any farther light into it being unsuccessful, he began to imagine the parents of the children had been compelled by necessity to expose them, and had only wrote in this mysterious manner to engage a better reception: he also accounted in his mind for their being left with him, as he being a batchelor, and having a large estate, it might naturally be supposed there would be fewer impediments to their being taken care of, than either where a wife was in the case, or a narrow fortune obliged the owner to preserve a greater œconomy in expences.

Being at last convinced within himself that he had now explained this seeming riddle, he took no farther trouble about whose, or what these children were, but resolved to take care of them during their infancy, and afterwards to put them into such a way as their genius's rendered them most fit for, in order to provide for themselves.

On his leaving the county, he ordered his housekeeper to furnish every thing needful for them as often as they wanted it, and to take care they were well used by the women with whom he had placed them; and delivered these commands not in a cursory or negligent manner, but in such terms as testified any failure of obedience on this point would highly incur his displeasure.

Nothing material happening during their infancy, I shall pass over those years in silence, only saying that as often as Dorilaus went down to his estate (which was generally two or three times a year) he always sent for them, and expressed

---

[4] *privity*: a secret matter, or plan.

a very great satisfaction in finding in their looks the charge he had given concerning them so well executed: but when they arrived at an age capable of entertaining him with their innocent prattle, what before was charity, improved into affection; and he began to regard them with a tenderness little inferior to paternal; but which still increased with their increase of years.

Having given them the first rudiments of education in the best schools those parts afforded, he placed Louisa with a gentlewoman, who deservedly had the reputation of being an excellent governess of youth, and brought Horatio in his own chariot up to London, where he put him to Westminster school, under the care of doctor Busby,[5] and agreed for his board in a family that lived near it, and had several other young gentlemen on the same terms.

What more could have been expected from the best of fathers! what more could children, born to the highest fortunes, have enjoyed! nor was their happiness like to be fleeting: Dorilaus was a man steady in his resolutions, had always declared an aversion to marriage, and by rejecting every overture made him on that score, had made his friends cease any farther importunities; he had besides (as has already been observed) no near relations, so that it was the opinion of most people that he would make the young Horatio heir to the greatest part of his estate, and give Louisa a portion answerable to her way of bringing up. What he intended for them, however, is uncertain, he never having declared his sentiments so far concerning them; and the strange revolutions happening afterwards in both their fortunes, preventing him from acting as it is possible he might design.

The education he allowed them indeed gave very good grounds for the above-mentioned conjecture — Louisa being taught all the accomplishments that became a maid of quality to be mistress of; and Horatio having gone thro' all the learning of the school, was taken home to his own house, from whence he was to go to Oxford, in order to finish his studies in the character of a gentleman-commoner.[6]

But when every thing was preparing for this purpose, he came one morning into the chamber of his patron, and throwing himself on his knees — Think me not, sir, said he, too presuming in this request I am about to make you. — I know that all that I am is yours. — That I am the creature of your bounty, and that, without being a father, you have done more for me than many of those, who are so, do for their most favourite sons. — I know also that you are

---

[5] *Westminster school, under the care of doctor Busby*: Westminster was, and is, a prestigious school, the existence of which can be traced back to at least the fourteenth century. Richard Busby (1606–95), a classicist, grammarian and strict disciplinarian, was headmaster of Westminster school from 1638 until his death.

[6] *gentleman-commoner*: formerly, one of a privileged class of undergraduates at the Universities of Oxford and Cambridge. Gentlemen-commoners were distinguished by special academic dress, by dining at a separate table, and by the payment of higher fees.

the best judge of what is fit for me, and have not the least apprehensions that you will not always continue the same goodness to me, provided I continue, as I have hitherto done, the ambition of meriting it. — Yet, sir, pardon me if I now discover a desire with which I have long laboured, of doing something of myself which may repair the obscurity of my birth, and prove to the world that heaven has endued this foundling with a courage and resolution capable of undertaking the greatest actions.

In speaking these last words a fire seemed to sparkle from his eyes, which sufficiently denoted the vehemence of his inward agitations. Dorilaus was extremely surprized, but after a little pause, what is it you request of me? said that noble gentleman, (at the same time raising him from that posture he was in) or by what means than such as I have already taken, can I oblige you to think that, in being my foundling, fortune dealt not too severely with you?

Ah! sir, mistake me not, I beseech you, replied the young Horatio, or think me wanting in my gratitude either to heaven or you. — But, sir, it is to your generous care in cultivating the talents I received from nature, that I owe this emulation, this ardour for doing something that might give me a name, which is the only thing your bounty cannot bestow. — My genius inclines me to the army. — Of all the accomplishments you have caused me to be instructed in, geography, fortification, and fencing, have been my darling studies. — Of what use, sir, will they be to me in an idle life? permit me then the opportunity of shewing the expence you have been at has not been thrown away. — I know they will say I am too young to bear a commission, but if I had the means of going a volunteer, I cannot help thinking but I should soon give proofs of the extreme desire I have to serve my country that way would well attone for my want of years.

The more he spoke, the more the astonishment of his patron increased: he admired the greatness of his spirit, but was troubled it led him into so dangerous a way of life. — He represented to him all the hardships of a soldier, the little regard that was sometimes paid to merit, and gave him several instances of gentlemen who had passed their youth in the service, and behaved with extreme bravery, yet had no other reward than their scars, and a consciousness of having done more than their duty: in war, said he, the superior officers carry away all the glory as well as profits of the victory; whereas in civil employments it is quite otherwise: in physic, in law, in divinity or in the state, your merits will be immediately conspicuous to those who have the power to reward you; and if you are desirous of acquiring a name, by which I suppose you mean to become the head of a family, any of these afford you a much greater prospect of success, and it lies much more in my power of assisting your promotion.

To these he added many other arguments, but they were not of the least weight with the impatient Horatio. He was obstinate in his intreaties, which he even with tears enforced, and Dorilaus, considering so strong a propensity as something supernatural, at last consented. — Never was joy more sincere and fervent than what this grant occasioned, and he told his benefactor that he doubted not but that hereafter he should hear such an account of his behaviour, as would make him not repent his having complied with his request.

The preparations for his going to Oxford were now converted into others of a different nature. — several of our troops were already sent to Flanders, and others about to embark, in order to open the campaign; so that there was but a small space between the time of Horatio's asking leave to go, and that of his departure, which Dorilaus resolved should be in a manner befitting a youth whom he had bred up as his own. He provided him a handsome field-equipage, rich cloaths, horses, and a servant to attend him; and while these things were getting ready, had masters to perfect him in riding, and those other exercises proper for the vocation he was now entering into, all which he performed with so good a grace, that not only Dorilaus himself, who might be suspected to look on him with partial eyes, but all who saw him were perfectly charmed.

He was more than ordinarily tall for his years, admirably well proportioned, and had something of a grave fierceness in his air and deportment, that tho' he was not yet sixteen, he might very well have passed for twenty: he was also extremely fair, had regular features, and eyes the most penetrating, mixed with a certain sweetness; so that it was difficult to say whether he seemed most formed for love or war.

Dorilaus thinking it highly proper he should take his leave of Louisa, sent for her from the boarding-school, that she might pass the short time she had to stay with her brother at his house, not without some hopes that the great tenderness there was between them might put Horatio out of his resolution of going to the army, who being now grown extremely dear to him, he could not think of parting with, tho' he had yielded to it, without a great deal of reluctance.

It is certain, indeed, that when she first heard the motive which had occasioned her being sent for, her gentle breast was filled with the most terrible alarms for her dear brother's danger; but the little regard he seemed to have of it, and the high ideas he had of future greatness, soon brought her to think as he did; and instead of disswading him from prosecuting his design, she rather encouraged him in it: and this gave the first testimony of the greatness of soul, no less to be admired than the courage and laudable ambition which actuated that of her brother.

Dorilaus beheld with an infinity of satisfaction the success of his endeavours, in favour of these amiable twins, and said within himself, how great a pity it would have been, if capacities such as theirs had been denied the means of improvement!

After the departure of Horatio, he kept Louisa some time with him, under pretence of shewing her the town, which she had never before seen; but in reality to alleviate that melancholy which parting from her brother had caused in him. He could not have taken a more effectual way; for there was such an engaging and sweet chearfulness in her conversation, added to many personal perfections, that it was scarce possible to think of any thing else when she was present. She had also an excellent voice, and played well on the bass viol and harpsichord, so that it is hard to say whether he found most satisfaction in hearing her or discoursing with her.

But how dangerous it is to depend on one's own strength, against the force of such united charms! Dorilaus, who, in the midst of a thousand temptations, had maintained the entire liberty of his heart, and tho' never insensible of beauty, had never been enslaved by it, was now by charms he least suspected, and at an age when he believed himself proof against all the attacks of love, subdued without knowing that he was so. — The tender passion stole into his soul by imperceptible degrees, and under the shape of friendship and paternal affection, met with no opposition from his reason, till it became too violent to be restrained; then shewed itself in the whole power of restless wishes, fears, hopes, and impatiences, which he had often heard others complain of, but not till now experienced in himself; all that he had before felt of love was languid, at best aimed only at enjoyment, and in the gratification of that desire was extinguished; but the passion he was possessed of for Louisa was of a different nature, and accompanied with a respect which would not suffer him to entertain a thought in prejudice of her innocence.

Many reasons, besides his natural aversion to marriage, concurred to hinder him from making her his wife; and as there were yet more to deter him from being the instrument of her dishonour, the situation of his mind was very perplexing. — He blushed within himself at the inclinations he had for a girl whom he had always behaved to as a child of his own, and who looked upon him as a father: not only the disparity of their years made him consider the passion he was possessed of as ridiculous, there was one circumstance, which, if at any time a thought of marrying her entered into his head, immediately extirpated it, which was, that there was a possibility of her being born not only of the meanest, but the vilest parents, who, on hearing her establishment, might appear and claim the right they had in her; and so, said he, I shall ally myself to, perhaps, a numerous family of vagabonds; at least, whether it be so or not, the manner in which these children were exposed, being publicly known, may furnish a pretence for any wretch to boast a kindred.

He was therefore determined to suppress a passion, which, as he had too much honour to seek the gratification of by one way, his prudence and character in the world would not allow him to think of by the other: and as absence seemed to him the best remedy, he sent her down into the country again with a precipitation, which made her (wholly ignorant of the real motive) fear she had done something to offend him. At parting, she entreated him to let her know if he had been dissatisfied with any thing in her behaviour. — Wherefore do you ask? said he with some emotion, which the poor innocent still mistook for displeasure; because, answered she, dropping some tears at the same time, that you banish me from your presence. Why, would you be glad to continue with me always? again demanded he. Yes indeed, said she; and if you loved me as well as you do my brother, you would never part with me; for I saw with what regret you let him go.

This tender simplicity added such fewel to the fire with which Dorilaus was enflamed, that it almost consumed his resolution: he walked about the room some time without being able to speak, much less to quiet the agitation he was in. At last, Louisa, said he, I was only concerned your brother made choice of an avocation so full of dangers; — but I never intended to keep him at home with me: — he should have gone to Oxford to finish his studies; and the reason I send you again to the boarding-school is that you may perfect yourself in such things as you may not yet be mistress of: — as for any apprehensions of my being offended with you, I would have you banish them entirely, for I assure you, I can find nothing in you but what both merits and receives my approbation.

She seemed extremely comforted with these words; and the coach being at the door, went into it with her accustomed chearfulness, leaving him in a state which none but those who have experienced the severe struggles between a violent inclination and a firm resolution to oppose it, can possibly conceive.

CHAP. II.

Relates the offers made by Dorilaus to Louisa, and the manner of her receiving them.

LOUISA was no sooner gone, than he wished her with him again, and was a thousand times about to send and have her brought back; but was as often prevented by the apprehensions of her discovering the motive. — He was now convinced that love does not always stand in need of being indulged to force its votaries to be guilty of extravagancies. — He had banished the object of his affections from his presence; he had painted all the inconveniences of pursuing his desires in the worst colours they would bear; yet all was insufficient! — Louisa was absent in reality, but her image was ever present to him. — Whatever company he engaged himself in, whatever amusement he endeavoured to entertain himself with, he could only think of her. — The Town without her seemed a desart, and every thing in it rather seemed irksome than agreeable: for several months did he endure this cruel conflict; but love and nature at last got the victory, and all these considerations which had occasioned the opposition subsided: he found it impossible to recover any tranquility of mind while he continued in this dilemma, and therefore yielded to the strongest side. All the arguments he had used within himself in the beginning of his passion seemed now weak and trifling: the difference of age, which he had thought so formidable an objection, appeared none in the light with which he at present considered it: he was now but in his fortieth year and the temperance he had always observed had hindered any decay either in his looks or constitution. — What censures the world might pass on his marrying one of her age and obscure birth, he thought were of little weight when balanced with his internal peace. — Thus was he enabled to answer to himself all that could be offered against making her his wife; and having thus settled every thing, as he imagined, to the satisfaction of his passion, became no less resolute in following the dictates of it than he had been in combating it while there was a possibility of doing so.

To this end he went down to his country seat, and as soon as he arrived sent to let Louisa know he would have her come and pass some time with him. She readily obeyed the summons, and found by his manner of receiving her that she was no less dear to him than her brother. As she had always considered him as a father, tho' she knew all her claim in him was compassion, she was far from suspecting the motive which made him treat her with so much tenderness; but he suffered her not long to remain in this happy ignorance. As he was walking with her one day in the garden, he purposely led her on that side where he had found Horatio and herself in the manner already related; and as they came towards the arbour, It was here, said he, that heaven put into my power the opportunity of affording my protection to two persons whom I think will not be ungrateful for what I have done. — I hope, Louisa, continued he, you will not at least deceive my good opinion of you; but as you have always found in me a real friend, you will testify the sense you have of my good wishes, by readily following my advice in any material point.

I should be else unworthy, sir, answered she, of the life you have preserved; and I flatter myself with being guilty of nothing which should give you cause to call in question either my gratitude or duty.

I insist but on the former, resumed he; nor can pretend any claim to the latter; — look on me therefore only as your friend, and let me know your sentiments plainly and sincerely on what I think proper to ask you. This she having assured him she would do, he pursued his discourse in these or the like terms:

You are now, said he, arrived at an age when persons of your sex ordinarily begin to think of marriage. — I need not ask you if you have ever received any addresses for that purpose; the manner in which you have lived convinces me you are yet a stranger to them; but I would know of you whether an overture of that kind, in favour of a man of honour, and who can abundantly endow you with the goods of fortune, would be disagreeable to you.

Alas! sir, replied she, blushing, you commanded me to answer with sincerity, but how can I resolve a question which as yet I have never asked myself? — All that I can say is, that I now am happy by your bounty, and have never entertained one wish but for the continuance of it.

On that you may depend, said he, while you continue to stand in need of it. But would it not be more pleasing to find yourself the mistress of an ample fortune, and in a condition to do the same good offices by others as you have found from me?   In fine, Louisa, the care I have taken of you would not be complete unless I saw you well settled in the world. — I have therefore provided a husband for you, and such a one as I think you can have no reasonable objection to.

Sir, it would ill-become me to dispute your will, answered she, modestly, but as I am yet very young, and have never had a thought of marriage, nor even conversed with any who have experienced that state, I should be too much at a loss how to behave in it, without being allowed some time to consider on its respective duties. — I hope therefore, sir, continued she, you will not oblige me to act with too much precipitation in an affair on which the happiness or misery of my whole future life depends.

Your very thinking it of consequence, said he, is enough to make you behave so, as to assure your happiness with a man of honour; and indeed Louisa, I love you too well to propose one to you whose principles and humour I could not answer for as well as my own.

Yet, sir, replied she, I have read that a union of hearts as well as hands is necessary for the felicity of that state; — that there ought to be a simpathy of soul between them, and a perfect confidence in each other, before the indissoluble knot is tied: — and this, according to my notion, can only be the result of a long acquaintance, and accompanied with many proofs of affection on both sides.

Were all young women to think as you do, said he with a smile, we should have much fewer marriages; they would indeed be happier; therefore I am far from condemning your precaution, nor would I wish you should give yourself to one till well assured he was incapable of treating you with less regard after marriage than before: — no, no, Louisa, I will never press you to become a wife, till you shall yourself acknowledge the man I offer to you as a husband is not unworthy of that title, thro' a want of honour, fortune, or affection.

As Louisa thought this must be the work of time, the chagrin she felt at the first mention of marriage was greatly dissipated; and she told him, that when she was once convinced such a person as he described honoured her so far as to think she merited his affection, she would do all in her power to return it.

The enamoured Dorilaus having now brought her to the point he aimed at, thought it best to throw off the mask at once, and leave her no longer in suspence. — Behold then in me, said he, the person I have mentioned: nor think me vain in ascribing those merits to myself which I would wish to be the loadstone of your affection. — My honour, I believe, you will not call in question: — my humour you have never found capricious, or difficult to please; and as for my love, you cannot but allow the conquering the aversion, which myself, as well as all the world, believed unalterable for a marriage state; besides a thousand other scruples opposed my entering into it with you, is a proof greater than almost any other man could give you. — There requires, therefore, my dear Louisa, no time to convince you of what I am, or assure you of what I may be; and I hope the affection you bore me, as a faithful friend, and the protector of your innocence, will not be diminished on my making this declaration.

The confusion in which this speech involved her is even impossible to be conceived, much less can any words come up to its description: she blushed; — she trembled; — she was ready to die between surprize, grief and shame: — fain she would have spoke, but feared, lest what she should say would either lose his friendship or encourage his passion. — Each seemed equally dreadful to her: — no words presented themselves to her distracted mind that she could think proper to utter, till he pressing her several times to reply, and seeming a little to resent her silence — Oh! sir, cried she, how is it possible for me to make any answer to so strange a proposition! — you were not used to rally my simplicity; nor can I think you mean what you now mention. If there wanted no more, said he, than to prove the sincerity of my wishes in this point to gain your approbation of them, my chaplain should this moment put it past a doubt, and confirm my proposal: — but, pursued he, I will not put your modesty to any farther shock at present; — all I intreat is, that you will consider on what I have said, and what the passion I am possessed of merits from you. In concluding these words he kissed her with the utmost tenderness, and quitted her to speak to some of the men who were at work in another part of the garden, leaving her to meditate at liberty on this surprizing turn in her affairs.

It was indeed necessary he should do so, for the various agitations she laboured under were so violent, as to be near throwing her into a swoon. — She no sooner found herself alone, than she flew to her chamber, and locked herself in, to prevent being interrupted by any of the servants; and as in all emotions of the mind, especially in that of a surprize, tears are a very great relief, her's found some ease from the sources of her eyes. — Never had the most dutiful child loved the tenderest of fathers more than she did Dorilaus; but then it was only a filial affection, and the very thoughts of his regarding her with that sort of passion she now found he did, had somewhat in them terribly alarming. — All she could do to reconcile herself to what seemed to be her fate was in vain. — This generous man who offers me his heart, said she, is not my father, or any way of my blood: — he has all the accomplishments of his whole sex centered in him. — I could wish to be for ever near him. — All that I am is owing to his goodness. — How wretched must I have been but for his bounty! — What unaccountable prejudice is this then that strikes me with such horror at his love! — what maid of birth and fortune equal to his own but would be proud of his addresses; and shall I, a poor foundling, the creature of his charity, not receive the honour he does me with the utmost gratitude! — shall I reject a happiness so far beyond my expectation! — so infinitely above any merit I can pretend to! — what must he think of me if I refuse him! — how madly stupid, how blind to my own interest, how thankless to him must I appear!   how will he despise my folly! — how hate my ingratitude!

Thus did her reason combat with her prejudice, and she suffered much the same agonies in endeavouring to love him in the manner he desired, as he had done to conquer the inclination he had for her, and both alike were fruitless. Yet was her condition much more to be commiserated: he had only to debate within himself whether he should yield or not to the suggestions of his own passion: she to subdue an aversion for what a thousand reasons concurred to convince her she ought rather to be ambitious of, and which in refusing she run the risque of being cast off, and abandoned to beggary and ruin; and what was still more hateful to her, being hated by that person who, next to her brother, she loved above all the world, tho' in a different way from that which alone could content him.

Dorilaus, who had taken the disorder he perceived in her for no other than the effects of a surprize, which a declaration, such as he had made, might very well occasion, was perfectly contented in his mind, and passed the night with much more tranquility than he had done many preceding ones, while he suffered his cruel reason to war against the dictates of her heart; but having now wholly given himself up to the latter, the sweet delusion filled him with a thousand pleasing ideas, and he thought of nothing but the happiness he should enjoy in the possession of the amiable Louisa. But how confounded was he, when the next day accosting her with all the tender transports of a lover, she turned from him, and burst into a flood of tears. How is this, Louisa, said he; do the offers I make you merit to be treated with disdain? has my submitting to be your lover forfeited that respect you were wont to pay me as a guardian! O do not, sir, accuse me of such black ingratitude, replied she; heaven knows with what sincere and humble duty I regard you, and I would sooner die than wilfully offend you; but if I am so unfortunate as not to be able to obey you in this last command, impute it, I beseech you, to my ill fate, and rather pity than condemn me.

You cannot love me then? cried he, somewhat fiercely. No other wise than I have ever done, answered she. My heart is filled with duty, reverence and gratitude, of which your goodness is the only source: as for any other sort of love I know not what it is; were it a voluntary emotion, believe me, sir, I gladly would give it entrance into my soul, but I well see it is of a far different nature.

Yet is your person at your own disposal, resumed he; and when possessed of that, the flame which burns so fiercely in my breast, in time may kindle one in yours. In speaking these words he took her in his arms, and kissed her with a vehemence which the prodigious respect she bore to him, as the patron and benefactor of herself and brother, could alone have made her suffer. — Her eyes however sparkled with indignation, tho' her tongue was silent, and at last bursting from his embrace, this, sir, cried she, is not the way to make me think as you would have me. As in this action he had no way transgressed the rules of decency, he could ill brook the finding her so much alarmed at it; and would have testified his resentment, had not the excess of his love, which is ever accompanied with an adequate share of respect, obliged him to stifle it. Well, Louisa, said he, looking earnestly upon her, ungenerously do you requite what I have done for you; but I, perhaps, may bring myself to other sentiments. — None, interrupted she, emboldened by the too great freedom she thought he had taken with her, can be so dreadful to me as those you now seem to entertain.

The look he gave her in hearing her speak in this manner, made her immediately repent having been so open; and in the same breath, because, pursued she, I look on it as the worst evil could befal me that I am compelled to oppose them.

Come, said he, again softened by these last words, you will not always oppose them: the fervor and constancy of my passion, joined with a little yielding on your side, will by degrees excite a tender impulse in you; and whatever is disagreeable at present, either in my person or behaviour, will wear off. — Permit me at least to flatter myself so far, and refuse me not those innocent endearments I have been accustomed to treat you with, before you knew me as a lover, or I indeed suspected I should be so.

He then kissed her again; but tho' he constrained himself within more bounds than before, those caresses which she received with pleasure, when thinking them only demonstrations of friendship, were now irksome, as knowing them the effects of love: she suffered him however to embrace her several times, and hold one of her hands close pressed between his, while he endeavoured to influence her mind by all the tender arguments his passion, backed with an infinity of wit, inspired; to all which she made as few replies as possible; but he contented himself, as love is always flattering, with imagining she was less refractory to his suit than when he first declared it.

Every day, and almost the whole day, did he entertain her on no other subject, but gained not the least ground on her inclinations; and all he could get from her was the wish of being less insensible, without the least indication of ever being so.

In this manner did they live together near three weeks; and how much longer he would have been able to restrain his impatience, or she to conceal the extreme regret in being compelled to listen to him, is uncertain: a law-suit required his presence to town, and Louisa was in hopes of being relieved for some time; but his passion was arrived at such a height that he could not support the least absence from her, and therefore brought her to London with him, so that her persecution ceased not, he never stirring from her but when the most urgent business obliged him to it.

One night happening to have stayed pretty late abroad, and in company, which occasioned his drinking more plentifully than he was accustomed, Louisa was retired to her chamber in order to go to bed: his love, ever uppermost in his head, would not permit him to think of sleeping without seeing her; accordingly he ran up to her room, and finding she was not undressed, told her he had something to acquaint her with, on which the maid that waited on her withdrew. Tho' the passion he was inspired with could not be heightened, his behaviour now proved it might at least be rendered more ungovernable by being enflamed with wine: He no sooner was alone with her, than he threw himself upon her as she was sitting in a chair, crying, O when my angel, my dear adored Louisa, will you consent to make me blest. — By heaven, I can no longer wait the tedious formalities your modesty demands. — I cannot think you hate me, and must this night ensure you mine. While he spoke these words his lips were so closely cemented to her's, that had there been no other hindrance, it would have been impossible for her to have reply'd. — But terrified beyond measure at the wild disorder of his looks, the expressions he made use of, and the actions that accompanied them, she wanted even the power of repulsing, till feeling her almost breathless, he withdrew his arms which he had thrown around her neck, and contenting himself with holding one of her hands, — Tell me, pursued he, when may I hope a recompence for all I have suffered? — I must, I will, have an end of all these fears of offending; — this cruel constraint; — this distance between us. — Few men, Louisa, in the circumstances we both are, would, like me, so long attend a happiness in my power to seize. — Trifle not therefore with a passion, the consequences of which there is no answering for.

O, sir! said she, with a trembling voice, you cannot, from the most generous, virtuous, and honourable man living, degenerate into a brutal ravisher. — You will not destroy the innocence you have cherished, and which is all that is valuable in the poor Louisa. She ended these words with a flood of tears, which, together with the sight of the confusion he had occasioned, made him a little recollect himself; and to prevent the wildness of his desires from getting the better of those rules he had resolved to observe, he let go her hand, and having told her he would press her no farther that night, but expected a more satisfactory answer the next day, went out of her chamber, and left her to enjoy what repose she could after the alarm he had given her.

CHAP. III.

Dorilaus continues his importunities, with some unexpected consequences that attended them.

POOR Louisa concealed the distraction she was in as much as possible she could from the maid, who immediately came into the room on Dorilaus having quitted it, and suffered her to undress, and put her to bed as usual; but was no sooner there, than instead of composing herself to sleep, she began to reflect on what he had said: — the words, *that there was no answering for the consequences of a passion such as his*, gave her the most terrible idea. — His actions, too, this night, seem'd to threaten her with all a virgin had to fear. — She knew him a man of honour, but thought she had too much reason to suspect that if she persisted in refusing to be his wife, that passion which had influenced him, contrary to his character, to make her such an offer, would also be too potent for any consideration of her to restrain him from proceeding to extremities. Having debated every thing within her own mind, she thought she ought not to continue a day longer in the power of a man who loved her to this extravagant degree: where to go indeed she knew not; — she had no friend, or even acquaintance, to whom she might repair, or hope to be received. — How could she support herself then? — which way procure the most common necessaries of life? — This was a dreadful prospect! yet appeared less so than that she would avoid: even starving lost its horrors when compared either to being compelled to wed a man whom she could not accept as a husband, or, by refusing him, run the risque of forfeiting her honour. — She therefore hesitated but a small time, and having once formed the resolution of quitting Dorilaus's house, immediately set about putting it into execution.

In the first place, not to be ungrateful to him as benefactor, she sat down and wrote the following letter to be left for him on the table:

> SIR,
>
> HEAVEN having rendered me of a disposition utterly incapable of receiving the honour you would do me, it would be an ill return for all the unmerited favours you have heaped upon me to prolong the disquiets I have unhappily occasioned by continuing in your presence; — besides, sir, the education you have vouchsafed to give me has been such, as informs me a person of my sex makes but an odd figure while in the power of one of yours possessed of

all the sentiments you are.

These, sir, are the reasons which oblige me to withdraw; and I hope, when well considered, will enough apologize for my doing so, to keep you from hating what you have but too much loved; for I beseech you to believe a great truth, which is, that the most terrible idea I carry with me is, lest while I fly the one, I should incur the other; and that, wheresoever my good or ill stars shall conduct me, my first and last prayers shall be for the peace, health, and prosperity of my most generous and ever honoured patron and benefactor.

Judge favourably, therefore, of this action, and rather pity than condemn the unfortunate

LOUISA.

Having sealed and directed this, she dressed herself in one of the least remarkable and plainest suits she had, taking nothing with her but a little linnen which she crammed into her pockets, and so sat waiting till she heard some of the family were stirring; then went down stairs, and being seen by one of the footmen, she told him she was not very well, and was going to take a little walk in hopes the fresh air might relieve her; he offered to wait upon her, but she refused, saying, she chose to go alone.

Thus had she made her escape; but, when in the street, was seized with very alarming apprehensions. — She was little acquainted with the town, and knew not which way to turn in search of a retreat. — Resolving, however, to go far enough, at least, from the house she had quitted, she wandered on, almost tired to death, without stopping any where, till chance directed her to a retired nook, where she saw a bill for lodgings on one of the doors. — Here she went in, and finding the place convenient for her present circumstances, hired a small, but neat chamber, telling the people of the house she was come to town in order to get a service, and till she heard of one to her liking, would be glad to do any needle-work she should be employed in.

The landlady, who happened to be a good motherly sort of woman, replied, that she was pleased with her countenance, or she would not have taken her in without enquiring into her character; and as she seemed not to be desirous of an idle life, she would recommend her to those that should find her work if she stayed with her never so long.

This was joyful news to our fair fugitive; and she blessed heaven for so favourable a beginning of her adventures. The woman was punctual to her promise; and being acquainted with a very great milliner, soon brought her more work than she could do, without encroaching into those hours nature requires for repose: but she seemed not to regret any fatigue to oblige the person who employed her, and sent home all she did so neat, so curious, and well wrought, that the milliner easily saw she had not been accustomed to do it for bread, and was very desirous of having her into the house, and securing her to herself. Louisa thinking it would be living with less care, agreed to go, on this condition, that she should be free to quit her in case any offer happened of waiting upon a lady. This was consented to by the other, who told her, that since she had that design, she could no where be so likely to succeed as at her house, which was very much frequented by the greatest ladies in the kingdom, she having the most Curiosities of any woman of her trade, which they came there to raffle for.

On this Louisa took leave of her kind landlady, who having taken a great fancy to her, and believing it would be for her advantage, was not sorry to part with her. A quite new scene of life now presented itself to her: — she found indeed the milliner had not made a vain boast; for her house was a kind of rendezvous, where all the young and gay of both sexes daily resorted. — It was here the marquis of W——r lost his heart, for a time, to the fine Mrs S — ge: — here, that the duke of G——n first declared his amorous inclinations for Mrs C——r: — here, that the seemingly virtuous lady B——n received the addresses of that agreeable rover Mr D——n: — here, that the beautiful dutchess of M—— gave that encouragement, which all the world had sighed for, to the more fortunate than constant Mr C——: in fine, it might properly enough be called the theatre of gallantry, where love and wit joined to display their several talents either in real or pretended passions.

Louisa usually sat at work in a back parlor behind that where the company were; but into which some of them often retired to talk to each other with more freedom.

This gave her an opportunity of seeing in what manner too many of the great world passed their time, and how small regard some of them pay to the marriage vow: every day presented her with examples of husbands, who behaved with no more than a cold civility to their own wives, and carried the fervor of their addresses to those of other men; and of wives who seemed rather to glory in, than be ashamed of a train of admirers. How senseless would these people think me, said she to herself, did they know I chose rather to work for my bread in mean obscurity, than yield to marry where I could not love. — Tenderness, mutual affection, and constancy, I find, are things not thought requisite to the happiness of a wedded state; and interest and convenience alone consulted. Yet she was far from repenting having rejected Dorilaus, or being in the least influenced by the example of others. — The adventures she was witness of made her, indeed, far more knowing of the world, but were far from corrupting those excellent morals she had received from nature, and had been so well improved by a strict education, that she not only loved virtue for its own sake, but despised and hated vice, tho' disguised under the most specious pretences.

Her youth, beauty, and a certain sprightliness in her air, was too engaging to be in the house of such a woman as Mrs C——ge, (for so this court-milliner was called) without being very much taken notice of; and tho' most of the gentlemen who came there had some particular object in view, yet that did not hinder them from saying soft things to the pretty Louisa as often as they had opportunity. Among the number of those who pretended to admire her was Mr B——n, afterwards lord F——h; but his addresses were so far from making any impression on her in favour of his person or suit, that the one was wholly indifferent to her, and the other so distasteful, that to avoid being persecuted with it, she entreated Mrs C——ge to permit her to work above stairs, that she might be out of the way of all such solicitations for the future, either from him or any other. This request was easily complied with, and the rather because she, who knew not the strength of her journey-woman's resolution, nor the principles she had been bred in, was sometimes in fear of losing so great a help to her business, by the temptations that might be offered in a place so much exposed to sight. Mr B——n no sooner missed her, than he enquired with a good deal of earnestness for her; and on Mrs C——ge's telling him she was gone away from her house, became so impatient to know where, and on what account she had left her, that this woman thinking it would be of advantage to her to own the truth, (for she did nothing without that view) turned off the imposition with a smile, and said, that perceiving the inclinations he had for her, she had sent her up stairs that no other addresses might be a hindrance to his designs. — This pleased him very well, and he ran directly to the room where he was informed she was, and after some little discourse, which he thought was becoming enough for a person of his condition to one of her's, began to treat her with freedoms which she could not help resisting with more fierceness than he had been accustomed to from women of a much higher rank; but as he had no great notion of virtue, especially among people of her sphere, he mistook all she said or did for artifice; and imagining she enhanced the merit of the gift only to enhance the recompence, he told he would make her a handsome settlement, and offered, as an earnest of his future gratitude, a purse of money. The generous maid fired with a noble disdain at a proposal, which she looked on only as an additional insult, struck down the purse with the utmost indignation, and cried, she was not of the number of those who thought gold an equivalent for infamy; and that mean as she appeared, not all his wealth could bribe her to a dishonourable action. At first he endeavoured to laugh her out of such idle notions as he called them, and was so far from being rebuffed at any thing she said, that he began to kiss and toy with her more freely than before, telling her he would bring her into a better humour; but he was wholly deceived in his expectations, if he had any of the nature he pretended, for she became so irritated at being treated in this manner, that she called out to the servants to come to her assistance, and protested she would not stay an hour longer in the house if she could not be secured from such impertinencies; on which he said she was a silly romantic fool, and flung out of the room.

Mrs C——ge hearing there had been some bustle, came up soon after and found Louisa in tears: she immediately complained of Mr B——n's behaviour to her, and said, tho' she acknowledged herself under many obligations to her for the favours she had conferred on her, she could not think of remaining in a place where, tho' she could not say her virtue had any severe trials, because she had a natural detestation to crimes of the kind that gentleman and some others had mentioned, yet her person was liable to be affronted. The milliner, who was surprized to hear her talk in this manner, but who understood her trade perfectly well, answered, that he was the best conditioned civil gentleman in the world; — that she did not know how it happened; — that she was certain indeed he loved her; and that it was in his power to make her a very happy woman if she were inclined to accept his offers; — but she would perswade her to nothing.

These kind of discourses created a kind of abhorrence in Louisa, as they plainly shewed her, what before she had some reason to believe, that she was in the house of one who would think nothing a crime that she found it in her own interest to promote. However, she thought it would be imprudent to break too abruptly with her, and contented herself for the present with engaging her promise that neither Mr B——n, nor any other person should for the future give her the least interruption of the like sort.

From this day, however, she was continually ruminating how she should quit her house, without running the risque of disobliging her so far as not to be employed by her; for tho' she found herself at present free from any of those importunities to which both by nature and by principles she was so averse, yet she could not answer to herself the continuing in a place where virtue was treated as a thing of little or no consequence, and where she knew not how soon she might again be subjected to affronts.

Amidst these meditations the thoughts of Dorilaus frequently intervened: she reflected on the obligations she had to him, and the mighty difference between the morals of that truly noble and generous man, and most of those she had seen at Mrs C——ge's: she wondered at herself at the antipathy she had to him as a husband, whom she so dearly loved and honoured as a friend; yet nothing could make her wish to be again on the same terms with him she had lately been. It also greatly added to her affliction that she knew not how to direct to her brother; for at the time of his departure, little suspicious of having any occasion to change the place of her abode, she had left the care of that entirely to Dorilaus. She was one morning very much lost in thought at the odd circumstances of her fortune, when a Gazette happening to lye upon the table, she cast her eye, without design, upon the following advertisement.

> WHEREAS a young gentlewoman has lately thought fit to abscond from her best friends, and with the most diligent search that could possibly be made after her has not yet been heard of, this is to acquaint her that if she pleases to return, she shall hereafter have no disturbance of that nature which it is supposed occasioned her withdrawing herself, but live entirely according to her own inclinations; and this the advertiser hereof gives his word and honour (neither of which she has any cause to doubt) faithfully to adhere to.
>
> It shall also be at her choice to live either at the house she quitted, or be again under the care of that gentlewoman who was entrusted with her education: she is therefore requested to conceal herself no longer, lest her youth, beauty, and inexperience of the town should betray her innocence into those very snares she fears to fall into.

The very beginning of this paragraph gave her a conjecture it was meant for no other than herself; and the more she read, the more she grew convinced of it. — It must be so, cryed she; every word, — every circumstance confirms it. — How unhappy am I that I cannot return so perfect an affection! — Instead of detesting my ingratitude, he only fears I should receive the punishment of it. — What man but Dorilaus would behave thus to the creature of his benevolence? — If I have any merits, do not I owe them to his goodness? — My brother and myself, two poor exposed and wretched foundlings, what but his bounty rear'd us to what we are? — Hard fate! — unlucky passion that drives me from his presence and protection.

Yet, would she say again, if he has indeed subdued that passion; — if he resolves to think of me as before he entertained it; if I were certain he would receive me as a child, how great would be the blessing!

This consideration had so much effect on her, that she was half determined to comply with the advertisement; but when she remembered to have read that where love is sincere and violent, it requires a length of time to be erased, and that those possessed of it are incapable of knowing even their own strength, and, as he had said to her himself, *that there was no answering for the consequences*, she grew instantly of another mind, and thought that putting herself again into the power of such a passion was running too great a hazard.

The continual agitations of her mind, joined to want of air, a quite different way of life, and perhaps sitting more closely to work than she had been accustomed to, threw her at length into a kind of languishing indisposition, which, tho' it did not confine her to her bed, occasioned a loss of appetite, and frequent faintings, which were very alarming to her. Mrs C——ge was extremely concerned to observe this change in her, and would have the opinion of her own physician, who said that she had the symptoms of an approaching consumption, and that it was absolutely necessary she should be removed into the country for some time.

Louisa readily complied with this advice, not only because she imagined it might be of service for the recovery of her health, but also as it furnished her with a pretence for leaving Mrs C—— ge's house, to which she was determined to return no more as a boarder. The good woman with whom she had lodged at first recommended her to a friend of her's at Windsor, where she immediately went, and was very kindly received.

CHAP. IV.

Louisa becomes acquainted with a lady of quality, part of whose adventures are also related, and goes to travel with her.

CHANGE of place affords but small relief to those whose distempers are in the mind: Louisa carried with her too many perplexing thoughts to be easily shook off, tho' the queen and court being then at Windsor, she had the opportunity of seeing a great many of the gay world pass daily by her window. — There also lodged in the same house with her a young widow of quality, who was visited by persons of the first rank; but as she was not of a condition to make one in any of these conversations, she reaped no other satisfaction from them than what the eye afforded.

As she was not, however, of a temper to indulge melancholy, she made it her endeavour to banish, as much as possible, all ideas which were displeasing from her mind: to this end, a fine harpsichord happening to stand in the dining-room, whenever the lady was abroad, she went in and diverted herself with playing. She was one day entertaining the woman of the house with a tune, which she accompanied with her voice, when the lady returning sooner than was expected, and hearing the instrument before she came up stairs, would needs know who had been making use of it; for Louisa hurried out of the room before she came in: the landlady, as there was no occasion to disguise the truth, told her that it was a young woman, who not being very well, had come down into the country for air.

She has had an excellent education, I am certain, said the lady, (who henceforward we shall call Melanthe) for in my life I never heard any body play or sing better: — I must be acquainted with her; on which the other said she would let her know the honour she intended her.

That very evening, as great ladies no sooner think of any thing but they must have it performed, was Louisa sent for into her apartment; and her countenance and behaviour so well seconded the good impression her skill in music had begun, that Melanthe became charm'd with her, and from that time obliged her to come to her every morning; and whenever she was without company, made her dine and sup with her. Being curious to know her circumstances, Louisa made no scruple of acquainting her with the truth, only instead of relating how she had been exposed in her infancy, said, that having the misfortune to be deprived of her parents, it was her intention to wait on a lady, and till she heard of one who would accept her service, she had work'd at her needle.

Melanthe then asked if she would live with her; to which the other gladly answering, she should think herself happy in such a lady; but you must go abroad then, said she, for I am weary of England, and am preparing to travel: as it is a route of pleasure only, I shall stay just as long as I find any thing new and entertaining in one place, then go to another till I am tired of that, and so on, I know not how long; for unless my mind alters very much, I shall not come back in some years.

Louisa was perfectly transported to hear her say this; she had a great desire to see foreign parts, and thought she could never have a better opportunity: she expressed the pleasure she should take in attending her wherever she went with so much politeness and sincerity, that Melanthe told her, it should be her own fault if she ever quitted her, and withal assured her, she would never treat her in any other manner than a companion, and that tho' she would make her a yearly allowance for cloaths and card-money, yet she would expect no other service from her than fidelity to her secrets, and affection to her person.

From the moment this agreement was made, the young Louisa regained her complection and her appetite; and being now initiated into the family of this lady, had no longer any care to take than to oblige her, a thing not difficult, Melanthe being good-natured, and strongly prepossessed in favour of her new friend, for so she vouchsafed to call her, and to use her accordingly.

As a proof of it, she made her in a very short time the confident of her dearest secrets: they were one day sitting together, when accidentally some mention was made of the power of love. You are too young, Louisa, said Melanthe, to have experienced the wonderful effects of that passion in yourself, and therefore cannot be expected to have much compassion for what it can inflict on others.

Indeed, madam, answered she, tho' I have never yet seen a man who gave me a moment's pain on that score, yet I believe there are no emotions whatever so strong as those of love, and that it is capable of influencing people of the best sense to things which in their nature they are most averse to.

Well, my dear, resumed the other, since I find you have so just a notion of it, I will confide in your discretion so far as to let you know, that but for an ungrateful man, I had not looked on my native country as a desart, and resolved to seek a cure for my ill-treated and abused tenderness in foreign parts.

My quality, continued she, I need not inform you of: you have doubtless heard that my family yields to few in antiquity, and that there is an estate belonging to it sufficient to support the dignity of its title; but my father having many children, could not give very great portions to the daughters: I was therefore disposed of, much against my inclinations, to a nobleman, whom my unlucky charms had so much captivated as to make him not only take me with no other dowry than my cloaths and jewels, but also to settle a large jointure upon me, which, he being dead, I at present enjoy. I cannot say that all the obligations he laid upon me could engage a reciprocal regard: — I behaved with indifference to him while living, and little lamented him when dead: not that I was prepossessed in favour of any other man; — my heart, entirely free, was reserved to be the conquest of the too charming perfidious Henricus, who arriving soon after my lord's decease, and bringing with him all the accomplishments which every court he had visited could afford, join'd to the most enchanting person nature ever formed, soon made me know I was not that insensible creature I had thought myself.

I happened to be at court when he came to kiss her majesty's hand on his return; and whether it was that my eyes testified too much the admiration the first sight of him struck me with, or that he really discovered something more attractive in me than any lady in the presence I know not, but he seemed to distinguish me in a particular manner, and I heard him say to my lord G——n in a whisper, that I was the finest woman had had ever seen: but what gave me more pleasure than even this praise, was an agreement I heard made between him and the same lord to go that evening to a raffle at Mrs C — rt-f — r's. I was one of those who had put in, tho' if I had not, I should certainly have gone for a second sight of him, who when he went out of the drawing-room seemed to have left me but half myself.

In fine, I went, and had there wanted any thing to have entirely vanquished me, my conqueror's manner of address had done it with a form less agreeable. — O Louisa, pursued she with a sigh, if you have never seen or heard the charming Henricus, you can have no notion of what is excellent in man; such flowing wit; — such softness in his voice and air; — but there is no describing what he is. He seemed all transport at meeting me there; among a number of ladies I alone engrossed him: he scarce spoke to any other; and being so fortunate to win the raffle, which was a fine inlaid India cabinet, instead of sending it to his own house, he privately ordered his servant to leave it at mine, lord G——n having, as he afterwards told me, informed him where I lived, and also all the particulars he wanted to know concerning me.

I was prodigiously surprized when I came home and found the Cabinet, which my woman imagined I had won by its being brought thither. It was indeed a piece of gallantry I had no reason to expect from one so perfect a stranger to me; and this, joined with the many complaisant things he said to me at Mrs C — rt-f — r's, flattered my vanity enough to make me think he was no less charmed with me than I too plainly found I was with him. I slept little that night, and pretty early the next morning received a billet from him to this effect:

MADAM,

I THOUGHT the cabinet we raffled for was more properly the furniture of a lady's closet than mine, especially one who must

daily receive a great number of such epistles as it was doubtless
intended by the maker to contain: happy should I think myself if
any thing of mine might find room among those which, for their
wit and elegance, may be more worthy of preserving, tho' none
can be for their sincerity more so than those which are dictated
by the eternally devoted heart of

HENRICUS.

You cannot imagine, my dear Louisa, how delighted I was with these few
lines; I enclosed them indeed in the cabinet given me by the author of them,
but laid up their meaning in my heart: — I was quite alert the whole day, but
infinitely more so, when in the evening my admired Henricus made me a
visit introduced by my lord H——, who had been one of my late husband's
particular friends, and had ever kept a good correspondence with me.

Henricus took not the least notice either of the cabinet or letter before him;
and as I imagined he had his reasons for it, I too was silent on that head; he took
the opportunity, however, while lord H—— was speaking to a young lady who
happened to be with me, to ask permission to wait on me with the hope of being
received on his own score as he was now on that of his friend. I told him that
merit, such as his, was sufficient to recommend him anywhere; and, besides, I
had an obligation to him which I ought to acknowledge. This was all either of
us had time to say; but it was enough to make me convinced he desired a more
particular conversation, and him, that it would not be unwelcome to me.

Thus began an acquaintance equally fatal to my peace of mind and reputation;
and having said that, it would be needless to repeat the circumstances of it,
therefore shall only tell you I was so infatuated with my passion, that I never
gave myself the trouble to examine into the nature of his pretensions, and lull'd
with the vows he made of everlasting love, resented not that he forbore pressing
to that ceremony which could alone ensure it: — yes, my Louisa, I will not
wrong him so far as to say he deceived me in this point; for tho' he protested
with the most solemn imprecations that he would never address any other
woman than myself, yet he never once mentioned marriage to me. — Alas! he
too well saw into my heart, and that all my faculties were too much his to be
able to refuse him any thing: — even so it proved; — he triumphed over all in
my power to yield; — nay, was so far subdued, that I neither regretted my loss,
nor used any endeavours to conceal it: — vain of being his at any rate, I thought
his love more glory to me than either fame or virtue; and while I was known to
enjoy the one, despised whatever censures I incurred for parting with the other:
in the Mall, the play-house, the ring,[7] at Bath or Tunbridge, he was always with

---

[7] *the ring*: Charles I created a circular track, known as the Ring, for members of the royal
court to drive their carriages around in the northern half of Hyde Park, London. The Park
was opened to the public in 1637, and it became a fashionable place to ride, drive and be seen.

me; nor would any thing have been a diversion to me had he been absent.

For upwards of a year I had no reason to complain of his want of assiduity to me, tho' I have since heard that even in that time he had other amours with women who carried them on with more prudence than I was mistress of; but I had afterwards a stabbing proof of his insincerity and inconstancy.

Perceiving a great alteration in his behaviour, that he visited me less frequently, and when he came, the ardours he was accustomed to treat me with still more and more languid and enforced, I upbraided him in terms which, tho' they shewed more love than resentment, and had he retained any tolerable remains of tenderness for me, must have been rather obliging than the contrary, he affected to take extremely ill, and told me plainly, that nothing was so dear to him as his peace, — that he was not of a temper to endure reproaches, and that, if I desired the continuance of our amour, I must be satisfied with him as he was. These cool, and indeed insolent replies made me almost distracted; and beginning to suspect he had some new engagement, I talked to him in a manner as if I had been assured of it: — he, perhaps, imagining it was so, made no efforts to cure my jealousy, but behaved with so cruel an indifference as confirmed my apprehensions.

Resolving to be convinced whether I really had any rival or not, I employed spies to observe wherever he went, and to whom; but alas, there required little pains to acquire the intelligence I sought. — I was soon informed that he was every day with the daughter of a little mechanic; — that he made her very rich presents, procured a commission in the army for one of her brothers, and in fine, that he was as much devoted to her as a man of his inconstant temper could be to any woman.

How severe a mortification was this to my pride! but it had this good attending it, that it very much abated my love: — to be abandoned for so mean a creature, and who had nothing but youth and a tolerable face to recommend her, shewed such a want of taste as well as gratitude, as rendered despicable in my eyes what had lately engrossed all my love and admiration. — The moment I received the information I sent for him; and forcing my countenance to a serenity my heart was a stranger to, told him it was only to take a last leave of a person whom I had been so far mistaken in as to think deserving my affection: that I desired to see him once more, but having now seen my error, desired he would desist his visits for the future. He asked me with the same calmness he had lately behaved with, what whim I had got into my head now. I, who had before determined not to feed my rival's pride by shewing any jealousy of her, only replied, that as amours, such as ours had been, must have an end some time or other, — I thought none could be more proper than the present, because I believed both of us could do it without pain.

Answer for yourself, madam, cried he with some emotion, for I could perceive my behaviour had a little stung his vanity: and resolute to give him in my turn all the mortification in my power, nay, said I, with a disdainful toss of my head, I do not enquire into your sentiments, — it is sufficient mine are to break off entirely with you — neither is it any concern to me how you may resent this alteration in my conduct, or dispose of yourself hereafter; but I once more assure you, with my usual frankness, that I now can see none of those perfections my foolish fancy formerly found in you, and cannot be complaisant enough to counterfeit a tenderness I neither feel nor think you worthy of.

The surprize he was in kept him silent for some moments; but recovering himself as well as he could, he told me, that if the levity of my nature had made me cease to love him, he could not have expected endearments should be converted into affronts; that if I was determined to see him no more he must submit, and should endeavour to make himself as easy as he could under the misfortune.

These last words were uttered with a kind of sneer, which was very provoking, however, I restrained my passion during the little time he stayed; but as soon as I found myself alone gave it vent in tears and exclamations, — since which I have been more at peace within myself; for tho' I cannot say I hate him, I am now far from loving him, and hope that time and absence may bring me to a perfect indifference.

Thus, Louisa, continued she, you see the beginning and end of an adventure which has made some noise in town, to be out of which I have taken a resolution to travel till the whole shall be forgotten, and I have entirely rooted out of my heart all manner of consideration for this ungrateful man.

Louisa thanked her for the condescension she had made her in entrusting her with so important a secret, and said every thing she could in praise of the resolution she had taken to leave England for a time, not only because it was exactly conformable to her own desires, but also that she thought it so laudable in itself. Melanthe then assured her that she was not capable of changing her mind in this particular, and that her equipage was getting ready at London for that purpose, so that she believed they should embark in a few days. Louisa, on hearing this, said, that she must then provide herself with some things it would be necessary for her to have in order to appear in the station her ladyship was pleased to place her; but the other, who, as may be seen by her history, never preserved a medium in any thing, would not suffer her to be at the least expence on that account, but took the care of furnishing her with every thing on herself; and accordingly sent a man and horse directly to her mercer's, draper's, milliner's, and other tradesmen, with orders to send down silks, laces, hollands,[8] and whatever else was requisite; which being brought, were put to be made fit for wearing by work-women at Windsor; so that now our Louisa

---

[8]   *hollands*: Holland cloth, a fine, plainwoven linen, especially from the Netherlands.

made as good a figure, and had as great a variety of habits as when under the guardianship of Dorilaus, and, to complete her happiness, this new benefactress grew every day more and more delighted with her company.

All being now prepared, they came to London, where they lay but one night before they took shipping for Helvoetsluys[9] in Holland, where, being safely landed, they proceeded to Utrecht, and so to Aix-la-Chapelle: there they stayed some weeks for the sake of the waters, air, and good company; and Louisa thought it so pleasant, that she would have been glad not to have removed for some time longer; but Melanthe was yet restless in her mind, and required frequent change of place. Here it was, however, that Louisa thought she might venture to write to Dorilaus, to ease him of that kind concern she doubted not but he was in for her welfare, by the advertisement already mentioned in the Gazette. The purport of her letter was as follows:

> *Ever Honoured Sir,*
>
> CHILD of your bounty as I am, I flatter myself that, in spight of my enforc'd disobedience, it would be a trouble to you to hear I should do any thing unworthy of that education you were pleased to bestow on me: I therefore take the liberty of acquainting you, that heaven has raised me a protectress in a lady of quality with whom I now am, as you will see by the date of this, at Aix-la-Chapelle. As all the favours I receive from her, or all the good that shall happen during my whole life is, and will be entirely owing to you as the fountain-head, it will always be my inclination, as well as duty, to pay you the tribute of grateful thanks. — Poor recompence, alas, for all you have done for me! yet those, with my incessant prayers to heaven, are all in the power of
>
> *Your most dutiful*
>
> LOUISA.

She took no notice of the advertisement, not only as she could not be positive it related to herself, as also because she thought, if he were certain she had read it, he might resent her not answering it, as discovering a too great diffidence of his honour. She added, however, a postscript, entreating him to let her brother know, that whatever happened, he should have no reason to find fault with her conduct.

After they left Aix-la-Chapelle, they took bye roads to avoid the armies; yet notwithstanding all their care, they now and then met parties who were out on foraging, but as it happened, they were always under the conduct of officers

---

[9] *Helvoetsluys*: Helvoetsluis, now a small city in the Western Netherlands. At the time of the United Provinces, it was a significant naval port.

who prevented any ill accident, so that our travellers met with no manner of interruption, but arrived safely at the magnificent city of Vienna, where was at that time an extreme gay court, affording every thing capable of diverting a much more settled melancholy than either Melanthe or her fair companion were possessed of.

The arch-dutchesses, Mary Elizabeth, and Mary Anna Josepha, afterward queen of Portugal,[10] had frequent balls and entertainments in their different drawing-rooms; to all which Melanthe, being a stranger and a woman of quality, was invited: she kept her promise with Louisa; and treating her as a young lady, whose friendship to her, and a desire of seeing the world had engaged to accompany her, she was received and respected as such; and by this means had an opportunity of shewing the skill she had in dancing, singing, music, and indeed all the accomplishments that a woman born and educated to the best expectations, is usually instructed in. As neither her lady nor herself understood the German language, and she spoke infinitely the best French, her conversation was the most agreeable, which, joined with a most engaging manner, and a peculiar sweetness in her voice, attracted all those civilities which the rank of the other demanded.

Possessed of so many charms, it would have been strange if, in a city throng'd like Vienna with young noblemen, who were continually coming from all parts of the empire, she had lived without some who pretended to somewhat more than mere admiration; but her heart had not refused the worthy Dorilaus to become the conquest of a German; nor was it here she was ordained to experience those anxieties in herself, she could but imperfectly conceive by the description she had from others.

Melanthe, however, whose sole aim was to drive all perplexing thoughts from her mind, encouraged a great number of visiters, so that her lodgings seemed a perfect theatre of gallantry; and Louisa having her share in all the amusements this lady prepared for the reception of those that came to see her, or were contrived for her entertainment by others, past her time in the most gay and agreeable manner imaginable, and by this means acquired the knowledge of almost the only thing she before was ignorant in, how to receive a multiplicity of company, yet to behave so as each should imagine themselves most welcome; — to seem perfectly open, without discovering any thing improper to be revealed; — to use all decent freedoms with the men, yet not encourage the least from them, and to seem to make a friend of every woman she conversed with, without putting trust in any; — and in fine, all the little policies which make up

---

[10] *The arch-dutchesses, Mary Elizabeth, and Mary Anna Josepha, afterward queen of Portugal*: Maria Elisabeth of Austria (1680–1741), Governor of the Netherlands from 1725 until her death; Maria Ana of Austria (1683–1754), wife of João V of Portugal and Regent during his final illness.

the art of what is called a polite address, and which is not be attained without an acquaintance with the court and great world.

This, I say, our amiable foundling was now well vers'd in, and practised among those who she found made a practice of it; but yet retained the same sincerity of mind, love of virtue, and detestation of vice, she brought with her from the house of Dorilaus: — neither was her youth too much dazzled with exterior splendor she beheld; and tho' she was well enough pleased with it, yet it did not in the least take her off from the duties of religion, or inspire her with any ambitious or aspiring wishes to become what she was forbid any probable expectation of. She knew the present fashion of her life was not an assured settlement, and therefore set not her heart upon it. Few at her years would have had the like prudence, or in time armed themselves, as she did, against any change that might befal her.

In this happy situation let us leave her for a while: the young Horatio claims his share of attention; and it is time to see what encouragement and success his martial ardor met with on the banks of the Danube.

CHAP. V.

Horatio's reception by the officers of the army; his behaviour in the battle; his being taken prisoner by the French; his treatment among them, and many other particulars.

THE extreme graceful person of Horatio, his youth, handsome equipage, and the letters sent by Dorilaus to several of the principal officers in his favour, engaged him a reception answerable to his wishes: but none was of greater service than the recommendation he had to colonel Brindfield,[11] who being in great favour with the duke of Marlborough,[12] was highly respected by the whole army. This gentleman made him dine frequently with him, and testified the regard he had for Dorilaus, by doing all the good offices he could to a youth whom he perceived by his letter he had a great concern for. He not only introduced him to the acquaintance of many officers of condition, but took an opportunity of presenting him to the duke himself, giving at the same time his grace an account that he was a gentleman whose inclinations to arms, and the honour of serving under his grace, had made him renounce all other advantages for the hope of doing something worthy of his favour. The duke looked all the time he was speaking very attentively on the young Horatio, and finding something in his air that corroborated the colonel's description, was pleased to say, that he was charm'd with his early thirst after fame; and then turning toward him, you will soon, pursued he, have an opportunity of seeing how the face of war looks near at hand: — I can tell you, that you must not always expect smiles. No, my lord, replied he, without being at all daunted by the presence of so great a man; but where we love all countenances are agreeable.

He arrived indeed opportunely to be a witness of the dangers of that glorious campaign which brought such shame to the French, such honour to the

---

[11]   *colonel Brindfield*: probably James Bringfield (d. 1706), equerry and aide-de-camp to the duke of Marlborough. There is a memorial tablet to Bringfield in the north aisle of the nave of Westminster Abbey, recording his death at the Battle of Ramillies in 1706.

[12]   *duke of Marlborough*: John Churchill, first duke of Marlborough (1650–1722), commander of the Allied armies from 1701–1711, and politician. The success of the Blenheim campaign of 1704 [see below, n. 13] secured Churchill's reputation as a brilliant military tactician, and brought him substantial property, wealth and honours.

English, and such real advantages to the empire.[13] Prince Eugene of Savoy,[14] and prince Lewis of Baden[15] were come to the duke's quarters, which were then at Mondesheim,[16] to consult on proper operations; the result was, that the duke and prince Lewis should join armies, and command each day alternately, and that prince Eugene should head a separate army and repair towards Philipsburg,[17] to defend the passage of the Rhine, the lines of Stolhoffen, and the country of Wirtenberg.[18]

The two armies joined at Westerstretton, thence proceeded by early marches towards Donawert, between which and Scellenberg[19] the enemy was encamped. Fatigued as they were, the duke made them pass over a little river and endeavour to force the intrenchments; which enterprize succeeded, notwithstanding all the advantages the confederate armies were in, and the others were obliged to retire with great precipitation, many of whom were drowned in endeavouring to pass the Danube.

---

[13] *that glorious campaign which brought such shame to the French, such honour to the English, and such real advantages to the empire*: The culmination of the campaign of 1704 was the heavy defeat of Franco-Bavarian forces in a battle fought in and around the villages of Blenheim (or Blindheim) and Oberglau, on the road between Höchstädt and Donauwörth, in Bavaria on 13 August (NS). After the defeat, Bavaria no longer posed a threat to Austria, which was secured as a member of the Grand Alliance. By the end of 1704, the Alliance had established a ring around France and Spain that allowed military offensives to be mobilized in all the theatres of war. (See John Hattendorf, *England in the War of the Spanish Succession. A Study of the Grand Strategy, 1702-1712* (New York: Garland, 1987), pp. 100-11). For details of the battles in which Marlborough and the allies were involved Haywood could have drawn on any number of contemporary accounts. Recent histories, from Haywood's point of view, were Thomas Lediard's three-volume *The Life of John, Duke of Marlborough, Prince of the Roman Empire* (1736), or John Bancks's *The History of John Duke of Marlborough, Prince of Mindelheim, Captain-General and Commander in Chief of the Armies of her Britannick Majesty* (1741).
[14] *prince Eugene of Savoy*: Eugène François, prince of Savoy-Carignan (1663-1736), who with John Churchill, duke of Marlborough [see above, n. 12], routed the Franco-Bavarian army at Blenheim in 1704.
[15] *prince Lewis of Baden*: Ludwig Wilhelm, Margrave of Baden-Baden (1655-1707), godson of Louis XIV. He served as commander of the imperial army of Leopold I, Archduke of Austria and Holy Roman Emperor (1640-1705) in the War of the Spanish Succession.
[16] *Mondesheim*: Mindelheim, a town about 90 km west of Munich. John Churchill, duke of Marlborough (see above, n. 12) was made Prince of Mindelheim by the Holy Roman Emperor, Joseph I (1678-1711) in 1705. Mindelheim was returned to the Elector of Bavaria under the terms of the Treaty of Utrecht (1714).
[17] *Philipsburg*: Philippsburg, a town in what is now the German state of Baden-Württemberg.
[18] *to defend the passage of the Rhine, the lines of Stolhoffen, and the country of Wirtenberg*: Ludwig Wilhelm, Margrave of Baden-Baden [see above, n. 15] constructed a defensive line in the Black Forest, at Stollhofen, which prevented a French advance from Strasbourg down the Rhine towards Württemberg.
[19] *Westerstretton ... Scellenberg*: Westerstetten, a village in what is now the German state of Baden-Württemberg; Schellenberg was a fortified ridge dominating the riverside city of Donauwörth, and the site of the Battle of Schellenberg in July 1704.

In this action was our young soldier initiated, and had the glory to be signalized by two remarkable accidents; one was, that pressing among the foremost in this hazardous attempt, he had his hat taken off by a cannon ball; and the other was, that seeing a standard about to be taken by the enemy, the person who carried it happening to be kill'd, he ran among those who were carrying it away, and being seconded by some others, retrieved that badge of English honour; and as this was done in sight of the duke, he rode up to him directly and presented it to him. Take it for your pains, cried he, you have ventured hard, and well deserve the prize. There was no time for thanks; the duke, who was almost every where at once, was immediately gone where he found his presence necessary, and Horatio returned to take the place of the dead cornet, doubly animated by the encouragement he had received.

This victory opening a way into the elector of Bavaria's dominions,[20] that poor country was terribly ravaged, no less than 300 towns, villages and castles being utterly consumed by a detachment of horse and dragoons the duke sent for that purpose. Some old officers told Horatio that now would be the time to make his fortune if he went with these squadrons, there being many rich things which would fall to the share of the plunderers; to which he answered, that he came to fight for the honour of his country, and not to rob for its disgrace. This they laughed at, and endeavoured to make him sensible, that the taking away an enemy's treasure was to take away their strength; but all they could say was ineffectual; he was not to be perswaded out of what he thought reason and justice: and this conversation being afterward repeated to the duke, he smil'd and said, he was yet too young to know the value of money.

After this, prince Lewis of Baden dividing from the duke, in order to undertake the siege of Ingolstadt,[21] our young cornet attended his grace to the relief of prince Eugene, who expected to be attacked by the united army of Bavarians and French, then encamped near Hockstadt.[22]

It would be needless to give any description of this famous battle, few of my readers but must be acquainted with it, so I shall only say, that among the number of those few prisoners the French had to boast of in attonement for so great a defeat, was the young brave Horatio, who fell to the lot of the baron de la Valiere, nephew to the marquis of Sille.[23] This nobleman being extremely taken with his person and behaviour, treated him in the politest manner; and

---

[20] *the elector of Bavaria's dominions*: Maximilian Emanuel Von Wittelsbach, Elector of Bavaria (1662–1726), ruled an area of the Holy Roman Empire roughly equivalent to present-day Upper and Lower Bavaria in Germany.

[21] *siege of Ingolstadt*: a siege of August 1704, preceding the Battle of Blenheim, designed to provide a further Danube crossing for Marlborough's army.

[22] *Hockstadt*: Höchstädt (see above, n. 13).

[23] *baron de la Valiere, nephew to the Marquis of Sille*: unidentified: Haywood may have borrowed the name from that of Louise de la Vallière (1644–1710), mistress of Louis XIV.

tho' he carried him with him into France, assured him, that it was more for the pleasure of entertaining him there than any other consideration. Horatio was not much afflicted at this misfortune, because it gave him an opportunity of seeing a country he had heard so much commended, and also to make himself master of a language, which, tho' he understood, he spoke but imperfectly.

The baron was not only one of the most gallant, but also one of the best humoured men in the world; he spared nothing during the whole time they tarried in his quarters, nor in their journey to Paris, which might contribute to make his prisoner easy under his present circumstances; and among other things, often said to him, if you and some others have fallen under the common chance of war, you have yet the happiness of knowing your army in general has been victorious, and that there are infinitely a greater number of ours, who, against their will, must see England, than there are of yours conducted into France.

On their arrival, Horatio wrote an account to Dorilaus of all had happened to him, not doubting but he would use his interest to have him either mentioned when there should come an exchange of prisoners, or that he would ransom him himself; but receiving no answer, he concluded his letter, by some accident, had miscarried, and sent another, but that meeting the same fate as the former, he wrote a third, accompanied with one to his sister directed to the boarding-school, where he imagined she still was: to this last, after some time, he had the following return from the governess:

> SIR,
>
> A LETTER directed for miss Louisa coming to my house, I was in debate with myself what to do with it, that young lady having been gone from me last September, since which time I never heard any thing of her: — at last I sent it to Dorilaus's country seat by a messenger, who brought it to me again, with intelligence he was gone with some friends into the north of Ireland, and that it was probable they had taken miss with them: — I then thought proper to open it, believing she had no secrets I might not be entrusted with, and finding it came from you, could do no less than give you this information to prevent your being under any surprize for not receiving answers to your letters. I am sorry to find by yours that you have had such ill success in your first campaign; but would not have you be cast down, since you need not doubt but on the return of Dorilaus you will have remittances for your ransom, or whatever else you may have occasion for.
>
> *I am,* SIR,
> *Your most humble and obedient Servant,*
> A. TRAINWELL.

This letter made him perfectly contented; he had no reason to question the continuance of Dorilaus's goodness to him, nor that he should attend this new proof of it any longer than the return of that gentleman to England should make him know the occasion he now had for it. He therefore had no anxious thoughts to interrupt the pleasures the place he was in afforded in such variety: he was every evening with the baron, either at court, the opera, the comedy, or some other gay scene of entertainment; was introduced to the best company; and his young heart, charm'd with the politeness and gallantry of that nation, and the little vanity to which a person of such early years is incident, being flattered with the complaisance he was treated with, gave him in a short time a very strong affection for them; but there was yet another and more powerful motive which rendered his captivity not only pleasing, but almost destroyed in him an inclination ever to see his native country again.

The baron de la Valiere had long been passionately in love with a young lady, who was one of the maids of honour to king James's queen: he went almost every day to St Germains,[24] in order to prosecute his addresses, and frequently took Horatio with him. The motive of his first introducing him to that court was, perhaps, the vanity of shewing him that no reverse of fate could make the French regardless of what was due to royalty, since the Chevalier St George[25] seem'd to want no requisite of majesty but the power; but he afterwards found the pleasure he took in those visits infinitely surpassed what he could have expected, and that his heart had an attachment, which made him no sooner quit that palace than he would ask with impatience when they should go thither again. The baron had a great deal of penetration; and as those who feel the power of love in themselves can easily perceive the progress it makes in others, a very few visits confirmed him that Horatio had found something there more attractive than all he could behold elsewhere: nor was he long at a loss to discover, among the number of beauties which composed the trains of the queen and princess, which of them it was that had laid his prisoner under a more lasting captivity than war had done.

Princess Louisa Maria Teresa, daughter of the late king James,[26] was then but in her thirteenth year; the ladies who attended her were all of them much of the same age; and to shew the respect the French had for this royal family, tho' in misfortunes, were also the daughters of persons whose birth and fortune might

---

[24] *St Germains*: the Château at Saint-Germain-en-Laye, gifted to James II by Louis XIV. Saint Germain is now an affluent suburb of Paris.
[25] *the Chevalier St George*: The Chevalier St George was one of the names given, usually by Jacobites, to James Francis Edward Stuart (1688–1766) son of James II. For Whigs, he was the 'Old Pretender'.
[26] *Princess Louisa Maria Theresa, daughter of the late king James*: Louise Marie Stuart (1692–1712), last child of James II [see above, n. 1]. She was born in the court in exile at Saint-Germain-en-Laye.

have done honour to the service of the greatest empress in the world; nor were any of them wanting in those perfections which attract the heart beyond the pomp of blood or titles; but she who had influenced that of our Horatio, was likewise in the opinion of those, who felt not her charms in the same degree he did, allowed to excel her fair companions in every captivating grace, and to yield in beauty to none but the princess herself, who was esteemed a Prodigy. This amiable lady was called Charlotta de Palfoy, only daughter to the baron of that name; and having from her most early years discovered a genius above what is ordinarily found in her sex, had been educated by her indulgent parents in such a manner, as nature lost nothing for want of the improvements of art; yet did not all the accomplishments she was mistress of give her the least air of haughtiness; on the contrary, there was a certain sweetness of temper in her which gave a double charm to every thing she said or did: she was all affability, courtesy and chearfulness; she could not therefore avoid treating so agreeable a stranger as Horatio with all imaginable marks of civility; but she had been a very small time acquainted with him before her liking ripened into a kind of tenderness little inferior to what he was possessed of for her; and tho' both of them were then too young to be able to judge of the nature of this growing inclination, yet they found they loved without knowing to what end.

As both the Chevalier St George and the princess his sister were instructed in the English language, and besides many of their court were natives of Great Britain, whose loyalty had made them follow the exil'd monarch,[27] the French belonging to them had also an ambition to speak in the same dialect: mademoiselle Charlotta being but lately come among them had not yet attained the proper accent, any more than Horatio had that of the French; so they agreed that to improve each other in the different languages, he should always speak to her in French, and she should answer him in English. This succeeded not only for the purpose it was intended, but likewise drew on a greater intimacy between them than might otherwise have happened, at least in so short a time.

The baron having a real friendship for Horatio, rejoiced to find he had so powerful an attachment to continue among them, and without taking any notice how far he saw into his sentiments, encouraged his visits at St Germains all he could. Thus indulged in every thing he wished, he began insensibly to lose all desires of returning to England, and receiving no letters either from Dorilaus or his sister, was as it were weaned from that affection he formerly bore to them, and in the room of that the new friendships he was every day

---

[27] *many of their court were natives of Great Britain, whose loyalty had made them follow the exil'd monarch*: The number of Jacobite exiles who left Britain and Ireland for France and settled in Paris and Saint-Germain-en-Laye between 1688 and 1692 has been estimated at 30,000 to 40,000. (See Nathalie Genet-Rouffiac, 'Jacobites in Paris and Saint-Germain-en-Laye', in *The Stuart Court in Exile and the Jacobites*, ed. by Eveline Cruickshanks and Edward Corp (London: Hambledon Press, 1995), p. 17.)

contracting took up his mind.

He was indeed used with so much love and respect by people in the most eminent stations, to whom the baron had introduced him, that it would have been ungrateful in him not to have returned it with the greatest good-will. Expressing one day some surprize at being so far forgotten by his friends in England, de la Valiere told him that he would not have him look on himself as any other than a guest in France, and that if he chose to quit that country, he should not only be at his liberty to return to England whenever he pleased, but also should be furnished with a sum sufficient for the expences of his journey; but added, that the offer he now made of depriving himself of so agreeable a companion was a piece of self-denial, than which there could not be a greater proof of a disinterested regard.

Horatio replied in the manner this generosity demanded, and said, that if there was any thing irksome to him in France, it was only his inability of returning the favours he had received: believe me, sir, pursued he, were I master of a fortune sufficient to put me above the necessity of receiving the obligations I now do, it would not be in the power of all I left in England to prevail on me to return; — it is here, and in the society of that company I at present, thro' your means, enjoy, that I would wish to pass my whole life.

The baron then told him he would find a way to make all things easy to him, and accordingly went the same day to monsieur the prince of Conti,[28] to whom he gave such an advantagious description of the courage and accomplishments of the English cornet, and the inclination he had to stay among them, that his highness told the baron, that he might acquaint him from him, that if he were willing to serve under him he should have a commission; or, if he rather chose a civil employment, he would use his interest to secure him such a one as might afford both honour and profit.

This the baron did not fail to communicate immediately to Horatio, who, charm'd with the generosity both of the one and the other, broke into the utmost encomiums of that nation — sure, said he, the French are a people born to inspire and instruct virtue and benevolence to all the kingdoms in the world! After the first raptures of his gratitude were over, being pressed by the baron to let him know which of the prince's offers he would chuse to accept; alas! replied he, this is a kind of unfortunate dilemma I am in; — my inclinations are for the army, and it would be the height of my ambition to serve under such generals as the French; but it would be unnatural in me to draw my sword against the land which gave me being: O would to God! continued he, there were an opportunity

---

[28] *prince of Conti*: The title 'prince of Conti' could, depending on the date, apply to Armand, prince of Conti (1629–1666), or one of his two sons. Louis Armand was second prince of Conti (1661–1685) and François Louis the third prince of Conti (1664–1709). The Conti family were a cadet branch of the reigning House of Bourbon and were therefore *princes du sang*, or Princes of the Blood.

for me to do it in any other cause! how gladly would I leave the best part of my blood to shew the sense I have of the generosity I have experienced.

The baron had nothing to offer in opposition to a sentiment which he found had so much of honour in it, and therefore acquainted the prince that he chose to accept his highness's favour in a civil employment; on which he was ordered to attend his levee[29] the next day.

His good friend accompanied him, and having presented him with the forms usual on such occasions, the prince received him very graciously, and was pleased to ask him several questions concerning the government of England at that time, the battle in which he had been taken, and many other things, to all which the young Horatio answered with so much discretion and politeness, as made the prince say to the baron, you have not flattered this gentleman in your description of him; for tho' I believe your friendship ready enough to give a just idea of him, yet, I assure you, his own behaviour is his best recommendation, and well entitles him to more than I find it in my power to do for him at present. I have been thinking for you, sir, continued he, turning to Horatio, and imagine that the employment I have found you will not be disagreeable to you: — one of the gentleman of the bed-chamber to the Chevalier St George being dead, there is a vacancy, which I will make interest shall be filled by no other than yourself; — you seem to be of much of the same age with him, and I daresay he will be extremely pleased in the choice I make of you to be near him: — it is not indeed, added he, a place of so advantage as I could wish, but there is a handsome pension annexed to it, which, with the honour, will, I believe, content you till something better presents itself.

From the first mention the prince made of the post he had found for him, the heart of Horatio leap'd in his breast with an agitation he had never felt before: the thoughts of living at St Germains in the same palace with mademoiselle Charlotta so transported him, that he scarce knew what he said; and the thanks he gave the prince were expressed with such hyperboles of gratitude, as made his highness think he had a higher idea of the employment than it indeed deserved; but the baron who knew the motive, and could not help smiling within himself, to prevent any other from suspecting it, however, told the prince, that it was not to be wondered at that he testified so high a satisfaction, since he was now to serve a family he had by nature a strong attachment to, and at the same time continue in a country he liked better than his own.

Horatio having by this time a little recovered himself, and sensible he had gone rather too far, seconded what the baron had said, and no more observations were made on it.

That same evening, the prince having made it his request, was Horatio

---

[29] *levee*: a reception of visitors on rising from bed, especially by royalty or a person of distinction.

permitted to kiss the hand of the Chevalier St George, and the ensuing day took possession of the apartment appropriated to the office bestowed on him.

After having received the congratulations of the whole court, who testified a great deal of satisfaction in having him among them, and paid his compliments in a particular manner to mademoiselle Charlotta, he took abundance of pleasure in viewing all the apartments of a palace famous for the birth of one of the greatest monarchs of the age,[30] and for being the asylum of the distrest royal family of England: when his attendance on his master gave him leisure, he frequently passed many hours together in a closet, where he was told the late king James used to retire every day to pray for the prosperity of that people who had abjur'd him. Young as Horatio was, and gay by nature, he sometimes loved to indulge the most serious meditations; and this place, as well as the condition of those he served, remonstrating to him the instability of all human greatness, he made this general reflection, that there was nothing truly valuable but virtue, because the owner could be deprived of that only by himself, and not by either fraud or force of others.

Indeed the behaviour of all the persons who composed this court could not but inspire those who saw it with sentiments of the nature I have described: the queen herself, tho' of too great a soul to shew any marks of repining at her fate, was never seen to smile: even the Chevalier St George and princess had both of them a very serious air, which denoted they had reflections more befitting their condition than their years; and those about them being most of them persons who had left the greatest part of their fortunes as well as kindred either in England, Scotland or Ireland, had their own misfortunes as well as that of the royal cause to lament, and therefore could not but wear a dejection in their countenances: in fine, every thing he saw seem'd an emblem of fallen majesty, except on drawing-room nights, and then indeed the splendour of Marli[31] and Versailles shone forth at St Germains in the persons of those who came to pay their compliments, among whom were not only the Dauphine[32] and all the princes of the blood, but even the grand monarch himself thought it not beneath his dignity to give this proof of his respect once or twice a week.[33]

---

[30] *a palace famous for the birth of one of the greatest monarchs of the age*: Louis XIV (1638–1715) was born at Saint-Germain-en-Laye, the country estate of his father, Louis XIII.

[31] *the splendour of Marli*: Louis XIV's château at Marly, in what is now Marly-le-Roi, in the western suburbs of Paris.

[32] *the Dauphine*: wife of the Dauphin, heir apparent to the French throne. Depending on the date, the title could apply to Marianne-Victoire, Princess of Bavaria (1660–1690), given the title *Dauphine* after her marriage to the Dauphin, Louis of France (1661–1711), only surviving child of Louis XIV and Maria Thérèse of Spain; or to Princess Adélaïde of Savoy (1685–1712), wife of Louis, Duke of Burgundy, later Dauphin of France (1682–1712).

[33] *the grand monarch himself thought it not beneath his dignity to give this proof of his respect once or twice a week*: An exaggeration, though contact between the English and French royal families was frequent between 1689 and 1715. Louis XIV visited James II at Saint-Germain-

This way of living, and the company he was now associated with, gave Horatio a manly way of thinking much sooner than otherwise perhaps he might have had, yet did not rob him of his vivacity: some of the queen's women, and the young ladies about the princess, particularly mademoiselle Charlotta, had a thousand sprightly entertainments among themselves, into which he, the baron de la Valiere, and some others who had attachments at that court, were always admitted.

But now the time had arrived in which he was to lose the society of that valuable friend; the campaign was ready to open, and he was obliged to head his troops and follow the marshals de Villars and Marsin[34] into Flanders.

All the conversation now turning on war, those martial inclinations, which love and the season of the year had occasioned to lye dormant for a while in the bosom of Horatio, now revived in him: he embraced the baron at taking leave of him with tears of affection and regret: how cruel is my fate, said he, to make me of a nation at enmity with yours, and that I can neither fight for you nor against you!

Well, my dear Horatio, replied the other, France may hereafter have occasion to employ your arm where there are no ties of duty to restrain you: — in the mean time, continued he with a smile, softer engagements may employ your thoughts; — mademoiselle Charlotta de Palfoy is a conquest worth pursuing.

This was the first hint the baron had ever given him of the discovery he had made of his sentiments, and it so much the more surprised him that he was told by another what he was not certain of himself: — he knew indeed the society of that young lady gave him infinite satisfaction, and that he was restless when absent from her; but these words, and the air with which they were spoke, shewed him more of his own heart than he had before examined into; — he blush'd excessively, and made no answer; on which, you have no cause, resumed the baron, to be asham'd of the passion you are inspired with, nor troubled at my discovery of it: — I assure you I have seen it a long time; and tho' you never honoured me with your confidence in that point, have taken all opportunities of doing justice to your merit in the conversations I have had with mademoiselle, who I had the satisfaction to find was not displeased with what I said on that head; and I flatter myself with having a good account of the progress you have made at my return.

I have too much experience of your friendship and goodness to me, replied

---

en-Laye thirty-six times in 1689, but the number of visits decreased as the French king grew older. (See Edward Corp, *A Court in Exile: The Stuarts in France, 1689–1718* (Cambridge: Cambridge University Press, 2004), pp. 166–67.)

[34] *the marshals de Villars and Marsin*: Claude Louis Hector, duc de Villars (1653–1734), an army officer who was awarded the marshal's baton after leading French troops to a victory over the imperial army in 1702; Ferdinand, comte de Marsin (1656–1706), who succeeded Villars as head of the Army of Germany in 1703.

Horatio, not to assure myself of your doing me all manner of kind offices; — I have indeed so great a regard for that lady you mention, that I know none of her sex who I so much wish should think well of me, yet is she utterly ignorant of the sentiments I have for her; and if I am possessed of that passion which they call love, which I protest I am not certain of myself, I have never made the least declaration that can give her room for any such thing.

The baron laughed heartily to hear him speak in this manner, and then told him there was no need of words to make known an inclination of that kind; — it was to be seen in every look and motion of the person inspired with it. — Mademoiselle de Palfoy, continued he, young as she is, I dare answer has penetration enough to see the conquest she has made, but has not yet learned artifice enough to conceal that she is at the same time subdued herself; — and if you would take the advice of a person who has some experience in these affairs, you will endeavour to engage her to a confession before too much observation on the behaviour of others to their lovers, shall teach her those imperious airs by which women frequently torment the heart that adores them, tho' their own perhaps in doing so feels an equal share.

Horatio, who had seen something like this between the baron and his mistress, found a great deal of reason in what he said, and promised to be guided by him, especially as he had encouragement enough to hope, by all the treatment he had found from Charlotta, that a declaration of love from him would not offend her beyond forgiveness.

From that time forward he therefore began to think in what manner he should first disclose the tender secret to the dear object of his affections: when absent from her he easily found words, but when present, that awe which is inseparable from a real passion struck him entirely dumb; and whenever he was about to open his mouth to utter what he intended, he had neither words nor voice; and tho' he saw her every day, was often alone with her, and had opportunity enough to have revealed himself, yet he could not get the better of his timidity for a great while, and perhaps should have been much longer under this cruel constraint, had not an accident favoured his wishes beyond what he could have hoped, or even imagined, and by shewing him part of what passed in her soul, emboldened him to unfold what his own laboured with on her account.

CHAP. VI.

Describes the masquerade at the dutchess of Main's; the characters and intrigues of several persons of quality who were there; the odd behaviour of a lady in regard to Horatio, and Charlotta's sentiments upon it.

THE dutchess of Main[35] was one of the gayest and most gallant ladies at the court of Lewis XIV. She was for ever entertaining the nobility with balls, masquerades, or concerts; and as she was of the blood royal, and highly respected not only on that score, but by the distinguish'd favour of the king, the Chevalier St George, and the princess his sister, frequently honoured her assemblies with their presence.

To divert those ladies whose husbands were gone to Flanders, as she said, she now proposed a masquerade; and the day being fixed, it was the sole business of the young and gay to prepare habits such as were suitable to their inclinations, or, as they thought, would be most advantagious to their persons.

The Chevalier St George was dressed in a rich Grecian habit of sky-coloured velvet embroidered with large silver stars: the top of his cap was encompassed with diamonds, rubies, emeralds, saphirs, amythists, and other precious stones of various colours, set in rows in the exact form of a rainbow; a light robe of crimson taffaty,[36] fringed with silver, was fastened by a knot of jewels on his left shoulder, and crossed his back to the right side, where it was tucked into a belt of the finest oriental pearls, and thence hung down and trail'd a little on the ground: in fine, there was nothing that exceeded the magnificence and eloquence of his appearance, or was in any measure equal to it in the whole assembly, except that of the princess Louisa his sister.

She would needs go as a Diana,[37] and obliged all her ladies to be habited like nymphs: no idea of this goddess, inspired either by the painter or the poet's art, can in any degree come up to that which the sight of this amiable princess gave every beholder. Conformable to the character she assumed, she had a large crescent of diamonds on her head, which had no other covering than a great

---

[35] *dutchess of Main*: Anne Louise Bénédicte de Bourbon-Condé, duchesse du Maine (1676–1753), daughter of the prince de Condé [see below, n. 42], and wife of Louis-Auguste de Bourbon, duc de Maine (1670–1736), legitimised son of Louis XIV and Madame de Montespan.

[36] *taffaty*: or taffeta, a name applied at different times to different fabrics, though usually referring to a glossy or lustrous silk.

[37] *Diana*: In Roman mythology, a goddess of the moon, and, as derived from the Greek Artemis, a virgin and a huntress.

quantity of the finest hair in the world, partly braided with pearls and emeralds, and partly flowing in ringlets down her alabaster neck: her garments were silver tissue, white and shining as the moon on a clear frosty night; and being buttoned up a little as for the conveniency of the chace, shewed great part of her fine proportioned ankle. In her hand she held an ivory bow, and an arrow of the same headed with gold; and on her shoulder was fixed a quiver curiously wrought and beset with jewels: her attendants, which were six in number, had their habits green, but made in the same fashion of the princess's, with bows and arrows in their hands, and quivers at their backs: all of them had their hair turned up under a caul[38] of silver net, from which hung little tossels of pearl intermixed with diamonds.

Next to this fair troop the dutchess of Main herself attracted the attention of the assembly: she was habited like an Indian queen, with robes composed of feathers so artfully placed, that they represented a thousand different kinds of birds and beasts, which, as she moved, seemed to have motion in themselves: on her head she had a lofty plume supported by a cap, and richly ornamented with precious stones; as were all her garments wherever the propriety of the fashion of them would give leave.

The young mademoiselle de Bourbon, in the habit of a sea-nymph, and mademoiselle de Blois,[39] in that of a Minerva,[40] ornamented and decorated according to their several characters, had also their share of admiration.

Nor did the marchionesses of Vallois and Lucerne,[41] both in the garb of shepherdesses, serve as mere foils to those I have mentioned: there was something even in this plainness that shewed the elegance of the wearer's taste.

The prince of Conde,[42] the dukes of Berry, Vendosme and Chartres,[43] the

---

[38] *caul*: a net for the hair, often richly ornamented.

[39] *mademoiselle de Bourbon ... mademoiselle de Blois*: Mlle de Bourbon, Louise Élisabeth de Bourbon (1693–1775), daughter of Louis III de Bourbon, prince de Condé and Louise Françoise, duchesse de Bourbon, a legitimised daughter of Louis XIV and Madame de Montespan; Mlle de Blois, Marie-Anne de Bourbon, later princesse de Conti (1666–1739), legitimised daughter of Louis XIV and his mistress, Louise de la Vallière.

[40] *Minerva*: a goddess traditionally associated with wisdom, she was the Roman goddess of crafts, and, as derived from the Greek Athena, a warlike figure who aided male heroes.

[41] *the marchionesses of Vallois and Lucerne*: the first of these may refer to Anne-Marie of Orléans (1669–1728), Mademoiselle de Valois, daughter of Philippe, duc d'Orléans [see below, n. 43]; the second may be Haywood's own invention.

[42] *prince of Conde*: Henri Jules de Bourbon, prince de Condé (1643–1709). As a member of the reigning House of Bourbon, he was a *prince du sang*.

[43] *the dukes of Berry, Vendosme and Chartres*: Charles, duc de Berri (1685–1714), third son of Louis, Dauphin of France, heir apparent to the French throne, and Marianne-Victoire, Princess of Bavaria [see above, n. 32], he was an army officer and one of the possible successors to the Spanish throne in the event of the death, or succession to the French throne, of his brother Philippe, duc d'Anjou (1683–1746); Louis-Joseph, duc de Vendôme (1654–1712), army officer, who led successful campaigns in Italy from 1702–1705; Philippe, duc d'Orléans (1674–1723), nephew of Louis XIV, who was given the title of duc de Chartres

young marquis de Montbausine,[44] the counts de Chenille, de Ranbeau, and the baron de Roche, had all of them habits extremely rich and well fancied, as were many others of whom it would be too tedious to make particular mention, and be likewise digressive to the matter I take upon me to relate; I shall therefore only say, that there was not one person of either sex, who did not endeavour to set themselves forth to all possible advantage.

Those gentlemen who attended the Chevalier St George were at their liberty to appear in what habit they pleased: Horatio knowing his charming Charlotta was a nymph of the forest, chose to be a hunter, and was accordingly dressed in green, with a little cap on his head and a javelin in his hand, as Acteon[45] is generally portrayed; and indeed had he studied what garb would have become him best, he could not have fixed on one more proper for that purpose.

Fine mademoiselle de Sanserre at least thought him more worthy her regard than any of those, the richness of whose habits made her know were of a higher rank: — she took particular notice of him, made him dance with her, and said a thousand gallant things to him; but he could very well have dispensed with hearing them, and found little satisfaction in any thing that deprived him of entertaining his dear Charlotta, who he easily knew by her air and shape from all those who were habited in the same manner. As he doubted not, however, but the person who had thus singled him out was a lady of condition, he returned her civilities with a politeness which was natural to him, but which had received great improvements since his arrival in France. She was no less charm'd with his conversation than she had been with his person, and impatient to know who he was, made an offer of shewing him her face on condition he would pluck off his mask at the same time: but this he would by no means agree to, because still hoping to get rid of her, and have some discourse with mademoiselle Charlotta, he did not think proper he should be known by any other, who might perhaps make remarks on his behaviour; and therefore excused himself from complying with her desires in terms as obliging as the circumstance would admit.

As she had displayed all her talents of wit and eloquence to engage him, she looked on the little curiosity she had been able to inspire in him as an affront, and vexed she had thrown away so much time on an insensible, as she called him, flung hastily away, and joining with some other company, left him at liberty to pursue his inclinations.

This lady had been a royal mistress, but not having the good fortune to be made a mother, was not honoured with any title; her being forsaken by the king, who indeed had few amours of any long continuance, did not in the least abate

---

at his birth in 1674.

[44] *marquis de Montbausine*: possibly Hercule de Rohan, duc de Montbazon (1568–1654).

[45] *Acteon*: Actaeon, who inadvertently came upon Artemis [see above, n. 37] bathing. The offended goddess turned him into a stag and he was torn apart by his own hounds.

the good opinion she had of her beauty; and to see herself followed by a train of lovers being the supreme pleasure of her life, she spared nothing to attract and engage: whenever she failed in this expectation it was a severe mortification; but her vanity and the gaiety of her humour would not suffer it to prey upon her spirits for above a minute, and she diverted the shock of a rebuff in one place by new attempts to conquer in another; therefore it is probable thought no more of Horatio after she had turned from him.

He now carefully avoided all that might interrupt his wishes, and seeing Charlotta had just broke off some conversation she had been entertained with, made what haste he could to prevent her from being re-engaged: — She immediately knew him; and as their mutual innocence made them perfectly free in expressing themselves to each other, she told him she was glad he was come; that they would keep together the whole masquerade, provided he did not think it a confinement, to prevent her being persecuted with the impertinencies of some people there, who she found thought a masque a kind of sanction for saying any thing.

It is not to be doubted but Horatio gave her all the assurances that words could form, of feeling the most perfect pleasure in her society, and that he should not, without the extremest reluctance, find himself obliged to abandon the happiness she offered him to any other person in the company: to recompence this complaisance, as she called it, she gave him a brief detail of the characters of as many as she knew tho' their habits; and in doing this discovered a sweet impartiality and love of truth, which was no small addition to her other charms. She blamed the baroness de Guiche[46] for not being able to return the affection of a husband who had married her with an inconsiderable fortune, and had since she had been his wife pardoned a thousand miscarriages in her conduct: — she praised the virtue of mademoiselle de Mareau, who being at fifteen the bride of a man of seventy, behaved to him with a tenderness, and exact conformity to his will, which, if owing alone to duty, was not to be distinguished from inclination: — she expressed a concern that the gaiety of the dutchess of Vendome[47] gave the world any room for censure, and highly condemned the duke for being guilty of actions which made her sometimes

---

[46] *baroness de Guiche*: probably referring to Marguerite Louise Suzanne de Béthune, duchesse de Guiche (1642–1726), wife of Guy-Armand de Gramont, comte de Guiche (1637–1674). The comte de Guiche, who had an affair with Henriette Anne, daughter of Charles I of England and wife of Louis XIV's brother Philippe, duc d'Anjou (1640–1701), figures prominently in Vol. I of Bussy-Rabutin's *Histoire Amoureuse des Gaules*, and in Madame de Lafayette's *Histoire de Madame Henriette d'Angleterre* (1720), translated into English as *Fatal Gallantry: or. The Secret History of Henrietta, Princess of England* (1722). This comte de Guiche was dead before the events represented in *The Fortunate Foundlings*.

[47] *dutchess of Vendome*: Marie Anne de Bourbon (1678–1718), daughter of Henri Jules, Prince de Condé [see above, n. 42] and Anne of Bavaria, Princess Palatine (1648–1723), and wife of Louis-Joseph, duc de Vendôme (1654–1712) [see above, n. 43].

give into parties of pleasure by way of retaliation: — but she was more severe on the indecorum of mademoiselle de Renville, who being known for the mistress of the duke of Chartres, and that she was supported by him, was fond of appearing in all public places. She could not help testifying a good deal of surprize, that any woman who pretended to virtue would admit her into their assemblies: not but she said the case of that lady was greatly to be pitied, who being high-born and bred had been reduced to the lowest exigencies of life, and from which to be relieved she had only consented to assist the looser pleasures of the amorous duke: but, added she, I would not methinks have her seem to glory in her shame, and in a manner of life which her misfortunes alone can render excusable; nor can I approve of the indulgence her mistaken triumph meets with, because it may not only destroy all notions of regret in herself for what her necessities oblige her to, but also make others, who have not the same pretence, find a kind of sanction for their own errors: — vice, said she, ought at least to blush, and hide itself as much as possible from view, lest by being tolerated in public it should become a fashion.

Horatio was so much taken up with admiring the justness of her sentiments, that awed by them, as it were, he could not yet, tho' mask'd, make any discovery of his own: she was about entering into a discourse with him concerning the first motives which had rendered some persons she pointed out to him unhappy in the marriage-state, which perhaps might have given him an opportunity for explaining himself, when a lady richly dress'd came up to them, and giving Horatio a sudden pluck by the arm; villain! cried she. Madam, returned he, strongly amazed. Is the trifling conversation of Sanserre, resumed she, or this little creature to be preferred to a woman of that quality you have dared to abuse? — but this night has convinced her of your perfidy: — she sends you this, continued she, giving him a slap over the face as hard as she could, and be assured it is the last present you will ever receive from her.

She had no sooner uttered these words than she flew quick as lightning out of the room, leaving Horatio in such a consternation both at what she said and did, as deprived him even of the thought of following her, or using any means to solve this riddle. — He was in a deep musing when mademoiselle Charlotta, possessed that moment with a passion she till then was ignorant of, said to him; I find, Horatio, you have wonderfully improved the little time you have been in France, to gain you a multiplicity of mistresses; but I am sorry my inadvertency in talking to a man so doubly pre-engaged, should cause me to be reckoned among the number. In speaking this she turned away with a confusion which was visible in her air, and the scarlet colour with which her neck was dyed. By heaven! cried he, in the utmost agitation, I know so little the meaning of what I have just now heard, that it seems rather a dream than a reality. O the deceiver! returned she, a little slackening her pace, will you pretend to have given no occasion for the reproach you have received: — great must have been your professions to draw on you a resentment such as I have been witness of; — but I shall take care to give the lady, whoever she is, no farther room for jealousy on my account; and as for mademoiselle Sanserre, I believe the stock of reputation she has will not suffer much from the addition of one more favourite to the number the world has already given her.

The oddness of the adventure, and the vexation he was in to find Charlotta seemed incensed against him for a crime of which he knew himself so perfectly innocent, destroyed at once all the considerations his timidity had inspired, and aiming only to be cleared in her opinion; — if there be faith in man, cried he, I know nothing of what I am accused: no woman but your charming self ever had the power to give me an uneasy moment; — it is you alone have taught me what it is to love, and as I never felt, I never pretended to that passion for any other.

Me! replied Charlotta, extremely confused; if it were so, you take a strange time and method to declare it in; — but I know of no concern I have in your amours, your gratitude, or your perfidy; and you had better follow and endeavour to appease your enraged mistress, than lose your time on me in vain excuses.

Ah mademoiselle! cried he, how unjust and cruel are you, and how severe my fate, which not content with the despair my real unworthiness of adoring you has plunged me in, but also adds to it the imputation of crimes my soul most detests: — I never heard even the name of the lady you mentioned till your lips pronounced it; and if it be she I danced with, I protest I never saw her face: and as for the meaning of the other lady's treatment of me, it must certainly be occasioned by some mistake, having offered nothing to any of the sex that could justify such a proceeding.

All the time he was speaking Charlotta was endeavouring to compose herself. — The hurry of spirits she had been in at the apprehensions of Horatio having any amorous engagements, shewing her how much interest she took in him, made her blush at having discovered herself to him so far; and tho' she could not be any more tranquil, yet she thought she would for the future be more prudent; to this end she now affected to laugh at the dilemma into which she told him he had brought himself, by making addresses in two places at the same time, and advised him in a gay manner to be more circumspect.

Thus was this beautiful lady, by her jealousy, convinced of her sensibility; and as difficult as Horatio found it to remove the one, he found his consolation in the discovery of the other.

From the time he had been disengaged from mademoiselle Sanserre, he had retired with Charlotta to one corner of the room; and the greatest part of the company being in a grand dance, the others were taken up in looking on them, so that our young lovers had the opportunity of talking to each other without being much taken notice of; but several of the masquers now drawing nearer that way, prevented Horatio from saying any thing farther at that time, either to clear his innocence or prosecute his passion; and Charlotta, glad to avoid a discourse on a subject she thought herself but ill prepared to answer, joined some ladies, with whom she stayed till the ball was near concluded.

Horatio after this withdrew to a window, and sheltered behind a large damask curtain, threw himself on a sopha he found there, and ruminated at full on the adventure had happened to him, in which he found a mixture of joy and discontent: the behaviour of Charlotta assured him he was not indifferent to her; but then the thoughts that he appeared in her eyes as ungrateful, inconstant and perfidious, made him tremble, lest the idea of what he seemed to be should utterly erace that favourable one she had entertained of what he truly was. By what means he should prove his sincerity he knew not; and as he was utterly unpractised in the affairs of love, lamented the absence of his good friend the baron de la Valiere, who he thought might have been able to give him some advice how to proceed.

He remained buried, as it were, in these cogitations, when a lady pluck'd back the curtain which screened him, and without seeing any one was there, threw herself on the sopha almost in his lap. — O heaven! cried she, perceiving what she had done, and immediately rose; but Horatio starting up, would not suffer her to quit the place, telling her, that since she chose it, it was his business to retire, and leave her to indulge whatever meditations had brought her thither. She thank'd him in a voice which, by its trembling, testified her mind was in some very great disorder; and added, if your good nature, said she, be equal to your complaisance, you will do me the favour to desire a lady, dressed in pink and silver, with a white sattin scarf cross her shoulder, to come here directly: — you cannot, continued she, be mistaken in the person, because there is no other in the same habit. Tho' Horatio was very loth to engage himself in the lady's affairs, fearing to give a second umbrage to mademoiselle Charlotta, yet he knew not how to excuse granting so small a request, and therefore assured her of his compliance.

Accordingly he sent his eyes in quest, which soon pointed out to him the person whom she had described: having delivered his message to her; Horatio! cried she, somewhat astonished, how came you employed in this errand? he knew her voice, and that it was mademoiselle de Coigney, the mistress of his friend the baron, on which he immediately told her how the lady had surprized him: she laughed heartily, and said no more but left him, and went to the window he had directed.

For a long time he sought in vain for an opportunity of speaking to the object of his affections: she was still engaged either in dancing or in different parties; and as his eyes continually followed her, he easily perceived she purposely avoided him. A magnificent collation being prepared in a great drawing-room next to that in which the company were, they all went in to partake of it. The entertainment was served up on two large tables; but as every one was mask'd, and the vizards so contriv'd, that those who wore them could eat without plucking them off, they sat down promiscuously without ceremony or any distinction of degrees, none being obliged to know another in these disguises; only the attendants of the Chevalier St George, and the princess Louisa, took care not to place themselves at the same they were, so by this means sat together; but a great number of others being mingled with them, no particular conversation could be expected.

Supper being over, they all returned to the ballroom; and Horatio having contrived it so as to get next Charlotta, she could not refuse him the offer he made her of his hand to lead her in; but as he was about saying something to her in a low voice, a man came hastily to him, and taking him a little on one side, presented him with a letter, and then retired with so much precipitation, that Horatio could neither ask from whom it came, nor well discern what sort of person it was that gave it him. He put it however in his pocket, designing to read it at more leisure, his curiosity for the contents not equalling his desire of entertaining mademoiselle Charlotta; but that young lady, whose jealousy received new fewel from this object, had slipt away before he could turn from the man, and had already mixed with a cluster of both sexes who had got into the room before them.

Horatio finding all attempts to speak to her that night would be ineffectual, went back into the drawing-room where they supped, and where but few people remaining he might examine the letter with more freedom. He saw it had no superscription; but supposing the inside would give him some satisfaction, he broke it open hastily and found in it these lines.

> WHETHER false or faithful still are you dear to me; and if I am in the least so to you, the treatment you received will be pardoned for the sake of the occasion: — I own that at a place where you might have been as particular as you pleased with me without suspicion, it enraged me to see you waste those precious moments with others which I flattered myself to have solely engrossed; — besides, the character of mademoiselle Sanserre is so well known, that I thought you would have avoided her of all others; yet had she forced herself upon you, sure you might afterwards have come to me, when I had given you so particular a description of the habit I should wear; but instead of making any excuse for a first transgression, you hurry to a second, and pay all your devoirs to another, whom indeed I knew not at that time, but am since informed she is one of the maids of honour to princess Louisa. —

I must confess I had not resolution enough to suffer so cruel an injustice, and being too much overcome by my passion to resent it as I ought, I left the place, and desired our friend to do it for me. — I find she somewhat exceeded her commission, but you must forgive her, since it was her love for me: — I am now at her house where I impatiently expect you. — The baron is secure for some hours; — those we may pass together, if you still think there is any thing worth quitting the masquerade for, to be found in the arms of

Yours, &c.

P.S. If you now fail, no excuse hereafter shall ever plead your pardon.

This letter confirmed Horatio in the belief he had before, that he had been mistaken by the lady for some favourite person; but who the lady was, he was as much in the dark as ever; nor would he have given himself any trouble concerning it, if he had not hoped by that means to have retrieved the good opinion of Charlotta. He was impatient however to shew her the letter, as he doubted not but she had seen it delivered to him; but with all his assiduity he could not obtain one word in private during the masquerade; and when it was broke up, which was not till near morning, and they returned to St Germains, it was impossible, because he knew she must be in the princess's chamber, as he in that of the Chevalier St George: he was therefore obliged to content himself with the hope that the next day would be more favourable.

CHAP. VII.

An explanation of the foregoing adventure, with a continuation of the intrigues of some French ladies, and the policy of mademoiselle Coigney in regard of her brother.

IT cannot be supposed that either of our young lovers enjoyed much true repose that night, tho' the fatigue of the dance might naturally require it: the one did but just know herself a lover before she felt the worst torments of that passion in her jealousy; and the other having been compelled, as it were, to lay open his heart in order to convince his charmer it had no object but herself in view, knew not but his temerity in doing so might be imputed to him as no less a crime than that from which he attempted to be cleared: each had their different anxieties; but those of Horatio were the least severe, because thro' all the indignation of his mistress he saw marks of an affection, which he could not have flattered himself with if they had not been evident; and conscious of his innocence, doubted not but time would both explain that and reconcile the offended fair: — whereas Charlotta was far from being able to assure herself of her lover's fidelity: she could not conceive how, in the compass of one night, such a plurality of mistakes should happen to the same man, and trembled at the reflection that this man, who possibly was the falsest of his sex, should not only have made an impression on her heart, but also, by the concern she had so unwarily expressed, have reason to triumph in his conquest: — ashamed therefore of what she felt and determined to make use of her utmost efforts to conceal it for the future, if not to conquer it, she thought to shun all occasions of seeing or speaking to this dangerous invader of her peace was the first step she ought to take; but how little is a heart, possessed of the passion her's was, capable of judging for itself, or maintaining any resolutions in prejudice of the darling object! — she had no sooner set it down as a rule to avoid him, than she began to wish for his presence, and contented herself with thinking she desired it only out of curiosity to hear what he would say, and to have an opportunity, by a rallying manner of behaviour, to destroy whatever conjectures he might have form'd in favour of his passion; but all this time she deceived herself, and in reality only longed for an interview with him, in hopes he would find means to justify himself. Horatio, who was impatient to attempt it, seeing her at a distance walking on the terrass with no other company than mademoiselle de Coigney, went immediately to join them, thinking that if the presence of this lady might be a bar to many things he wanted to say to Charlotta, it would be of service to him another way, by preventing her from making him any reproaches.

As soon as he came near, I owe you little thanks, Horatio, said mademoiselle de Coigney laughing, for the interruption you gave me last night. In the multiplicity of those reflections which his own affairs had occasioned him, he had entirely forgot the lady in the window; and imagining some other accident had happened which should make him appear yet more guilty in the eyes of Charlotta, ask'd her, with some impatience, what she meant? don't you remember, answered she, that you brought me a message from a certain lady? Yes, madam, said he, and in that, thought I did no more than my duty obliged me to, as she seemed under some perplexity, which I supposed she was impatient to acquaint you with.

You judged rightly, indeed, resumed de Coigney; but had you known how gladly I would have dispensed with the honour of her confidence, I dare answer you would have spared it me: — I'll tell you, my dear, pursued she turning to Charlotta, for the secrets of this lady are pretty universal; and I am certain I have heard from no less than fifty different persons, that very affair she was in such a hurry to inform me of last night: you must needs have heard of the affair between madam la Boissy and the chevalier de Mourenbeau? frequently, replied Charlotta; her ridiculous jealousies of him have long been the jest of the whole court; and I never go to Marli or Versailles, but I am told of some new instance of it. And yet to relate a long story of her passion, and his ingratitude, said mademoiselle de Coigney, was I last night dragged into a dark corner, and deprived for an hour together of all the pleasures of the masquerade: it seem she had over-heard some gallant things between him and the daughter of the count de Granpree, and that gave her the occasion of running into a recapitulation of all the professions of constancy he had made to herself, the proofs she had given him of a too easy belief, and the little regard he now paid to her peace of mind. — I was obliged to affect a pity for her misfortunes, and gratitude for the trust she reposed in me, tho' neither the one nor the other merited in reality any thing but contempt.

One often suffers a good deal from one's complaisance this way, said Charlotta; and for my part there is nothing I would more carefully avoid than secrets of this nature; but you have not told me how far Horatio was accessary to bringing you into this trouble.

He then said he would save mademoiselle de Coigney the labour, and immediately related how the lady they were speaking of threw herself upon him, and afterwards enjoined him to deliver the message. But, added he, I think last night was one of the most unfortunate ones I have ever known, since, with all the care I could take, I was continually prevented by other people's concerns from prosecuting my own. — I was not only insulted and reproached for being mistaken for some other person, for it could happen no other way, but also soon after received a letter no less mysterious to me than the blow, which doubtless came from the same quarter: as there is no name subscribed, or if there were, I should look on myself as under no obligation of secrecy, I will beg leave to communicate it to you, ladies.

With these words he took the letter out of his pocket and held it open between them: Charlotta conquered her impatience so far as not to take it out of his hand; but mademoiselle Coigney snatched it hastily, imagining she knew the hand; nor was she deceived in her conjecture: she had no sooner lightly read it over; — see here, mademoiselle Charlotta, said she, a new proof of madam de Olonne's[48] folly, and my brother's continued attachment to that vile woman.

Charlotta then looked over the letter with a satisfaction that was visible in her countenance; and as soon as she had done, then it is plain, said she, that Horatio was mistaken for monsieur de Coigney: but how it happened so is what I cannot conceive.

I can easily solve the riddle, replied mademoiselle de Coigney: I heard my brother say he intended to wear a hunting dress at the masquerade; but being disappointed of going to it, by his most christian majesty sending for him to Marli, I suppose too suddenly for him to give notice of his enforced absence to madame d'Olonne, and Horatio by chance appearing in the same habit which he had doubtless told her he would be in, and their sizes being pretty much alike, she might very well be deceived, and also have a seeming reason for the jealousy and rage her letter testifies.

Nothing could exceed the joy Horatio felt at this unexpected eclaircisement[49] of his innocence, which was also doubled by the pleasure which, in spight of all her endeavours to restrain it, he saw sparkle in the eyes of his beloved Charlotta. Neither of them, however, had any opportunity of expressing their sentiments at this time, de Coigney continuing with them till dinner, when they all separated to go their respective tables.

The next day afforded what in this he had sought in vain: — he found her alone in her own apartment; and having broke the ice, was now grown bold enough to declare his passion with all the embellishments necessary to render it successful: mademoiselle Charlotta knew very well what became the decorum of her sex, and was too nice an observer of it not to behave with all the reserve imaginable on this occasion. All the freedom she had been accustomed to treat him with, while ignorant of his or her own inclination, was now banished from her words and actions, and she gravely told him, that if he were in earnest, it was utterly improper for her to receive any professions of that kind without

---

[48] *madam de Olonne*: Catherine-Henriette d'Angennes, comtesse d'Olonne (1634–1714). A notorious female libertine, the comtesse d'Olonne figures prominently in Volume I of Bussy-Rabutin's *Histoire Amoureuse des Gaules*.

[49] *eclaircisement*: *éclaircissement*, a clearing up or explanation of what is unknown or obscure.

the approbation of monsieur de Palfoy her father; and as there was but little probability of his granting it, on many considerations, she would wish him to quell in its infancy an affection which might otherwise be attended with misfortunes to them both.

It is certain, indeed, that in this she spoke no more than what her reason suggested: she knew very well that her father had much higher expectations in view for her, and that on the least suspicion of her entertaining a foreigner, and one who seemed to have no other dependance than that of favour, she should be immediately removed from St Germains; so that it behoved her to be very circumspect in any encouragement she gave him: but tho' she spoke to him in this manner, it was not, as her actions afterwards fully demonstrated, that she really designed what she said should make him desist his pretensions, but that he should be careful how he let any one into the secret of his heart. She foresaw little prospect of their love ever being crown'd with success, yet found too much pleasure in indulging it to be able to wish an extinction of it, either in him or herself; and in spight of all the distance she assumed, he easily perceived that whatever difficulties he should have to struggle with in the prosecution of his addresses, they would not be owing to her cruelty. They were both of them too young to attend much to consequences; and as securing the affections of each other was what each equally aimed at, neither of them reflected how terrible a separation would be, and how great the likelihood that it must happen they knew not how soon.

As the remonstrances of mademoiselle Charlotta had all the effect she intended them for on Horatio, he so well commanding himself that no person in the world, except the baron de la Valiere, who was absent, had the least intimation of his passion, they might probably have lived a long time together in the contentment they now enjoyed, had not an accident, of which neither of them could have any notion, put a stop to it.

Horatio thought no more of the affair of madame de Olonne and monsieur de Coigney, from the time he had been cleared of having any concern with that lady, yet was that night's adventure productive of what he looked upon as the greatest misfortune could befal him. But to make this matter conspicuous to the reader, it is necessary to give a brief detail of the circumstances that led to it.

This lady, who was wife to the baron de Olonne,[50] was one of the most beautiful, and most vicious women in the kingdom; she entertained a great number of lovers; but there was none more attached to her, or more loved by her than young monsieur de Coigney: he had for a long time maintained a criminal correspondence[51] with her, to the great trouble of all his friends, who

---

[50] *baron de Olonne*: Louis de la Trémoille, comte d'Olonne (1626–1686).
[51] *a criminal correspondence*: legally, adultery, but also used as a euphemism for any illicit sexual act between a man and a woman.

endeavoured all they could, but in vain, to wean him from her: he had lately a rencounter with one of her former lovers, which had like to have cost him his life; and it was with great difficulty, and as much as the relations on both sides could do, by representing to the king that they were set upon by street-robbers, that they avoided the punishment the law inflicts on duelists. De Coigney was but just recovered of the hurts he had received, when, so far from resolving to quit the occasion of them, he made an appointment to meet her at the masquerade: — they had described to each other the habit they intended to wear, when, as he was preparing for the rendezvous, an express came from the king, commanding his immediate attendance at Marli, where the court then was: this was occasioned by old monsieur de Coigney, who having, by some spies he kept about his son, received intelligence of this assignation, had no other way to disappoint it than by the royal authority, which he easily procured, as he was very much in favour with his majesty, and had laid the matter before him.

The person who came with the mandate had orders not to quit the presence of young Coigney, but bring him directly; by which means he was deprived of all opportunity of sending his excuses to madame d'Olonne, who coming to the masquerade big with expectation of seeing her favourite lover, and finding him, as she imagined, engaged with others, and wholly regardless of herself, was seized with the most violent jealousy; and not being able to continue in a place where she had received so manifest a slight, desired mademoiselle de Freville, her confidante and companion, to upbraid him with his inconstancy; which request she complied with in the manner already related, and which gave mademoiselle Charlotta such matter of disquiet.

The amorous madame de Olonne, however, having given full vent to the first transports of her fury, could not hinder those of a softer nature from returning with the same violence as ever; and for the gratification of them wrote that letter which Horatio received, and occasioned afterwards the explanation of the whole affair, which explanation he then thought fortunate for him; but by a whimsical effect of chance it proved utterly the reverse.

Mademoiselle de Coigney, who had the most tender affection for her brother, and passionately wished to make him break off all engagements with a woman of madame de Olonne's character, and who might possibly bring him under many inconveniencies, took the hint which mademoiselle Charlotta unthinkingly gave, by telling her how she had been affronted on his account by de Freville, of putting something into his head which might probably succeed better than all the attempts had hitherto been practised to make him quit his present criminal amour.

The first time she saw mademoiselle de Freville, she told her as a great secret that her brother was fallen in love with mademoiselle Charlotta, and that she believed it would be a match, for he had already engaged friends to sollicit monsieur de Palfoy on that score. This she knew would be carried directly to madame de Olonne, and doubted not but it would increase her jealous rage, that all he could say in his defence would pass for nothing: she also added, that he was in the masquerade that night, tho' for some private reasons best known to himself, said she, he had ordered his people to give out he was gone to Marli.

De Freville, who was the creature of madame de Olonne, no sooner received this intelligence than she flew with it to her, as mademoiselle de Coigney had imagined: neither did it fail of the desired effect. When he came to visit her, as he did on the moment of his return from Marli, the violence of her temper made her break out into such reproaches and exclamations, as a man had need to be very much in love to endure: he endeavoured to make her sensible of her error by a thousand protestations; but the more he talked of Marli and the king's command, the more she told him of Charlotta and the masquerade; and almost distracted to find he still persisted in denying he was there, or had ever made such tender protestations to that lady, she proceeded to such extravagancies as he, who knew himself innocent, could not forbear replying to in terms which were far from being softening: — in fine, they quarrelled to a very high degree, and some company happening to come in at the same time, hindered either of them from saying any thing which might palliate the resentment of the other.

Before they had an opportunity of meeting again, mademoiselle de Coigney saw her brother; and artfully introducing some discourse of mademoiselle Charlotta de Palfoy, began to run into the utmost encomiums on that lady's beauty, virtue, wit, and sweetness of disposition, and at last added, that she should think herself happy in having her for a sister. Young de Coigney listened attentively to what she said: he had often been in her company, but being prepossessed with his passion for madame de Olonne, her charms had not that effect on him as now that the behaviour of the other had very much lessened his esteem of her.

He replied, that he knew no lady more deserving than the person she mentioned, and should be glad if, by her interest, he might have permission to visit her: this was all mademoiselle de Coigney wanted; she doubted not but if he were once engaged in a honourable passion, it would entirely cure him of all regard for madame de Olonne, and as she knew he had a good share of understanding, thought that when he should come to a more near acquaintance with the perfections of Charlotta, the loose airs of the other would appear in their true colours, and become as odious to him as they once had been infatuating.

Finding him so well inclined to her purpose, she took upon herself the care of introducing him, as it was indeed easy to do, considering the intimacy there was between her and Charlotta. That young lady received him as the brother of a person she extremely loved; and little suspecting the design on which he came, treated him with a gaiety which heightened her charms, and at the same time flattered his hopes, that there was something in his person not disagreeable to her.

Mademoiselle de Coigney took care that every visit he made to Charlotta should be reported to de Olonne, which still heightening her resentment, together with his little assiduity to moderate it, made a total breach between them, to the great satisfaction of all his friends in general. Those of them whom mademoiselle had acquainted with the stratagem by which she brought it about, praised her wit and address; and as they knew the family and fortune of mademoiselle Charlotta, encouraged her to do every thing in her power for turning that into reality which she at first had made use of only as a feint for the reclaiming of her brother.

The young gentleman himself stood in need of no remonstrances of the advantages he might propose by a marriage with Charlotta; her beauty and the charms of her conversation had made a conquest of his heart far more complete than any prospect of interest could have done: not only de Olonne, but the whole sex would now in vain have endeavoured to attract the least regard from him, and as he was naturally vain, he thought nothing but Charlotta de Palfoy worthy of him.

The success he had been accustomed to meet in his love affairs, emboldened him to declare himself much sooner than he would have done had he followed the advice of his sister, and too soon to be received in a manner agreeable to his wishes by a lady of Charlotta's modesty and delicacy, even had she not been prepossessed in favour of another; for tho' she respected him as the brother of her friend, that consideration was too weak to hinder her from letting him know how displeasing his pretensions were to her, and that if he persisted in them she should be obliged to refuse seeing him any more. He was now sensible of his error, and endeavoured to excuse it by the violence of his passion, which he said would not suffer him to conceal what he felt; but as, when a heart is truly devoted to one object, the sound of love from any other mouth is harsh and disagreeable; the more he aimed to vindicate himself in this point the more guilty he became, and all he said served only to increase her dislike.

Mademoiselle de Coigney after this took upon her to intercede for her brother's passion, but with as ill success as he had done; and being one day more importunate than usual, mademoiselle Charlotta grew in so ill a humour, that she told her she was determined to give no encouragement to the amorous addresses of any man, unless commanded to do so by those who had the power of disposing her; but, added she, I would not have monsieur de Coigney make any efforts that way; for were he to gain the consent of my father, which I am far from believing he would do, I have so little inclination to give him those returns of affection he may expect, that in such a case I should venture being guilty of disobedience.

Is there any thing so odious then, madam, in the person of my brother? said de Coigney with a tone that shewed how much she was picqued. I never gave myself the trouble of examining into the merits either of his person or behaviour, replied she; but to deal sincerely with you, I have a perfect aversion to the thoughts of changing my condition, and if you desire the friendship between us should subsist, you will never mention any thing of it to me; — and as to your brother, when I am convinced I shall receive no farther persecutions from him of the nature I have lately had, he may depend upon my treating him with my former regard; till then, you will do me a favour, and him a service, to desire he would refrain his visits.

These expressions may be thought little conformable to the natural politeness of the French, or to that sweetness of disposition which mademoiselle Charlotta testified on other occasions; but she found herself so incessantly pressed both by the brother and the sister, and that all the denials she had given in a different manner had been without effect, therefore was obliged to assume a harshness, which was far from being natural to her, in order to prevent consequences which she had too much reason to apprehend.

Horatio soon discovered he had a rival in monsieur de Coigney; and tho' he easily saw by Charlotta's behaviour that he had nothing to fear on this score, yet the interruptions he received from the addresses of this new lover, made him little able to endure his presence, and he sometimes could not restrain himself from saying such things as, had the other not been too much buoyed up with his vanity to take them as meant to himself, must have occasioned a quarrel.

She made use of all the power she had over him to curb the impetuosity of his temper whenever he met this disturber of his wishes; but his jealousy would frequently get the better of the respect he paid her, and they never were together in her apartment without filling her with mortal fears. She therefore found it absolutely necessary to get rid of an adorer she hated, in order to hinder one she loved from doing any thing which might deprive her of him; and tho' she had a real friendship for mademoiselle de Coigney, yet she chose rather to break with her, than run the hazard she was continually exposed to by her brother's indefatigable pursuit.

But all her precaution was of no effect, as well as the enforced patience of Horatio: what most she trembled at now fell upon her, and by a means she had least thought of. Madame de Olonne, full of malice at being forsaken by her lover, and soon informed by whose charms her misfortune was occasioned, got a person to represent to the baron de Palfoy the conquest his daughter had made in such terms, as made him imagine she encouraged his passion. Neither the character, family, or fortune of de Coigney being equal to what he thought

Charlotta might deserve, made him very uneasy at this report; and as he looked on her not having acquainted him with his pretensions as an indication of her having an affection for him, he resolved to put a stop to the progress of it at once, which could be done no way so effectually as by removing her from St Germains.

To this end the careful Father came himself to that court, and waited on the princess: he told her highness, that being in an ill state of health and obliged to keep much at home, Charlotta must exchange the honour she enjoyed in her service, for the observance of her duty to a parent, who was now incapable of any other pleasures than her society.

The princess, to whom she was extremely dear, could not think of parting with her without an extreme concern, but after the reasons he had given for desiring it, would offer nothing for detaining her, on which she was immediately called in, and made acquainted with this sudden alteration in her affairs.

CHAP. VIII.

The parting of Horatio and mademoiselle Charlotta, and what happened after she left St Germains.

A PEAL of thunder hurtling over her head, could not have been more alarming to mademoiselle Charlotta than the news she now heard; but her father commanded, the princess had consented, and there was no remedy to be hoped: she took leave of her royal mistress with a shower of unfeigned tears, after which she retired to her apartment to prepare for quitting it, while the baron went to pay his compliments to some of the gentlemen at that court.

To be removed in this sudden manner she could impute to no other motive than that the love of Horatio had by some accident been betrayed to her father, (for she never so much as thought of monsieur de Coigney;) and the thoughts of being separated from him was so dreadful, that till this fatal moment she knew not how dear he was to her: — to add to the calamity of her condition, he was that morning gone a-hunting with the Chevalier St George, and she had not even the opportunity of giving him the consolation of knowing she bore at least an equal part in the grief this unexpected accident must occasion. Mademoiselle de Coigney came to take leave of her, as did all the ladies of the queen's train as well as the princess's, and expressed the utmost concern for losing so agreeable a companion; but these ceremonies were tedious to her, and as she could not see Horatio, she dispatched every thing with as much expedition as her secret discontent would allow her to do, and then sent to let her father know she was ready to attend him.

When they were in the coach both observed a profound silence for some time; at last, I hope Charlotta, said the baron, you have no extraordinary reasons to be troubled at leaving St Germains? none, my lord, answered she, of so much moment to me as the fears my sudden removal is owing to your being dissatisfied with my conduct. I flatter myself, resumed he, you are conscious of nothing which should authorize such an apprehension: — you have had an education which ought to inform you that persons of your sex and age are never to act in any material point of themselves: — but courts are places where this lesson is seldom practised; and tho' the virtues of the English queen and princess are a shining example to all about them, yet I am of opinion that innocence is safest in retirement.

As she was fully convinced in her own mind that it was only owing to some jealousy of her behaviour that she had been taken from St Germains, and also that it was on the score of Horatio, she would not enquire too deeply for fear of giving her father an opportunity of entering into examinations, which she thought she could not answer without either injuring the truth, or avowing what would not only have incensed him to a very great degree, but also put him upon measures which would destroy even the most distant hope of ever seeing Horatio more. He, on his side, would not acquaint her with the sentiments which the above-mentioned suggestions had inspired him with, thinking he should discover more of the truth by keeping a watchful eye over her behaviour without seeming to do so.

During the time of their little journey from the palace of St Germains to Paris, where monsieur the baron de Palfoy ordinarily resided, nothing farther was discoursed on: but when they arrived, and mademoiselle Charlotta had opportunity of reflecting on this sudden turn, she gave a loose to all the anxieties it occasioned: — she was not only snatch'd from the presence of what was most dear to her on earth, but as she had no confidante, nor durst make any, was also without any means either of conveying a letter to him, or receiving the least intelligence from him.

She had been in Paris but a very little time before she perceived the baron artfully kept her in the most severe restraint under a shew of liberty; pretending to her, as he had done to the princess, that he was not well enough to go abroad, he would stay at home whole days together, and oblige her to read, or play to him on the spinnet, which frequently she did with an aking heart; and when she went out, it was always in company with a relation whom he kept at his house on purpose, as he said, as a companion to divert her, but in reality to be a spy over all her actions; and had orders to dive, by all the insinuations she was mistress of, into her very thoughts. All this mademoiselle Charlotta had penetration enough to discover, and, spite of the discontent she laboured under, so well concealed what they endeavoured to find out, that all the traps laid for her were wholly ineffectual.

But in what manner did the enamoured Horatio support so cruel an affliction! he was no sooner informed at his return from hunting of what had happened, than he was seized with agonies, which, in the force he did himself to conceal, threw him into a fever that had confined him to his bed for several days: as his passion for mademoiselle Charlotta was not in the least suspected, every body imputed his disorder to be occasioned by having over-heated himself in the chace, and during his indisposition was visited by all the court: — the Chevalier St George sent two or three times a day to enquire of the health of his countryman, as he was pleased to call him, and gave him many other tokens how greatly he was in his favour; but all the civilities he received were not capable of lessening the anguish of his mind, which kept his body so weak, that tho' youth and an excellent constitution threw off the fever in a short time, yet he was unable to quit his chamber in near three weeks, and when he did, appeared so wan and so dejected, that he seemed no more than the shadow of the once gay and sprightly Horatio.

But while he was thus sinking under the burden of his griefs, and despairing ever to see his adorable Charlotta any more, fate was providing for him a relief as unexpected as the cause of his present unhappy situation had been, and to the very same person also was he indebted both for the one and the other.

Young monsieur de Coigney was not less alarmed than Horatio at the removal of Charlotta, tho' it had not the same effect on him; he was continually teizing his sister to make her a visit and repeat her intercessions on his behalf; but she had received such tart answers on that score, that she was very unwilling to undertake the embassy: however, she complied at last, and was received by mademoiselle Charlotta in the most obliging manner, but had not the least opportunity of executing her commission, that lady having a good deal of company with her, whom she purposely detained in order to avoid entering into any particular conversation with her, till the hour she knew her attendance on the queen would oblige her to take leave.

The baron de Palfoy was at that time abroad; but when he was informed who had been there, was a little disturbed that the sister of de Coigney endeavoured still to keep up her intimacy with his daughter, not doubting but she had either brought some letter or message from him, as he was fully perswaded in his mind that there was a mutual affection between them; but he took no notice of it as yet, thinking that probably she might make a second visit, and that then he should be better able to judge of the motive.

In the mean time the father of monsieur de Coigney being informed of these proceedings, thought it beneath his son to carry on a clandestine courtship; and the great share he possessed of the royal favour, he having been instrumental in some point in the parliament of Paris, rendered him vain enough to imagine his alliance would not be refused, tho' there was a superiority both of birth and fortune on the side of monsieur the baron de Palfoy.

In a perfect confidence of succeeding in his request, he went to his house, and, after some little preparation, proposed a match between his son and mademoiselle de Palfoy. The baron was not at all surprized at what he said, because he expected, if the young people were kept asunder, an offer would be made of this kind; and after hearing calmly all he had to say, in order to induce him to give his consent, he told him, that he was very sorry he had asked a thing which it was impossible to grant, because he already determined to dispose otherwise of his daughter. Monsieur de Coigney then asked to whom. I know not as yet, replied the other, but when I said I had determined to dispose her otherways, I only meant to one who is of blood at least equal to her own, and who has never, by any public debaucheries, rendered himself contemptible to the discreet part of mankind.

De Coigney knew not how either to put up or resent this affront; he knew very well that his son had behaved so as to give cause for it, yet thought he had other perfections which might over-balance what, by a partial indulgence, he looked upon only as the follies of youth; and as for the reflection on his family, he told the other, that whatever he was he owed to the merit of his ancestors, not his own, and that he doubted not but his son would one day raise his name equal to that of Palfoy. In fine, the pride of the one, and the vanity of the other, occasioned a contest between them, which might have furnished matter for a scene in a comedy had any poet been witness of it: the result of it was that they agreed in this to be mutually dissatisfied with each other, never to converse together any more, and to forbid all communication between their families.

The baron went immediately to his daughter's chamber, and having ordered her maid, who was then doing something about her, to leave the room, I have wondered, Charlotta, said he, with a countenance that was far from betraying the secret vexation of his mind, that you have never, since your coming to Paris, expressed the least desire of making a visit at St Germains, tho' the duty you owe a princess, who seems to have a very great affection for you, might well have excused any impatience you might have testified on that score; besides, you owe a visit to mademoiselle de Coigney.

The princess merits doubtless all the respect I am able to pay her, answered she; but, my lord, as it was your pleasure to remove me from that palace, I waited till your command should licence my return; as for mademoiselle de Coigney, the intimacy between us will excuse those ceremonies which are of little weight where there is a real friendship.

These words confirming all the baron's suspicions, he thought there was no need of farther dissimulation, and the long-conceived indignation burst out in looks more furious than the trembling Charlotta had ever seen in him before. — Yes, degenerate girl! said he, I have but too plain proofs of the friendship in which you have linked yourself with the family of the de Coigney's; but tell me, continued he, how dare you engage yourself so far without my knowledge? could you ever hope I would consent to an alliance with de Coigney?

De Coigney! cried she, much more assured than she had been before the mention of that name, heaven forbid you should have such a thought!

The resolution and disdain with which she spoke these words a little surprized him: what, cried he, have you not encouraged the addresses of young de Coigney, and even proceeded so far as to make his father imagine there required no more than to ask my consent to a marriage between you!

How much courage does innocence inspire? Charlotta, of late so timid and alarmed while she thought Horatio was in question, was now all calmness and composure, when she found de Coigney the person for whom she had been suspected. She confessed to her father, with the most settled brow, that he had indeed made some offers of an affection for her, but said, she had given him such answers, as nothing but the height of arrogance and folly could interpret to his advantage; and then, on the baron's commanding her, acquainted him with every particular that had passed between that young gentleman, his sister, and herself, touching the affair she was accused of.

She was so minute in every circumstance, answered with such readiness to all the questions he asked of her, and seemed so perfectly at ease, as indeed she was, that the baron could no longer have any doubts of her sincerity, and was sorry he had taken her so abruptly from St Germains: he now told her, that she was at liberty to visit there as frequently as she pleased, only, as he had been affronted by old monsieur de Coigney, as well as to silence all future reports concerning the young gentleman, he expected she would break off all acquaintance with mademoiselle. She assured him of her obedience in this point, and added, that she could do it without any difficulty; for tho' she was a lady who had many good qualities, and one for whom she once had a friendship, yet the taking upon her to forward her brother's designs had occasioned a strangeness between them, which had already more than half anticipated his commands.

Monsieur the baron de Palfoy was now as well satisfied with his daughter as he had lately been the reverse, and she was allowed once more all those innocent liberties which the French ladies, above those of any other nation in the world, enjoy.

It is not to be doubted but that the first use she made of liberty was to go to St Germains: she had heard from mademoiselle de Coigney, when she came to visit her, that Horatio had been very much indisposed, and at that time was not quite recovered, and was impatient to give him all the consolation that the sight of her could afford; but fearing she should not have an opportunity of speaking to him in private, she wrote a letter, containing a full recital of the reason which had induced her father to take her from St Germains, and the happy mistake he had been in concerning de Coigney; concluding with letting him know he might sometimes visit her at Paris as an indifferent acquaintance, not the least suspicion being entertained of him, and the baron now in so good a humour with her, that it would not be easy for any one to make him give credit to any informations to her prejudice. The whole was dictated by a spirit of tenderness, which, tho' it did not plainly confess an affection, implied every thing an honourable lover could either expect or hope.

On her arrival at St Germains, where there was an extreme full court to congratulate the princess Louisa, on the great victories lately gained by Charles XII.[52] the brave king of Sweden, to whom she had been some time

---

[52] *the great victories lately gained by Charles XII*: By 1704 Charles XII of Sweden (1682–1718) had secured the capitulation of Denmark-Norway after it occupied the duchy of Holstein-

contracted,[53] she passed directly to her highness's apartment; and the Chevalier St George being then with her, those of his Gentlemen who had attended him thither, were waiting in the antichamber: among them was Horatio: the alteration of his countenance on sight of her, after this absence, was too visible not to have been remarked, had not all present been too busy in paying their compliments to her, to take any notice of it. He was one of the last that approached, being willing to recover the confusion he felt himself in, lest it should have an effect on his voice in speaking to her. She, more prepared, received his salute with the same gay civility she did the others, but at the same instant slipped the letter she had brought with her into his hand.

Any one who is in the least acquainted with the power of love, may guess the transports of Horatio at this condescension; but, impatient to know the dear contents, he went out of the room as soon as he found he could do it without being observed, and having perused this obliging billet, found in it a sufficient cordial to revive that long languishment his spirit had been in.

At his return he found her engaged in conversation with several gentlemen and ladies: he mingled in the company, but could expect no other satisfaction from it than being near his dear Charlotta, and hearing her speak. The Chevalier St George soon after came out, and he was obliged with the rest of his train to quit the place, which at present contained the object of his wishes. She went in immediately after the princess, so he saw her no more that day at St Germains.

All that now employed his thoughts was a pretence to visit her at her father's house; for tho' she had told him in her letter that he might come as an ordinary acquaintance, yet knowing that the continuance of their conversation depended wholly on the secrecy of it, he was willing to avoid giving even the most distant occasions of suspicion.

Fortune, hitherto favourable to his desires, now presented him with one more ample than any thing his own invention could have supplied him with: happening to be in Paris in the company of some friends, with whom he stayed later than ordinary, he was hurrying thro' the streets in order to go to the inn where his servant and horses waited for him, when he heard the clashing of swords at some distance from him: guided by his generosity, he flew to the place

---

Gottorp; defeated the Russian army at Narva in November 1700; and gained victories over the army of Augustus II [see below, n. 57] at Dvina in 1701, Kliszów in 1702, and Pultusk in 1703. For accounts of the campaigns in which Charles XII of Sweden was involved, Haywood could have drawn on Daniel Defoe's *The History of the Wars, of his Present Majesty Charles XII. King of Sweden* (1715); Voltaire's *Histoire de Charles XII: Roi de Suède* (1731), available in English by 1732; and Gustaf Adlerfelt's *The Military History of Charles XII. King of Sweden*, translated from French into English by Henry Fielding in 1740. [See also below, nn. 100, 117.]
[53] *the brave king of Sweden, to whom she had been some time contracted*: The idea of a marriage between Charles XII of Sweden and James Francis Edward Stuart's daughter, Princess Louise Marie, was a product of the Jacobite imagination. See Niall MacKenzie, 'Charles XII of Sweden and the Jacobites', *Royal Stuart Papers*, 62 (2002), p. 11.

where the noise directed him, and saw by the lights, which hang out very thick in that city, one person defending himself against three who pressed very hard upon him, and had got him down just as Horatio arrived to his relief: he ran among the assailants; and either the greatness of his courage, or the belief that others would come to his assistance, threw them into such a consternation, that they all sought their safety in their flight, while the person they had attacked got up again and thanked his deliverer, without whose timely aid, he said, he could have expected nothing but death: those who set upon him being robbers, and, as he perceived by their behaviour, desperate wretches, who were for securing themselves by taking the lives, as well as the money, of those who were too weak to resist them: he pointed to a dead body on the ground, who he told Horatio was his servant, and had been killed in his defence.

But how transported was our young lover when he found that the person to whom he had done so signal a piece of service, was the father of his mistress. As he perceived he had some wounds, tho' they proved but slight, he compleated the obligation he had begun to confer, by supporting him under the arm till he got home, where the baron made him enter with him, and would have prevailed with him to stay all night; but Horatio told him he could not well dispense with being absent from his post; that it was highly proper he should return to St Germains that night late as it was, but would do himself the honour of waiting on him the next day to enquire after the state of the wounds he had received.

Mademoiselle Charlotta was gone to bed; but being rouzed by the accident, no sooner was informed by the surgeons, who were immediately sent for, that there was nothing dangerous in the hurts her father had received, than she blessed heaven for making Horatio the instrument of his preservation. The sense the baron seemed to have of this obligation, and the praises he bestowed on the gallant manner in which the young gentleman came to his relief, made her almost ready to flatter herself that fate interested itself in behalf of their love; and indeed monsieur the baron, notwithstanding the haughtiness of his nature, had the most just notions of gratitude; and to testify it to Horatio, would have refused him scarce any thing except his daughter. But however that should happen, she still found more and more excuses for indulging the inclinations she had for him; and tho' she yet had never given him any such assurances, yet she resolved in her own mind to live only for him.

The baron being obliged to keep his bed for several days, Horatio had a pretence for repeating his visits to him during this time of confinement, and afterwards went often by invitation; the other, besides the obligation he had to him, finding something extremely pleasing in his conversation, to which (not to take from Horatio's merits) the obsequiousness he found no difficulty in himself to behave to a Man of his age, his quality, and above all, the father of Charlotta, not a little contributed.

The lovers now had frequent opportunities of entertaining each other both at Paris and St Germains: nor were any of those demonstrations which virtue and innocence permitted, wanting between them, to render them as perfectly easy as people can possibly be, who have yet something to desire, and much to fear. But as smooth as now their fortune seemed, they knew not how soon a storm might arise, and give a sudden interruption to that felicity they enjoyed. — The charms of Charlotta were every day making new conquests; and among the number of those who pretended to admire her, how probable was it that some one might be thought worthy by her father, and she be compelled to receive the addresses of a rival. These were reflections too natural not to occur to them both, and whenever they did, could not fail of embittering those sweets the certainty of a mutual affection had otherwise afforded.

They now had no trouble from monsieur de Coigney; his father, in order to make him forget a hopeless passion, had found an employment for him which obliged him to go many leagues from Paris; and since the conversation already mentioned at the baron's, his sister and mademoiselle Charlotta, by command of their respective parents, as well as their own inclinations, broke off all correspondence, nor even spoke to each other, unless when happening to meet in a visit there was no avoiding it; and then it was in such a distant manner, and with so much indifference, that none would have imagined they ever had been intimate friends and companions.

CHAP. IX.

A second separation between Horatio and Charlotta, with some other occurrences.

THE season of the year now having put an end to the campaign, and the French, as well as confederate armies, being retired into their winter quarters, the baron de la Valiere, who had always a special permission from the general, returned to Paris: Horatio promised himself much satisfaction in the renewed society of this friend, and no sooner heard he was on the road than he went to meet him. The baron, charm'd with this proof of his affection and respect, received him as a brother, and there was little less freedom used between them.

After the mutual testimonies and good-will were over, de la Valiere began to ask him concerning mademoiselle Charlotta; on which Horatio acquainted him with her being removed from St Germains, and the occasion of it, not omitting the arrogance with which old monsieur de Coigney had behaved to her father, and the resentment now between the families.

Well, said the baron, but I hope you have been more successful, at least with the young lady: I will never trust more the intelligence of the eyes, if yours did not hold a very tender intercourse; and I protest to you, my dear Horatio, that amidst all the toils and dangers of war, my thoughts were often at St Germains, not envying, but congratulating the pleasures you enjoyed in the conversation of that amiable lady.

I doubt not, relied Horatio with a smile, but we had you with us at a place which contained mademoiselle de Coigney; and I am of opinion too she was no less frequently in the camp with you; for in spite of all the reserve she affected while you were present, she never heard the bare mention of your name without emotions, which were very visible in her countenance.

I would not be vain, replied the baron, but I sometimes have flattered myself with the hope I was not altogether indifferent to her; tho' for two whole years I have constantly made my addresses to her, I never could obtain one soft confession to assure my happiness: — but let me know how you have proceeded on the score of mademoiselle Charlotta? believe me, I am not so engrossed by my own affairs, as not to give attention to those of a friend.

Horatio, who had been engaged by Charlotta to preserve an inviolable secrecy in every thing that had passed between them, without any exception of persons, would fain have turned the conversation on some other topic: he truly loved the baron, had the highest opinion of his discretion, and would have trusted him with the dearest secrets of his life, provided they related to himself alone; but he had given his word, his oath, his honour to Charlotta, and durst not violate them on any consideration; yet, loth to refuse or deceive his friend, he found himself in the most perplexing dilemma. As often as the other spoke of Charlotta, he answered with something of de Coigney; but all his artifice was ineffectual, and the baron at last saw thro' it, and assuming a very grave countenance, I perceive, Horatio, said he, you do not think me worthy your confidence, and I was to blame to press you to reveal what you resolve to make a mystery of.

These words made a very deep impression on the grateful soul of him they were addressed to; and equally distressed between the necessity of either disobliging a person whose generosity he had experienced, or falsifying the promise he had made to Charlotta, at last an expedient offered to his mind how to avoid both, and yet not be guilty of injuring the truth.

Alas! my lord, answered he, you little know the heart of Horatio, if you imagine there be any thing there that would hide itself from you: — I freely confess, the charms of mademoiselle Charlotta had such an effect on me, that, had I been in circumstances which in the least could have flattered me with success, I should long ago have avowed myself as her lover: but when I reflected on the disparity between us, the humour of her father, and a thousand other impediments, I endeavoured to banish so hopeless a passion from my breast, and was the more confirmed in my resolution to do so by the ill treatment monsieur de Coigney received: — besides, her removal from St Germains, depriving me in a great measure of those opportunities I had before of entertaining her, might very well contribute to wean off a passion, not settled either by time or expectation, of ever being gratified; and I hope, continued he, I shall always have so much command over myself as not to become ridiculous by aiming at impossibilities.

Whether the baron gave any credit to what he said on this account or not, he had too much politeness to press him any farther; and the discourse soon after taking another turn, Horatio was very well pleased to think he had got off so well.

De la Valiere having related to him some particulars of the late campaign, which the public accounts had been deficient in, they passed from that to some talk of the brave young king of Sweden, a topic which filled all Europe with admiration: but the French being a people in whom the love of glory is the predominant passion, were more than any other nation charmed with the greatness of that prince's soul.

What indeed has any hero of antiquity to boast of in competition with this northern monarch, who conquered and gave away kingdoms for the benefit of others, disdaining to receive any other reward for all his vast fatigues, than the pleasure of giving a people that person whom he judged most worthy to reign over them!

The baron, who had attended the Count de Guiscard[54] when he was residentiary ambassador from his most christian majesty at the Swedish court, had an opportunity of seeing more of this monarch than any other that Horatio was acquainted with; he therefore, on his requesting it, informed him how, at the age of eighteen, he threw off all magnificence, forsook the pomp and delicacies of a court he had been bred in, and undertook, and compleated the delivery of his brother-in-law, the Duke of Holstein,[55] from the cruel incursions of the Danes, who had well nigh either taken or ravaged the greatest part of his territories. He also set forth, in its proper colours, the base part which Peter Alexowitz, czar of Muscovy,[56] and Augustus, king of Poland,[57] acted against a prince who was then employing his arms in the cause of justice; the latter of these bringing a powerful army to take from him one part of his dominions; and the former, at the head of 100,000 men, were plundering the other: but when he concluded his little narrative, by reciting how this young conqueror, with a handful of brave Swedes, animated by the example of their king, put entirely to route all that opposed him, Horatio felt his soul glow with an ardour superior even to that of love: he longed to behold a prince who seemed to have all the virtues comprized in him, and whose very thoughts, as well as actions, might be looked on as supernatural.

He is, however, greatly to be pitied, said the baron de la Valiere, that the wars he is engaged in, and which, in all probability will be of long continuance, hinders him from the possession of the most amiable princess in the world, and I dare answer, at least if I may credit those about her, she wishes he were of a less martial disposition.

He will be the more worthy of her, cried Horatio interrupting him, and the immortal fame of his actions be a sufficient attonement for all the years of expectation that may be its purchase.

From the time Horatio had this discourse with the baron, the king of Sweden was ever uppermost in his thoughts: he had always reflected that, in the station he then was, it would be impossible to obtain any more of mademoiselle Charlotta than her heart, at least while the baron de Palfoy lived, and that a thousand accidents might deprive him of all hopes of ever being more happy; but, said he to himself, were I among the number of those who attend this hero

---

[54] *Count de Guiscard*: Louis, comte de Guiscard (1651–1720).
[55] *the Duke of Holstein*: Frederick IV, duke of Holstein-Gottorp (1671–1702), who married Charles XII's sister, princess Hedvig Sophia.
[56] *Peter Alexowitz, czar of Muscovy*: Peter I, Tsar of Russia (1672–1726).
[57] *Augustus, king of Poland*: Augustus II (1670–1733), king of Poland from 1697–1706 and 1709–1733. As Elector of Saxony, he was formerly Frederick Augustus I.

in his martial exploits, I might at least have the opportunity of proving how far fortune would befriend me; — who knows but I might be able to do something which might engage that just and generous monarch to raise me to a degree capable of avowing my pretensions even to her father, and the same blessed day that joined our principals, might also make me blessed in the possession of my dear Charlotta.

With these ideas did he often flatter himself; but the manner in which he should accomplish his desires was yet doubtful to him. The chevalier St George treated him with so much kindness, that he had no room to doubt his having a great share in his favour; and was fully perswaded, that if he communicated his intentions to him, he would vouchsafe to give him letters of recommendation to a prince who was to be his brother-in-law: but this he feared to ask, lest it should be looked upon as ingratitude in him to desire to leave a court where he had been so graciously received, and had many favours, besides the perquisites of his post, heaped upon him, not only by the chevalier himself, but also by the queen and princess, who, following the example of the late king, behaved with a kind of natural affection to all the English.

He sometimes communicated his sentiments on this head to mademoiselle Charlotta, who was too discreet not to allow the justice of them; and well knew, that in the station her lover now was, they could never be on any other terms with each other than those they were at present: her reason, therefore, and the advantage of her love, made her sometimes wish he would follow the dictates of so laudable an ambition; but then the dangers he must inevitably be exposed to in following a monarch who never set any bounds to his courage, and the thoughts how long it might possibly be before she saw him again, alarmed all her tenderness; and he had the satisfaction of seeing the tears stand in her eyes whenever they had any discourse of this nature; and tho' her words assured him that it was her opinion he could not take a more ready way to raise his own fortune, yet her looks at the same time made him plainly see how much she would suffer in his taking that step.

Many reasons, both for and against following his inclination in this point, presented themselves to him; and he had no sooner, as he thought, determined for the one, than the other rose with double vehemence and overthrew the former. In this fluctuating situation of mind did he remain for some time, and perhaps had done so much longer, had not an accident happened which proved decisive, and indeed left him no other party to take than that he afterwards did.

Charlotta, now being entirely mistress of herself, gave him frequent meetings at the Tuilleries,[58] judging it safer to converse with him there than at the house

---

[58] *the Tuilleries*: The Tuileries Gardens, beside the Tuileries Palace, developed and landscaped by Louis XIV's gardener André le Nôtre in 1664.

of any person, whom, in such a case, must be the confidante of the whole affair; whereas, if they were seen together in the walks, it might be judged they met by accident, and not give any grounds of suspicion, which hitherto they had been so fortunate as to avoid.

It was in one of those appointments, when entered into a very tender conversation, they forgot themselves so far as to suffer the moon to rise upon them: the stillness of the evening, and the little company which happened to be there that night, seemed to indulge their inclinations of continuing in so sweet a recess: — they were seated on a bench at the foot of a large tree, when Charlotta, in answer to some tender professions he had been making, said, depend on this, Horatio, that as you are the first that has ever been capable of making me sensible of love, so nothing shall have power to change my sentiments while you continue to deserve, or to desire I should think of you as I now do. He shall not continue long to desire it, — cried a voice behind them, and immediately rushed from the other side of the thicket a man with his sword drawn, and ran full upon Horatio, who not having time to be upon his guard, had certainly fallen a victim to his rival's fury, had not a gentleman seized his arm, and, by superior strength, forced him some paces back. — Are you mad, monsieur, said he; do you forget the place you are in, or the danger you so lately escaped for an enterprize of this nature?

Mademoiselle Charlotta, now a little recovered from her first surprize, and knowing it was young monsieur de Coigney who had given her this alarm, had presence enough of mind to ask how he dared, after he knew her own and father's resolution, to disturb her, or any company she had with her? he made no reply, but reflecting that there were other ways than fighting, by which he might be revenged, went hastily away with that friend who had hindered him from executing his rash purpose; but they could hear that he muttered something which seemed a menace against them both.

How impossible it is to express the consternation our lovers now were in: they found by the repetition monsieur de Coigney made of the words she spoke, that what they had so long and so successfully laboured to conceal, was now betrayed: — betrayed to one who would not fail to make the most malicious use of the discovery, and doubted not but the affair would become the general talk, perhaps to the prejudice of Charlotta's reputation; but the least thing either of them could expect, was to be separated for ever.

Horatio, full of disturbed emotions, conducted his disconsolate mistress to the gate of the Tuilleries, and there took a farewel of her, which he had too much reason to fear would be his last, at least for a long time. He was tempted by his first emotions to seek de Coigney, and call him to account for the affront he had put upon him, and either lose his own life, or oblige the other to secrecy; but then he considered, that there was some probability he would not dare to own that he had given himself any concern about mademoiselle Charlotta, after the injunction laid on him by his father, much less as he had attempted a duel in her cause, having, as has already been mentioned, been before guilty of a like offence against the laws, which in that country are very strict, on account of madame de Olonne; and this prevailed with him to be passive as to what had happened, till he should hear how the other would behave, and find what turn the affair would take.

Charlotta in the mean time was in the most terrible anxieties: — she could not imagine what had brought monsieur de Coigney, who she thought had been many miles distant, so suddenly to Paris: but on making some private enquiry, she was informed, that having met some difficulty in the execution of his office, he had taken post, in order to lay his complaints before the king, and had arrived that very day. — She now blamed her own inadvertency in holding any discourse with Horatio, of a nature not proper to be over-heard, in a place so public as the Tuilleries, where others, as well as he, might have possibly been witnesses of what was said.

Young monsieur de Coigney suffered little less from the turbulence of his nature, and the mortification it gave his vanity, to find a person, whom he looked upon as every way his inferior, preferred to him. His thoughts were wholly bent on revenge; but in what manner he should accomplish it, he was for some time uncertain: when he acquainted his father with the discovery he had made, and the resentment he had testified against this unworthy rival, as he called him, the old gentleman blamed him for taking any notice of it. Let them love on, son, said he; let them marry; — we shall then have a fine opportunity of reproaching the haughty baron with his new alliance. This did not however satisfy monsieur de Coigney: all the love he once had for mademoiselle Charlotta was now turned to hate; and in spite of his father's commands not to meddle in the affair, he could not help throwing out some reflections among his companions, very much to the disadvantage of the young lady's reputation. But these might possibly have blown over, as he had but a small time to vent his malice. His father knowing the violence of his temper, in order to prevent any ill consequences, compelled him to return to his employment; taking upon himself the management of that business which had brought him so unluckily to Paris.

But mademoiselle de Coigney had no sooner been informed of the discovery he had made, than she doubted not it was on the score of Horatio that he had met with such ill success in his courtship; and also imagined, that it had been owing to some ill impressions mademoiselle Charlotta had given the baron de Palfoy, that her father had been treated by him in the manner already recited. She complained of it to the baron de la Valiere, and told him, her whole family had been affronted, and her brother rendered miserable, for the sake of a young man, who, said she, can neither have birth or fortune to boast of, since he has been so long a prisoner without any ransom paid, or interposition offered to redeem him.

The baron was too generous not to vindicate the merits of Horatio, as much as was consistent with his love and complaisance for his mistress: he was notwithstanding very much picqued in his mind that a person, to whom he had given the greatest proofs of a sincere and disinterested friendship, should have concealed a secret of this nature from him, and the more so, as he had seemed to expect and desire his confidence. From this time forward he behaved to him with a coldness which was sufficient to convince the other of the motive, especially as he found mademoiselle de Coigney took all opportunities of throwing the most picquant reflections on him. It is certain that lady was so full of spight at the indignity she thought her family had received, that she could not help whispering the attachment of Horatio and Charlotta, not only at St Germains, but at Paris also, with innuendo's little less cruel than those her brother had made use of to his companions; so that between them, the amour was talked of among all who were acquainted with either of them.

At length the report reached the ears of the baron de Palfoy, who, tho' he did not immediately give an entire credit to it, thought it became him to do every thing in his power to silence it.

Accordingly he called his daughter to him one day, and having told her the liberty which the world took in censuring her conduct on Horatio's account, commanded her to avoid all occasions of it for the future, by seeing him no more.

The confusion she was in, and which she had not artifice wholly to conceal from the penetrating baron, more convinced him, than all he had been told, that there was in reality some tender intercourse between them; but resolving to be fully ascertained, he said no more to her at that time, but dispatched a messenger immediately to St Germains, desiring Horatio to come to him the same day.

The lover readily obeyed this summons, but not without some apprehensions of the motive: the hints daily given him, joined to the alteration, not only in the behaviour of mademoiselle de Coigney, but likewise of the baron de Valiere, gave him but too just room to fear his passion was no longer a secret.

The father of Charlotta received him with great courtesy, but nothing of that pleasantness with which he had looked on him ever since he had defended him from the robbers. Horatio, said he, I am indebted to you for my life, and would willingly make what recompence is in my power for the obligation I have to you: — think therefore what I can do for you; and if your demands exceed not what is fit for you to ask, or would become me to grant, you may be assured of my compliance.

The astonishment Horatio was in at these words is impossible to be expressed;

but having an admirable presence of mind, my lord, answered he, I should be unworthy of the favours you do me, could I be capable of presuming on them so far as to make any requests beyond the continuance of them.

No, Horatio, resumed the baron, I acknowledge my gratitude has been too deficient, since it has extended only to those civilities which are due to your merit, exclusive of any obligation; the conversation we have had together has hitherto afforded a pleasure to myself, and it is with a good deal of mortification I now find a necessity to break it off: — I would therefore have the satisfaction of doing something that might convince you of my esteem, at the same time that I desire you to refrain your visits.

Not all Horatio's courage could enable him to stand this shock, without testifying some part of what passed in his mind: — he was utterly incapable of making any reply, tho' the silence of the other shewed he expected it, but stood like one confounded, and conscious of deserving the banishment he heard pronounced against him. — At last recollecting himself a little, — my lord, said he, I see not how I can be happy enough to preserve any part of your esteem, since looked upon as unworthy an honour you were once pleased to confer upon me.

You affect, said the baron, a slowness of apprehension, which is far from being natural to you, and perhaps imagine, that by not seeming to understand me, I should believe there were no grounds for me to forbid you my house; but, young man, I am not so easily deceived; and since you oblige me to speak plain, must tell you, I am sorry to find you have entertained any projects, which, if you had the least consulted your reason, you would have known could never be accomplished. — In fine, Horatio, what you make so great a mystery of, may be explained in three words: — I wish you well as a friend, but cannot think of making you my son: — I would recompence what you have done for me with any thing but my daughter, and as proof of my concern for your happiness, I exclude you from all society with her, in order to prevent so unavailing a passion from taking too deep a root.

Ah, my lord, cried Horatio, perceiving all dissimulation would be vain, the man who once adored mademoiselle de Palfoy can never cease to do so. He ought therefore, replied the baron, without being moved, to consider the consequences well before he begins to adore: — if I had been consulted in this matter I should have advised you better; but it is now too late, and all I can do is to prevent your ever meeting more: — this, Horatio, is all I have to say, and that if in any other affair I can be serviceable to you, communicate your request in writing, and depend upon its being granted.

In speaking these last words he withdrew, and left Horatio in a situation of mind not easy to be conceived. — He was once about to entreat him to turn back, but had nothing to offer which could make him hope would prevail on him to alter his resolution. — He never had been insensible of the vast disparity there was at present between him and the noble family of de Palfoy: he could expect no other, or rather worse treatment than what he had now received, if his passion was ever discovered, and had no excuse to make for what himself allowed to be so great a presumption.

With a countenance dejected, and a heart oppressed with various agitations, did he quit the house which contained what was most valuable to him in the world, while poor Charlotta endured, if possible, a greater shock.

The baron de Palfoy, now convinced that all he had been informed of was true, was more incensed against her than he had been on the mistaken supposition of her being influenced in favour of monsieur de Coigney: he had no sooner left Horatio than he flew to her apartment, and reproached her in terms the most severe that words could form. — It was in vain she protested that she never had any design of giving herself to Horatio without having first received his permission. — He looked on all she said as an augmentation of her crime, and soon came to a determination to put it past her power to give him more cause for concern than she had already done.

Early next morning he sent her, under the conduct of a person he could confide in, to a monastery about thirty miles from Paris, without even letting her know whither she was being carried, or giving her the least notice of her departure till the coach was at the door, into which he put her himself with these words, — adieu Charlotta, expect not to see Paris, or me again, till you desire no more to see Horatio.

CHAP. X.

The reasons that induced Horatio to leave France; with the chevalier St George's behaviour on knowing his resolution. He receives an unexpected favour from the baron de Palfoy.

WHILE Charlotta, under the displeasure of her father, and divided, as she believed, for ever from her lover, was pursuing her melancholy journey, Horatio was giving way to a grief which knew no bounds, and which preyed with the greater fierceness on his soul, as he had no friend to whom he could disburden it. The baron's estrang'd behaviour was no small addition to his other discontents, and he lamented the cruel necessity which had enforced him to disoblige a person to whom he owed so many favours, and whose advice would now have been the greatest consolation.

He could not now hope Charlotta would be permitted to come to St Germains, and doubted not but her father would take effectual methods to prevent her visiting at any place where even accident might occasion a meeting between them: he knew the watch had been set over her on the account of monsieur de Coigney, and might be assured it would not now be less strict, and that it would be equally impossible for either to communicate their thoughts by writing as it was to see each other.

He was in the midst of these reflections when he heard, by some people who were acquainted with the baron de Palfoy, that he had sent his daughter away, but none knew where: this, instead of lessening his despair, was a very great aggravation of it: — he imagined she was confined in some monastery, and was not insensible of the difficulties that attend seeing a young lady who is sent there purposely to avoid the world; yet, said he to himself, I could be happy enough to discover even to what province she was carried, I would go from convent to convent till I had found which of them contain her.

It was in vain that he made all possible enquiry: every one he asked was in reality as ignorant as himself. — The baron de Palfoy had trusted none, so could not be deceived by those persons who had the charge of conducting her, and of their fidelity he had many proofs. Yet how impossible is it for human prudence to resist the decrees of fate. — The secret was betrayed, without any one being guilty of accusing the confidence reposed in them, and by the strangest accident that perhaps ever was, Horatio learned all he wished to know when he had given over all his endeavours for that purpose, and was totally despairing of it.

He came one day to Paris, in order to alleviate his melancholy, in the company of some young gentlemen, who had expressed a very great regard for him; but his mind being taken up with various and perplexed thoughts on his entrance to that city, he mistook his way, and turned into the rue St Dennis instead of the rue St Honore, where he had been accustomed to leave his horses and servant. — He found his error just as he was passing by a large inn, and it being a matter of indifference to him where he put up, would not turn back, but ordered his man to alight here. — I forgot where I was going, said he, but I suppose the horses will be taken as much care of at this house as where we used to go. I shall see to that, replied the fellow. Horatio stepped into a room to take some refreshment while his servant went to the stable, but had not been there above a minute before he heard very high words between some people in the yard; and as he turned towards the window, saw a man in the livery of the baron de Palfoy, and whom he presently knew to be the coachman of that nobleman. He was hot in dispute with the innkeeper concerning a horse which he had hired of him, and, as the other insisted, drove so hard that he had killed him. The coachman denied the accusation; but the innkeeper told him he had witnesses to prove the horse died two hours after he was brought home, and declared, that if he had not satisfaction for his beast, he would complain to the baron, and if he did not do him justice, have recourse to law. — There was a long argument between them concerning the number of miles, the hours they drove, and the weight of the carriage. — Among other things the innkeeper alledged, that he saw them as he passed his corner, and there were so many trunks, boxes, and other luggage behind and before the coach, besides the company that was in it, that it required eight horses instead of six to draw it. Why then, said the coachman, did it not kill our horses as well as yours; if they had been equally good, they would have held out equally. — I do not pretend mine was as good, replied the innkeeper, I cannot afford to feed my horses as my lord does; but yet he was a stout gelding, and if he had not been drove so very hard, and perhaps otherwise ill used into the bargain, he would have been alive now.

All this was sufficient to make Horatio imagine it was for the journey which deprived him of his dear Charlotta, that this horse had been hired, so tarried in the place where he was till the debate was over, which ended not to the satisfaction of the innkeeper, who swore he would not be fooled out of his money. As soon as the coachman was gone, Horatio called him in, and asked what was the matter, and who it was that endeavoured to impose upon him? on which the innkeeper readily told him, that on such a day this coachman came to him and hired a horse in order to make up a set to go to Rheines in Champaigne,[59] my lord-baron having three or four sick at the stable at that time. — Two days after, said he, my horse was brought home all in a foam, and

---

[59] *Rheines in Champaigne*: Reims, a city 130 km north-east of Paris that was and is still a centre for the production of champagne.

fell down dead in less than three hours, and yet this rascally coachman refuses to pay me for him.

Horatio humoured him in all he said, and let him go on his own way till he had vented his whole stock of railing, and then asked him what company were in the coach. The innkeeper replied, that there was one man and two women, but did not know who they were, for their faces were muffled up in their hoods. This was sufficient for him to be assured it was no other than Charlotta, with her woman, and some friend whom the baron had sent with them. The day mentioned, being the very same he had been informed she was carried away, was also another confirmation; and he had not only the happiness of knowing where his mistress was, but of knowing it by such means as could give the baron no suspicion of his being acquainted with it, and therefore make him think it necessary to remove her.

Having gained this intelligence, which yet he was no better for than the hope of being able to get a sight of her thro' the grate,[60] which he was resolved to accomplish some way or other, he resumed his design of going into the army of the king of Sweden. As a perfect knowledge of the many excellent qualities of the chevalier St George, made him regard and love him with an affection beyond what is ordinarily to be met with from a servant to his master, he felt an extreme repugnance to quit him, and yet more in breaking a matter to him which, while it testified a confidence in the goodness of him whose assistance he must implore, he thought, at the same time, would be looked on as ingratitude in himself; and he was some time deliberating in what manner he should do it; and it would have been perhaps a great while before he could have found words which he would have thought proper for the purpose, if he had not taken an opportunity, which, without any design of his own, offered itself to him.

The chevalier St George took a particular pleasure in the game of Chess; and Horatio having learned it among the officers in Campaine,[61] frequently played with him: they were one evening at this diversion, when the lover of Charlotta having his mind a little perplexed, placed his men so ill, that the chevalier beat him out at every motion. How is this, Horatio, cried he; you used to play better than I, but now I have the advantage of you. — May you always have it, sir, replied he with the utmost respect, over all who pretend to oppose you. — Chess is a kind of emblem of war, where policy should go hand in hand with courage; and there is a great master in that art, whom if I were some time to serve under, I flatter myself that I should be able to know how to move my men with better success than I have done to night; but then my skill should be employed only against such as are your enemies.

You mean my brother Charles of Sweden, said the chevalier smiling, but

---

[60] *grate*: the grille allowing communication between nuns and visitors.
[61] *Campaine*: here, a military campaign.

I believe he seldom plays. Never, but when kingdoms are at stake, resumed Horatio; and if a day should come when you, sir, shall attempt the prize, how fortunate would it be for me to have learned to serve you as I am obliged to by more than my duty, by the most natural and inviolable attachment of my heart, which would render it the greatest blessing I could receive from heaven. I believe, indeed, returned the chevalier St George, you love me enough to fight in my cause whenever occasion offers. I would not only fight, but die, cried Horatio warmly; yet I would wish to have the skill to make a great number of your enemies die before me. Well, said the chevalier, we will talk of this to-morrow; in the mean time play as well as you can against me at St Germains: in another place perhaps you may play for me. Horatio made no other reply to these words than a low bow, and then elating his hands and eyes to heaven, as internally praying for the opportunity his master seemed to hint at.

The impression this little conversation made on the mind of the chevalier St George, proved itself in its effects the very next day. Horatio being ordered to come into his chamber early in the morning, — I have been thinking on what passed last night between us, said he, and if you have a serious Intention of doing what you seem to hint at, will contribute all I can to forward you.

Ah sir! cried Horatio, falling at his feet, impute not, I beseech you, this desire in me to any thing but the extreme desire I have to render myself worthy of the favours you have been pleased to confer upon me, and to be able to serve you whenever any happy occasion shall present itself.

No more, Horatio, replied the chevalier, with a sweetness and affability peculiar to himself; I am perfectly assured of your duty and affection to me, and am so far from taking it ill that you desire to quit my court on this score, that I think your ambition highly laudable: — I will write letters of recommendation, with my own hand, to my brother Charles, and to some others in his camp; which I doubt not but will procure you a reception answerable to your wishes: — therefore, as it is a long journey you are to take, the sooner you provide for your departure the better: — I will order you out of my privy purse 2000 crowns towards your expences.

Horatio found it impossible to express how much this goodness touched his soul; nor could do it any otherwise than by prostrating himself a second time, embracing his knees, and uttering some incoherent acclamations, which more shewed to his master the sincerity of his gratitude, and the perfect love he bore him, than the most elegant speeches could have done.

After all possible demonstrations of the most gracious benignity on the one side, and reverence on the other, Horatio quitted the presence, and went to Sir

Thomas Higgons,[62] who at that time was privy purse,[63] and one of the finest gentleman that ever England bred, and acquainted him with the chevalier St George's goodness to him, and the change that was going to be made in his fortune: he thanked him in the politest manner for being made the first that should congratulate him, and told him, he did not doubt but he should see him return covered with laurels, and enriched with honours, by the most glorious and grateful monarch the world had to boast of. The whole court, whose esteem the good qualities, handsome person, and agreeable behaviour of Horatio had entirely gained, seemed to partake in his satisfaction, and he was so engrossed with the preparations for his departure, and receiving the compliments made him, that tho' he was far from forgetting Charlotta, yet the languishment which her absence had occasioned was entirely banished, and he now appeared all life and spirit. — So true it is that idleness is the food of soft desires.

It must be confessed, indeed, that love had a very great share in reviving in him those martial inclinations, which for a time had seemed lulled to rest, since it was to render himself in a condition which might give him hope of obtaining the object of his love that now pushed him on to war. He resolved also to make Rheines in his way to Poland, where the king of Sweden was then pursuing conquests, and see, if possible, his dear Charlotta before he left France; and as he was of a more than ordinary sanguine disposition, he was much sooner elated with the prospect of success in any undertaking he went about, than dejected at the disappointment of it.

The baron de la Valiere, whose friendship over-balanced his resentment, now gave an instance of his generosity, which, as things stood of late between them, Horatio was far from expecting. That nobleman came to his apartment one day with a letter in his hand, and accosting him with the familiarity he had been accustomed to treat him with before their estrangement, — Horatio, said he, I cannot suffer you to leave us without giving you what testimonies of good-will are in my power: — you are now going among strangers, and tho' after the recommendations I hear you are to carry with you from the chevalier St George, nothing can be added to assure you of the king of Sweden's favour, yet as many brave actions are lost for want of a proper recommendation of them, and the eyes of kings cannot be every where, it may be of some service to you to have general Renchild[64] your friend: I once had the honour of a particular

---

[62] *Sir Thomas Higgons*: Thomas Higgons, Jacobite Sir Thomas Higgons (1688/9–1733), was gentleman usher of the privy chamber at the Stuart court in exile at Saint-Germain-en-Laye. He was active in the Jacobite Rebellion of 1715.

[63] *privy purse*: here, the holder of the office of Privy Purse, a member of the court responsible for managing the sovereign's finances. The Privy Purse is that part of public revenue set aside for the private expenses of the monarch.

[64] *general Renchild*: Karl Gustaf Rehnskiöld (1651–1722), Swedish Field-marshal, created count in 1707.

acquaintance with that great man, and I believe this letter, which I beg the favour of you to deliver to him, will in part convince him of your merit, before you may have an opportunity of proving it to him by your actions.

Horatio took the letter out of his hand, which he had presented to him at the conclusion of his speech; and charmed with this behaviour, the satisfaction I should take, said he, in this mark of your forgiving goodness, would be beyond all bounds, were I not conscious how far I have been unworthy of it; and I fear the same goodness, always partial to me, may have in this paper (meaning the letter) endeavoured to give the general an idea of me which I may not be able to preserve.

I look upon myself to be the best judge of that, replied the baron with a smile; and you may remember, that on a very different occasion I saw into your sentiments before you were well acquainted with the nature of them yourself.

As Horatio knew these words referred to the discourse that had passed between them concerning his then infant passion for mademoiselle Charlotta he could not help blushing; but de la Valiere perceiving he had given him some confusion, would have turned the discourse, had not the other thought fit to continue it, by letting him know the real motive which had constrained him to act with the reserve he had done on that score.

The baron de la Valiere assured him that he should think no more of it; and tho' at first he had taken it a little amiss, yet when he came to reflect on the circumstance, he could not but confess he should have behaved in the same manner himself.

The renewal of the former friendship between them, greatly added to the contentment Horatio at present enjoyed; but soon after he received such an augmentation of it, as he could never have imagined, much less have flattered himself with the hope of.

Some few days before his departure, a servant of the baron de Palfoy came to him to let him know his lord sent his compliments, and desired to speak with him at his own house. The message seemed so improbable, that Horatio could scarce give credit to it, and imagined the man had been mistaken in the person to whom he delivered it, till he repeated over and over again that it was to no other he was sent.

Had it been any other than the father of mademoiselle Charlotta, who had invited him to a house he had once been forbid, he scarce would have obeyed the summons; but as it was he, the awful person who gave being to that charmer of his soul, he sent the most respectful answer, and the same day took horse for Paris, and attended the explanation of an order which at present seemed so misterious to him.

The baron was no sooner informed he was there, than he came into the parlour with a countenance, which had in it all the marks of good humour and satisfaction; Horatio, said he, after having made him seat himself, I doubt not but you think me your enemy, after the treatment I gave you the last time you were here; but I assure you, I suffered no less myself in forbidding you my house, than you could do in having what you might think an affront put upon you: — but, continued he after a pause, you ought to consider I am a father, that Charlotta is my only child, that my whole estate, and what is of infinite more consideration with me, the honour of my family, must all devolve on her, and that I am under obligations not to be dispensed with, to dispose of her in such a manner as shall not any way degrade the ancestry she is sprung from. — I own your merits: — I also am indebted to you for my life: — but you are a foreigner, your family unknown, — your fortune precarious: — I could wish it were otherwise; — believe, I find in myself an irresistable impulse to love you, and I know nothing would give me greater pleasure than to convince you of it. — In fine, there is nothing but Charlotta I would refuse you.

The old lord uttered all this with so feeling an accent that Horatio was very much moved at it; but unable to guess what would be the consequence of this strange preparation, and not having any thing to ask of him but the only thing he declared he would not grant, he only thanked him for the concern he was pleased to express, and said, that perhaps there might come a time in which the obscurity he was in at present would be enlightened; at least, cried he, I shall have the satisfaction of endeavouring to acquire by merit what I am denied by fortune.

I admire this noble ambition in you, replied the baron de Palfoy; pursue these laudable views, and doubt not of success: it would be an infinite pleasure to me to see you raised so high, that I should acknowledge an alliance with you the greatest honour I could hope: and to shew you with how much sincerity I speak, — here is a letter I have wrote to count Piper, the first minister and favourite of the king of Sweden;[65] when you deliver this to him, I am certain you will be convinced by his reception of you, that you are one whose interest I take no inconsiderable part in.

With these words he gave him a letter directed, as he had said, but not sealed, which Horatio, after he had manifested the sense he had of so unhoped for an obligation, reminded him of. As it concerns only yourself, said the baron, it is proper you should read it first, and I will then put on my signet.

Horatio on this unfolded it, and found it contained such high commendations of him, and such pressing entreaties to that minister to contribute all he could to his promotion, that it seemed rather dictated by the fondness of a parent, than by one who had taken such pains to avoid being so. O, my lord! cried he, as soon as he had done perusing it, how much do you over-rate the little merit I

---

[65] *count Piper, the first minister and favourite of the king of Sweden*: Carl, count Piper (1647–1716), Swedish statesman, ennobled in 1679.

am master of, yet how little regard a passion which is the sole inspirer of it! what will avail all the glory I can acquire, if unsuccessful in my love!

Let us talk no more of that, said the baron de Palfoy, you ought to be satisfied I do all for you in my power to do at present: — other opportunities may hereafter arrive in which you may find the continuance of my friendship, and a grateful remembrance of the good office you did me; but to engage me to fulfil my obligations without any reluctance on my part, you must speak to me no more on a theme which I cannot hear without emotions, such as I would by no means give way to.

Horatio gave a deep sigh, but presumed not to reply; the other, to prevent him, turned the conversation on the wonderful actions of that young king into whose service he was going to enter; but the lover had contemplations of a different nature which he was impatient to indulge, therefore made his visit as short as decency and the favour he had just received would permit. The baron at parting gave him a very affectionate embrace, and told him, he should rejoice to hear of his success by letters from him as often as the places and employments he should be in would allow him to write.

Let any one form, if they can, an idea suitable to the present situation of Horatio's mind at so astonishing an incident: impossible was it for him to form any certain conjecture on the baron de Palfoy's behaviour; some of his expressions seemed to flatter him with the highest expectations of future happiness, while others, he thought, gave him reason to despair: — sometimes he imagined that it was to his pride and the greatness of his spirit, which would not suffer him to let any obligation go unrequited, that he owed what had been just now done for him. — But when he reflected on the contents of the letter to count Piper, he could not help thinking they were dictated by something more than an enforced gratitude: — he remembered too that he promised him the continuation of his friendship, and had given some hints during the conversation, as if time and some accidents, which might possibly happen, might give a turn to his affairs even on Charlotta's account. — On the whole it appeared most reasonable to conclude, that if he could by any means raise his fortune in the world to the pitch the baron had determined for his daughter, he would not disapprove their loves; and in this belief he could not but think himself as fortunate as he could expect to be, since he never had been vain enough to imagine, that in his present circumstances he might hope either the consent of the father, or the ratification of the daughter's affection.

Every thing being now ready for his departure, he took leave of the chevalier St George, who seemed to be under a concern for losing him, which only the knowledge how great an advantage this young gentleman would receive by it, could console: the queen also gave him a letter from herself to her intended son-in-law; and the charming princess Louisa, with blushes, bid him tell the king of Sweden, he had her prayers and wishes for success in all his glorious enterprizes.

Thus laden with credentials which might assure him of a reception equal to the most ambitious aim of his aspiring soul, he set out from Paris, not without some tender regret at quitting a place where he had been treated with such uncommon and distinguished marks of kindness and respect. But these emotions soon gave way to others more transporting: — he was on his journey towards Rheines, the place which contained his beloved Charlotta; and the thoughts that every moment brought him still nearer to her filled him with extacies, which none but those who truly love can have any just conception of.

CHAP. XI.

Horatio arrives at Rheines, finds means to see mademoiselle Charlotta, and afterwards pursues his journey to Poland.

THE impatience Horatio had to be at Rheines made him travel very hard till he reached that city; nor did he allow himself much time for repose after his fatigue, till having made a strict enquiry at all the monasteries, he at length discovered where mademoiselle Charlotta was placed.

Hitherto he had been successful beyond his hopes; but the greatest difficulty was not yet surmounted: he doubted not but as such secrecy had been used in the carrying her from Paris, and of the place to which she had been conveyed, that the same circumspection would be preserved in concealing her from the sight of any stranger that should come to the monastery: — he invented many pretences, but none seemed satisfactory to himself, therefore could not expect they would pass upon others. — Sometimes he thought of disguising himself in the habit of a woman, his youth, and the delicacy of his complexion making him imagine he might impose on the abbess and nuns for such; but then he feared being betrayed, by not being able to answer the questions which would in all probability be asked him. — He endeavoured to find out some person that was acquainted there; but tho' he asked all the gentlemen, which were a great many, that dined at the same Hotel with him, he was at as great a loss as ever. He went to the chapel every hour that mass was said, but could flatter himself with no other satisfaction from that than the empty one of knowing he was under the same roof with her; for the gallery in which the ladies sit, pensioners,[66] as well as those who have taken the veil, are so closely grated, that it is impossible for those below to distinguish any object.

He was almost distracted when he had been there three or four days without being able to find any expedient which he could think likely to succeed: — he knew not what to resolve on; — time pressed him to pursue his journey; — every day, every hour that he lost from prosecuting the glorious hopes he had in view, struck ten thousand daggers to his soul: — but then to go without informing the dear object of his wishes how great a part she had in inspiring his ambition, — without assuring her of his eternal constancy and faith, and receiving some soft condescensions from her to enable him to support so long an absence as he in all probability must endure. — All this, I say, was a shock

---

[66] *pensioners*: a pensioner could lodge in a convent or monastery for the payment of a sum of money.

to thought, which, had he not been relieved from, would perhaps have abated great part of that spirit which it was necessary for him to preserve, in order to agree with the recommendatory letters he carried with him.

He was just going out of the chapel full of unquiet meditations, when passing by the confessional, a magdalen[67] curiously painted which hung near it attracted his eyes: as he was admiring the piece, something fell from above and hit against his arm; he stopped to take it up, and found it a small ivory tablet: he looked up, but could see the shadow of nothing behind the grate: imagining it only an accident, and not knowing to whom to return it, he put it in his pocket, but was no sooner out of the chapel than curiosity excited him to see what it contained, which he had no sooner done than in the first leaf he found these words:

> As I imagine you did not come this long journey without a desire to see me, it would be too ungrateful not to assist your endeavours: — come a little before vespers, and enquire of the portress for mademoiselle du Pont; — say you are her brother, and leave the rest to me.

There was no name subscribed; but the dear characters, tho' evidently wrote in haste and with a pencil, which made some alteration in the fineness of the strokes, convinced him it came from no other than Charlotta; and never were any hours so tedious to him as those which past between the receiving this appointment, and that of the fulfilling it.

At length the wish'd-for time arrived, and he repaired to the gate, where telling the portress, as he was ordered, that he was the brother of mademoiselle du Pont, he was immediately brought into the parlour, where he had not waited long before a young lady appeared behind the grate: as he found it was not her he expected, he was a little at a loss, and not without some apprehensions that his imagination had deceived him: I know not, madame, said he, if chance has not made me mistaken for some happier person: — I thought to find a sister here. — No, replied she laughing, Horatio shall find me a sister in my good offices; — mademoiselle Charlotta will be here immediately; — she has counterfeited an indisposition to avoid going to vespers, and obtained permission for me to stay with her; — so that every thing is right, and as soon as the choir is gone into chapel you will see her. It would be needless to repeat the transports Horatio uttered on this occasion, so I shall only say they were such as convinced mademoiselle du Pont, that her fair friend had not made this condescension to a man ungrateful for, or insensible of the obligation. He was

---

[67] *a magdalen*: From the Counter-Reformation onwards St Mary Magdalene, who is one of the witnesses to Christ's resurrection in the gospels of Matthew and John, was portrayed as a type of the sinful but penitent woman — possibly a repentant prostitute.

indeed so lost in them, that he scarce remembered to pay those compliments to the lady for her generous assistance which it merited from him; but she easily forgave any unpoliteness he might be guilty of on that score; and he so well attoned for it after he had given vent to the sudden emotions of his joy, that she looked upon him as the most accomplished, as well as the most faithful of his sex. They had entered into some discourse of the rules of the monastery, and how impossible it would have been for him to have gained an interview with mademoiselle Charlotta, but by the means she had contrived; — she told him that young lady had seen him for several days, and not doubting but it was for her sake he came, had resolved to run any risque rather than he should depart without obtaining so small a consolation as the sight of her was capable of affording. Horatio, by the most passionate expressions, testified how dearly he prized what she had seemed to think of so little value, when the expected charmer of his soul drew near the grate. — All that can be conceived of tender and endearing past between them; but when he related to her the occasion of his coming, and that change of life he now was entering upon, she listened to him with a mixture of pleasure and anxiety: — she rejoiced with him on the great prospects he had in view; but the terror of the dangers he was plunging in was all her own. She was far, however, from discouraging him in his designs, and concealed not her admiration of the greatness of his spirit, and that love of glory which seemed to render him capable of undertaking any thing.

But when she heard in what manner her father had treated him, she was all astonishment: as she knew his temper perfectly well, she was certain he would not have acted in the manner he did without being influenced to it by a very strong liking for Horatio; for tho' gratitude for the good office he had received at his hands might have engaged him to make some requital, yet there were several expressions which Horatio, who remembered all he said, with the utmost exactness repeated to her, that convinced her he would not have made use of, if he had not meant the person better than he at present would have him think he did; and that there was in reality nothing restrained him from making them as happy as their mutual affection could desire, but the pride of blood and the talk of the world, which the disparity of their present circumstances would occasion. As she doubted not but the courage and virtue of Horatio would remove that impediment, by acquiring a promotion sufficient to countenance his pretensions, she had now no other disquiet than what arose from her fears for his safety, which she over and over repeated, conjuring him, in the most tender terms, not to hazard himself beyond what the duties of his post obliged him to: — this, said she, shall be the test of my affection to you; for whenever I hear you run yourself into unnecessary dangers, I will conclude from that moment you have ceased to remember, or pay any regard to my injunctions or repose.

Horatio kissed her hand thro' the grate, and told her, he would always set too great a value on a life she was so good to wish the continuance of, not to take all the care of it that honour would admit; but she would not give him leave to add any asseverations to this promise, which, said she, you will every day be tempted to break; — the enterprizing disposition of the prince you are going to serve, added to your own sense of glory, will make it very difficult for you not to be the foremost in following wherever his royal example leads the way: — nor would I wish you to purchase security by the price of infamy; but as you go in a manner such as will in all probability place you near his person, methinks it would be easy for you, by now and then mentioning the princess Louisa, to rouse in him these soft emotions which might prevent him from too rashly exposing a life she had so great an interest in.

How great a pity was it this tender conversation between two persons who had so pure a passion for each other, who had been absent some time, and who knew not when, or whether they ever should meet again, could not be indulged with no longer continuance! but now mademoiselle du Pont, who had been so good as to stand at some little distance, while they entertained each other, as a watch to give them notice of any interruption, now warned them that they must part: — divine service was over, and the abbess and nuns were returning from the chapel.

Short was the farewel the lovers took; mademoiselle Charlotta had told him it would be highly improper he should run the hazard of a discovery by coming there a second time, which would probably incense her father so much, as to convert all the favourable intentions he now might have towards them into the reverse, and he was therefore oblig'd to content himself with printing with his lips the seal of his affection on her hand, which he had scarce done before, on a second motion by mademoiselle du Pont, she shot suddenly from the place and went to her chamber, that no suspicions might arise on her being found so well as to have been able to quit it.

As he had passed for the brother of mademoiselle du Pont, she stayed some little time with him: this lady, whom Charlotta in this exigence had made her confidante, had a great deal of good nature, and seeing the agony Horatio was in, endeavoured to console him by all the arguments she thought might have force; — she told him, that in the short time she had been made partaker of mademoiselle Charlotta's secrets, she had expressed herself with a tenderness for him, with which he ought to be satisfied, and that she was convinced nothing would ever be capable of making the least alteration in her sentiments.

While she was speaking in this manner, Horatio remembered he had not given Charlotta her tablet, which he now took out of his pocket, and with the same pencil she had made use of, and which was fastened to it, wrote in the next leaf to that she had employed these words:

I GO, most dear and adorable Charlotta; whether to live or die I know not, but which ever is my portion, the passion I have for you is rooted in my soul, and will be equally immortal: life can give no joy but in the hope of being yours, nor death any terrors but being separated from you: — O! let nothing ever prevail on you to forget so perfect an attachment; but in the midst of all the temptations you may be surrounded with, think that you have vouchsafed to encourage my hopes, presuming as they are, and if once lost to them, what must be the destiny of

HORATIO.

Having thus poured out some part of the overflowings of his heart, he entreated mademoiselle du Pont to give it to her, which she assured him she would not only do, but also be a faithful monitor for him during the whole time she should be happy enough to enjoy the company of that lady.

Horatio now having fulfilled all his passion required of him, quitted Rheines the next day, no less impatient to pursue his other mistress, glory!

But let us now see in what manner his beautiful sister Louisa, whom we left at Vienna, was all this while engaged.

CHAP. XII.

Continuation of the adventures of Louisa: her quitting Vienna with Melanthe, and going to Venice, with some accidents that there befel them.

NOT all the gaieties of the court of Vienna, had power to attach the heart of Melanthe, after she heard that a great number of young officers, just returned from the campaign in Italy, and other persons of condition, were going to Venice, in order to partake the diversions of the near approaching carnival: she was for following pleasure every where, and having seen all that was worth observing in Germany, was impatient to be gone where new company and new delights excited her curiosity.

Having therefore obtained proper passports, they set out in company with several others who were taking the same rout, and by easy journeys thro' Tyrol, at length arrived at that republic, so famous over all Europe for its situation, antiquity, and the excellence of its constitution.[68]

Here seemed to be at this time an assemblage of all that was to be found of grand and polite in the whole christian world; but none appeared with that splendor and magnificence as did Lewis de Bourbon, prince of Conti:[69] he had in his train above fifty noblemen and gentlemen of the best families in France, who had commissions under him in the army, and seemed proud to be of his retinue, less for being of the blood royal, than for the many great and amiable qualities which adorned his person. This great hero had been a candidate with Augustus, elector of Saxony, for the crown of Poland[70]; but the ill genius of that kingdom would not suffer it to be governed by a prince whose virtues would doubtless have rendered it as flourishing and happy as it has since that unfortunate rejection been impoverished and miserable. Bigotted to[71] a family whose designs are plainly to render the crown hereditary, they not only set aside

---

[68] *that republic, so famous over all Europe for its situation, antiquity, and the excellence of its constitution*: Venice enjoyed a reputation for unusually stable political arrangements. The Venetian institutions of the Maggior Consiglio (Great Council), the senate and the Doge appeared to embody a vision of the ideal state as one that combined the best elements of democracy, aristocracy and monarchy.

[69] *Lewis de Bourbon, prince of Conti*: François-Louis de Bourbon, prince de Conti (1664–1709).

[70] *a candidate with Augustus, elector of Saxony, for the crown of Poland*: François-Louis de Bourbon, prince de Conti [see above, n. 69] was proclaimed king of Poland in 1697, but by the time he reached Danzig, he found Augustus II [see above, n. 57] already in possession of the throne.

[71] *Bigotted to*: prejudiced against.

that great prince, under the vain and common-place pretence, that on electing him they might be too much under the influence of France; but also afterward, as resolved to push all good fortune from them with both hands, refused Stanislaus, a native of Poland,[72] a strict observer of its laws, and a man to whose courage, virtue, and every eminent qualification even envy itself could make no objection, and thereby rendered their country the seat of war and theatre of the most terrible devastations of all kinds. But of this infatuation of the Poles I shall have occasion hereafter to speak more at large, and should not now have made any mention of it, had not the presence of that hero, whom they first rejected, rendered it the general subject of discourse at Venice. Numberless were the instances he gave of a magnanimity and greatness of mind worthy of a more exalted throne than that of Poland; but I shall only mention one, which, like the thumb of Hercules,[73] may serve to give a picture of him in miniature.

Having the good fortune one night to win a very great sum at public gaming, just as he sweep'd the stakes, a noble Venetian, who by some casualties in his life was reduced in his circumstances, could not help crying out, heavens! how happy would such a chance have made me! these words, which under the extreme difficulties he was under forced from him, without being sensible himself of what he said, were over-heard by the prince, who turning hastily about, instead of putting the money in his own pocket, presented it to him, saying, I am doubly indebted to chance, sir, which has made me master of this; since it may be of service to you, I beseech you therefore to accept it with the respects of a prince, whose greatest pleasure in life is to oblige a worthy person.

It would take up too much time to expatiate on the grateful acknowledgments made by the Venetian, or the admiration which the report of this action being immediately spread, occasioned; but, added to others of a little less conspicuous nature, it greatly served to convince those who before were ignorant of it, how blind the Polanders had been to their own interest.

Among the concourse of nobility and gentry, whom merely the love of pleasure had drawn hither, and for that end were continually forming parties, Melanthe never failed of making one either in one company or the other: Louisa, whom that lady still treated with her former kindness, or rather with an increase of it, was also seldom absent, and when she was so, the fault was wholly her own inclination: but in truth, that hurry of incessant diversion, which at first had seemed so ravishing to her young and inexperienced mind, began, by a more perfect acquaintance with it, to grow tiresome to her, and she rather chose sometimes to retire with a favourite book into a closet, than to go to the most elegant entertainment.

---

[72] *Stanislaus, a native of Poland*: nobleman Stanislaus Leszczyński (1677–1766), palatine of Poznańia [see below, n. 83] and leader of a Polish patriot group.

[73] *the thumb of Hercules*: referring to the idea that the stature of Hercules could be calculated from the size of his thumb alone. (See John Mennes, *Wit Restor'd* (1658): 'Hercules tall stature might be guessed/But by his thumb, the Index of the rest'.)

It is certain, indeed, that her disposition was rather inclined to serious than the contrary, and that, joined with the reflections which her good understanding was perpetually presenting her with, on the uncertainty of her birth, the precariousness of her dependance, and her enforced quitting the only person from whom she could expect the means of any solid establishment in the world, had rendered her sometimes extremely thoughtful, even in the midst of those pleasures that are ordinarily most enchanting to one of her sex and age. But as she never was elated with the respect paid to her supposed condition, so she never was mortified with the consciousness of her real one, to a behaviour such as might have degraded the highest birth; neither appearing to expect it, or be covetous of honours, nor meanly ashamed of accepting them when offered. And while by this prudent management she secured herself from any danger of being insulted whenever it should be known who she was, she also gave no occasion for any one to make too deep an enquiry into her descent and fortune.

But now the time was arrived when those deficiencies gave her more anxiety than hitherto they had done; and love in one moment filled her with those repinings at her fate, which neither vanity or ambition would ever have had power to do.

Melanthe here, as at Vienna, received the visits of all whose birth, fortune, or accomplishments, gave them a pretence; but there was none who paid them so frequently, or which she encouraged with so much pleasure as those of the count de Bellfleur, a French nobleman belonging to the above-mentioned prince of Conti: she often told Louisa, when they were alone, that there was something in the air and manner of behaviour of this count, which had so perfect a resemblance with that of Henricus, that tho' it reminded her of that once dear and perfidious man, she could not help admiring and wishing a frequent sight of him. This was spoke at her first acquaintance with him; but after some little time she informed her, that he had declared a passion for her. He is not only like Henricus in his person, said she, but appears to have the same inclinations also: — he pretends to adore me, continued she with a sigh, and spares no vows nor presents to assure me of it: — something within me tempts me to believe him, and yet I fear to be a second time betrayed.

Ah! madam, cried Louisa, in the sincerity of her heart, I beseech you to be cautious how you too readily give credit to the protestations of a sex, who, by the little observations I have made, take a pride in deceiving ours; — besides, the count de Bellfleur is of a nation where faith, I have heard, is little to be depended on.

Those who give them that character, replied Melanthe, do them an infinite injustice: — in politics, I allow, they have their artifices, their subterfuges, as well as in war; but then they put them in practice only against their enemies, or such as are likely to become so: — wherever they love, or have a friendship, their generosity is beyond all bounds. —

She pursued this discourse with a long detail of all she had ever read or heard in the praise of the French, and did not forget to speak of the prince of Conti as an instance of that gallant spirit with which that people are animated.

Louisa knew her temper, and that it would be in vain to urge any thing in contradiction to an inclination she found she was resolved to indulge; but she secretly trembled for the consequence, the count having said many amorous things to herself before he pretended any passion for Melanthe; and tho' he had of late desisted on finding how little she was pleased with them, yet that he had done so was sufficient to convince her he was of a wavering disposition. Melanthe was not, however, to be trusted with this secret; she loved him, and jealousy, added to a good share of vanity, would, instead of engaging any grateful return for a discovery of that nature, have made her hate the person he had once thought of as worthy of coming in any competition with herself. She therefore indeed thought it best not to interfere in the matter, but leave the event wholly to chance.

The evening on the day in which this discourse had past between them, they went to a ball, to which they had been invited by one of the Magnifico's.[74] The honour of the prince's company had been requested; but he excused himself on account, as it was imagined, of his being engaged with a certain German lady, who also being absent, gave room for this conjecture: most of the gentlemen who had followed his highness from France were there, among whom was the count de Bellfleur, and a young gentleman called monsieur du Plessis,[75] who, by a fall from his horse, had been prevented from appearing in public since his arrival. The gracefulness of his person, the gallant manner in which he introduced himself, and the brilliant things he said to the ladies, on having been so long deprived of the happiness he now enjoyed, very much attracted the attention of the company; but Louisa in particular thought she had never seen any thing so perfectly agreeable: a sympathy of sentiment, more than accident, made him chuse her for his partner in a grand dance then leading up; and the distinction now paid her by him gave her a secret satisfaction, which she had never known before on such an occasion, tho' often singled out by persons in more eminent situations.

The mind which, whenever agitated by any degree of pain or pleasure,

---

[74] one of the Magnifico's: Magnifico was originally an honorary title applied to a Venetian magnate, but could also signify a great or noble person.

[75] du Plessis: 'Plessis' is the name of a noble French family dating back to the twelfth century. Haywood may have borrowed the name from that of Alexandre de Choiseul, comte du Plessis-Praslin (1634–1672), who in Madame de Lafayette's Histoire de Madame Henriette d'Angleterre, [see above n. 46] carries love-letters between Princess Henrietta Maria (1644–1670) and René de Bec-Crispin, marquis de Vardes (1620–1688).

never fails to discover itself in the eyes, now sparkled in those of Louisa with an uncommon lustre, nor had less influence over all her air: — her motions always perfectly easy, gentle, and graceful, especially in dancing, were now more spirituous, more alert than usual; and she so much excelled herself, that several, who had before praised her skill in this exercise, seemed ravished, as if they had seen something new and unexpected: — her partner was lavish in the testimonies of his admiration, and said, she as much excelled the ladies of his country, as they had been allowed to excel all others.

The encomiums bestowed on her, and more particularly those she received from him, still added fresh radiance to her eyes, and at the same time diffused a modest blush in her cheeks which heightened all her charms. — Never had she appeared so lovely as at this time; and the count de Bellfleur, in spight of his attachment to Melanthe, felt in himself a strong propensity to renew those addresses which her reserved behaviour alone had made him withdraw and carry to another; but the lady to whom for some days past he had made a shew of devoting himself was present, and he was ashamed to give so glaring an instance of his infidelity, which must in all probability render him the contempt of both.

This night, however, lost Melanthe the heart she had thought herself so secure of; but little suspecting her misfortune, she treated the inconstant count with a tenderness he was far from deserving; and having transplanted all the affection she had once for Henricus on this new object, told him, at a time that such discovery was least welcome to him, that she was not insensible of his merit, nor could be ungrateful to his passion, provided she could be convinced of the sincerity of it. He had gone too far with her now to be able to draw back, therefore could not avoid repeating the vows he before had made, tho' his heart was far from giving any assent to what his tongue was obliged to utter; but blinded by her own desires, she perceived not the change in his, and appointed him to come the next day to her lodgings, promising to be denied to all other company, that she might devote herself entirely to him.

It is possible he was so lost in his passion for Louisa, as not to be sensible of the condescension made him by Melanthe; but it is certain, by the sequel of is behaviour, that he was much less so than he pretended.

The ball being ended, these ladies carried with them very different emotions, tho' neither communicated to the other what she felt. Melanthe had a kind of awe for those virtuous principles she observed in Louisa, tho' so much her inferior and dependant, and was ashamed to confess her liking of the count should have brought her to such lengths; not that she intended to keep it always a secret from her, but chose she should find it out by degrees; and these thoughts so much engrossed her, that she said little to her that night. Louisa, for her part, having lost the presence of her agreeable partner, was busy supplying that deficiency with the idea of him; so that each having meditations of her own of the most interesting nature, had not leisure to observe the thoughtfulness of the other, much less to enquire the motive of it.

One of the great reasons we find love so irresistable, is, that it enters into the heart with so much subtilty, that it is not to be perceived till it has gathered too much strength to be repulsed. If Louisa had imagined herself in any danger from the merits of monsieur du Plessis, she would at least have been less easily overcome by them: — she had been accustomed to be pleased with the conversation of many who had entertained her as he had done, but thought no more of them, or any thing they said, when out of their company; but it was otherways with her now: not a word he had spoke, not a glance he had given, but was imprinted in her mind: — her memory ran over every little action a thousand and a thousand times, and represented all as augmented with some grace peculiar to himself, and infinitely superior to any thing she had ever seen: — not even sleep could shut him out; — thro' her closed eyes she saw the pleasing vision; and fancy, active in the cause of love, formed new and various scenes, which to her waking thoughts were wholly strangers.

Melanthe also past the night in ideas which, tho' experienced in, were not less ravishing: she was not of a temper to put any constraint on her inclinations; and having entertained the most amorous ones for the count de Bellfleur, easily overcame all scruples that might have hindered the gratification of them: — her head ran on the appointment she had made him: — the means she would take to engage his constancy, — resolved to sell the reversion of her jointure and accompany him to France, and flattered herself with the most pleasing images of a long series of continued happiness in the arms of him, who was now all to her that Henricus had ever been.

Full of these meditations she rose, and soon after received from the subject of them a billet, containing these words:

To the charming MELANTHE.

MADAM,

THO' the transporting promise you made me of refusing admittance to all company but mine, is a new instance of your goodness, yet I cannot but think we should be still more secure from interruption at a place I have taken care to provide. Might I therefore hope you would vouchsafe to meet me about five in the evening at the dome of St Mark,[76] I shall be ready with a Gondula

---

[76] *the dome of St Mark*: The Basilica di San Marco, chief monument of Venice, has five domes or *cupolas*. Construction of the original building began in CE 828, to house the (supposed) body of St Mark. In the thirteenth century the domes were raised so that they could be seen from the sea.

to conduct you to a recess, which seems formed by the god of love himself for the temple of his purest offerings, than which none can be offered with greater passion and sincerity than those of the adorable Melanthe's

Most devoted, and

Everlasting Slave,

DE BELLFLEUR.

P.S. To prevent your fair friend Louisa from any suspicion on account of being left at home, I have engaged a gentleman to make her a visit in form, just before the time of your coming out: — favour me, I beseech you, with knowing if my contrivances in both these points have the sanction of your approbation.

Tho' Melanthe, as may have been already observed in the foregoing part of her character, was no slave to reputation in England, and thought herself much less obliged to be so in a place where she was a stranger, and among people who, when she once quitted, she might probably never see again, yet she looked on this caution in her lover as a new proof of his sincerity and regard for her. She was also fond of every thing that had an air of luxury, and doubted not to find the elegance of the French taste in the entertainment he would cause to be prepared for her reception, therefore hesitated not a moment to send him the following answer:

To the engaging count DE BELLFLEUR.

SENSIBLE, as you are, of the ascendant your merits have gained over me, you cannot doubt of my compliance with every thing that seems reasonable to you: — I will not fail to be at the place you mention; but oh! my dear count, I hope you will never give me cause to repent this step; — if you should, I must be the most miserable of all created beings; but I am resolved to believe you are all that man ought to be, or that fond tenacious woman can desire; and in that confidence attend with impatience the hour in which there shall be no more reserve between us, and I be wholly yours.

MELANTHE.

Thus every thing being fixed for her undoing, she spent the best part of the day in preparing for the rendezvous: nothing was omitted in the article of dress, which might heighten her charms and secure her conquest: — the glass was consulted every moment, and every look and various kind of languishment essayed, in order to continue in that which she thought would most become the occasion. As she ordinarily past a great deal of time in this employment, Louisa was not surprized that she now wasted somewhat more than usual; and the discourse they had together while she was dressing, and all the time of dinner, being very much on the ball and the company who were at it, her thoughts were so much taken up with the remembrance of du Plessis, that she perceived not the hurry of spirits which would else have been visible enough to her in all the words and motions of the other, and which increased in proportion as the hour of her appointment drew nearer.

At length it arrived, and a servant came into the room and acquainted Louisa a gentleman desired to speak with her: she was a little surprized, it being usual for all those who visited there to expect their reception from Melanthe; but that lady, who doubted not but it was the same person the count had mentioned in his letter, prevented her from saying any thing, by immediately giving orders for the gentleman to be admitted.

But with what strange emotions was the heart of Louisa agitated, when she saw monsieur du Plessis come into the room! and after paying his respects to Melanthe in the most submissive manner, accosted her, with saying he took the liberty of enquiring of her health after the fatigue of the last night; but, added he, the question, now I have the happiness of seeing you, is altogether needless: those fine eyes, and that sprightly air, declare you formed for everlasting gaiety, and that what is apt to throw the spirits of others into a languor, serves but to render yours more sparkling.

Louisa, in spite of the confusion she felt within, answered this compliment with her accustomed ease; and all being seated, they began to enter into some conversation concerning the state with which the Magnifico's of Venice are served, the elegance with which they entertain strangers, and some other topics relating to the customs of that republic, when all on a sudden Melanthe starting up, cried, bless me! I had forgot a little visit was in my head to make to a monastery hard by: — you will excuse me, monsieur, continued she, I leave your partner to entertain you, and fancy you two may find sufficient matter of conversation without a third person. She had no sooner spoke this than she went out of the room, and left Louisa at a loss how to account for this behaviour, as she had not before mentioned any thing of going abroad. She would have imagined her vanity had been picqued that monsieur du Plessis had particularized her in this visit; but as she seemed in perfect good humour at going away, and knew she thought it beneath her to put any disguise on her sentiments, she was certain this sudden motion must have proceeded from some other cause, which as yet she could form no conjecture of.

This deceived lady, however, was no sooner out of the room, than monsieur du Plessis drawing nearer to Louisa, how hard is my fate, madame, said he, in a low voice, that I am compelled to tell you any other motive than my own inclination has occasioned my waiting on you: — heaven knows it is an honour I should have sought by the lowest submissions, and all the ways that would not have rendered me unworthy of it; but I now come, madame, not as myself, but as the ambassador of another, and am engaged by my word and honour to plead a cause which, if I succeed in, must be my own destruction.

Louisa was in the utmost consternation at the mystery which seemed contained in these words: she looked earnestly upon him while he was uttering the latter part, and saw all the tokens of a serious perplexity in his countenance, as well as in the accents with which he delivered them; but not being willing to be the dupe of his diversion, thought it best to answer as to a piece of railery, and told him, laughing, she imagined this was some new invention of the frolics of the season, but that she was a downright English-woman, understood nothing beyond plain speaking, and could no ways solve the riddle he proposed.

What I say, may doubtless appear so, madame, replied he, and I could wish it had not been my part to give the explanation; but I cannot dispense with the promise I have made, and must therefore acquaint you with the history of it.

After the ball, continued he, monsieur the count de Bellfleur desired me to accompany him to his lodgings, and, as soon as we were alone, told me, he had a little secret to acquaint me with, but that, before he revealed it, he must have the promise of my assistance. As he spoke this with a gay and negligent air, I imagined it a thing of no consequence, or if it were, he was a man of too much honour, and also knew me too well to desire or expect I would engage in any thing unbecoming that character: indeed I could think of nothing but an amour or a duel, tho' I was far from being able to guess of what service I could be to him in the former. I was, however, unwarily drawn in to give my word, and he then made me the confident of a passion, which, he said, had received its birth from the first moment he beheld the Belle Angloise, for by that term, pursued he, bowing, he distinguished the adorable Louisa: that he had made some discovery of his flame, but that finding himself rejected, as he thought, in too severe a manner, and without affording him opportunity to attest his sincerity, he had converted his addresses, tho' not his passion, to a lady who, he perceived, had the care of her, acting in this manner, partly thro' picque at your disdain, and partly to gratify his eyes with the sight of you, which he has reason to fear you had totally deprived him of but for this stratagem. He confessed to me that he found the object of his pretended ardours infinitely more kind than she who inspires the real ones: but this gratification of his vanity is of little consequence to his peace; — he engaged me to attend you this day, to conjure you to believe his heart is incapable of being influenced by any other charms, and whatever he makes shew of to Melanthe, his heart is devoted wholly to you, — begs you to permit him to entertain you without the presence of that lady, the means of which he will take care to contrive; and charged me to assure you, that there is no sacrifice so great, but he will readily offer it to convince you of the sincerity of his attachment.

This, madame, added he, is the unpleasing task my promise bound me to perform, and which I have acquitted myself of with the same pain that man would do who, by some strange caprice of fate, was constrained to throw into the sea the sum of all his hopes.

The indignation which filled the virtuous soul of Louisa, while he was giving her this detail of the count's presumption, falsehood, and ingratitude, prevented her from giving much attention to the apology with which he concluded. Never, since the behaviour of Mr B——n at Mrs C — g — 's, had she met with any thing that she thought so much merited her resentment: — so great was her disdain she had not words to express it, but by some tears, which the rising passion forced from her eyes: — Heaven! cried she, which of my actions has drawn on me this unworthy treatment? — This was all she was able to utter, while she walked backward and forward in the room endeavouring to compose herself, and form some answer befitting of the message.

Monsieur du Plessis looked on her all this while with admiration: all that seemed lovely in her, when he knew no more of her than that she was young and beautiful, was now heightened in his eyes almost to divine, by that virtuous pride which shewed him some part of her more charming mind. What he extremely liked before, he now almost adored; and having, by the loose manner in which the count had mentioned these two English ladies, imagined them women of not over-rigid principles, now finding his mistake, at least as concerning one of them, was so much ashamed and angry with himself for having been the cause of that disorder he was witness of, that he for some moments was equally at a loss to appease, as she who felt was to express it.

But being the first that recovered presence of mind; madame, I beseech you, said he, involve not the innocent with the guilty: — I acknowledge you have reason to resent the boldness of the count; but I am no otherwise a sharer in his crime than in reporting it; and if you knew the pain it gave my heart while I complied with the promise I was unhappily betrayed into, I am sure you would forgive the misdemeanor of my tongue.

Sir, answered she, I can easily forgive the slight opinion one so much a stranger to me as yourself may have of me; but monsieur the count has been a constant visiter to the lady I am with, ever since our arrival at Venice; and am very certain he never found any thing in my behaviour to him or any other person, which could justly encourage him to send me such a message: — a message, indeed, equally affrontive to himself, since it shews him a composition of arrogance, vanity, perfidy, and every thing that is contemptible in man. — This, sir, is the reply I send him, and desire you to tell him withall, that if he persists in giving me any farther trouble of this nature, I shall let him know my sense of it in the presence of Melanthe.

Monsieur du Plessis then assured her he would be no less exact in delivering what she said, than he had been in the observance of his promise to the other, and conjured her to believe he should do it with infinite more satisfaction. He then made use of so many arguments to prove, that a man of honour ought not to falsify his word, tho' given to an unworthy person, that she was at last won to forgive his having undertaken to mention any thing to her of the nature he had done.

Indeed, the agitations she had been in were more owing to the vexation that monsieur du Plessis was the person employed, than that the count had the boldness to apply to her in this manner; but the submission she found herself treated with by the former, convincing her that he had sentiments very different from those the other had entertained of her, rendered her more easy, and she not only forgave his share in the business which had brought him there, but also permitted him to repeat his visits, on condition he never gave her any cause to suspect the mean opinion the count had of her conduct had any influence on him.

CHAP. XIII.

Louisa finds herself very much embarrassed by Melanthe's imprudent behaviour. Monsieur du Plessis declares an honourable passion for her: her sentiments and way of acting on that occasion.

AFTER the departure of monsieur du Plessis, Louisa fell into a serious consideration of what had passed between them: not all the regard, which she could not hinder herself from feeling for that young gentleman, nor the pleasure she took in reflecting on the respect he paid her, made her unmindful of what she owed Melanthe: the many obligations she had received from her, and the friendship she had for her in return, made her think she ought to acquaint her with the baseness of the count de Bellfleur, in order to prevent an affection which she found she had already too much indulged from influencing her to grant him any farther favours; but this she knew was a very critical point to manage, and was not without some apprehensions, which afterward she experienced were but too well grounded; that when the lady found herself obliged to hate the man she took pleasure in loving, she would also hate the woman who was the innocent occasion of it. Few in the circumstances Louisa was, but would have been swayed by this consideration, and chose rather to see another become the prey of perfidy and deceit, than fall the victim of jealousy herself; but the generosity of her nature would not suffer it to have any weight with her, and she thought she could be more easy under any misfortunes the discovery might involve her in, than in the consciousness of not having discharged the obligations of duty and gratitude in revealing what seemed so necessary to be known.

With this resolution, finding Melanthe was not come home, she went into her chamber in order to wait her return, and relate the whole history to her as she should undress for bed. But hour after hour elapsing without any appearance of the person she expected, she thought to beguile the tedious time by reading; and remembering that Melanthe had a very agreeable book in her hand that morning, she opened a drawer, where she knew that lady was accustomed to throw any thing in, which she had no occasion to conceal; but how great was her surprize when, instead of what she sought, she found the letter from the count de Bellfleur which Melanthe, in the hurry of spirits, had forgot to lock up. As it lay open and was from him, she thought it no breach of honour to examine the contents, but in doing so was ready to faint away between grief and astonishment.

She was not insensible that Melanthe was charmed with this new lover, and had always feared her liking him would sway her to some imprudencies, but could not have imagined it would have carried her, at least so soon, to such a guilty length as she now found it did.

Convinced by the hour in which she went out, and alone, that she had complied with the appointment, and that all she would have endeavoured to prevent was already come to pass, she now considered that the discovery she had to make would only render this indiscreet lady more unhappy, and therefore no longer thought herself obliged to run any risque of incurring her ill-will on the occasion; but in her soul extremely lamented this second fall from virtue, which it was impossible should not bring on consequences equally, if not more shameful than the first.

Good God! cried she, how is it possible for a woman of any share of sense, and who has been blessed with a suitable education, to run thus counter to all the principles of religion, honour, virtue, modesty, and all that is valuable in our sex? and yet that many do, I have been a melancholy witness: — and then again, what is there in this love, resumed she, that so infatuates the understanding, that we doat on our dishonour, and think ruin pleasing? — Can any personal perfections in a man attone for the contempt he treats us with in courting us to infamy! — the mean opinion he testifies to have of us sure ought rather to excite hate than love; our very pride methinks, should be a sufficient guard, and turn whatever favourable thoughts we might have of such a one, unknowing his design, into aversion, when once convinced he presumed upon our weakness.

In these kind of reasonings did she continue some time; but reflecting that the trouble she was in might put Melanthe on asking the cause, it seemed best to her to avoid seeing her that night, so retired to her own room and went to bed, ordering the servants to tell their lady, in case she enquired for her, that she was a little indisposed.

While Louisa was thus deploring a misfortune she wanted power to remedy, the person for whom she was concerned past her time in a far different manner: the count omitted nothing that might convince her of his gallantry, and give her a pretence for flattering herself with his sincerity: — he swore ten thousand oaths of constancy, and she easily gave credit to what she wished and had vanity enough to think she merited: — he had prepared every thing that could delight the senses for her reception at the house to which he carried her; and she found in herself so little inclination to quit the pleasures she enjoyed, that it was as much as the little remains of decency and care of reputation could do, to make her tear herself away before midnight.

In the fulness of her heart she had doubtless concealed no part of this adventure from Louisa, but on hearing she was gone to rest, and not very well, would not disturb her. The first thing she did in the morning was to run into the chamber and enquire after her health, which she did in so affectionate and tender a manner, that it very much heightened the other's trouble for her.

It is certain that, setting aside too loose a way of thinking of virtue and religion, and adhering to that false maxim, that a woman of rank is above censure, Melanthe had many amiable qualities, and as she truly loved Louisa, was alarmed at her supposed indisposition, which, to conceal the perplexity her mind was in, she still continued to counterfeit, as well as to avoid going to a masquerade, to which they had some days before been invited, and which the present situation of her thoughts left her no relish for.

Melanthe would fain have perswaded her that the diversion would contribute to restoring her; but she entreated to be excused, and the other went without her.

Monsieur du Plessis in the mean time having informed the count de Bellfleur, how much it was in vain for him to flatter himself with any hopes of Louisa, that proud and inconstant nobleman was extremely mortified, and said, that since she was so haughty, he was resolved to try some way or other to get her into his power, as well out of revenge as inclination. This, the other represented to him, would be a very ungenerous way of proceeding; and said, that as she refused his addresses merely out of a principle of virtue, and not for the sake of a more favoured rival, he ought to content himself; but these arguments were lost on a man whom pride of blood, and an affluence of fortune, had rendered too insolent and headstrong to think any thing reason which opposed his will; and they parted not well satisfied with each other, tho' du Plessis concealed part of the dislike he had of his principles and manner of behaviour, on account of a long friendship between their families, and also as the count was his superior in birth, in years, and in the post he held in the army.

He had no sooner left him than he came to Louisa, thinking it his duty to give her warning of the count's design, and that it would be a proper prelude to something else he had to say. As the servants knew she was not perfectly well, they told him, they believed she would see no company; but on his entreating it, and saying he had something of moment to impart, one of them went in and repeated what he had said, on which she gave leave for his admission.

He rejoiced to find her alone, as he came prepared to reveal to her more secrets than that of the count's menace; but the pleasure he took in having so favourable an opportunity was very much damped, by seeing her look more pale than usual, and that she was in a night-dress. Fearful that this change proceeded from what had passed between them the day before, he asked with a hastiness, that shewed the most kind concern, if she were well. No otherways disordered, answered she, than in my mind, and that not sufficiently to have any effect over my health; but to confess the truth, monsieur, said she, the continual round of diversions this carnival affords, has made what the world calls pleasure, cease to be so with me; and I find more solid satisfaction in retirement, where I am in no danger of being too much flattered or affronted.

Ah! madam, cried he, I see the audacity of the count dwells too much upon your thoughts, and tremble to relate the business on which I came, and which it is yet necessary you should know. You mistake me, monsieur, replied she; a common foe of virtue, such as the count, is incapable of taking up my thoughts one moment; it is only those I love can give me real pain.

I understand you, madam, resumed he, and am too much interested in your concern not to simpathize on the occasion: the misfortunes, such as I fear will attend the too great sensibility of Melanthe, may give you so terrible an idea of love in general, that it will be difficult to persuade you there can be any lasting happiness to be found in that passion: — but, charming Louisa, continued he, if you will make the least use of your penetration, and examine with a desire of being convinced, you will easily distinguish the real passion from the counterfeit: that love, whose supremest pleasure is in being capable to give felicity to the beloved object; and that wild desire, which aims at no more than a self-gratification: — the one has the authority of heaven for its sanction; — the other no excuse but nature in its depravity. From all attempts of the one, I am confident, your virtue and good sense will always defend you; but to fly with too great obstinacy the other, is not to answer the end of your creation; and deny yourself a blessing, which you seem formed to enjoy in the most extensive degree.

Both the voice and the manner in which monsieur du Plessis spoke, gave Louisa some suspicion of what he aimed at in this definition, and filled her at the same time with emotions of various kinds; but dissembling them as well as she could, and endeavouring to turn what he said into raillery, you argue very learnedly on the subject, it must be confessed, answered she smiling; but all you can urge on that head, nor the compliment you make me, can win me to believe that love of any kind is not attended with more mischief than good: — where it is accompanied with the strictest honour, constancy, purity, and all the requisites that constitute what is called a perfect passion, there are ordinarily so many difficulties in the way to the completion of its wishes, that the breast which harbours it must endure a continual agitation, which surely none would chuse to be involved in.

Ah! madam, how little you are capable of judging of this passion, said he; there is a delicacy in love which renders even its pains pleasing, and how much soever a lover suffers, the thoughts of for whom he suffers is more than a compensation: I am myself an instance of this truth: — I am a lover: — conscious unworthiness of a suitable return of affection, and a thousand other impediments lie between me and hope, yet would I not change this dear anxiety for that insipid ease I lived in before I saw the only object capable of making me a convert to love. — It is certain my passion is yet young; but a few days has given it root which no time, no absence, no misfortune ever can dislodge. — The charming maid is ignorant of her conquest: — the carnival draws near to a conclusion. — I must return to the army, and these cruel circumstances oblige me either to make a declaration which she may possibly condemn as too abrupt, or go and leave her unknowing of my heart, and thereby deprive myself even of her pity: — Which party, madam, shall I take? — Will the severe extreme, to which I am driven, be sufficient to attone for a presumption which else would merit her disdain?

Louisa must have been as dull as she was really the contrary, not to have known all this was meant to herself; and the pleasing confusion which this discovery infused thro' all her veins, made her at the same time sensible of the difference she put between him and all those who before had entertained her on that subject; but not knowing presently whether she ought to attribute it to her good or ill fortune, she was wholly at a loss how to behave, and, to avoid giving any direct answer, still affected an air of pleasantry.

See, cried she, the little reason you have to speak in praise of love; for if pity be all you have to hope for from your mistress, I am afraid the consolation will be no way adequate to the misfortune.

Yet if you vouchsafe me that, replied he, kissing her hand, I never shall complain. Me! interrupted she, pretending the utmost astonishment, and drawing her chair somewhat farther from him. Yes, beautiful Louisa, resumed he; it is you alone who have been capable of teaching me what love truly is: — your eyes, at first sight, subdued my heart; but virtue has since made a conquest of my soul: — if I dare hope to make you mine, it is only by such ways as heaven, and those who have the power of disposing you, shall approve: — in the mean time I implore no more than your permission to admire you, and to convince you, by all the honourable services in my power to do you while you continue here, how much my words are deficient to denote my meaning.

Louisa, now finding herself under a necessity of answering seriously, told him, that if it were true he had sentiments for her of the nature he pretended, they would not only merit, but receive the most grateful acknowledgments on her part; but at the same time she should be sorry he had entertained them, and would wish him not to indulge a prospect which could last no longer than while both remained in Venice, and must infallibly vanish on their separation.

No, madam, replied he, when the next campaign is over, I shall return to France; and sure the distance between that kingdom and England is not so great, but a less motive than yourself would easily carry me thither; and such credentials also of who, and what I am, as, I flatter myself, would not appear contemptible in the eyes of your friends: — the prospect therefore is not so visionary as you seem to think, provided I have your consent.

The mention he made of her friends reminding her of her destitute condition, gave her the utmost shock; which not being able to overcome, she remained silent some moments; but at last perceiving he waited her reply, monsieur, said she, there may be a thousand indissoluble bars between us which you do not think of.

None, interrupted he eagerly, but what such love as mine will easily surmount: — it is true, I am ignorant of your condition in the world; but if it be superior to mine, the passion I am possessed of will inspire me with means to raise me to an equality; and if inferior, which heaven grant may be the case, it will only give the opportunity of proving that I love Louisa for Louisa's self, and look upon every thing she brings beside as nothing.

The emphasis he gave these words manifesting their sincerity, could not but give new charms to the person who spoke them: Louisa thought she might, without a blush, testify the sense she had of his generosity; but tho' what she said was perfectly obliging to him, yet she concluded with letting him know, there still was something that rendered the accomplishment of what he seemed to wish impossible.

Then your heart is already engaged, cried he, or you are predestined by your parents to some happier man? Without either of these, answered she, there may be reasons to prevent our ever meeting more; — therefore I owe so much to the honourable offers you are pleased to make me, as to wish you to overcome whatever inclinations you may have for one who I once more assure you never can be yours.

It would be impossible to express the distraction monsieur du Plessis testified at this expression: — a thousand times over did he repeat that dreadful word NEVER; — then added, neither engaged by love or promise, yet never can be mine! does my ill fate come wrap'd to me in riddles! — yet many things have seemed impossible that are not so in themselves: — O Louisa! continued he, if there be any thing beside my want of merit that impedes my wishes, and you delight not in my torment, speak it I conjure you.

There is a necessity of denying you this also, said Louisa; but to shew you how little I am inclined to be ungrateful, be certain that I have the highest idea of your merits, and prize them as much as I ought to do.

These last words, obliging as they were, could not console monsieur du Plessis for the cruelty, as he termed it, of refusing to let him know what this invincible obstacle was which put a stop to any further correspondence between them: he spared neither prayers nor tears to draw the secret from her, but all were ineffectual; and she at last told him, that if he pressed her any farther on that head, she must for the future avoid his presence.

This was a menace which he had not courage to dare the execution of, and he promised to conform to her will, tho' with such agonies as shewed her how much he valued even the little she was pleased to grant; but it was not in the power of her perswasions to prevail on him to make any efforts for the vanquishing his passion; he still protested that he neither could cease to love her, and her alone, nor even to wish an alteration of his sentiments.

By what has been already said of the extreme liking which the first sight of this young gentleman inspired Louisa with, it may easily be supposed she could not hear his complaints, and be witness of the anxieties she was enforced to inflict on him, without feeling at least an equal share: she endeavoured not to conceal the pity she had for him; but he now found that was far from being all he wanted, because it forwarded not, as he at first imagined, the progress of his hopes, but rather shewed them at more distance than ever.

The business of his love so engrossed his thoughts during this visit, that he almost forgot to mention any thing of the count's designs upon her, and she as little remembered to remind him of it, tho' he told her on his entrance, that he had something to acquaint her with on this subject, and it was not till he was going to take leave that it came into his head. When he had related it to her, she assured him that she took the caution he gave her as a new proof of his friendship, which, said she, I shall always prize. At parting, she permitted him to salute her, and gave her promise not to refuse seeing him while they continued in that city; but told him at the same time, that he must not expect any thing from his repeated visits more than she had already granted.

He durst not at that time press her any farther, but fetched a deep sigh as he went out of the room, accompanied with a look more expressive than any words could be of the discontent he laboured under, while she, oppressed beneath the double weight of his and her own grief, remained in a condition he was little able to form any conjecture of.

Pleased as she was with the presence of the only man who had ever had power of inspiring her with one tender thought, yet a thousand times she had wished him gone before he went, that she might be at liberty to give vent to the struggling passions which were more than once ready to throw her into a swoon. The perfections she saw in the person of her lover; — the respect he treated her with, notwithstanding the violence of the passion he was possessed of; — the sincerity that appeared in all his looks and words; — the generosity of his behaviour in regard to her fortune; — all the qualifications that would have made any other woman blessed in the offer of such a heart, served but to make her wretched, since she could not look on herself in a condition capable of accepting it.

Alas! du Plessis, cried she, little do you think to whom you would ally yourself: — you would, you say, despise a portion, but would you marry a foundling, a child of charity, one that has neither name nor friends, and who, in her best circumstances, is but a poor dependant, a servant in effect, tho' not in shew, and owes her very cloaths to the bounty of another? — Oh! why did the mistaken goodness of Dorilaus give me any other education than such as befitted my wretched fortune! Better I had been bred an humble drudge, and never been taught how to distinguish merit: — What avail the accomplishments that cost him so much money, and me so much pains to acquire, but to attract a short-liv'd admiration, which, when I am truly known, will be succeeded with an adequate derision: — Could I but say I was descended from honest, tho' mean parents, I would not murmur at my fate, but I have none, — none to own me; — I am a nothing, — a kind of reptile in humanity, and have been shewn in a genteel way of life only to make my native misery more conspicuous.

Thus did love represent her unhappy circumstances in their worst colours, and render her, which till now she had never been, thankless to heaven for all the good she had received, since it seemed to deny her the only good her passion coveted, that of being in a condition to reward the affection of her dear du Plessis.

A torrent of tears at length somewhat mitigated the violence of her passion, and unwilling to be seen by Melanthe in the present confusion of her thoughts, she went to bed, leaving the same orders as she had done the night before.

CHAP. XIV.

The base designs of the count de Bellfleur occasion a melancholy change in Louisa's way of life; the generous behaviour of monsieur du Plessis on that occasion.

HAD the agonies Louisa suffered been of very long continuance, she must have sunk underneath them; but grief is easily dissipated in a young heart, and she awoke more tranquil. — The principles of religion grew stronger as her passion weaker, and she reflected that she ought to submit in every thing to the will of heaven, which sometimes converts what seems the greatest evil into good. — The offer of such a match as monsieur du Plessis, a man she loved, and who was master of accomplishments which might excuse the most violent passion, appeared indeed a happiness she would have gloried in had she been really such as he took her for; but then she had known him but a very short time, had no experience of his principles or humour; and tho' he seemed all honour, could not assure herself that the generosity which so much engaged her might not be all artifice; at least she found to think so would most contribute to her ease, therefore indulged it as much as she was able. She condemned herself for having given monsieur du Plessis permission to continue his visits, after having assured him he had nothing to hope from them, because a further conversation might only serve to render both more unhappy. She resolved however to give him no opportunity of talking to her of his passion, and in order to avoid thinking of it herself as much as possible, to go, as usual, into all company that came to Melanthe, and partake of every diversion that offered itself.

Accordingly she forced herself to a gaiety, she was far from feeling, vainly imagining that by counterfeiting a chearfulness, she should in time be able to resume it; but du Plessis hung too heavy at her heart, and when she affected the greatest shew of mirth, it was often interrupted with sighs, which she was not always sensible of herself. He visited her almost every day under one pretence or other; but she took such care never to be alone at the times when she could possibly expect him, that he had not the least opportunity to renew his addresses, any otherways than by his looks, which, notwithstanding, were perfectly intelligible to her, tho' she seemed not to observe them.

Melanthe, no longer able to keep the secret of her amour, finding Louisa, as she thought, had entirely regained her former sprightliness, acquainted her with all that had passed between herself and count de Bellfleur; which, tho' the other was no stranger to, she seemed astonished at, and could not help telling her, that she feared the consequence of an intrigue of that nature would one day be fatal to her peace. Yet, said Melanthe, where one loves, and is beloved, it is hard to deny oneself a certain happiness for the dread of an imaginary ill. — In fine, my dear Louisa, I found I could not live without him; and heaven will sure excuse the error of an inclination which is born with us, and which not all our reason is of force to conquer. — But, added she, you always seem to speak of the count, as of a man that wanted charms to excuse the tenderness I have for him; and, I have observed, deny him those praises which I have heard you bestow very freely on persons that have not half his merit.

Louisa knew how vain it was to contest with inclination, in persons who are resolved to indulge it, and also that all advice was now too late, began to repent of what she said. If, madam, replied she, after a little pause, I have seemed unjust to the count's perfections, it was only because I feared you were but too sensible of them; for otherwise, it must be owned, he has a person and behaviour extremely engaging; but as the carnival will put an end to all acquaintance we have contracted here, it gives me pain to think how you will support a separation.

Perhaps it may not happen so soon as you imagine, said Melanthe: — tho' the carnival, and with it all the pleasures of this place will soon be over, our loves may be continued elsewhere: — suppose, Louisa, we go to France, added she with a significant smile, that shewed it was her intention to do so.

Some company coming in, prevented any farther discourse on this head for the present; but afterward she confirmed what she had now hinted at, and told Louisa, that she had resolved to pass some little time in seeing those places which were in her way to France, and afterwards meet the count at Paris, on his return from the campaign. Louisa, unable to determine within herself whether she ought to rejoice, or be sad at this intended journey, fell into a sudden thoughtfulness, which the other at that time took no notice of, but it served afterwards to corroborate the truth of something she was told, and proved of a consequence little to be foreseen.

The inconstant count, in the mean time, satiated with Melanthe, and as much in love with Louisa as a man of his temper could be, was contriving all the ways his inventive wit could furnish him with to get handsomely rid of the one, and attain the enjoyment of the other. As he had spent many years in a continual course of gallantry, and had made and broke a thousand engagements, he easily found expedients for throwing off his intercourse with Melanthe, but none that could give him the least prospect of success in his designs on Louisa while they lived together and continued friends: to part them therefore was his aim, and to accomplish it the following method came into his head.

On his first acquaintance with these ladies his design was wholly on Louisa, but meeting a rebuff from her, his vanity rather than his inclinations had made him turn his devoirs to Melanthe, who too easily yielding to his suit, served but to heighten his desires for the other: the extravagant fondness of that unhappy woman rendering her visibly uneasy at even the ordinary civilities she saw him behave with to any other, discovered to him that jealousy was not the least reigning foible of her soul, and the surest means to make her hate that person whom it was not the interest of his passion she should continue to love. When they were alone together one day at the place of their usual rendezvous, in the midst of the most tender endearments, he asked suddenly if she had ever made Louisa the confident of his happiness. She was a little surprized at the question, but answered that she had not, and desired to know the reason of that demand; because, cried he, I am very certain she is no friend to our loves; and by the manner in which she behaves to me, whenever she has the least opportunity of shewing her ill humour, I imagined she either knew or suspected the affair between us.

Melanthe, conscious she had hid nothing from her, and also sensible of the little approbation she gave to her intrigue, was very much picqued that she should have done any thing to make the count perceive it; — whatever she suspects, cried she, haughtily, she ought not to treat with any ill manners a person whom I avow a friendship for. Vanity, answered he, sometimes gets the better of discretion in ladies of her years: — she knows herself handsome, and cannot have a good opinion of the man who prefers any charms to her own. — I imagine this to be the cause why she looks on me with such disdain, and, whenever you are not witness of her words, is so keen in satyrical reflections. — On our first acquaintance she looked and spoke with greater softness, and I can impute it to no other motive than the pride of beauty, that this sudden change has happened.

All the time he was speaking, the soul of Melanthe grew more and more fired with jealousy. — It is natural for every one to imagine whatever they like is agreeable to others. The distaste which Louisa had on many occasions testified for the count, seemed now to have been only affected: — the melancholy she had been in, and the deep resvery she remembered she had fallen into when first she informed her of their amour, joined to convince her, that the advice she gave proceeded from a motive very different from what she pretended.

The wily count saw into the workings of her soul; and while he seemed as if he would not discover the whole of his sentiments for fear of disobliging her, threw out the plainest hints, that Louisa had made him advances which would have been very flattering to a heart not pre-engaged, till Melanthe, not able to contain her rage, broke out into the severest invectives against the innocent Louisa. — The ungrateful wretch! cried she, how dare she presume to envy, much less to offer an interruption to my pleasures! — What, have I raised the little wretch to such a forgetfulness of herself, that she pretends to rival her mistress and benefactress! In the height of her resentment, she related to the count in what manner she had taken her into her service; but that finding her, as she imagined, a girl of prudence, she had made her a companion during her travels, and as such treated her with respect, and made others do so too; — but, said she, I will reduce her to what she was, and since she knows not how to prize the honour of my friendship, make her feel the severities of servitude.

Nothing could be more astonishing, and at the same time more pleasing to count Bellfleur than this discovery: what he felt for Louisa could not be called love, he desired only to enjoy her; and the knowledge of her meanness, together with Melanthe's resentment, which he doubted not but he should be able to improve to the turning her out of doors, made him imagine she would then be humbled enough to accept of any offers he might make her.

Pursuant to this cruel aim, he told Melanthe, that now not thinking himself under any obligation to conceal the whole of the affair, he must confess Louisa had not only made him advances, but gone so far as to discover a very great passion for him. — As I had never, said he, given her the least room to hope I was ambitious of any favours from her of that nature, I could not help thinking she was guilty of some indecencies ill-becoming a woman of condition, as well as infidelity to her friendship for you, whom she might well see I adored: — but alas! I little suspected the obligations she had to you, and now I know what she is, am in the utmost consternation at her ingratitude, impudence and stupidity. Heavens! added he, could she have the vanity to imagine that the genteel garb you put her in, could raise her to such an equality, as to make me hesitate one moment if I should give the balance of merit on her side, and quit the amiable Melanthe for the pert charms of her woman?

Melanthe, believing every thing he said on this occasion, was ready to burst with indignation; which impatient to give vent to, parted from her lover much sooner than she was accustomed, in order to wreak on the poor Louisa all that rage and malice could suggest.

That innocent maid, little suspecting the misfortune that was falling on her, was at ombre[77] with some ladies who came to visit them, when the furious Melanthe came home, and taking this opportunity of heightening her intended revenge by making it more public, — so, minx, said she to her, after having made her compliments to the company, you ape the woman of fashion exceeding well, as you imagine; but hereafter know yourself, and keep the distance that becomes you. With these words she gave her a push from the table in so rough a manner, that the cards fell out of her hand.

It is hard to say whether Louisa herself, or the ladies who were present, were most astonished at this behaviour; every one looked one upon another

---

[77] *ombre*: a trick-taking card game for three people using forty cards, popular in the eighteenth century.

without speaking for some time: at last Louisa, who wanted not spirit, and on this occasion testified an uncommon presence of mind, — if I have seemed otherways than what I am, madam, it was your commands obliged me to it: — I never yet forgot myself, and shall as readily resume what distance you are pleased to enjoin me. Insolent, ungrateful wretch, cried Melanthe, vexed to the soul to find her seem so little shocked at what she had done, if I permitted you any liberties, it was because I thought you merited them; — but get out of my sight, and dare not to come into it again till I send for you. I shall obey you, madam, replied Louisa, and perhaps be as well pleased to be your servant as companion.

This resignation and seeming tranquility under an insult, she expected would have been so mortifying, was the greatest disappointment could be given to Melanthe, and increased her rage to such a degree, that she flew to her as she was going out of the room, and struck her several blows, using at the same time expressions not decent to repeat, but such, as in some unguarded moment, women of quality level themselves with the vulgar enough to be guilty of. This is a behaviour, madam, said Louisa, which demeans yourself much more than me, and when reason gets the better of your passion, I doubt not but you will be just enough to acknowledge you have injured me.

She got out of the room with these words, but heard Melanthe still outrageous in her reproaches; but determined not to answer, made what haste she could into her own chamber, where having shut herself in, she gave a loose to the distraction so unexpected an event must naturally occasion.

Pride is a passion so incident to human nature, that there is no breast whatever that has not some share of it; and it would be to describe Louisa such as no woman ever was, or ever can be, especially at her years, to say she was not sensibly touched at the indignity she had received from a person, who, but a few hours before, had treated her as pretty near an equality with herself. — Nor was her amazement inferior to her grief, when after examining, with the utmost care, all her words and action, she could find nothing in either that could possibly give occasion for this sudden turn.

From the present, she cast her thoughts back on the past incidents of her life, and comparing them together, how cruelly capricious is my fate, said she, which never presents me with a good but to be productive of an adequate evil! — How great a blessing was the protection and tenderness I found from Dorilaus, yet how unhappy did the too great increase of that tenderness render me! — What now avails all the friendship I received from Melanthe, but to make me the less able to support her ill usage! — And what, of what advantage is it to me that I am beloved by a man the most worthy to be loved, since I am of a condition which forbids me to give any encouragement to his, or my own wishes!

In this manner did she pour forth the troubles of her soul, till the hour of supper being arrived, Melanthe's woman knocked at the chamber, and Louisa having opened it, she told her that she was sorry to see such an alteration in the family, but it was her ladyship's pleasure that she should eat at the second table. It is very well, said Louisa, resolving, whatever she endured, not to let Melanthe see any thing she could do disturbed her too much, and in saying so, went with her into the hall and sat down to table, but with what appetite I leave the reader to guess.

Melanthe, who now hated her to a greater degree than ever she had loved her, gave to the ladies who were with her the whole history of Louisa, as far as she knew it, and rather aggravated, than any way softened the mean condition from which she had relieved her; but when they asked her what that unhappy creature had done to forfeit a continuance of her goodness, she only answered in general, that she had found her to be an ungrateful and perfidious wretch.

As she mentioned no particular instance on which this accusation was grounded, every one was at liberty to judge of it as they pleased. — The accomplishments Louisa was mistress of, made every one convinced she had been educated in no mean way, tho' by some accidents she might have been reduced to the calamities Melanthe had so largely expatiated upon, and more there were who pitied her than approved the behaviour of her superior: — some indeed, who had envied the praises they had heard bestowed on her, were rejoiced at her fall, and made it a matter of mirth wherever they came; — and others again thought themselves affronted by having a person, who they now found was no more than a servant, introduced into their company, and would never visit Melanthe afterward the whole time she stayed in Venice.

The affair, however, occasioned a great deal of discourse: monsieur du Plessis heard of it the next day related after different fashions. The concern he was in was conformable to the passion he had for the fair occasion, and both beyond what is ordinarily to be found in persons of his sex. Impatient to know the truth he went to Melanthe's, and she happening to be abroad, he desired to speak to Louisa, but was told she was indisposed, and could see no company. These orders had been given by Melanthe, but were very agreeable to Louisa herself, who desired to avoid the sight of every one she had conversed with in a different manner from what she could now expect; but of the whole world this gentleman she most wished to shun.

He concealed the trouble he was in as well as he was able, and affecting a careless air, told the person who answered him, that he only came to ask if she had heard the last new song, and that he would send it to her.

The moment he came home he sat down and wrote the following billet.

To the ever charming LOUISA.

THAT invincible bar you mentioned, yet made so great a secret of, is at last revealed, and I should be unworthy of the blessing

I aspire to, if I were unable to surmount it. Cruel Louisa! you little know me, or the force of that passion you have inspired, to imagine that any difference which chance may have put between us, can make the least alteration in my sentiments! — It is to your own perfections I have devoted my heart, not to the merit or grandeur of your ancestors. What has my love to do with fortune, or with family! — Does a diamond lose any thing of its intrinsic value for being presented by an unknown, or an obscure hand?

— My eyes convince me of the charms of my adored Louisa; my understanding shews me those of her mind; and if heaven vouchsafes to bless me with so rich a jewel, I never shall examine whence it came. — If therefore I am not so unhappy as to be hated by you, let not vain punctilioes divide us, and, as the first proof of my inviolable passion, permit me to remove you from a place where you have met with such unworthy treatment: — I hope you wrong me not so far as to suspect I have any other designs on you than such as are consistent with the strictest honour; but to prevent all scruples of that nature from entering your gentle breast, I would wish to place you in a convent, the choice of which shall be your own, provided it may be where I sometimes may be allowed to pay my vows to you thro' the grate, till time shall have sufficiently proved my fidelity, and you shall prevail on yourself to recompence my flame, by bestowing on me your hand and heart: — the one I would not ask without the other; but both together would render the happiest of mankind

Your eternally devoted
DU PLESSIS.

P.S. As I perceive it will be next to an impossibility to gain a sight of you while you continue with that ungenerous woman, I entreat to know by a line how I stand in your opinion, and if the offers I make you, in the sincerity of my soul, may be thought worthy of your acceptance.

This epistle he ordered his valet de chambre to give to her own hand, if there were a possibility of it; and the fellow so well executed his commission, being acquainted with Melanthe's servants, that he was carried directly up to her chamber. She was a little surprized to see him, because he knew it was contrary to Melanthe's commands that any one should see her; and doubted not but to find she was treated with any kind of respect, would enhance her ill humour to her. But she said nothing that discovered her sentiments on this point, and with all the appearance of a perfect ease of mind, asked what he had to deliver to her.

Only a song, mademoiselle, answered he, which my master ordered me to give you, and to desire you will let him know how you like it: — he says it might be turned into an admirable duetto, and begs you would employ your genius on that score and send it by me.

Poor Louisa, who took his words literally, and thought her present circumstances too discordant for the fulfilling his request, opened the supposed piece of music with an aking heart; but when she had perused it, and found the artifice her lover had made use of to communicate his generous intentions to her, it is extremely fine, said she to the valet, and I will do what he requires to the best of my power, but fear I shall not be able to give it such a turn as he may expect. If you please, continued she, to wait a little, I shall not be long before I dispatch you. In speaking these words she went into her closet, and read over and over the offers he had made, in which, with the strictest examination, she could find nothing but what indicated the most perfect love, honour, and generosity. In the first transports of her soul she was tempted to comply; but her second thoughts were absolutely against it. — Those very reasons which would have prevailed with almost any other woman, made her obstinate to refuse: — the more she found him worthy, the less could she support the thoughts of giving him a beggar for a wife; and the more she loved him, the less could she consent to be obliged to him; so she took but a small time for consideration, before she returned an answer in these terms:

> To the most accomplished, and most generous monsieur DU PLESSIS.
>
> AS it was not owing to my pride or vanity, but merely compliance with the will of Melanthe, that my real meanness was made a secret, I find it revealed without any mortification; but, monsieur, the distance between us is not shortened by being known: as the consciousness of my unworthiness remains with me, and ever must do so, I again repeat the impossibility of accepting your too generous passion, and, after this, you will not wonder if I refuse those other obliging offers you are so good to make. — I left my native country with Melanthe, devoted myself to her service while she was pleased to continue me in it, and only wait her commands for my doing so, or to return to England. — I believe, by what her woman told me this day, the latter will be my fate. — Think not, however, most truly worthy of your whole sex, that I want eyes to distinguish your merits, or a heart capable of being influenced by them, perhaps too deeply for my own future peace: — this is a confession I would not have made, were I ever to see you more; but as I am determined to shut myself from all the world during my abode at Venice, I thought I owed this recompence to the generous

affection you express for me, and had rather you should think any thing of me, than that I am ungrateful.

LOUISA.

P.S. I beg, monsieur, after this, you will not attempt either to speak or write to me.

When she had sent this away, she fell into fresh complainings at the severity of her fate, which constrained her to refuse what most she languished for: — the uncertainty how she should be disposed of was also a matter of grief: — she was at this time a prisoner in Melanthe's house: she had sent several messages to that lady, by her woman, entreating to know in what she had offended, but could receive no other answer than abuses, without one word which gave her the least light into the cause of this strange treatment; but that morning she was informed, by the same woman, that her lady protested she should never more come into her presence, and that she would send her home: this, as she had wrote to monsieur du Plessis, seemed highly probable, as there was no appearance of a reconciliation; and the thoughts in what manner she should begin her life again, on her return, filled her with many anxieties, which, joined to others of a different nature, rendered her condition truly pitiable.

It was in the midst of these perplexing meditations, that word was brought her from Melanthe, that she must prepare for her departure on the ensuing day. It was in vain she again begged leave to see her, and to be made acquainted with the reason of her displeasure; but the other would not be prevailed upon, but sent her a purse sufficient to defray the expences of her journey to England, and bid her woman tell her she had no occasion to repine, for she turned her away in a much better condition than she had found her.

CHAP. XV.

Louisa is in danger of being ravished by the count de Bellfleur; is providentially
rescued by monsieur du Plessis, with several other particulars.

LOUISA packed up her things, as she had been commanded, tho' with what
confusion of mind is not easy to be expressed; and, when she was ready to
go, wrote a letter to Melanthe, thanking her for all the favours she had received
from her, acknowledging them to be as unmerited as her late displeasure, which
she conjured her to believe she had never, even in thought, done any thing justly
to incur; — wished her prosperity, and that she might never find a person less
faithful to her interests than she had been. Having desired her woman to deliver
this to her, she took leave of the servants, who all loved her extremely, and saw
her go with tears in their eyes.

The rout she intended to take was to Padua by water, thence in a post chaise
to Leghorn,[78] where she was informed, it would be easy to find a ship bound for
England; to what port was indifferent to her, being now once more to seek her
fortune, tho' in her native country, and must trust wholly to that providence for
her future support, which had hitherto protected her.

Accordingly she took her passage to Padua in one of those boats, which are
continually going between Venice and that city; and it being near the close of
day when she landed, was obliged to go into an inn, designing to lye there that
night, and early in the morning set out for Leghorn.

She was no sooner in bed than, having never been alone in one of those
places before, a thousand dreadful apprehensions came into her head: all the
stories she had been told, when a child, of robberies and murders committed
on travellers in inns, were now revived in her memory: — every little noise she
heard made her fall into tremblings; and the very whistling of the wind, which
at another time would have lulled her to sleep, now kept her waking: but these
ideal terrors had not long possessed her, before she had an occasion of real ones,
more shocking than her most timid fancy could have suggested.

The wicked count de Bellfleur, who had taken care to prevent the passion
he had excited in Melanthe against her from growing cool, learned, from that
deceived lady, in what manner she intended to dispose of her; and no sooner
heard which way she went than, attended by one servant, who was the confidant
and tool of all his vices, he took boat for Padua, and presently finding out, by
describing her, at what inn she was lodged, came directly thither; and, having

---

[78] *Leghorn*: Livorno, on the west coast of Italy.

called the man of the house, asked him if such a young woman were not lodged there, to which being answered in the affirmative, he told him that she was his wife; — that being but lately married to her, in compliance with her request, he had brought her to see the diversions of the carnival, and that she was eloped, he doubted not, but for the sake of a gallant, since he loved her too well to have given her any cause to take so imprudent a step.

The concern he seemed to be under gained immediate credit to all he said, which he easily perceiving, I know, said he, that if I have recourse to a magistrate I shall have a grant, and proper officers to force her to return to her duty; but I would feign reclaim her by fair means: — it is death to me to expose her; and if my perswasions will be effectual, the world shall never know her fault.

The innkeeper then told him she was gone to bed, but he would wait on him to her chamber, and he might call to her to bid her open the door. No, answered the count, if she hears my voice she may, perhaps, be frighted enough to commit some desperate action: — you shall therefore speak to her, and make some pretence for obliging her to rise.

On this they both went up, and the man knocked softly at first, but on her not answering immediately, more loud. — She, who heard him before, but imagining something of what she had heard of others was now going to happen to herself, was endeavouring to assume all the courage she could for supporting her in whatever exigence heaven should reduce her to: — at last she asked who was there, and for what reason she was disturbed. The innkeeper then said he wanted something out of the room, and she must needs open the door. This she refused to do, but got out of bed and began to put on her cloaths, resolving to dye as decently as she could, verily believing they were come to rob and murder her.

The man, who spoke all by the count's direction, then told her, that if she would not open the door, he must be obliged to break it, and presently beat so violently against it, that the poor terrified Louisa expected it to burst, so thought it would be better to unbolt it of her own accord, than, by a vain resistance, provoke worse usage than she might otherwise receive: but what was her astonishment when she beheld the count de Bellfleur! On the first moment the words monsieur du Plessis repeated to her, that *he would have her one way or another*, came into her mind, and made her give a great shriek; but then almost at the same time the thought that he might possibly be sent by Melanthe to bring her back, somewhat mitigated her fears. — Unable was she to speak, however; and the consternation she appeared to be in at his presence, joined with his taking her by the hand and bidding her to be under no apprehensions, confirmed the truth of what he had told the innkeeper, who thinking he had no other business there, and they would be soonest reconciled when alone, left them together and went downstairs.

When the count saw he was gone, — I could not support the thoughts of seeing you no more, my dear Louisa, said he; I have heard Melanthe's cruel usage of you, and also that your condition is such, that you have no friends in England to receive you if you should prosecute your journey: — I come therefore to make you an offer, which, in your present circumstances, you will find it imprudent, I believe, to reject: — I long have loved you, and if you will be mine, will keep you concealed at a house where I can confide, till my return to the army; then will take the same care of you, and place you somewhere near my own quarters; and, as I shall go to Paris as soon as the next campaign is over, will there provide for you in as handsome a manner as you can wish; — for be assured, dear lovely girl, that no woman upon earth will ever be capable of making me forsake you.

That she had patience to hear him talk so long in this manner, was wholly owing to the surprize and fear she had been in, and perhaps had not yet recovered enough from, to make any reply to what he said, if he had contented himself only with words; but his actions rouzing a different passion in her soul, she broke from his arms, into which he had snatched her at the conclusion of this speech, and looking on him with eyes sparkling with disdain and rage, — perfidious man! cried she, is this, — this the consequence of the vows you made Melanthe; and do you think, after this knowledge of your baseness, I can harbour any idea of you, but what is shocking and detestable!

I never loved Melanthe, by heaven, resumed he; she made me advances, and not to have returned them would have called even my common civility in question; — but from the first moment I saw your beauties, I was determined to neglect nothing that might give me enjoyment of them: — fortune has crowned my wishes, you are in my power, and it would be madness in you to lose the merit of yielding, and compel me to be obliged to my own strength for a pleasure I would rather owe to your softness: — come, come, continued he, after having fastened the door, let us go to bed; — I will save your modesty, by pulling your cloaths off myself. In speaking this he catched hold of her again, and attempted to untye a knot which fastened her robe de chambre at her breast. On this she gave such shrieks, and stamped with her feet so forcibly on the ground, that the innkeeper fearing the incensed husband, as he supposed him to be, was going to kill her, ran hastily up stairs, and called to have the door opened, saying, he would have no murder in his house.

The artful count immediately let him in, and told him, he need be under no apprehensions, his wife was too dear to him to suffer any thing from his resentment; and all the noise you heard, said he, was only because I insisted on her going to bed. By these words Louisa discovered how he had imposed upon the man, and cried out she was not his wife; but as she spoke very bad Italian, and the man understood no French, the count being very fluent in that language, had much the advantage, the innkeeper was fully satisfied, and they were again left alone, having a second opportunity to prosecute his villainous attempt.

You see, said he, how much in vain it is for you to resist: — would it not be wiser in you, therefore, to meet my flames with equal warmth; — to feign a kindness even if you have none, and thereby oblige me to use you with a future tenderness: — believe I love you now with an extravagance of fondness: — it is in your power to preserve that affection for ever: — give me then willingly that charming mouth.

He had all this time been kissing her with the utmost eagerness, so that with all her struggling she had not been able either to disengage herself from his embrace, or to utter one word; and he was very near forcing from her yet greater liberties, when all at once heaven gave her strength to spring suddenly from him, and running to a table where he had laid his sword, she drew it out of the scabbard with so much speed, that he could not prevent her, and making a push at him with one hand, kept him from closing with, or disarming her, till with the other she had plucked back the bolt of the door.

In this posture she flew down stairs, and reached the hall before he overtook her, quite breathless and ready to faint. He was going to lay hold of her, when he found himself seized behind by two persons, whom, on turning to examine the reason, he found was monsieur du Plessis and the innkeeper. He started at the sight of that gentleman, and was going to say somewhat to him in French, when the innkeeper told him, the young woman should be molested no farther till he knew the truth of the affair; for, said he, there is a person, meaning monsieur du Plessis, who is just come in, and says she has no husband, and belongs to an English lady of quality now in Venice: — I will therefore take care of her this night, and if you have any real claim to her, you may make it out before the magistrate to-morrow.

The count was so enraged to find it had been by monsieur du Plessis he had been disappointed, that he snatched his sword from Louisa, who had all this time held it in her hand, and made so furious a thrust at him, that, had he not been more than ordinarily nimble in avoiding it, by stepping aside, it must have infallibly gone thro' his body. — He immediately drew and stood on his defence, but the innkeeper and several other people, whom Louisa's cries had by this time brought into the hall, prevented any mischief.

The confusion of voices and uproar which this accident occasioned, would suffer nothing to be heard distinctly; but the guilt of count Bellfleur might easily be read in his looks, and not able to stand the test of any enquiry, he departed with his servant, casting the most malicious reflections as he went out, both on Louisa and her deliverer.

Du Plessis less affected, because innocent, gave every one the satisfaction they desired: he said that the young lady being of English birth, came along with a lady of her own country, to visit several parts of Europe merely for pleasure; that the lady was still at Venice, and that on some little disgust between them, she who was there, meaning Louisa, had quitted her, and was now returning home by the way of Leghorn; of the truth of what he told them, he added, they might be informed, by sending to Venice the next day.

He also said, that having a business to be negotiated in England, he had followed this young lady, in order to beg the favour of her to deliver letters to some friends he had there, not having the opportunity of making this request before, by reason of her departure having been so sudden, that he knew nothing of it before she was gone.

The truth of all this Louisa confirmed, and on farther talk of the affair, acquainted them, that the gentleman who had occasioned this disturbance, for she forbore mentioning his name, had often sollicited her love on unlawful terms, and being rejected by her, had taken this dishonourable way of compassing his desires, at a place where he knew she was alone, and wholly a stranger.

The fright and confusion she had been in, had rendered her so faint, that it was with infinite difficulty she brought out these words; but having something given her to refresh her spirits, and being conducted into another room out of the crowd, she began, by degrees, to recover herself.

Monsieur du Plessis then informed her, that on coming to Melanthe's, and hearing she was gone, he immediately took boat, resolving to prevail on her to alter her resolution of going to England, or dye at her feet: that he easily found the inn she was at, and that the man of the house presently told him, such a person as he described was there; but that he understood she had eloped from her husband, who had pursued, and was now above with her.

Never, said this faithful lover, did any horror equal what I felt at this intelligence! — The base count de Bellfleur came presently into my mind: I thought it could be no other who had taken this abhored method of accomplishing the menaces you may remember I repeated to you. — I was going to fly up stairs that instant, but was withheld, and found it best to argue the man into reason, who, I found, was fully prepossessed you were his wife: as I was giving some part of your history, I saw the count's man passing thro' the hall; he saw me too, and would have avoided me, but I ran to him, seized him by the throat, and asked him what business had brought either him or his master to this place: the disorder he was in, and the hesitation with which he spoke, together with refusing to give any direct answer, very much staggered the innkeeper, who was just consenting to go up with me to your chamber, and examine into the truth of this affair, when we saw you come down, armed as your virtue prompted, and at the same time flying from the villain's pursuit.

Louisa could not help confessing that she owed the preservation of her honour wholly to him; for, said she, the people were so fully persuaded not only that I was his wife, but also that I had fled from him on some unwarrantable intent, that all I did, or could have done, would only have served to render me more guilty in their opinion; and it must have been by death alone I could have escaped the monster's more detested lust.

Monsieur du Plessis now made use of every argument that love and wit could inspire, to prevail with her to accept of the offer contained in the letter he had wrote to her; and concluded with reminding her, that if the charming confession her answer had made him was to be depended upon, and that she had indeed a heart not wholly uninfluenced by his passion, she would not refuse agreeing to a proposal, which not the most rigid virtue and honour could disapprove.

Louisa on this replied with blushes, that since, by the belief she should never see him more, she had been unwarily drawn in to declare herself so far, she neither could, nor would attempt to deny what she had said; but, added she, it is perhaps, by being too much influenced by your merits, that I find myself obliged to refuse what you require of me: — I cannot think, cried she, of rendering unhappy a person who so much deserves to be blessed: — and what but misery would attend a match so unequal as yours would be with me! — How would your kindred brook it! — How would the world censure and ridicule the fondness of an affection so ill placed! — What would they say when they should hear the nobly born, the rich, and the accomplished monsieur du Plessis, had taken for his wife a maid obscurely descended and with no other dowry than her virtue! — My very affection for you would, in the general opinion, lose all its merit, and pass for sordid interest: — I should be looked upon as the bane of your glory; — as one whose artifices had ensnared you into a forgetfulness of what you owed to yourself and family, and be despised and hated by all who have a regard for you. — This, monsieur, continued she, is what I cannot bear, neither for your sake nor my own, and entreat you will no farther urge a suit, which all manner of considerations forbid me to comply with.

The firmness and resolution with which she uttered these words, threw him into the most violent despair; and here might be seen the difference between a sincere and counterfeited passion: the one is timid, fearful of offending, and modest even to its own loss; — the other presuming, bold, and regardless of the consequences, presses, in spight of opposition, to its desired point.

Louisa had too much penetration not to make this distinction: she saw the truth of his affection in his grief, and that awe which deterred him from expressing what he felt: — she sympathized in all his pains, and for every sigh his oppressed heart sent forth, her own wept tears of blood; yet not receding from the resolution she had formed, nothing could be more truly moving than the scene between them.

At length he ceased to mention marriage, but conjured her to consider the snares which would be continually laid, by wicked and designing men, for one so young and beautiful: — that she could go nowhere without finding other Bellfleurs; and she might judge, by the danger she had just now so narrowly escaped, of the probability of being involved again in the same: — he represented to her, in the most pathetic terms, that her innocence could have no sure protection but in the arms of a husband, or the walls of a convent; and on his knees beseeched her, for the sake of that virtue which she so justly prized, since she would not accept of him for the one, to permit him to place her in that other only asylum for a person in her circumstances.

Difficult was it for her to resist an argument, the reason of which she was so well convinced of, and could offer nothing in contradiction to, but that she had a certain aversion in her nature to receive any obligations from a man who had declared himself her lover, and who might possibly hereafter presume upon the favours he had done her.

It was in vain he complained of her unjust suspicion in this point, which, to remove, he protested to her that he would leave the choice of the monastery wholly to herself: that in whatever part she thought would be most agreeable, he would conduct her; and that, after she was entered, he would not even attempt to see her thro' the grate, without having first received her permission for his visit. Not all this was sufficient to assure her scrupulous delicacy: she remained constant in her determination; and all he could prevail on her, was leave to attend her as far as Leghorn, to secure her from any second attempt the injurious count might possibly make.

After this they entered into some discourse of Melanthe, and whether it would be proper for Louisa to write her an account of this affair, and the count's perfidiousness. Monsieur du Plessis said, he thought that the late usage she had received from that lady, deserved not she should take any interest in her affairs; but it was not this that hindered Louisa from doing it: — the remembrance of the kindness she had once been treated with by her, more than balanced, in her way of thinking, all the insults that succeeded it; and when she reflected how much Melanthe loved the count, and that she had already granted him all the favours in her power, it seemed to her rather an act of cruelty than of friendship, to acquaint her with this ingratitude, and thereby anticipate a misfortune, which, perhaps, by his artifices and continued dissimulation, might be for a long time concealed: therefore, for this reason, she exacted a promise from monsieur du Plessis not to make any noise of this affair at his return to Venice, unless the count, by some rash and precipitate behaviour, should enforce him to it.

This injunction discovered so forgiving a sweetness of disposition in the person who made it, that monsieur du Plessis could not restrain testifying his admiration by the most passionate exclamations; in which perhaps he had continued longer, had not the eyes of the fair object discovered a certain languishment, which reminded him, he should be wanting in the respect he professed, to detain her any longer from that repose, which seemed necessary, after the extraordinary hurry of spirits she had sustained; therefore having taken his leave of her for that night, retired to a chamber he had ordered to be got ready for him, as did she to that where she had been so lately disturbed: but all those who are in the least capable of any idea of those emotions, which agitated the minds of both these amiable persons, will believe neither of them slept much that night.

CHAP. XVI.

The Innkeeper's scruples oblige Louisa to write to Melanthe: her behaviour on the discovery of the count's falshood. Louisa changes her resolution, and goes to Bolognia.

MONSIEUR du Plessis, having found it impossible to dissuade Louisa from going to England, now bent his whole thoughts to perform his promise of conducting her to Leghorn, in the most commodious manner he could; accordingly he rose very early, and calling for the man of the house, desired he would provide a handsome post chaise, and if he knew any fellows whose integrity might be relied on, he thought necessary to hire two such, who, furnished with fire-arms, might serve as a guard against any attack the count might take it into his head to make.

But the innkeeper had now entertained notions that forbid him to correspond with the designs of monsieur: some of his neighbours, who had heard of last night's accident, whispered it in his ears, that it would not be safe for him to let these young people depart together; that he could not be assured the person, who pretended to be the husband, might not be so in reality; and if he should come again with proper officers and proofs to claim his wife, it might be of dangerous consequence to him to have favoured her escape; and that the only way he had to secure himself from being brought into trouble, was to lay the whole affair before the podestat.[79] This advice seemed to him too reasonable not to be complied with: he went directly to that magistrate, and while the lover was speaking to him, officers came in to seize both him and Louisa, and carry them before the podestat.

Monsieur du Plessis was very much surprized and vexed at this interruption, and the more so, as he feared it would terrify Louisa to a greater degree than the nature of the thing required; but in this he did injury to her courage: when she was called up and informed of the business, she surrendered herself with all the dauntlessness of innocence to the officers, and suffered them to conduct her, with du Plessis, to the house of the podestat.

Both of them flattered themselves with the belief, that when he should come to hear the story, they would be immediately discharged; but he happened to be one of those who are over wary in the execution of their office; and he only told them, that what they said might be true, but he was not to take things on the bare word of the parties themselves; and that therefore they must be confined

---

[79] *podestat: podestà*, a civic magistrate or governor, especially of an Italian city.

till either the person who claimed the woman for his wife, should bring proofs she was so, or she should be able to make out he had no right over her.

That is easy for me to do, said Louisa; I am only concerned that this gentleman, meaning du Plessis, should be detained on an account he has no manner of interest in. The podestat answered, it was unavoidable, because as the person, who said he was her husband, had accused her of an elopement, there was all the reason in the world to suppose, that if it were so, it was in favour of this gentleman, by the rage he was informed he had testified in finding him at Padua.

Louisa gave only a scornful smile, denoting how much she disdained a crime of the nature she was suspected of, and followed one of the officers, who conducted her to the place appointed for her confinement.

Monsieur du Plessis was touched to the soul at the indignity he thought offered to this sovereign of his affections; but he restrained himself when he considered that it had the sanction of law, which in all nations must be submitted to; and he only told the podestat, that the virtue of that lady would soon be cleared, to the confusion of those who had presumed to traduce it.

As, after they were under confinement, they had no opportunity of advising each other what to do, monsieur du Plessis, uneasy at the injustice done him, wrote immediately to the prince of Conti, in these terms:

To his Royal Highness the Prince of CONTI.

IT is with the extremest reluctance I give your royal highness this trouble, or find myself obliged to accuse the count de Bellfleur of an action so dishonourable to our nation; but as I am here under confinement for preventing him from committing a rape on a young English lady, who failing to seduce at Venice, he followed hither; and under the pretence of being her husband, gained the people of the house on his side, and had infallibly compassed his intent, had it not been for my seasonable interposition: I am too well convinced of the justice I presume to implore, to doubt if your highness will oblige him to clear up the affair to the podestat, on which she will be at liberty to prosecute her journey, and I to throw myself, with the utmost gratitude and submission, at your feet, who have the honour to be

Your royal highness's
Most devoted

Padua.

DU PLESSIS.

Louisa, who was ignorant what her lover had done, and knew no other way, than by writing to Mclanthe, to extricate herself from this trouble, sent a letter to her, the contents whereof were as follows:

MADAM,

ON what imagined cause whatever you were pleased to banish me, I am certain you have too much goodness to suffer any one, much less a person you have once honoured with your friendship, to remain in prison for a crime it is impossible for me to be guilty of: — I am sorry I must accuse a person so dear to you; — but it is, madam, no other than the unworthy count de Bellfleur, who followed me hither, came into the inn where I was lodged, into the very chamber, and oh! I tremble while I relate it, had proceeded yet farther; and I had been inevitably lost, had not heaven sent me a deliverer in the unexpected arrival of monsieur du Plessis, who is also a prisoner as well as myself, for the timely rescue he gave me. You will wonder, doubtless, by what law either I should be confined for endeavouring to defend my chastity, or he, for generously assisting me; but the detested artful count had pretended himself my husband; and under the sanction of that name it was, that he met no opposition to his wicked will from the people of the house, and rendered them regardless of my shrieks and cries. — The magistrates are yet dubious of the truth; and till it can be proved what I really am, both myself and monsieur du Plessis must continue where we are: — have pity on me, therefore, I conjure you, madam, and write to the podestat: I have already told him I had the honour to belong to you; — a line from you will confirm it, and once more set at liberty a maid, who will ever remember all your favours with the greatest gratitude, and your withdrawing them as the worst misfortune could have befallen,

MADAM,

From the prison   Your most faithful, and
at Padua.   *Most humble servant,*

LOUISA.

These letters were sent away by special messengers, who had orders to be as expeditious as possible in the delivery of them.

But while these accidents happened at Padua, Melanthe was not without her share of inquietudes at Venice: she had not seen her beloved count in two whole days, and, tho' she sent several times to his lodgings, could hear nothing but that he was not yet come home. As her vanity would not suffer her to think herself neglected, without having received some glaring proofs of it, she feared some misfortune had befallen him, and exposed herself not a little in the enquiries she made after him, among all those who she could imagine were able to inform her any thing concerning him.

At length some person, who happened to see him take boat, told her he was gone to Padua, which being the rout she knew Louisa had taken, and she had also informed him, a sudden thought started into her head that he was gone in pursuit of her. — It now seemed not impossible, but that all he said concerning his dislike of her might be artifice; and that the love of variety might prevail on him at last to comply with the advances he pretended she had made him. — The privacy with which he went, none of his acquaintance knowing any thing of his journey, seemed to favour this opinion; and never was a heart more racked with jealousy and suspence, than that of this unhappy, and too easily deceived lady.

She had sometimes an inclination to go to Padua in person, and endeavour to find out what business had carried him thither; and her impatience had doubtless got the better of her prudence in this particular, if, sending once more to his lodgings, she had not heard he was returned. — On this she expected to see him in the evening, and flattered herself with his being able to make some reasonable excuse for his absence; but finding he came not, she was all distraction, and sent a billet to him next morning, requiring him to come to her immediately on the receipt of it; but as he was at that time in too ill a humour to think of entertaining her, sent her an answer by word of mouth, that he was indisposed, and would wait on her on his recovery. — This message seemed so cold, and so unlike the passion he had hitherto professed for her, that it threw her into almost convulsive agonies. — A masquerade was to be that night at the house of a person of quality: she sent again to know if he intended to be there, and, if he did, what habit he would wear, it being customary with them, ever since their amour, to acquaint each other with their dresses, that they might not mistake, by addressing to wrong persons. His reply was, he would go if health permitted, but as to what he should wear he had not as yet thought of it.

What, if he has not thought of it! cried she haughtily, when she heard these words; — the knowledge that I shall be there, ought now to make him think of it. — Pride, love, and the astonishment at this sudden change in his behaviour, rendered her wholly forgetful of what she owed her sex and rank; and as she was just going to his lodgings, in order to upbraid him with his indifference, and prove what it was she now had to depend on from him, when the messenger from Louisa arrived and delivered her letter, which contained a sad eclaircisement of all she wanted to be informed of.

At first reading it, she seemed like one transfixed with a clap of thunder: — she had indeed been jealous, suspicious, fearful of her fate; but so glaring, so impudent a treachery had never entered her head, that any man could be guilty of, much less one whom her too fond passion had figured to her imagination, as possessed of all the virtues of his sex. It seemed too monstrous to be true; and she had accused the innocent Louisa as the inventor of this falshood, merely in revenge for her late treatment, had there been the least shadow of a pretence for doing so: — gladly would she have encouraged such a hope, but common sense forbid it; — all circumstances seemed to concur, in proving that he was indeed that villain which the letter represented him; and that surprize, which had in a manner stupified her on the discovery, was succeeded by a storm of mingled grief and rage, which no words can sufficiently describe: — she exclaimed against fate, cursed all mankind, and accused every thing as accessory to her misfortune, but that to which alone she owed it, her own imprudence.

The disorders of her mind had such an effect on her body, that she fell into fits, and a physician was sent for, who, tho' esteemed the most skilful in that country, found it required all his art to prevent a fever: she continued, however, for five days in a condition, such as permitted her not to do any thing either for the satisfaction of her own impatient curiosity, or to comply with the just request Louisa had made; and had not monsieur du Plessis's letter to the prince been more successful, they must both have continued where they were, perhaps for a considerable time.

That, however, had all the effect could be expected from a prince of so much honour: he immediately sent for the count de Bellfleur; and easily finding, by the confusion with which he replied to his examination, and the little low evasions he was obliged to have recourse to, that the affair was as monsieur du Plessis had represented, gave him a severe check, and ordered him to depart immediately from Venice, where he told him, he had given such occasion to call the honour of the French nation in general in question; and to repair with all expedition to his winter quarters. Which command he instantly obeyed, without taking any leave of Melanthe, or perhaps even thinking on her.

At the same time the prince dispatched his gentleman of horse to Padua, with necessary instructions for clearing up the affair; on which the prisoners were discharged, and their pardon asked by the podestat for doing what, he said, the duties of his post had alone obliged him too; tho' it is certain he had exercised his authority with greater strictness than the necessity of the thing required; since, if the count had been in reality the husband of Louisa, it would have been more easy for him to bring proofs of it, than for those under confinement to invalidate his claim.

After the proper compliments to the gentleman who had taken this trouble, monsieur du Plessis entreated he would excuse him to the prince, that he retarded the thanks he had to pay his royal highness, till his return from conducting Louisa some part of her journey, which being a piece of gallantry the lady herself seemed well pleased with, was easily complied with by the other.

This faithful lover had now a full opportunity to entertain his mistress with his passion, and represented it to her with so much force and eloquence, together with the dangers she would be continually exposed to, that she had at length no words to form denials, and gave him leave to conduct her to some monastery in Italy, the choice of which she left to him, till the campaign was over. This was indeed all he presumed to request of her at present. It may happen, said he, that your lover may fall a victim to the fate of war, among many other more brave and worthy men, who doubtless will not survive the next battle, and you will then be at liberty to pursue your inclinations either to England or elsewhere; and be assured of this, that I shall take care, before the hour of danger, to leave you mistress of a fortune, sufficient to protect you from any future insults of the nature you received from Melanthe.

The tender soul of Louisa was so much dissolved at these words, that she burst into a flood of tears, and cried out, Oh! too generous du Plessis, think not I will survive the cruel hour which informs me all that is valuable in man has ceased to be! — Take, — oh! take no care for me; when you are no more, nothing this world affords can enable me to drag on a wretched life!

What must be the transport of a man, who loved like him, to hear a mouth accustomed to the greatest reserve, utter exclamations so soft, so engaging, so convincing to him that he was no less dear to her than he could even wish to be! — He threw himself at her feet, and even thought that posture not humble enough to testify, as it deserved, his gratitude and joy. But she not suffering him to continue in it, he took the hand that raised him, kissed off the tears which had fallen from her eyes upon it, with speechless extacies, and seemed almost beside himself at the concern she could not yet overcome, on the bare imagination of losing him in the way he mentioned. If you love me, said she tenderly, you will endeavour to preserve yourself: — I have now put myself under your protection, by consenting to do as you would have me, and have no other from whom I would receive those favours I expect from you: — think not, therefore, that I will perform my promise, unless you give me yours, not to be so covetous of fame as to court dangers, nor, in too eager a pursuit of glory, to lose the remembrance of what you owe to love.

Oh thou divinest softness! cried he, be assured I will put nothing to the venture that might take me from Louisa! — Your kindness, my angel, has shewed me the value of life, and almost made a coward of your lover: — no farther will I go than the duties of my post oblige me, and that honour, which to forfeit, would render me unworthy of your care.

Louisa now found herself so much at ease, in having discovered a secret she had so long laboured with, and suffered an infinity of pain in the concealing of, that nothing could be more chearful than her looks and behaviour. He, on the other hand, was all rapture, yet did it not make him in the least forgetful of the rules he had prescribed himself, or give her modesty any room to repent the confession she had made in favour of his passion: — the conversation between them was all made up of innocence and love; and every hour they passed together, rendered them still dearer to each other.

Monsieur du Plessis having thus gained the point his soul was set on, began to consider in what part of Italy it would be best to place his dear Louisa: as Bolognia was a free country, under the jurisdiction of the Pope,[80] he thought she would there be the least subject to alarms, on account of the army's continual marches and countermarches thro' most other parts of Italy. He therefore got a post-chaise, and by easy journeys conducted her thither; and having made an agreement with the lady abbess of the Augustines,[81] she was welcomed into the convent by the holy sisterhood with all imaginable good-nature and politeness.

It would be endless to recite the farewels of these equally sincere, and passionate lovers; so I shall only say, that never any parting was more truly touching; and the grief, which both of them endured, was only alleviated by the confidence they had in each other's affection, and the mutual promises of communicating the assurances of persevering in it, by letters as often as opportunity would permit.

Melanthe being recovered of the indisposition of her body, tho' not of her mind, was informed of every particular of her perfidious lover's conduct; but as he had quitted Venice before she did her chamber, was obliged to bear the load of discontent her too easy belief had brought upon her, without even the poor ease of venting it in reproaches on him. The carnival soon after ending, and finding that change of place was no defence from misfortunes of the kind she had sustained, without she could also change her way of thinking, she took the first convenience that offered, and returned to England, rather in worse humour than she had left it.

---

[80] *as Bolognia was a free country, under the jurisdiction of the Pope*: from 1506–1860 the Italian state of Bologna was one of the Papal States, under the sovereign rule of the Pope.
[81] *the Augustines*: the order of St Augustine, a Roman Catholic religious order dating back to the thirteenth century.

CHAP. XVII.

Horatio arrives at Warsaw, sees the coronation of Stanislaus and his queen: his reception from the king of Sweden: his promotion: follows that prince in all his conquests thro' Poland, Lithuania and Saxony. The story of count Patkul and madame de Ensilden.

WHILE these things were transacting in Italy, Horatio, animated by love and glory, was pursuing his journey to Poland. His impatience was so great, that he travelled almost night and day, already imitating the example of the master he was going to serve; no wood, no river was impassable to him that shortened the distance to the place he so much longed to approach: and thus by inuring himself to hardship, became fitly qualified to bear his part in all the vast fatigues to which that prince incessantly exposed his royal person.

Not a city, town, or even village he passed thro', but ecchoed with the wonders performed by the young king of Sweden: — new victories, new acquisitions met him wherever he came: — all tongues were full of his praises; and even those who had been ruined by his conquests, could not help speaking of him with admiration. — Horatio heard all this with pleasure, but mixed with a kind of pain that he was not present at these great actions. — How glorious is it, cried he to himself, to fight under the banners of this invincible monarch! — What immortal honour has not every private man acquired, who contributed the least part to successes that astonish the whole world!

But notwithstanding his eagerness which carried him thro' marshes, over mountains, and ways, which to an ordinary traveller would have seemed impassable, he met with several delays in his journey, especially when he got into Germany, where they were extremely scrupulous; and he was obliged to wait at some towns two or three days before he could obtain passports: he also met several parties of flying horse and dragoons, who were scouting about the country, as he drew nearer Saxony;[82] but his policy furnished him with stratagems to get over these difficulties, and he got safe to Punitz, in the Palatinate of Posnania,[83] where a great part of the king of Sweden's army was encamped. — He immediately demanded to be brought to the presence of the

---

[82] *Saxony*: in the eighteenth century, an electorate of the Holy Roman Empire in north-east Germany, bordered by Brandenburg-Prussia to the north, the Polish-Lithuanian Commonwealth to the east, and Austria to the south.

[83] *Punitz, in the Palatinate of Posnania*: the modern town of Poniec, 335 km west of Warsaw. The Palatinate of Poznańia (or Posnania) was part of Greater Poland, an historical region of west-central Poland.

grand marshal Renchild, to whom he delivered the letter of the baron de la Valiere, and found the good effects of it by the civilities with which that great general vouchsafed to treat him. He would have had him stay with him; but Horatio, knowing the king was at Warsaw, was too impatient of seeing that monarch to be prevailed upon, on which he sent a party of horse to escort him to that city.

He had the good fortune to arrive on the very day that Stanislaus and his queen were crowned,[84] and was witness of part of the ceremony. The king of Sweden was there incognito, and being shewn to Horatio, he could not forbear testifying his surprize to see so great a prince, and one who, in every action of his life, discovered a magnanimity even above his rank, habited in a manner not to be distinguished from a private man; but it was not in the power of any garb to take from him a look of majesty, which shewed him born to command not only his own subjects, but kings themselves, when they presumed to become his enemies. There was a fierceness in his eyes, but tempered with so much sweetness, that it was impossible for those who most trembled at his frowns to avoid loving him at the same time.

Stanislaus had in him all that could attract respect and good wishes; beside the most graceful person that could be imagined, he had a certain air of grandeur, joined with an openness of behaviour, that shewed him equally incapable of doing a mean or dishonourable action: his queen was one of the greatest beauties of her time; and every one present at their coronation confessed, that never any two persons more became a throne, or were more worthy of the dignity conferred upon them.

The whole court was too much taken up that day, for Horatio to think of presenting himself before the king of Sweden; but the officer, who commanded the party that general Renchild had sent with him, introduced him in the evening to count Hoorn, governor of Warsaw,[85] who provided him an apartment, and the next morning introduced him to count Piper. That minister no sooner read the baron de Palfoy's letter, and heard he had others to deliver to the king from the chevalier St George, and the queen dowager of England,[86] than he treated him with the utmost marks of esteem; and assured him that, since he had an inclination to serve his majesty, he would contribute every thing in his power to make him not repent the long fatigues he had undergone for that purpose; but, said he with a smile, you will have no need of me; you bring, I perceive, recommendations more effectual, and have besides, in yourself, sufficient to

---

[84] *the very day that Stanislaus and his queen were crowned*: Stanislaus was crowned on 24 September [N.S.], 1705, along with his wife, Catherine Opalińska (1680–1747).

[85] *count Hoorn, governor of Warsaw*: Arvid Bernard, count Horn (1664–1742), Swedish officer and councillor.

[86] *queen dowager of England*: Mary of Modena (1658–1718), wife of James II and mother of James Francis Edward Stuart, or the 'Old Pretender'.

engage all you have to wish from a monarch so just and generous as ours.

Horatio replied to this compliment with all humility; and as the count perceived by his accents that he was not a Frenchman, tho' he spoke the language perfectly well, he asked him of what country he was; to which Horatio replied, that he was of England, but made him no farther acquainted with his affairs, nor that the motive of his having remained so long in France, was because he was not ransomed by his friends: not that he concealed this out of pride, but he knew the character of most first ministers, and thought it not prudence to unbosom himself to one of those, whose first study, when they come into that employment, is to discover as much as they can of others, without revealing any thing of themselves. For this reason he was also very sparing of entering into any discourse of the chevalier's court, or of that of the king of France, and answered all the questions put to him by the count, that his youth, and being of foreign extraction, hindered him from being let into any secrets of state.

After a pretty long conversation, the count led him to the king of Sweden's apartment, where, just as they were about to enter, he asked him if he could speak Latin; for, said he, tho' his majesty understands French, he never could be brought to speak it, nor is pleased to be addressed in that language. Horatio thanked him for this information, and told him, that tho' he could not boast of being able to deliver himself with an affluence[87] becoming the presence of so great a prince, yet he would chuse rather to shew his bad learning, than his want of ambition to do every thing that might render himself acceptable.

As he spoke these words, he found himself in his presence. — The king was encompassed by the officers of the army, to whom he was giving some directions; but seeing count Piper, and a stranger with him, he left off what he was saying, and, without giving him time to speak, cried, Count, who have you brought me here? One, it may please your majesty, replied he, who brings his credentials with him, and has no need of my intercession to engage his welcome. While the count was making this reply, the king, who had an uncommon quickness in his eyes, measured Horatio from head to foot; and our young soldier of fortune, without being daunted, put one knee to the ground, and delivered his packet with these words: — The princes, by whom I have the honour to be sent, commanded me to assure your majesty, that they participate in all your dangers, rejoice in all your glories, and pray, that as you only conquer for the good of others, the sword you draw, in the cause of justice, may at last be sheathed in a lasting and universal peace.

I am afraid it will be long before all that is necessary for that purpose is accomplished, said the king; wrong, when established, not easily gives place to right; — but we are yet young enough to hope it.

He broke open his letters as he spoke this; and while he was examining

---

[87] *affluence*: an obsolete synonym for fluency (*OED*).

them, took his eyes off the paper several times to look on Horatio, and then read again.

When he had done, I am much obliged said he, to the zeal these letters tell me you have expressed for my service, and shall not be ungrateful: — we are here idle at present, but shall not long be so; and you will have occasions enough to prove your courage, and gratify that love of arms which, my brother informs me, is the predominant passion of your soul.

After this he asked him several questions concerning the chevalier St George, the queen, and princess Louisa; to which Horatio answered with great propriety, but mingled with such encomiums of these royal persons, as testified his gratitude for the favours he received from them. But when he mentioned the princess, and delivered the message she sent by him, a more lively colour flushed into the king's cheeks, and he replied, well, we shall do all we can to comply with her commands; then turned quick about, and resumed the discourse he was in, before Horatio's entrance, with his officers, as much as to say, the business of his love must not interrupt that of the war; and Horatio had afterwards the opportunity of observing, that tho' he often looked upon the picture of that amiable princess, which he always wore in his bosom, yet he would on a sudden snatch his eyes away, as fearing to be too much softened.

Horatio was ordered to be lodged in the castle where the garrison was kept; but he was every day at the king's levee, and received the most extraordinary marks of his favour and affection; for which, as he looked upon himself entirely indebted to the recommendations of his friends in France, he wrote letters of thanks, and an account of all that happened to him.

Poland now being entirely subdued by the valour and fortune of Charles XII. and having received a king of his nomination, submitted chearfully, glad to see an end of devastation, as they then flattered themselves; but the troubles of that unfortunate kingdom were yet to endure much longer. — Augustus, impatient of recovering what he had lost, and the czar of Muscovy jealous and envious of the king of Sweden's glory, came pouring with mighty armies from Saxony and Russia. Shullenburgh,[88] the general of the former, had passed the Oder; and the other, at the head of a numerous body, was plundering all that came in his way, and putting to the sword every one whom he even suspected of adhering to king Stanislaus: so that nothing now was talked of but war, and the means concerted how to put a stop to the miseries these two ambitious princes made, not only in that country, but all the adjacent parts.

It was agreed that general Renchild should go to meet Shullenburgh, and the two kings drive out the Muscovites; who being divided into several parties, Stanislaus went at the head of one army, and the king of Sweden led another; and taking different routs, had every day what he called skirmishes, but what

---

[88] *Shullenburgh*: Saxon commander Johann Matthias von Schulenburg (1661–1747).

the vanquished looked upon as terrible battles.

The king of Sweden, before their departure from Warsaw, told Horatio that all his officers were gallant men, and it was not his custom to displace any one for meer favour to another; he must therefore wait till the fate of war, or some other accident, made a vacancy, before he could give him a commission; in the mean time, said he, with a great deal of sweetness, you must be content to be only my aid-de-camp. On this Horatio replied to his majesty, with as much politeness as sincerity, that it was the post he wished, tho' dare not presume to ask; for he looked upon the honour of being near and receiving the commands of so excellent a monarch, preferable to the highest commission in the army.

Thus, highly contented with his lot, did he attend the king, thro' rivers, lakes, marshes, and all the obstacles nature had thrown in the way of this conqueror; and whenever they came to any battle, was so swift in bearing his commands to the general, and in returning to him in which line soever he was, that Poniatosky[89] gave him the name of the Mercury[90] to their Jove; nor did he less signalize his valour; he fought by the side of the king like one who valued not life, in competition with the praises of his master. In an engagement where they took the baggage of Augustus, he did extraordinary service; and a colonel then being killed on the spot, the king presently cried out, Now here is a regiment for my Horatio. Our young warrior thanked him on his knees, but beseeched he might not be removed from him, again protesting that he could no where deserve so well as where he was animated by his royal presence. This Charles XII. took very kindly, and told him, he should have his desire; but, said he, I must also have mine: — I will continue you my aid-de-camp, but you shall accept the commission, and the lieutenant colonel shall command the regiment in your absence.

He also allotted him so large a share in the prize taken in this battle, that Horatio was already become rich enough to avow his pretensions to the daughter of the baron de Palfoy; but, dear as he was to him, his love and admiration of the king of Sweden, joined to the ambition of desiring still more than he had received, kept him from entertaining the least desire of quitting the service he was in.

In eight or nine weeks did the two kings clear the country round, and drove their enemies into the heart of Lithuania.[91] As they were about to return, they were met by the welcome news that general Renchild had been no less successful, and entirely routed the whole army of Shullenburgh, and also that

---

[89] *Poniatosky*: count Stanislaw August Poniatowski (1676–1762) a Polish-Lithuanian general in both the Swedish and Polish-Lithuanian armies.

[90] *Mercury*: traditionally, the messenger of the gods.

[91] *Lithuania*: In the eighteenth century, Lithuania was one part of the extensive Commonwealth of Poland-Lithuania, a union formalised by the Union of Lublin in 1659.

the diet of Ratisbon,[92] fearing the king of Sweden would enter Germany, had come to a resolution to declare him an enemy to the empire, in case he offered to pass the Oder with his army.

They could not have taken a more effectual step to bring on what they dreaded, than by daring him to it by this menace. He took but little time for consideration, before he determined to carry the war into Saxony, and drive Augustus from his electorate, as he had done from his kingdom.

He had no sooner made known his resolution, than the troops began to march, and with a chearfulness and alacrity, which shewed they had no will but that of their king: — indeed he seemed the soul of this mighty body, of which every single man was a member, and actuated only by him.

It is certain his heart was set on establishing Stanislaus on the throne, and he knew no better way of preventing Augustus from molesting him, than by calling off all communication between his electorate and Poland: — accordingly he bent his course to Saxony, marched thro' Silesia and Lusatia,[93] plundered the open country, laid the rich city of Leipsic,[94] and other towns, under contribution, and at length camped at Alranstadt, near the plains of Lutsen,[95] whence he sent to the estates of Saxony, to give him an estimate of what they could supply, and obliged them to levy whatever sums he had occasion for: not that he had the least spark of avarice in his nature, but his hatred to Augustus, who had by his injustice made him become his enemy, was so great, that it extended to all those of his country, so far, as to humble and impoverish the once opulent inhabitants, making them not only support his numerous army, but laid on them besides many unnecessary imposts, which he divided among his soldiers, so that they were all cloathed in gold and silver, and every private man had the appearance of a general, the king himself still preserving his usual plainness; but he loved, he said, to see the Saxon riches upon Swedish backs.

Horatio now had a second opportunity of writing to France, which he did not fail to do, and, as there was no talk of the army decamping for some time, let his friends know he hoped to hear from them at Alranstadt.

Augustus, in the mean time deprived of every thing, and a wanderer in that kingdom where he had lately reigned, sent a mean submission to him, entreating peace, and that he might have leave to return to his electorate. This was granted by the conqueror, on condition he would renounce, for ever, all

---

[92] *diet of Ratisbon*: The Imperial Diet, or general assembly of imperial states of the Holy Roman Empire, meeting at Ratisbon, now Regensburg in Germany.
[93] *Silesia and Lusatia*: Silesia is now a region of south-western Poland, while Lusatia is now part of the German states of Saxony and Brandenberg that border modern-day Poland.
[94] *Leipsic*: Leipzig, in the German federal state of Saxony.
[95] *Alranstadt, near the plains of Lutsen*: present-day Altranstädt, a village in the German state of Saxony; present-day Lützen, a town in the German state of Saxony-Anhalt, around 10 km west of Leipzig.

thoughts of re-entering Poland, or giving any disturbance to Stanislaus. But as the treaty was going to be signed, the czar sent an army of 20,000 men to his relief, who defeated general Mayerfeild,[96] whom the king had left to guard that kingdom; and the dethroned monarch once more entered Warsaw, the capital of Poland, in triumph.

Charles XII. was so exasperated when he received this intelligence, that he gave immediate orders to decamp, resolving he should not long enjoy the benefit of his breach of faith; but the pusilanimity of Augustus prevented him: that prince was afraid the czar should discover the peace he had been secretly negotiating, and withdrew his troops; and as he had neither any of his own, nor money to assist him, he sent the articles demanded of him by the king of Sweden, signed with his own hand, and set out to Alranstadt, hoping, by his presence and persuasions, to molify his indignation, and be permitted to enjoy his Saxony in peace.

What more could the utmost ambition of man require than the king of Sweden now received, to see a prince, so lately his equal and inveterate enemy, come to solicite favour of him in his camp, almost at his feet; but whatever were his sentiments on this occasion he concealed them, and tho' he could not but despise such an act of meanness, he treated him with the utmost politeness, tho' without making any abatement of the demands he had exacted from him. On the contrary, he insisted on his delivering up to him general Patkul, ambassador from the czar,[97] who at that time was a prisoner in Saxony, being determined to put him to death as a traitor, having been born his subject, and now entered into the service of his sworn enemy.

Augustus beseeched him in the most abject manner to relinquish this one point, and remonstrated to him that the czar, his present master, would look on it as the utmost indignity offered to himself in the person of his ambassador: he assured him he hated Patkul, but feared the giving him up would be resented by all the princes of Europe. All he could urge on this head was to no effect; the king of Sweden was not to be moved from any resolution he had once made; and the unfortunate Patkul was sent to Alranstadt and chained to a stake for three whole months, and afterwards conducted to Casimir,[98] where he was to receive his sentence.

Horatio, who was an entire stranger to the motive of this behaviour in the

---

[96] *general Mayerfeild*: Johan August Meijerfeldt (1664–1749), Swedish officer and governor of Pomerania.

[97] *general Patkul, ambassador from the czar*: nobleman Johann Reinhold von Patkull (1660–1707), who, as a Livonian, was a Swedish subject [see below, n. 99]. He was the leader of a movement resisting the introduction of absolute monarchy by Charles XI, Charles XII's father, and in 1694 had been sentenced to death. He acted as an intermediary between Russia, Denmark and Saxony, all enemies of Sweden.

[98] *Casimir*: Patkull was executed at the castle at Kazimierz, near the city of Poznań.

king, and had never seen any thing before in him that looked like a cruel disposition, was one day mentioning his surprize at it to a young officer with whom he had contracted a great intimacy, on which he gave him the following account:

This Patkul, said he, is a Livonian[99] born, which, tho' a free country, is part of the dominions annexed to the crown of Sweden: Charles XI. began to introduce a more absolute form of government than was consistent with the humour of that people; his son has been far from receding in that point, and Patkul being a person of great consideration among them, stood up for their liberties in a manner which our king could not forgive: — he ordered him to be seized, but he made his escape, and was proscribed in Sweden; on which he entered into the service of king Augustus, and was made his general; but on some misunderstanding between him and the chancellor, he quitted Poland and went to Russia, where he got into great favour with the czar, was highly promoted, and sent his residentiary ambassador in Saxony. Augustus, whose fate it has been to disoblige every body, on some pretence clapp'd into prison the representative of his only friend, and now, we see, has given him up to death, to satiate the demands of his greatest enemy.

Horatio could not keep himself from falling into a deep musing at the recital of this adventure: he thought Patkul worthy of compassion, yet found reasons to justify the king's resentment: and as this officer had often disburthened himself to him with the greatest freedom, he had no reserve toward him, and this led them into a discourse on arbitrary power. — Horatio said, that he could not help believing that nature never intended millions to be subjected to the despotic will of one person, and that a limited government was the most conformable to reason. The officer agreed with him in that; except the person who ruled had really more perfections than all those he ruled over and if so, said he, and his commands are always calculated for the happiness of the subject, they cannot be more happy than in implicite obedience. True, replied Horatio, I am confident such a prince as ours knows how to chuse for his people much better than they do themselves; but how can they be certain his descendants will have the same virtues; and when once an absolute power is granted to a good prince, it will be in vain that the people will endeavour to wrest it from the hands of a bad one. — Never can any point be redeemed from the crown without a vast effusion of blood, and the endangering such calamities on the country, that the relief would be as bad as the disease. Upon the whole, therefore, I cannot think Patkul in the wrong for attempting to maintain the liberty of his country, tho' I do for entering the service of the avowed enemy of his master.

---

[99] *Livonian*: a native of Livonia, an historical region around the Gulf of Riga, corresponding to most of modern Latvia and Estonia. Livonia had become part of the Swedish empire in 1629.

It is that, I believe, resumed the other, that the king chiefly resents: his majesty is too just to condemn a man for maintaining the principles he was bred in, however they may disagree with his own; but to become his enemy, to enlist himself in the service of those who aim at the destruction of his lawful prince, is certainly a treason of the blackest dye.

As they were in this discourse, colonel Poniatosky came in, and hearing they were speaking of Patkul, — I have just now, said he, received a letter from one of my friends in Saxony concerning that general, which deeply affects me, not for his own, but for the sake of a lady, to whom, after a long series of disappointments, he was just going to be married, when Augustus, against the law of nations, made him a prisoner. I will relate the whole adventure to you, continued he; on which the others assuring him they should think themselves obliged to him, he went on.

When he first entered into the service of Augustus, he became passionately in love with madam d'Ensilden,[100] a young lady, whose beauty, birth, and fortune rendered her worthy the affections of a man of more honour than he had testified in his public capacity: her friends at least thought so; and chancellor Flemming[101] making his addresses to her at the same time, had the advantage in every thing but in her heart: there Patkul triumphed in spight of all objections: and tho' king Augustus vouchsafed to sollicite in behalf of his favourite, her constancy remained unshaken as a rock; which so incensed a monarch haughty and imperious in his nature, before humbled by our glorious Charles, that he made use of his authority, and forbid her to think of marrying any other: to which she resolutely answered, that she knew no right princes had to interfere with the marriages of private persons; but since his majesty commanded it, she would endeavour to obey and live single. This not satisfying the king, he hated Patkul from that moment; and the rivals soon after meeting in madam d'Ensilden's apartment, some hot words arose between them, which being by Flemming reported to his master, he sent, in the moment of his passion, to require Patkul to resign his office of general: he did so, but with a murmur that was far from abating the royal resentments; and he had then ordered him into confinement, but that private intelligence being given him, he made his escape before the officers, commissioned for that purpose, reached his house. He then went to the czar, who knowing him an experienced general, of which at that time he stood greatly in need, gladly received him; and it was there he first merited the

---

[100] *madam d'Ensilden*: Voltaire alludes briefly to Patkull's impending marriage to Fraülein von Einsiedel of Saxony in Book 3 of his *Histoire de Charles XII*. Defoe does not refer to the engagement, but Adlerfelt mentions a prospective marriage to an unnamed 'Saxon lady of birth, merit and beauty' (Gustavus Adlerfeld, *The Military History of Charles XII, King of Sweden: Translated into English*, 3 vols (1740), II, p. 369.)

[101] *chancellor Flemming*: Jakob Heinrich, Count Flemming (1667–1728) Saxon officer and minister. The arranged marriage to Flemming is Haywood's invention.

hate of all good men, by countenancing and abetting those ambitious projects his new master was then forming against the king of Sweden: but see the fate of treason, he persuaded him to enter into an alliance with Poland and Saxony against Sweden, which laid the foundation of this unjust war, and for which Augustus has so dearly paid; and being sent Ambassador, in order to negotiate these affairs, again renewed those of his love. Augustus, now obliged to the czar for the preservation of his dominions, durst not openly espouse chancellor Flemming, but no sooner heard that the marriage was near being compleated, than he ventured every thing to prevent it; and, under a pretence of his own forging, confined Patkul in the castle of Konisting, where he lay a considerable time; the czar being too much taken up with combating the fortune of our victorious king, to examine into this affair, and besides, unwilling to break with Augustus, as things then stood. Madam d'Ensilden did all this time whatever could be expected from a sincere affection, in order to procure his enlargement; but the interest of her friends, at least of those who would be employed in this intercession, were infinitely too weak to oppose that of Flemming and the king's own inclination, so that he remained a prisoner, without being permitted either to write to madam d'Ensilden or see her, till the time of his being delivered into our hands. But on hearing he was so, my friend informs me her great spirit, which till now had made her support her misfortune without discovering to the world any part of the agonies she sustained, in an instant quite forsook her: she abandoned herself to despair and grief, equally exclaiming against the Czar, Augustus, and Charles XII; has ever since shut herself up in her apartment, which she has caused to be hung with black, the windows closed, and no light but what a small lamp affords, and only adds more horror to the melancholy scene: she weeps incessantly, and, as she expects her lover will obtain no mercy, declares, she only waits till she hears the sentence of his fate is given, to dye, if possible, at the same moment of his execution.

I must confess, continued Poniatofsky, the history of this lady's sufferings touch me very much; and tho' I think her lover well worthy of the death he will undoubtedly receive, could wish some unexpected chance might once more set him free, and in a condition to recompence so tender a passion, which Augustus has now no longer any power to oppose.

Horatio had a heart too tender, and too sensible of the woes of love, not to be greatly affected with this passage; and as they were all young, and probably had each of them a lady to whom their affections were given, could not help simpathizing in the misfortunes of two persons who seemed to have fallen into them merely by the sincere attachment they had for each other.

CHAP. XVIII.

King Stanislaus quits Alranstadt to appease the troubles in Poland: Charles XII. gives laws to the empire: a courier arrives from Paris: Horatio receives letters which give him great surprize.

AUGUSTUS being able to obtain no better conditions from the king of Sweden, than leave to return to his almost ruined electorate, took leave of his conqueror with an almost broken heart. — Intelligence soon after arriving that Poland was half demolished by the violence of different factions, who, in the absence of both their kings, contended with equal fury for the sovereign power, Stanislaus took an affectionate farewell of his dear friend and patron, and went to appease the troubles of that kingdom, and make himself peaceably acknowledged for what he was, their lawful king, not only by election, but by the gift of the conqueror, Charles XII. of Sweden. He was attended by 10,000 Swedish horse, and twice the number of foot, in order to make good his claim against any of his rebellious subjects.

Charles having now accomplished all he could desire in relation to the Polish affairs, began to grow weary of the idle life he led at Alranstadt, and was thinking which way he should turn his arms; he had been ill used by the czar, who, as has been before observed, plotted his destruction while a minor, and began hostilities when he thought him not in a condition to defend himself, much less to make any reprisals: his resentment therefore against him was no less implacable than it had been against Augustus. — But the emperor had also disobliged him. Count Zobor, the chamberlain,[102] had taken very indecent and unbecoming liberties with his character, in the presence of his own Ambassador at Vienna; and that court had given shelter to 1500 Muscovites, who having escaped his arms, fled thither for protection. As he was now so near, he therefore thought best to call the emperor first to account, and then proceed to attack the czar.

To this end he sent to demand count Zobor, and the 1500 Muscovites should be given into his hands: the timid emperor complied with the first, and sent his chamberlain to be punished as the king thought fit; but it was not in his power to acquiesce the other; the Russian envoy, then at Vienna, having intelligence of it, provided for their escape by different routs. The king of Sweden then sent a second mandate, requiring protection for all the Lutherans

---

[102] *Count Zobor, the chamberlain*: baron Czobor, Maximilian Adam Czoborszentmihály (d. 1728), son-in-law of prince Johann Adam Andreas of Liechtenstein.

throughout Germany, particularly in Silesia, and that they should be restored to all the liberties and privileges established by the treaty of Westphalia.[103] The emperor, who would have yielded any thing to get the king of Sweden out of his neighbourhood, granted even this, disobliging as it was to the pope and his own catholic subjects: and having ratified these concessions, the king vouchsafed to let his chamberlain return, without any other punishment than imprisonment, so long as these affairs remained in agitation.

Having thus given laws to Germany and terror to the emperor, he resolved to turn where he might expect more opposition; and accordingly he ordered count Piper to acquaint the officers, that they must now begin to think of preparing for a march.

In the mean time ambassadors from all the courts of Europe were sent to his camp, most of them being apprehensive that they should be the next who felt the terror of his arms: but those who had nothing of this kind to dread, and more really his friends, made use of all the arguments in their power to prevail on him to return to Stockholm. France in particular sent courier after courier, remonstrating to him that his glory was complete; that he had already exceeded Alexander, and should now return covered, as he was, with lawrels, and let his subjects enjoy the blessing of his presence. The court of St Germains added their entreaties to that of Versailles, but each were equally ineffectual; nor could even the thoughts of the beautiful princess Louisa, his betrothed spouse, and whom he was to marry at the end of this war, put a stop to the vehemence of his impatience to revenge the many injuries he had received from the czar of Muscovy.

These were the sentiments by which this conquering monarch were agitated; but Horatio, tho' no less fond of glory, had a softness in his nature, which made him languish for the sight of his dear Charlotta, whom he had been absent from near two years; and being now blessed with a fortune from the plunder of Saxony, which might countenance his pretensions to her, passionately longed for an opportunity of returning without incurring the censure of cowardice or ingratitude. By these couriers he received letters from the baron de la Valiere, and several others of his friends, but none from the father of Charlotta; nor did any of them make any mention of that lady, tho' he knew the passion he had for her was now no secret to any of them.

He was very much surprized that the baron de Palfoy had not wrote, because as he had in a manner promised to correspond with him by desiring him to write, he had a right to expect that favour when they came to Alranstadt; for till then it was scarce possible, by reason of the army's continual and uncertain

---

[103] *the treaty of Westphalia*: The Treaty, or Peace, of Westphalia (1648), which reinstated the terms of the League of Augsburg (1555). The League of Augsburg had established the principle that the religion of states could be determined by their rulers.

motions; but he was much more so, that the baron de la Valiere had not been so good as to give him some information of an affair, of which he could be insensible his peace so much depended: that he did not do it, he therefore presently concluded, was owing to the having nothing pleasing to acquaint him with.

As love is always apprehensive of the worst that can possibly befal, he thought now of nothing but her being obliged to give her hand to some rival approved by her father: — what avails it, cried he, that fortune has raised me to an equality with her, if, by other means, I am deprived of her!

He was beginning to give way to a despair little befitting a soldier, when another courier arriving from Versailles with dispatches to the king, he also received a packet, in which were three letters. The first he cast his eye upon had on it the characters of Charlotta: amazed and transported he hastily broke the seal, and found it contained these lines:

To Colonel HORATIO.

SIR,

I HAVE the permission of my father to pursue my inclinations, in giving you this testimony how sincerely I congratulate your good fortune; tho' I ought not to call it by that name, since I find every-body allows your rewards have not exceeded your merits; but as neither has been found deficient either for your ambition or the satisfaction of your friends, all who are truly such think you ought to content, and run no future hazards. — Be assured you have many well-wishers here, among the number of whom you will be guilty of great injustice not to place

CHARLOTTA DE PALFOY.

How well were all the late anxieties he had endured attoned for by this billet; it was short indeed, and wrote with a more distant air than he might have expected, had the dear authoress been at liberty to pursue the dictates of her heart; but as it informed him it was permitted by her father, and was doubtless under his inspection, the knowledge that he had authorized her to write at all, was more flattering to his hopes of happiness than all she could have said without that Sanction. After having indulged the raptures this condescention excited, he proceeded to the rest, and found the next he opened was from the baron de Palfoy, who expressed himself to him in these terms:

To Colonel HORATIO.

I THINK myself obliged to you for so much exceeding the character I gave you; but I value myself on knowing mankind, and am glad to find I was not deceived in you, when I expected

you to do more than I durst venture on my own opinion to assure
the count. He tells me, in a letter I received from him the last
courier, that the victorious Charles XII. himself cannot behave
with greater bravery in the time of action, nor more moderation
after it is over. — This is a great praise, indeed, from such a man as
he; and I acquaint you with it not to make you vain, for that would
blemish the lustre of your other good qualities, but that you may
know how to make proper acknowledgements to that minister.

Our court, I know, makes pressing instances to the king of
Sweden not to carry on the war any farther: I wish they may
succeed, or if they should not, that you might be able to find some
opportunity of quitting the service for reasons which you will
see in a letter that accompanies this, and to which nothing can
be added to convince you what part you ought to take. — I shall
therefore say no more than that I am, with a very tender regard,

Yours,

PALFOY.

Rejoiced as he was at receiving a letter from the father of his mistress, wrote
in a manner which he might look upon as a kind of confirmation he no longer
would be refractory to his wishes, the latter part of it contained an enigma he
could by no means comprehend. — It seemed impossible to him there could
be any reasons prevalent enough to make him quit, with honour, a prince
who had so liberally rewarded his service; but hoping a further explanation,
he lost not any time in conjectures; and tearing open the other letter without
giving himself time to examine the hand in which it was directed, found, to
his inexpressible astonishment, the name of Dorilaus subscribed. It was indeed
wrote by that gentleman, and contained as follows:

Dear Horatio,

ACCIDENTS, which at our parting neither of us could foresee,
have doubtless long since made you cease to hope any continuance
of that kindness my former behaviour seemed to promise;
but never, perhaps, did heaven deal its blessings with a more
mysterious hand than it has done to you. — That seeming neglect
in me, at a time when you were a prisoner among strangers,
and had most need of my assistance, had the appearance of the
greatest misfortune could befal you; yet it has been productive of
the greatest good, and laid the foundation of a happiness which
cannot be but lasting. — I reserve the explanation of this riddle
till you arrive at Paris, where I now am, and intend to continue
my whole life. — That I impatiently desire to see you, ought to be

a sufficient inducement for you to return with as much expedition as possible: — I will therefore make this experiment of that affection, I might add duty, you owe me, and only give you leave to guess what recompence this proof of your obedience will entitle you to. — If therefore the king of Sweden is resolute to extend his conquests, entreat his permission to resign: I know the obligations you have to that excellent prince; but I know also you have others to me which cannot be dispensed with: — besides, his majesty's affairs cannot suffer by the loss of one man: yours will be in danger, if not totally ruined, by your continuance with him, and myself deprived at the same time of the only remaining comfort of my days. — Your sister left me soon after you did: — she went to Aix-la-Chapelle, since which I have never been able to hear any thing of her. — Let me not lose you both; if you have any regard for your own interest, or the peace of him you have ever found a father in his care and affection, and whom you will now find so more than you can possibly expect.

DORILAUS.

Impossible it is to conceive, without being in the very circumstances Horatio was, what a strange variety of mingled passions agitated his breast on having read, and considered these letters: — to find such unhoped condescensions from the baron de Palfoy, and that Dorilaus was still living, and had the same, if not more tender inclinations than ever, the latter of which he had long since ceased to hope, was sufficient to have overwhelmed even the most phlegmatic person with an excess of joy: — but then the dark expressions in both these letters put his brain on the rack. — The baron had seemed to refer to an explanation of what he darkly hinted at in the letter of Dorilaus, but that he found rather more obsolete:[104] he could imagine nothing farther than that Dorilaus having resolved to make him his heir, as he remembered some people said before he left England, on the knowledge of that intelligence the baron de Palfoy had consented to his marriage with mademoiselle Charlotta, and this, her being permitted to write to him confirmed. — This indeed was the supreme aim of his desires; and this it was made him quit St Germains, in hope of raising himself to a condition which might enable her to own her affection to him without a blush: but transporting as this idea was, it was mingled with disquiet, to reflect on the terms which both the Baron and Dorilaus seemed to insist on for the accomplishment of his wishes, tho' he impatiently longed to see Dorilaus after so long an absence. — Tho' in the possession of Charlotta all his hopes were centered, yet to leave a prince who had so highly favoured him,

---

[104] *obsolete*: a now archaic synonym for obscure or indistinct (*OED*).

and under whose banners he had gained so much consideration, was a piece of ingratitude, which it was worse than death for him to be guilty of. — No! said he, it would be to render me unworthy of all the blessings they make me hope, should I purchase them on such conditions! — How can they demand them of me! — The Baron, Charlotta, and Dorilaus, have all of them the highest notions of honour, generosity and gratitude, and can they approve that in me, which I am certain they would not be guilty of themselves! — Sure it is but to try me, they seem to exact what they are sensible I cannot yield to, without the breach of every thing that can entitle me to esteem or love!

Thus did he argue with himself for one moment; the next, other reasons, directly opposite to these, presented themselves. — Dorilaus, cried he, demands all my obedience; — all my gratitude: — without his protection I had been an outcast in the world! — Whatever honours, whatever happiness I enjoy, is it not to him I owe them! Can I refuse then to comply with commands, which, he says, are necessary to his peace! — Besides, was it not Charlotta that inspired this ardor in me for great actions! Was not the possession of that charming maid, the sole end I proposed myself in all I have undertaken! and shall I, by refusing her request, madly run the risque of losing her for ever! — Does she not wish, her father persuade, and Dorilaus enjoin me to return! — Does not love, friendship, duty call me to partake the joys that each affords! — And shall I refuse the tender invitation! — No! the world cannot condemn me for following motives such as these; and even the royal Charles himself is too generous not to acquit me of ingratitude or cowardice.

It must indeed be confessed he had potent inducements for his return to Paris, to combat against those of continuing in the king of Sweden's service; and both by turns appeared so prevalent, that it is uncertain which would have got the better, had not an accident happened, which unhappily determined him in favour of the latter.

Colonel Poniatosky, who had attended Stanislaus into Poland, now the disturbances of that kingdom were quieted, on hearing the king of Sweden was on some new expedition, obtained leave of Stanislaus to return to the camp, and implored his majesty's permission to be one of those who should partake the glorious toils he was now re-entering into. To which he replied, that he should be glad to have him near his person, but feared he would be wanted in Poland. No, may it please your majesty, resumed Poniatosky, there seems to be no longer any business in that kingdom for a soldier: — all seem ready to obey the royal Stanislaus out of affection to his person, and admiration of those virtues they are now perfectly convinced of; nor is Augustus in a condition to violate the treaty of resignation: — refuse me not therefore I beseech your majesty, continued he, falling upon both his knees, what I look on as my greatest happiness, as it is my greatest glory.

The king seemed very well pleased at the emphasis with which he expressed himself; and having raised him from the posture he was in, be it so, cried he, henceforward we will be inseparable.

Horatio was charmed with this testimony of love and zeal in a person, who had doubtless friends and kindred who would have been glad he had less attachment to a service so full of dangers as that of the king of Sweden, and somewhat ashamed he had ever entertained a thought of quitting it, resolved, as he had been more obliged, not to show less gratitude than Poniatosky. Therefore, without any further deliberation, retired to his quarters, and prepared the following answers to the letters had been brought him. As all things in a lover's heart yields to the darling object, the first he wrote was to his mistress.

To mademoiselle DE PALFOY.

WITH what transports I received yours, adorable Charlotta, I am little able to express! — To find I am not forgotten! — That what I have done is approved by her for whom alone I live, and whose praise alone can make me vain, so swallowed up all other considerations, that it had almost made me quit Alranstadt that moment, and fly to pour beneath your feet my gratitude and joy! — But glory, tyrannic glory, would not suffer me to obey the soft impulse, nor re-enjoy that blessing, till conscious I deserved it better! — My friends over-rate my services; and tho' that partial indulgence is the ultimate of my ambition, I dare not abuse what they are so good to offer.

To feast my long, long famished sight with gazing once more on your charms, I would forgo every thing but the hope of rendering myself one day more worthy of it! — Too dear I prize the good wishes you vouchsafe to have for me, not to attempt every thing in my power to prevent the disappointment of them: the little I have yet done, alas! serves but to prove how much the man, who has in view rendering himself acceptable to the divine Charlotta, dares to do, when dangers worthy of his courage present themselves. — A small time may, perhaps afford me an opportunity: — yet did you know how dear this self-denial costs me, you would confess it the greatest proof of affection ever man gave: — permit me therefore to gratify an ambition which has no other aim than a justification of the favours I receive: — continue to look with a favourable eye on my endeavours, and they cannot then fail of such success, as may give me a claim to the title of my most adored and loved Charlotta's

Everlasting Slave,
HORATIO.

To her father he wrote in the following manner:

To the baron DE PALFOY.

    My Lord,

THE favours your goodness confers upon me are such as can be equalled by but one thing in the world, and that is my just and grateful sense of them. — Charming would be the toils of war, did all employed in them meet a recompence like mine! — Is there a man so mean, so poor in spirit, that praises such as I receive might not animate to actions worthy of them! — What acknowledgements can I make the count suitable to the immense obligations I owe him, for inspiring your lordship with sentiments, which, tho' the supreme wish of my aspiring soul, I never durst allow myself to hope; and which afford a prospect of future accumulated blessings, such as I could scarce flatter myself with being real, were not the transporting idea in some measure confirmed to me, by your having given a sanction to a correspondence I so lately ever dared of obtaining! Blessed change! — Extatic condescensions! — Fortune has done all she can for me, and anticipated all the good that, after a long train of services and approved fidelity, I scarce should have presumed to hope! — Oh my lord! I have no words to thank you as I ought! It is deeds alone, and rendering myself worthy of your indulgence, that must preserve your good opinion, and keep you from repenting having overwhelmed me with this profusion of happiness! — Yet how joyfully could I now pursue the rout to Paris, and content myself with owing every thing merely to your goodness, were I not with-held by all the considerations that ought to have weight with a man of honour! — My royal general is inflexible to the persuasions of almost all the courts in Christendom, and hurried by his thirst of fame, or some other more latent motive, has given orders to prepare for a march, where, or against whom, is yet a secret to the army; but by the preparations for it, we believe they are not short journeys we are to take. — Should I now quit a service where I have been promoted so much beyond my merit, what, my lord, but cowardice or ingratitude could be imputed to me as the motive! — Not all my reasons, powerful as they are, would have any weight with a prince, who is deaf to every thing but the calls of glory; and I must return loaden with his displeasure, and the reproaches of all I leave behind! — Now to return is certain infamy! — To go, is in pursuit of honour! — Your lordship will not therefore be surprized I make choice of the latter, since no hazard can be equal to that of forfeiting the little reputation I have acquired, and which alone can render me worthy any part of the favours I have received.

I am,

With the extremest respect and submission,

Your lordship's
Eternally devoted servant,

HORATIO.

The last and most difficult task he had to go thro', was the refusal he must give to Dorilaus, who had laid his commands on him in such express terms; and it was not without a great deal of blotting, altering, and realtering, he at length formed an epistle to him in these terms:

> *To my more than father, my only patron, protector, and benefactor, the most worthy* DORILAUS.

> *Most dear and ever honoured Sir,*

> To hear you are living, and still remember me with kindness, affords too great a transport to suffer me to throw away any thought either on the motives of your long silence, or that happiness, which you tell me, I may expect has been the produce of it: — it is sufficient for me to know I am still blessed in the favour of the most excellent person that ever lived, and am not in the least anxious for any explanation of any farther good.

> To tell you with how much ardency I long to throw myself at your feet, to relate to you all the various accidents that have befallen me since first you condescended to put me in the paths of glory, and to pour out my soul before you with thanksgiving, would be as impossible as it is for me at present to enjoy that blessing! — The king's affairs, it is true, would suffer nothing by my absence; but, sir, what would the world say of me, if, after a whole year of inactivity and idleness, I flew, on the first appearance of danger, and forsook a prince, by whom I have been so highly favoured? — Instead of the character I have always been ambitious of attaining, should I not be branded with everlasting infamy! — Put not therefore, I beseech you, to so severe a test that love and duty, to which you cannot have a greater claim than I a readiness to pay? — Did you command my life, it is yours: — I owe it to you, and with it all that can render it agreeable; but, sir, my honour, my reputation, must survive when I am no more, it

was the first, and will be the last bent of my desires. No perils can come in any degree of competition with those of being deprived of that, nor any indulgencies of fortune compensate for the loss of it: — pardon then this enforced disobedience, and believe it is the only thing in which I could be guilty of it. — I very much lament my sister's absence, as I find by yours she went without your permission: time and reflection will doubtless bring her to a more just sense of what she, as well as myself, ought to have of your goodness to us, and make her return full of sincere contrition for having offended you. I should implore your favourable opinion of her actions in the mean time, were it not all the interest I have in you too little to apologize for my own behaviour. — All, sir, I dare to implore is pardon for myself, and that you will be assured no son, no dependant whatever, would more rejoice in an opportunity of testifying his duty, affection, gratitude and submission, than him who is now constrained by ties, which I flatter myself you will not hereafter disapprove, to swerve in some measure from them, and whose soul and all the faculties of it are

Entirely devoted to you.
Horatio.

These dispatches being sent away, he became more composed, and set his whole mind on his departure, and taking leave of those friends and acquaintance he had contracted at Leipsic and Alranstadt; the time of the army marching being fixed in a few days, tho' what rout they were to take none, except count Piper, general Renchild, count Hoorn, and some few others of the cabinet council, were made privy to.

CHAP. XIX.

The king of Sweden leaves Saxony, marches into Lithuania, meets with an instance of Russian brutality, drives the czar out of Grodno,[105] and pursues him to the Borysthenes.[106] Horatio, with others, is taken prisoner by the Russians, and carried to Petersburg, where they suffer the extremest miseries.

THE word at length being given, the tents were struck, the trumpets sounded, and the whole army was immediately in motion. Never was a more gay and glorious sight; the splendor of their arms, and the richness of their habits blazed against the sun; but what was yet more pleasing, and spread greater terror among their enemies, was the chearfulness that sat on every face, and shewed they followed with the utmost alacrity their beloved and glorious monarch.

It was in the latter end of September, a season extremely cold in those parts, that they began their march; but hardships were natural to the king of Sweden's troops; and as they perceived they were going into Lithuania, a place where their valour had been so well proved against the invading Muscovites, their cheeks glowed with a fresher red on the remembrance of their former victories. They passed near Dresden, the capital of the electorate of Saxony, and made Augustus tremble in his palace, tho' the word of the king, which ever was inviolable, had been given that he should enjoy those dominions in peace.

During the course of this, the czar had fallen upon the frontiers of Poland above twenty times, not like a general, desiring to come to a decisive battle, but like a robber, plundering, ravaging, and destroying the defenceless country people, and immediately flying on the approach of any troops either of Charles XII. or king Stanislaus. The Swedes in their march met several parties sent on these expeditions, but who retired on sight of the army into the woods, and were most of them either killed or taken by prisoners by detachments sent in pursuit of them by the king of Sweden.

In their march towards Grodno they found the remains of an encampment, several pieces of cannon and ammunition of all sorts, but not one creature to guard it, the troops to whom it belonged having all dispersed and hid themselves. On examining the tents, they were surprized by the sight of a very beautiful woman, who was lying on the ground in one of them, with three

---

[105] Grodno: *Grodno, now a city in western Belarus, close to its borders with Poland and Lithuania.*
[106] Borysthenes: *an ancient, classical name for the River Dnieper.*

others, who seemed endeavouring to comfort her, and, by the respect they paid her, that they were her dependants; but had all of them their garments torn and bloody, their hair hanging in strange disorder about their ears, their flesh discoloured with bruises and other marks of violence, and, as well as their disconsolate superior, were spectacles of the utmost distress.

The king of Sweden himself, followed by general Hoorn, Poniatosky, Horatio, and several others, who hardly ever lost sight of him, came into this tent, and, being touched with so moving a scene, demanded the Occasion; on which the prostrate lady being told who it was that spoke, started suddenly up, and throwing herself at his feet: — Oh king! cried she in the German language, as famous for justice as being invincible in war, revenge the cause of helpless innocence and virtue! — Oh let the murderous brutal Russians find heaven's vindictive arm in you its great viceregent. — She was able to utter no more: the inward agonies she sustained, on being about to relate the story of her wrongs, became too violent for speech, and she sunk motionless on the earth. Two of the women, assisted by some Swedes, carried her out of the tent, as thinking the open air most proper to revive her; and she who remained, satisfied the king's curiosity in these words:

May it please your majesty, said she, my mistress, that afflicted lady who just now implored your royal pity, is of the noble family of Casselburgh, in Saxony, only daughter to the present count: her person, before these heavy misfortunes fell upon her, was deservedly reputed one of the most beautiful that graced the court of Dresden: her birth, her youth, her charms, and the great fortune it was expected she would be mistress of, attracted a great number of persons who addressed her for marriage: her own inclinations, as well as the count her father's commands, disposed of her to Emmermusky, a Polish nobleman; and she had been scarce one month a bride, before they unhappily took this journey to visit my lord's mother who lives at Travenstadt. — In our way we met a party of straggling Muscovites, who, notwithstanding the strict league between our elector and the czar, and the knowledge they had by our passports that we were Saxons, stripped us of every thing, killed all our men-servants, and having given my lord several wounds, left him for dead upon the place, then dragged us miserable women to the camp. — My lady, in the midst of faintings, and when she was incapable even of flying to death for refuge, was brutally ravished, and we her wretched attendants suffered the same abuse. — Shame will not let me, continued she, blushing and weeping, acquaint your majesty with the shocking and repeated violations we were compelled to bear! — the wretches casting lots who first should satisfy his monstrous desires! — We were all bound to trees, and without any means of opposition but our shrieks and cries to unrelenting heaven! — My lord having a little recovered himself, had crawled, as well as his wounds would give him leave, after us, and arrived even while the horrid scene was acting: rage giving him new strength and spirits, he snatched a sword that lay upon the earth, and sent to perdition the villain who was about to add to the dishonour which had been, alas! but too much completed by others. The death of their companion incensed the accursed Muscovites, they turned upon him, and in a moment laid him dead at the feet of his ruined and almost expiring wife! After having satiated their wicked will, they left us, bound as we were, where we continued the remainder of the day and whole night, and had doubtless perished thro' hunger and extreme cold, if a second party had not passed that way, who having been out on a maroding, were then returning to the camp. — Being actuated by somewhat more compassion than the former, one of the officers made us be untied, and having heard our story, blamed the cruelty with which we had been treated, and brought us to his tent, the same we are now in, and ordered something should be given for our refreshment; but my lady has continued obstinate to dye, and to that end has refused all subsistence. This, oh invincible monarch! is the sad history of our misfortunes: — misfortunes, which, alas! can never be retrieved, nor admit any consolation but in the hope of vengeance!

Here a torrent of tears closed the sad narration; and the king cried out, turning as he spoke to us that followed him, — It is the cause of heaven and earth, my friends, said he, to punish these barbarians, and shew them that there is a God; for sure at present they are ignorant of it!

The generous monarch after this gave orders that these afflicted and abused women should be escorted to a place of safety, and for that purpose halted for a space of two days, then proceeded towards Grodno with such expedition, that after-ages will look upon it as incredible that so large an army, and also encumbered with a great quantity of baggage, could have marched in the time they did.

But the king of Sweden was on fire to encounter in person the czar of Muscovy, who, with about 2000 men, was then in that city: so great was his impatience, that he galloped before his troops, not above 600 of those best mounted being able to keep pace with him, till he came in sight of the south gate, which gave him entrance without any opposition, while the czar and his forces made their escape out at the north gate, not doubting but the king of Sweden's whole army were come up with him.

He was afterward so much vexed and ashamed to think he had quitted the town to no more than 600 of the enemy, that, to retrieve a mistake which he feared might be looked on as cowardice, being informed that the body of the army was near five leagues off, he sent a party of 1500 horse in order to surprize the king and his few guards. The Muscovites entered by night; but the alarm being given, the fortune which still had waited on the Swedish armies, immediately put them all to the rout; and the army soon after arriving, the conqueror lost no time, but pursued those that remained alive into the forest of Mensky,[107] on the other side of which the czar had then entrenched himself, and had made the general rendezvous of the Russian army, which was continually divided into parties; and sometimes falling on the Swedes in the rear, and sometimes in the flank, very much annoyed them in their march: these brave men had also other difficulties to encounter with; the forest was so extremely thick, that the infantry were obliged to fell down trees every moment, during the whole time of their passage, to make way for the baggage and troops.

Their industry and vigour surmounting all these obstacles, they once more found themselves in an open country, but on the banks of a river, on the opposite side of which were 20,000 Muscovites placed to oppose their crossing. The king made no delay, but quitting his horse, threw himself into the river, and was instantly followed by all the foot, while the troops under the command of general Renchild and Hoorn, galloped round thro' the morass in which that river ended, and both together charged the army, who, after some faint shew of resistance, fled with the utmost precipitation. The whole army being now joined marched on toward the Borysthenes, but with fatigues which are impossible to be described: Horatio still kept close to the king, and whether he fought or marched, was on foot or on horseback, was always in his sight ready to bear his commands to the generals, or assist him in the time of danger. More than once had the conqueror been indebted to this young warrior, for turning the point of the destructive sword from giving him the same death he was dealing about to others; yet in all the dangers he had been in never had he received one wound, and this often made the king say, who was a firm believer in predestination, that heaven designed him for a soldier: his fortune, his valour, his activity, added to his obliging and modest behaviour, indeed rendered him so dear to his royal master, that there were very few, if any, to whom he gave greater marks of his favour. And had Dorilaus, or even Charlotta herself, all tender as she was, and trembling for the hazards she knew he had been exposed to, seen him thus caressed and honoured by the most glorious prince and greatest hero in the world, they could scarce have wished him to quit the post he was in, much less persuaded him to do it.

He hitherto indeed had experienced only the happiness of a martial life, for the fatigues, hardships, and dangers of it he as little regarded as the intrepid and indefatigable prince he served; but now arrived the time which was to inflict on him the worst miseries of it, and make him almost curse a vocation he had been in his soul so much attached to.

The king of Sweden, with his usual success having passed the Borysthenes, encountered a party of 10,000 Muscovites and 6000 Calmuck Tartars;[108] but

---

[107] *Mensky*: now the city of Minsk, capital of Belarus.

[108] *Calmuck Tartars*: Tartars (or Tatars) were natives of a huge tract of central Asia extending

they gave way on the first onset and fled into a wood, where the king, following the dictates of his great courage more than prudence, pursuing them, fell into an ambuscade, which, throwing themselves between him and three regiments of horse that were with him, hem'd him in, and now began a very unequal fight. — Many of the gallant Swedes were cut to pieces, and the Muscovites made quite up to his majesty: — two aid-de-camps were killed within his presence, his own horse was shot under him, and as an equerry was presenting him with another, both horse and man was struck dead in the same moment. — Horatio immediately alighted in order to mount the king, who now on foot behaved with incredible valour, in that action was surrounded and taken prisoner, as were several others that had fought near his person. He had the satisfaction, however, while they were disarming and tying his hands, to see colonel Dardoff[109] with his regiment force thro' the Calmucks, and arrive timely enough to disengage the king, after which the army recovering its rank, and pouring in upon the enemy, he was not without hopes of regaining his liberty; but he was sat upon a horse and bound fast to the saddle, and compelled, with the others that were taken with him, to accompany the Muscovites in their flight, so was ignorant in what manner this re-encounter ended. Soon after repairing to the czar's quarters, these unfortunate officers of the king of Sweden were, with some others who had before become their prize, sent under a strong guard to Petersburg, and thrown altogether in a miserable dungeon.

It would be impossible to describe the horrors of this place: — light there was, but it was only so much as just served to shew to each of these unhappy sufferers the common calamity of them all. — The roof was arched indeed, but so low, that the shortest among them could scarce stand upright: — no kind of furniture, not even straw to cover the damp earthen floor, which served them for a seat by day and bed at night. Inured as they had been to hardships, the noisomeness of this dreaded vault killed many of them, and among the rest a young Swedish officer named Gullinstern, one with whom Horatio had contracted a very intimate friendship, and who, for his many excellent qualities, had been so dear to the king, that seeing him one day greatly wounded, and in danger of being taken prisoner, that generous prince obliged him to mount on his own horse, and fought on foot himself till another could be brought.

The sight of this gentleman expiring in his arms, filled Horatio with so poignant an anguish, that he wanted but little of following him; and, indeed, had it not been for the sanguine hopes that the king would in a short time complete the ruin of the czar, and not only restore them liberty, but also add

north and eastwards from the Caspian Sea, while Calmuck (or Kalmuck) distinguished those living on the Sea's north-western shores. Tartars were reputed to be fierce and pitiless fighters.

[109] *colonel Dardoff*: Johan Valentin von Daldorff (1665–1715), Swedish officer.

vengeance to it for the ill treatment they had found in his dominions, few, if any of them, had been able to support the miseries inflicted on them by these inhuman wretches, who, not content with burying them in a manner alive, for the dungeon they were in was deep underground, and allowing them no other food than bread and water once in four and twenty hours, made savage sport at their condition, ridiculed the conquests of their king, and spoke in the most opprobrious terms of his royal person, which, when some of them were unable to restrain themselves from answering in a manner befitting their duty and love of justice, they were silenced by the most cruel stripes.

Thus were the officers of the king of Sweden, the meanest of whom were fit to be generals in any other army, subjected to the servile taunts, and insolent behaviour of wretches undeserving to be ranked among the human species.

A very little time had doubtless made them all find graves among these barbarians; scarce a day passed over without their company decreasing by two or three, who were no sooner dead than dragged out by the heels, and thrown like dogs into a pit without the least funeral rites. But providence at length thought fit to send them a relief by means they least expected.

In one of the incursions made by the Muscovites into Poland, a very beautiful lady, whose father had been killed in asserting the cause of Stanislaus, was made prisoner: prince Menzikoff,[110] who commanded these batallions, saw her, and became enamoured of her charms: she was destitute of all friends, and in the conqueror's power, so thought it best to yield what otherwise she found him determined to seize: in fine, she was his mistress; and her ready compliance with his desires, together with the love she either had or feigned to have for him, afterward gained her an absolute ascendant over him. Every one knows the interest he had with the czar; and he so far exerted it, as to get this fair favourite lodged in the palace, where she was served with the same state and respect as if she had been his wife.

This lady, whose name was Edella, happened to be walking with some of her attendants near where these unfortunate gentlemen were buried, at a time when three of them were dragged to their wretched sepulchre, was touched with compassion to see any thing that had a human shape thus coarsely treated, tho' after death, and had the curiosity to order one of her people to enquire who those persons were, and what they had done, which hindered them from being allowed a christian burial.

She was no sooner informed that they were Swedish prisoners, than her soul shuddered at the thoughts of the Russian barbarity; and not doubting but their usage during life had been of a piece with that after their death, she resolved, if possible, to procure some abatement of the miseries of those who yet survived.

To this end she made it her business to examine what number of prisoners

---

[110] *prince Menzikoff*: Russian prince Alexander Danilovich Menshikov (1673–1729).

had been brought, of what condition they were, and where lodged; and being well acquainted with all she wanted to know, went to the governor of Petersburg, and so well represented how dishonourable it was to the czar, and how opposite to the law of nations, to treat prisoners of war in a worse manner than felons, that he knowing the power of prince Menzikoff, and fearing to disoblige one so dear to him by a refusal, consented they should be removed into an upper part of the prison where they would have more air, and also that they should have an allowance of meat every day.

As the governor was a true Muscovite in his nature, and had an implacable hatred to the king of Sweden and all that belonged to him, this was gaining a great deal; but it was not enough to satisfy the charitable disposition of Edella; after their removal, she went in person to visit those of them whom she heard were gentlemen, and finding them covered only in rags, which some of the soldiers had put on them after having stripped them of their own rich habits, she ordered others lined with furs to be made for them, to defend them from the coldness of the season; and not content to retrench a great part of her own table, sold several fine jewels, and other trinkets the prince had bestowed on her, to supply them with wine, and whatever necessaries she supposed them to be accustomed to. That she might be certain those entrusted by her did not abuse her good intentions, she went often to the prison herself to see how they were served, and would sometimes enter into discourse with them concerning the battles they had been in, the settlement of Stanislaus, and many other things relating to the Polish affairs. The gallant and courtly manner in which Horatio expressed himself on every occasion, made her take a particular pleasure in hearing him speak: that rough blunt behaviour to which she had been accustomed since her being brought a captive into Muscovy, gave double charms to the politeness with which she found herself entertained by our young warrior; his blooming years, and the gracefulness of his person, contributed not a little also towards rendering every thing he said more agreeable. Her liking of him grew by degrees into a friendship, no less tender than one feels for very near relations, and who have never done any thing to disoblige us, are more endeared by being under undeserved calamity: but as the inclination she had for him was perfectly innocent, and no ways prejudicial to the prince who was in possession of her person, she made no secret of it either to himself or those she conversed with, and was always talking of the wit, delicacy and handsomeness of one of those prisoners, whom it was well known were pensioners to her bounty. But how dangerous it is to be too open before persons who, void of all true generosity, or the least principle of honour themselves, never fail to put the worst construction on the actions of others. Edella was very near being undone by her sincerity in acknowledging the distinction she paid to merit, or the compassion she felt for misfortunes, in a country where humanity to enemies is looked upon as a crime, friendship to those of the same party altogether unknown, and even common civility never practised but for the gratification of self-interest, or some favourite passion.

This beautiful Polander however being treated by the Muscovites, on account of the influence she had over the prince Menzikoff, with as much complaisance as it was in their power to shew, imagined their disposition less savage than it was in reality; and when she testified the pity she had for those unhappy gentlemen, it was with design to excite it in others, and engage with her in petitioning the czar, at his return, for their enlargement, there being no cartel or exchange of prisoners subsisting between him and the king of Sweden.

Among the number she hoped to gain to her party was Mattakesa, the relique of a general who had been in great favour with his prince. This lady, who could speak French, having learned it of a recusant that took shelter in Russia, consented to go with her one day to the prison, and no sooner saw Horatio, than, unfortunately for him, Edella, and herself, she became charmed with him: as she was of the number of those who think nothing a crime that suits their own inclination, she took not the least pains to subdue the growing passion, but rather indulged it, in order to receive the highest degree of pleasure in the gratification. She doubted not but Edella was her rival, and that it was for his sake alone she had been so beneficent to his fellow-sufferers; to supplant her, therefore, was the first step she had to take, and she resolved to omit nothing for that purpose.

CHAP. XX.

The treachery of a Russian lady to her friend: her passion for Horatio: the method
he took to avoid making any return, and some other entertaining occurrences.

IT is easy to believe that Horatio, tho' relieved from that extremity of misery
he suffered while in the dungeon, was far from being able to content himself
with his present condition: — a thousand times he reproached himself for
pursuing the dictates of a glory which now seemed so tyrannic: — Have I, cried
he, hazarded the eternal displeasure of the best of men, — refused the invitation
of the adorable Charlotta, — slighted the condescentions of her father, — been
deaf both to interest and love, to become a prisoner to the worst of barbarians!
— Who now will pity me! — Or if they yet will be so good, how shall I acquaint
them with my wretched fate! — Nay, were there even a possibility of that, what
would the compassion of the whole world avail, since a slave to those, who,
contrary to the law of nations, and even common humanity, refuse, on any
terms, to release the wretches fallen into their savage power!

In this manner did he bewail himself night and day, and indeed had but too
just reasons for doing so: — he had heard that the last time the czar had been
at Petersburg, he had sent all the prisoners he had then taken to Siberia, and
other provinces of the greater Tartary,[111] where they were compelled, without
any distinction, to do the work of horses rather than men, and doubted not but
at his next return all those now in his power would meet the same fate, tho'
the generous king of Sweden had sent back the Muscovites he had taken, by
1500 and 2000 at a time. — This, however, may be said in favour of the czar,
that by the many attempts he made to civilize his barbarous subjects, it must
be supposed he would have been glad to have imitated this generosity, had it
been consistent with his safety; but the case had this difference, Charles XII.
feared not the number of the Muscovites, but the czar feared the courage of the
Swedes.

What also increased the affliction of these gentlemen, was, that being
debarred from all intelligence, they could hear nothing of their king, whom
each of them loved with a kind of filial affection and duty. — Horatio and two
others had been witnesses of the extreme danger in which they left him; and
tho' at the time they were seized he had killed thirteen or fourteen Muscovites
with his own hand, and they perceived general Dardoff had come to his relief,

---

[111] *the greater Tartary*: also known as Tartary, the region inhabited by Tartars (or Tatars)
[see above, n. 108].

yet they could not be certain of his safety; till at length the sweet-conditioned Edella perceiving the despair they were in on this account, informed them that his majesty was not only well, but as successful as ever; that he had passed far into Ukrania,[112] had defeated the Muscovites in five battles, and so far reduced the czar, that he had condescended to make some overtures of peace; which having been rejected, it was the common opinion, that in a very short time the Swedes would enter Moscow, and become arbiters of Russia as they had been of Poland.

Adequate to their late grief was the satisfaction at this joyful news: — Horatio was transported above his companions, and threw himself at the feet of the fair intelligencer; but she desired they would all of them moderate their contentment so as to hinder the guards, who had the care of them, from perceiving it, because, said she, it might not only draw on yourselves worse treatment, but also render me being suspected of being against the interest of a court, on which my fate has reduced me to become a dependant.

Horatio, as well as the others, assured her he would take care to manage the felicity she had bestowed upon them, so as not to be any way prejudicial to her; and she took her leave, promising to be with them again in a few days, and bring them farther information, a courier from the camp, she said, being expected every hour.

But while this compassionate lady was pleasing herself, by giving all the ease in her power to the distressed, the cruel Mattakesa was plotting her destruction. — She had several of her kindred, and a great many acquaintance in the army, who were in considerable posts, to all of whom she exclaimed against the loose behaviour, as she termed it, of Edella, and represented her charities to the prisoners as the effects of a wanton inclination: — this she doubted not but would come to prince Menzikoff's ears, and perhaps incense him enough to cause her to be privately made away with; for as she imagined nothing less than the most amorous intercourse between her and Horatio, she thought it unadvisable to declare the passion she had for him, till a rival so formidable, by the advantages she had over her in youth and beauty, should be removed.

This base woman therefore impatiently waited the arrival of the next courier, to find how far her stratagem succeeded; and the moment she heard he had delivered his dispatches, flew to the apartment of Edella, in hopes of being informed of what she so much desired to know.

She was not altogether deceived in her expectations: she found that lady drowned in tears, with a letter lying open before her; and on her enquiring, with a shew of the utmost concern, the motives of her grief, the other, who

---

[112] *Ukrania*: a region roughly corresponding to the modern state of Ukraine, which in the early eighteenth century was divided between Russia, Poland-Lithuania and the Ottoman empire.

looked on her as her real friend, replied, alas! Mattakesa, I have cruel enemies; I cannot guess for what cause, for willingly I never gave offence to any one; — but see, continued she, how barbarously they have abused my innocence, and represented actions, which, heaven knows, were influenced only by charity and compassion as the worst of crimes! with these words she gave her the letter which she had just received from the prince.

Mattakesa took it with a greedy pleasure, and found it contained these lines:

To EDELLA.

MADAM,

I LEFT you in a place, furnished, as I thought, with every thing necessary for your satisfaction; but I find I was mistaken in your constitution, and that there was something wanting; which, rather than not possess, you must have recourse to a prison to procure: — ungrateful as you are to the affection I have treated you with, I am sorry for your ill conduct, and could wish you had been, at least, more private in your amours: few men but would have sent an order for removing you and the persons, for whose sake you have made these false steps, into a place where you would have cause to curse the fatal inclination that seduced you: think therefore how much you owe a prince, who, instead of punishing your faults, contents himself with letting you know he is not ignorant of them. — If you make a right use of the lenity I shew on this occasion, you may perhaps retrieve some part of the influence you once had over me; but see the Swedish prisoners no more, if you hope or desire ever to see

MENZIKOFF.

Mattakesa affected the greatest astonishment on having read this letter; and after having cursed the persons that put such vile suspicions into the prince's head, asked her what she intended to do.

What can I do! answered the sorrowful Edella, but write to my lord all the assurances that words can give him, which heaven knows I can truly do, that I never wronged him either in wish or thought; and that since there are people so cruel to misinterpret to my dishonour, what was nothing but mere charity, to obey his commands with the utmost punctuality, and never set my foot into that prison more?

Her false friend could not but approve her resolution, yet told her it was pity that ill tongues should deprive those unfortunate gentlemen of the relief she had hitherto afforded them, or herself of the pleasure she took in their conversation.

As for the first, said Edella, heaven may perhaps raise them other friends more capable of assisting them; and as to the other, were it infinitely greater, it would be my inclination, as it is my duty, to sacrifice every thing to the will of a prince whom I love, and to whom I am so much obliged.

Mattakesa having thus compassed her design, so far as to be under no apprehensions of being interrupted by her imagined rival, tho' she had rather she had been poisoned or strangled, went directly to the prison and told the gentlemen, it was with the utmost concern she must acquaint them that Edella would never visit them any more, nor continue the weekly pension she had hitherto allowed them.

Those among them who understood her, and the others to whom Horatio interpreted what she said, looked upon one another with a great deal of consternation, as imagining one of them had done something to offend her, and thereby the rest were thought unworthy of her favours. — Every one endeavoured to clear himself of what he easily saw his companions suspected him guilty of; till Mattakesa, with a scornful smile, told them, that it was not owing to the behaviour of any of them, but to Edella's own inconstant disposition, that they owed the withdrawing of her bounty; but to console them for the loss of it, she promised to speak to some of her friends in their behalf, and also to contribute something herself towards alleviating their misfortunes; but, added she, I am not the mistress of a prince and first favourite, so have it not in my power to act as the generosity of my nature inclines me to do.

She stayed with them a considerable time, and entertained them with little else than railing on Edella; and to make her appear as odious and contemptible as she could to Horatio, insinuated it was for the sake of a young needy favourite she had been obliged to withdraw the allowance they had from her.

On taking leave she found means to slip a little billet into Horatio's hands, unperceived by any of the company, which, as soon as he had a convenient opportunity, he opened, and found these words in French:

To the agreeable HORATIO.

Sir,

Tho' I have not perhaps so much beauty as Edella, I have twice her sincerity, and not many years older: such as I am, however, I fancy you will think a correspondence with me of too much advantage to be refused: — if you will counterfeit an indisposition, to-morrow I will out of excessive charity visit you, and bring you a refreshment, I flatter myself, will not be disagreeable to a man in your circumstances: — farewell; — be secret, — and love as well as you can.

Yours,

MATTAKESA.

Of all the accidents that had befallen Horatio since his leaving England, none ever so much surprized him as the prodigious impudence of this lady: he had heard talk of such adventures, but never till now believed there could be any such thing in nature, as a woman that offered herself in this manner, without the least sollicitation from the person on whom she wished to lavish what ought only to be the reward of an approved, or at least a shew of the most violent passion.

The dilemma he was in how to behave, was also equal to his astonishment: — had she been the most lovely of her sex, as she was very much the reverse, the ever present idea of his dear Charlotta would have defended his heart from the invasions of any other charms; but he needed not that pre-engagement to make him look with detestation on a woman of Mattakesa's principles: — when he reflected on what she had said concerning Edella, he found her base, censorious, and unjust: — and when he considered the manner in which she proceeded in regard to himself, he saw a lewdness and audacity which rendered her doubly odious to him: — he doubted not but she was wicked and subtle enough to contrive some means of revenging herself, in case she met with a disappointment in her wishes, yet had too great an abhorrence to be able to entertain one thought of gratifying them.

As he was young and inexperienced in the world, he would have been glad of some advice how to act so as not to incur her resentment, yet avoid her love; but the strict notions he had of honour remonstrated to him that he ought not to betray a secret of that nature, tho' confided in him by an ill woman. — Her baseness, cried he to himself, would be no excuse for mine; and it is better for me to risque whatever her malice may inflict, than forfeit my character, by exposing a woman who pretends to love me.

These thoughts kept him waking the whole night; and his restlessness being observed by an old Swedish officer who lay with him, he was very much importuned by him to discover to him the occasion. — Horatio defended himself for a good while by the considerations before recited; but at length reflecting that the person who was so desirous of being let into the secret, had a great deal of discretion, he at length suffered himself to be prevailed upon, and told him what Mattakesa had wrote to him, for he did not understand a word of French, so could not read the letter.

This officer no sooner heard the story, than he laughed heartily at the scruples of Horatio, in thinking himself bound to conceal an affair of this nature with a woman of the character Mattakesa must needs be: — he also rallied his delicacy, as he termed it, in hesitating one moment whether he should gratify the lady's inclinations. — One would imagine, said he, that so long a fast from love as we have had, should render our appetites more keen: — what, tho' Mattakesa be neither handsome nor very young, she is a woman, and amorous, and methinks there should be no other excitements to a young man like you.

Horatio, tho' naturally gay, was not at present in a disposition to continue this raillery, and told his friend, he looked on this inclination of Mattakesa to be as great a misfortune as could happen to them; for, said he, as it is wholly out of my power to make her any returns, that violence of temper which has transported her to forget the modesty of her sex, will probably, when she finds herself rejected, make her as easily throw off all the softness of it; and you may all feel the effects of that revenge she will endeavour to take on me.

The other was entirely of his opinion; and they both agreed that some way ought to be thought on to avert the storm, her resentment might in all probability occasion.

After many fruitless inventions, they at last hit on one which had a prospect of success: they had in their company a gentleman called Mullern, nephew to chancellor Mullern,[113] who had attended the king in all his wars: he was handsome, well made, and his age, tho' much superior to that of Horatio, yet was not so far advanced as to render him disagreeable to the fair sex: he was of a more than ordinary sanguine disposition, and had often said, of all the hardships their captivity had inflicted on them, he felt none so severely as being deprived of a free conversation with women. — In the ravages the king of Sweden's arms had made in Lithuania, Saxony and Poland, he was sure to secure to himself three or four of the finest women; and tho' he had often been checked by his uncle, and even by the king himself, for giving too great a loose to his amorous inclinations, yet all their admonitions were too weak to restrain the impetuosity of his desires this way. To him, therefore, they resolved to communicate the affair; and as he was in other respects the most proper object among them to succeed in supplanting Horatio, so he was also by being perfectly well versed in the French language, which the rest were ignorant of.

Accordingly they told him what had happened, shewed him the letter, and how willing Horatio would be to transfer all the interest he had in this lady to him, if he could by any means ingratiate himself into her favour. Mullern was transported at the idea; and the stratagem contrived among them for this purpose was executed in the following manner:

Mattakesa was punctual to the promise she had made in her letter; and when she came into the room, where she usually found the gentlemen altogether, it being that where they dined, and saw not Horatio, she doubted not but he had observed her directions, and pretended himself indisposed, so asked for him, expecting to be told that he was ill; but when they answered he was gone with one of the keepers to the top of the round tower, in order to satisfy his curiosity in taking a view of the town, she was confounded beyond expression, and could not imagine what had occasioned him to slight an assignation, she had flattered

---

[113] *chancellor Mullern*: Gustav Henrik von Müllern (1664–1719), Swedish official.

herself he would receive with extacy.

As she was in a little resvery, endeavouring to comprehend, if possible, the motive of so manifest a neglect, Mullern drew near to her, and beginning to speak of the beauties of that fine city which the czar had erected in the midst of war, he told her, that having a little skill in drawing, he had ventured to make a little sketch of it in chalk on the walls of the room where he lay, and entreated her in the most gallant manner to look upon it, and give him her opinion how far he had done justice to an edifice he so much admired.

It cannot be supposed that Mattakesa had in her soul any curiosity to see a work of this nature, yet, to hide as much as she could the disorder she was in at her disappointment, gave him her hand, in order to be conducted to the place where he pretended to have been exercising his genius.

As soon as they were entered he threw the door, as if by accident, which having a spring lock, immediately was made fast. — She either did not, or seemed not to regard what he had done; but casting her eyes round the room, and seeing nothing of what he had mentioned, — Where is this drawing? cried she. In my heart, adorable Mattakesa, answered he, falling at her feet at the same time: — it is not the city of Petersburg, but the charming image of its brightest ornament, that the god of love has engraven on my heart in characters too indelible ever to be erased: — from the first moment I beheld those eyes my soul has been on fire, and I must have consumed with inward burnings had I not revealed my flame: — pardon, continued he, the boldness of a passion which knows no bounds; and tho' I may not be so worthy of your love as the too happy Horatio, I am certainly not less deserving of your pity.

Surprize, and perhaps a mixture of secret satisfaction, prevented her from interrupting him during the first part of his discourse; but rage, at the mention of Horatio, forced from her this exclamation: — has the villain then betrayed me! cried she. No, madam, replied he, justice obliges me to acquit him, tho' my rival. — He had the misfortune in putting your billet into his pocket, to let it fall: — I took it up unseen by him, — opened it, read it, and must confess, that all my generosity to my friend was wholly swallowed up in my passion for you. — I returned not to him that kind declaration you were pleased to make him, and he is ignorant of the blessing you intended for him: — if the crime I have been guilty of seem unpardonable in your eyes, command my death, I will instantly obey you, for life would be a torment under your displeasure; and if, in my last moments, you vouchsafe some part of that softness to the occasion of my fate, that you so lavishly bestowed on the fortunate Horatio, I will bless the lovely mouth that dooms me to destruction!

He pronounced all this with an emphasis, which made her not doubt the power of her charms; and surveying him while he was speaking, found enough in his person to compensate for the disappointment she had met with from Horatio: besides, she reflected, that if what he had told her concerning the dropping her letter was a fiction, it was however an ingenious one, and shewed his wit, as well as love, in bringing both himself and his friend off in so handsome a manner. She was infatuated with the praises he gave her; — the pathetic expressions he made use of, assured her of the ardency of his desires, and as she could not be certain of being able to inspire Horatio with the same, she wisely chose to accept the present offer, rather than wait for what might perhaps at last deceive her expectations. She made, however, no immediate answer; but her eyes told him she was far from being displeased with what he had said, and gave him courage to take up one of her hands and kiss it, with an eagerness which confirmed his protestations.

At last, — Well, Mullern, said she, looking languishingly on him, since chance has made you acquainted with my foible, I think I must bribe you to secrecy, by forgiving the liberties you take with me: — and if I were convinced you really love me as well as you pretend, might indulge you yet farther. — An unaccountable caprice indeed swayed me in favour of Horatio, but I am now half inclinable to believe you are more deserving my regard; — but rise, continued she, I will hear nothing from you while in that posture.

Mullern, who was no less bold in love than war, immediately obeyed her, and testified his gratitude for her condescention, by giving a sudden spring and snatching her to his breast, pressed her in so arduous a manner, that she would have been incapable of resisting, even tho' she had an inclination to do so: but she, no less transported than himself, returned endearment for endearment, and not only permitted, but assisted all his raptures, — absolutely forgot Horatio, as well as all sense of her own shame, and yielded him a full enjoyment without even an affectation of repugnance.

Both parties, in fine, were perfectly satisfied with each other, and having mutually sworn a thousand oaths of fidelity which neither of them, it is probable, had any intention to keep, Mullern took upon himself the care of continuing to entertain her in private as often as she came to the prison, and in return she made him a present of a purse of gold, after which they passed into the outer room to prevent censures on their staying too long together.

On their return they found Horatio with the other gentlemen. Abandoned as Mattakesa was, she could not keep herself from blushing a little at the sight of him; but soon recovering herself by the help of her natural audacity, — Well, Horatio, said she, what do you think of the little French epigram I put into your hands yesterday; — has it not a very agreeable point?

Horatio had such an aversion to all kinds of deceit, that even here, where it was so necessary, he could not, without some hesitation, answer to what she said in these words. — Some accident or other, cried he, deprived me of that pleasure you were so good to intend me; for when I put my hand in my pocket thinking to read it, I perceived I was so unhappy as to have lost it: — I looked for it in vain: — it was irrecoverably gone, and I am an utter stranger to its contents.

And ever shall be so, replied she tartly, only to punish your carelessness of a lady's favour; know, that it was a piece of wit which would have been highly agreeable to you: — but don't expect I shall take the pains to write it over again, or even tell you the subject on which it turned.

Horatio cooly said, he could not but confess he had been to blame, and must therefore allow the justice of her proceeding. As none present besides himself, his bedfellow, and Mullern, knew the truth of this affair, what passed between them was taken by the others as literally spoken, and little suspected to couch the mystery it really did.

Mullern, after this, by the assistance of Horatio and the old officer, had frequent opportunities of gratifying his own and the amorous Mattakesa's desires. — The testimonies she gave him how well she was pleased with his conversation, were for the common good of his companions. — Horatio was easy in finding himself out of all danger of any solicitations he was determined never to acquiesce in; and those three who were in the secret passed their time pleasantly enough, whenever they had an opportunity of talking on this adventure, without any of the others being witnesses of what they said.

CHAP. XXI.

The prisoners expectations raised: a terrible disappointment: some of the chief carried to prince Menzikoff's palace: their usage there. Horatio set at liberty and the occasion.

OUR captives had soon after a new matter of rejoicing: a Polander in the service of Muscovy, who had been taken prisoner by the Swedes, and was discharged and sent home, with a great number of others, by the unparallel'd generosity of Charles XII. was one of the guards who now did duty in the prison. It was often his turn to bring them their poor allowance of provision; and having some pity for their condition, as well as gratitude for a people who had used him and his companions in a different manner, told them, that they might be of good heart, for, said he, you will soon be set at liberty: — our emperor has enough to do to keep his ground in Ukrainia: Charles is as victorious as ever: — the prince of the Cosaques,[114] one of the bravest men on earth, next to himself, has entered into an alliance with him: — king Stanislaus is sending him succours from Poland: — a powerful reinforcement is coming to him from Lithuania; and when these armies are joined, as I believe they already are, nothing can withstand them: — you will hear the Swedish march beat from these prison walls, — and perhaps see your present conquerors change places with you; and, to confirm the truth of what I say, continued he, I can further assure you that the czar, before I left the camp, was in the utmost confusion: — his council, as well as army, were at a stand, and he had twice made overtures of peace, and been refused.

This was an intelligence which might well be transporting to the king of Sweden's officers: — the thoughts of seeing him enter Petersburg a conqueror, — of once more embracing their old friends and companions, and of triumphing over those who had so cruelly abused the power the chance of war had put into their hands, made them all, in their turns, hug and bless the kind informer: — they also asked him several questions concerning the generals; and each being more particular concerning those they had the greatest interest in, received from this honest soldier all the satisfaction they could desire.

---

[114] *Cosaques*: from the Turkish 'kazak', or outlaw, the term is often used to refer to Turkic and Slavic horsemen from Southern Russia. In 1709, some sided with the Swedes, while others were 'pummeled into submission and alliance' by Tsar Peter. (See Cathal J. Nolan, *Wars of the Age of Louis XIV 1650–1715: An Encyclopedia of Global Warfare and Civilization* (Westport, CT: Greenwood Press, 2008), p. 93.)

As couriers were continually arriving from the army, there passed few days without hearing some farther confirmation of their most sanguine expectations; but at length the guard being again changed, they lost all further intelligence, and were for several months without being able to hear any thing of what passed. They doubted not, however, but as things were in so good a disposition, every day brought them nearer to the completion of their wishes; and it was this pleasing prospect which alleviated their misfortunes, and enabled them to sustain chearfully those hardships which, almost ever since the withdrawing of Edella's bounty, they had laboured under. — Mattakesa, in the beginning of her amours with Mullern, had indeed made him some presents, which he shared with his companions; but either the natural inconstancy of her temper making her grow weary of this intrigue for the sake of another, or her circumstances not allowing her to continue such Donations, she soon grew sparing of them, and at length totally desisted her visits at the prison.

As, ever since the compassionate Edella had procured them to be removed from the dungeon, they had enjoyed the privilege of walking on the leads, and going up to the round tower, which being of a very great height, not only overlooked the town, but the country round for a considerable distance, they frequently made use of this indulgence, at first for no other purpose than to have the benefit of the open air, but now in hope of seeing their beloved prince at the head of a victorious army approaching to give them liberty and relief. — But, alas! how terrible a reverse of their high-raised expectations had inconstant fortune in store for them. — One day as they were sitting together, discoursing on the usual topics with which they entertained each other, and endeavoured to beguile the tedious time, they heard a confused noise as of some sudden tumult. — Tho' they had now been above a year in Russia, none of them could speak the language well enough to be understood, so could receive no information from the guard, even should they have proved good-natured enough to be willing to satisfy their curiosity, so they all run hastily up to the round tower, whence they easily perceived the town in great confusion, and the people running in such crowds, that in the hurry many were trampled to death in endeavouring to pass the gates: — at a distance they perceived standards waving in the air, but could not yet distinguish what arms they bore. — A certain shivering and palpitation, the natural consequence of suspence, ran thro' all their nerves, divided as they were at this sight, between hope and fear; but when it drew more near, — when, instead of Swedish colours they beheld those of Russia; — when, in the place where they expected to see their gallant king coming to restore them once more to freedom, they saw the implacable czar enter in triumph, followed by those heroes, the least of whom had lately made him tremble, now in chains, and exposed to the ribald mirth and derision of the gaping crowd, they lost at once their fortitude, and even all sense of expressing their grief at this misfortune:

— the shock of it was so violent, it even took away the power of feeling it, and they remained for some moments rather like statues carved out by mortal art, than real men created by God, and animated with living souls. A general groan was the first mark they gave of any sensibility of this dreadful stroke of fate; but when recruited spirits once more gave utterance to words, how terrible were their exclamations! Some of them, in the extravagance of despair, said things relating to fate and destiny, which, on a less occasion, could have little merited forgiveness.

Unable either to remove from the place, or view distinctly what their eyes were fixed upon, they stayed till the whole cavalcade was passed, then went down and threw themselves upon the floor, where their ears were deafen'd by the noise of guns, loud huzza's, and other testimonies of popular rejoicings, both within and without the prison walls. — What have we now to expect? cried one, — endless slavery: — chains, infamy, lasting as our lives, replied another. Then let us dye, added a third. Right, said his companion fiercely; — the glory of Sweden is lost! — Let us disappoint the barbarians, these Russian monsters, of the pleasure of insulting us on our country's fall.

In this romantic and distracted manner did they in vain endeavour to discharge their breasts of the load of anguish each sustained. — Their misfortune was not of a nature to be alleviated by words; — it was too mighty for expression; and the more they spoke, the more they had yet to say. — For three whole days they refused the wretched sustenance brought to them; neither did the least slumber ever close their eyelids by night: on the fourth the keeper of the prison came, and told them they must depart. — They endeavoured not to inform themselves how or where they were to be disposed of; in their present condition all places were alike to them, so followed him, without speaking, down stairs, at the bottom of which they found a strong guard of thirty soldiers, who having chained them in a link, like slaves going to be sold at the market, conducted them to a very stately palace adjoining that belonging to the czar.

They were but eight in number, out of fifty-five who had been taken prisoners at the time Horatio was, and were thrown altogether in the dungeon, the others having perished thro' cold and the noysomeness of the place, before Edella had procured them a more easy situation; but these eight that survived were all officers, and most of them men of distinguished birth as well as valour, tho' their long imprisonment, scanty food, and more than all, the grief they at present laboured under, made them look rather like ghosts, than men chose out of thousands to fight always near the king of Sweden's person in every hazardous attempt.

They were placed in a stately gallery, and there left, while the officer, who commanded the party that came with them, went into an inner room, but soon after returned, and another person with him; on which, the first of this unhappy string was loosed from his companions, and a signal made to him to enter a door, which was opened for him, and immediately closed again.

For about half an hour there was a profound silence: our prisoners kept it thro' astonishment; and the others, it is to be supposed, had orders for doing so. — At the end of that time the door was again opened, and the chain which fastened the second Swede to the others, was untied, and he, in like manner as the former, bid to go in. — In some time after, the same ceremony was observed to a third; — then to a fourth, fifth, sixth, and seventh: — Horatio chanced to be the last, who, tho' alarmed to a very great degree at the thoughts of what fate might have been inflicted on his companions, went fearless in, more curious to know the meaning of the mysterious proceeding, than anxious for what might befal him.

He no sooner passed the door, than he found himself in a spacious chamber richly adorned, at the upper end of which sat a man, leaning his head upon his arm in a thoughtful posture. — Horatio immediately knew him to be prince Menzikoff, whom he had seen during a short truce between the czar and king Charles of Sweden, when both their armies were in Lithuania. There were no other persons present than one who had the aspect of a jew, and as it proved was so, that stood near the prince's chair, and a soldier who kept the door.

Horatio was bid to approach, and when he did so, — you are called hither, said the jew in the Swedish language, to answer to such questions as shall be asked you, concerning a conspiracy carried on between you and your fellow-prisoners with the enemies of Russia. Horatio understood the language perfectly well, having conversed so long with Swedes, but never could attain to a perfect pronounciation of it, so replied in French, that he knew the prince could speak French, and he would therefore answer to any interrogatories his highness should be pleased to make without the help of an interpreter.

Are you not then a Swede? said the prince. Horatio then told him that he was not, but came into the service of the king of Sweden merely thro' his love of arms.

On these words Menzikoff dismissed the jew, and looked earnestly on him; wan and pale as he was grown thro' his long confinement, and the many hardships he had sustained, this prince found something in him that attracted his admiration. — Methinks, said he, since glory was your aim, you might as well have hoped to acquire it under the banners of our invincible emperor.

Alas! my lord, replied Horatio with a sigh, that title, till very lately, was given to the king of Sweden, and, I believe, whatever fate has attended that truly great prince, those who had the honour to be distinguished by him, will never be suspected either of cowardice or baseness. — It was by brave and open means our king taught his soldiers the way to victory, not by mean subterfuges and little plots: — I cannot therefore conceive for what reason I am brought hither to be examined on any score that has the appearance of a conspiracy.

Yes, replied the prince fiercely, you and your fellow-prisoners have endeavoured to insinuate yourselves into the favour of persons whom you imagined entrusted with the secrets of the government: — being prisoners of war, you formed contrivances for your escape, and attempted to inveigle others to accompany your flight.

That every tittle of this accusation is false, my lord, cried Horatio, there needs no more than the improbability of it to prove. — Indeed the cruel usage we sustained, might have justified an attempt to free ourselves, yet did such a design never enter our heads: — we were so far from making use of any stratagems for that purpose, that we never made the least overture to any of the guards, who were the only persons we were allowed to converse with.

How! said the prince interrupting him, were not your privileges enlarged by the interposition of a lady? — Did not she make you considerable allowances out of her own purse, and frequently visit you to receive your thanks? — And were you not emboldened by these favours to urge her to reveal what secrets were in her knowledge, and even to assist you in your escape? — You doubtless imagined you could prevail on her also to go with you: — part of this, continued he, she has herself confessed: — it will therefore be in vain for you to deny it: — if you ingenuously reveal those particulars she has omitted, you may hope to find favour; but if you obstinately persist, as your companions have done, in attempting to impose upon me, you must expect to share the same fate immediately.

In speaking these words he made a sign to the soldier, who throwing open a large folding door, discovered a rack on which one of the Swedish officers was tied, and the others stood near bound, and in the hands of the executioner.

This sight so amazed Horatio, that he had not the power of speaking one word; — till Mullern, who happened to be the person that was fastened on the rack, cried out to him, — Be not lost in consternation, Horatio, said he; are we not in the hands of Muscovites, from whom nothing that is human can be expected? — rather prepare yourself to disappoint their cruelty, by bravely suffering all they dare inflict.

Hold then, said Horatio, even Muscovites would chuse to have some pretence for what they do; and sure the first favourite and generalissimo of a prince, who boasts an inclination to civilize his barbarous subjects, will not, without any cause, torture those whom chance alone has put into his power, and who have never done him any personal injury. — By heaven, pursued he, turning to the prince, we are all innocent of any part of those crimes laid to our charge: — time, perhaps, if our declarations are ineffectual, will convince your highness we are so, and you will then regret the injustice you have done us.

You are all in one story, cried the prince, but I am well assured of the main point: — the particulars is all I want to be informed of: — but since I am compelled to speak more plain, which of you is it for whose sake you all received such instances of Edella's bounty? — Whoever tells me that, even tho' it be the person himself, shall have both pardon and liberty.

Impossible is it to express the astonishment every one was in at this demand: five of them had not the least notion of what it meant; but Mullern, Horatio, and that friend to whom he had shewn the letter of Mattakesa, had some conjecture of the truth, and presently imagined that lady had been the incendiary to kindle the flame of jealousy in the prince's breast. The affair, however, was of so nice a nature, that they knew not how to vindicate Edella without making her seem more guilty, so contented themselves with joining with the others, in protesting they knew of no one among them who could boast of receiving any greater favours from her than his fellows, but that what she did was instigated merely by compassion, since she had never seen, or knew any of them who were, till after she had moved the governor in their behalf: — they acknowledged she had been so good as to come sometimes to the prison, in order to see if those she entrusted with her bounty had been faithful in the delivery of it; but that she never made the least difference between them, and never had conversation with any one of them that was not in the presence of them all. Mullern could not forbear adding to this, that he doubted not but the persons who had incensed his highness into groundless surmises, were also the same who had hindered her, by some false insinuations or other, from continuing the allowance her charity allowed them, and for the want of which they had since been near perishing.

Prince Menzikoff listened attentively to what each said, and with no less earnestness fixed his eyes on the face of every one as they spoke. — Finding they had done, he was about giving some orders on their account, when the keeper of the prison came hastily into the room, and having entreated pardon for the interruption, presented a letter to the prince, directed for brigadier Mullern, and brought, he said, just after the prisoners were carried out.

Menzikoff commended his zeal in receiving and bringing it to him, as it might possibly serve to give some light into the affair he was examining.

Having perused it, he demanded which of them was named Mullern? I am, replied the brave Swede; and neither fear, nor am ashamed of any thing under that name.

Hear then what is wrote to you by a lady, resumed the prince, with a countenance more serene than he had worn since their being brought before him, and presently read with a very audible voice these words:

> THAT you have been so long without seeing me, my dear
> Mullern, or hearing from me, is not owing to any decrease in my
> affection, but to the necessity of my affairs: — if you have any
> regard for me remaining, I conjure you, if ever you are asked any

questions concerning the frequent visits I have made you, to say I was sent by Edella, and that I was no more than her emissary in the assistance you received from me: — add also, that you have reason to believe her charity was excited by her liking one of your company: mention who you think fit; but I believe Horatio, as the youngest and most handsome, will be the most likely to gain credit to what you say. — Depend upon it, that if you execute this commission artfully, I will recompence it by procuring your liberty: — nor need you have any scruples concerning it, for no person will be prejudiced by it, and the reputation preserved of

Yours,

MATTAKESA.

I suppose, said the prince, as soon as he had done reading, turning to Horatio, you are the person mentioned in the letter? Tho' I neither desire nor deserve the epithets given me there my lord, replied he, yet I will not deny but I am called Horatio.

Well, resumed the prince with a half smile, I am so well pleased with the conviction this letter has given me, that I shall retain no resentment against the malicious author of it.

He then ordered Mullern to be taken from the rack, which had never been strained; nor had he any intention, as he now assured him, to put him to the torture, but only to intimidate him, being resolved to make use of every method he could think of for the full discovery of every thing relating to the behaviour of his beloved Edella. — The other gentlemen had also their fetters taken off, and the prince asked pardon of them severally for the injury he had done them; then made them sit down and partake of a handsome collation at that table, before which they had so lately stood as delinquents at a bar.

The Russians are excessive in their carouses,[115] and prince Menzikoff being now in an admirable good humour, made them drink very freely: — to be the more obliging to his guests, he began the king of Sweden's health in a bumper of brandy, protesting at the same time, that tho' an enemy to his master, he loved and venerated the hero: Horatio on this ventured to enquire in what condition his majesty was; to which the prince replied, that being greatly wounded, he was obliged to leave the field, and, it was believed, had took the road towards the dominions of the grand signior,[116] some of the Russian troops having pursued him as far as the Borysthenes, where, by the incredible valour of a few that attended him, they had been beat back.

The Swedish officers knew it must be bad indeed when their king was

---

[115] *carouses*: drinking bouts.
[116] *the dominions of the grand signior*: the Ottoman empire.

compelled to fly; and this renewed in them a melancholy, which it was not in the power of liquor, or the present civilities of the prince to dissipate: they also learned that the generals Renchild, Slipenbock, Hamilton, Hoorn, Leuenhaup, and Stackelburg,[117] with the prince of Wirtemburg,[118] count Piper, and the flower of the whole army, were prisoners at Muscow.

The misfortune of these great men would have been very afflicting to those who heard it, could any thing have given addition to what they knew before. — Prince Menzikoff was sensible of what they felt, and to alleviate their grief, assured them, that he would take upon him to give them all their liberty, without even exacting a promise from them never more to draw their swords against the czar, in case the king of Sweden should ever be able to take the field again.

So generous a proceeding both merited and received their utmost acknowledgements: but he put an end to the serious demonstrations they were about to make him of their gratitude, by saying, — I pay you no more than I owe you: — I have wronged you: — this is but part of the retaliation I ought to make: — besides, added he laughing, Mattakesa promised Mullern his freedom; and as she has done me the good office, tho' undesignedly, of revealing to me her own treachery, I can do no less than assist her in fulfilling her covenant.

To prove how much he was in earnest, he called his secretary, and ordered him to make out their passports with all expedition, that they might be ready to depart next morning; after which he made them repose themselves in his palace the remainder of the night; which being in a manner vastly different from what they had been accustomed to of a long time, indeed ever since their quitting Alranstadt, they did not fail to do so, notwithstanding the discontent of their minds.

Prince Menzikoff, being now convinced of the fidelity of Edella, passed into her apartment, where the reconciliation between them took up so much time, that it was near noon next day before he appeared: his new guests had not quitted their chambers much sooner; but after reproaching themselves for having been so tardy, went altogether to take leave of the prince, and accept the passports he had been so good to order. As they were got ready, he gave them immediately into their hands, and told them, they were at liberty to quit Petersburg that moment, if they pleased; or if they had any curiosity to take a view of that city, they might gratify it, and begin their journey the next morning. As it was now so late in the day, they accepted his highness's offer, and

---

[117] *Slipenbock ... Stackelburg*: Swedish officers Wolmar Anton von Schlippenbach, (1658–1739); Hugo Johan, baron Hamilton (166?-1748); Adam Ludwig, count Lewenhaupt, (1659–1719); and Berndt Otto Stackelburg (1662–1734), Swedish general. The same list of prisoners is given by Defoe and Adlerfelt, but not Voltaire.

[118] *the prince of Wirtemburg*: Prince Maximilian Emanuel of Württemberg (1689–1709), Colonel of Swedish dragoons.

walked out to see a place which had excited so much admiration in the world, since from a wild waste, in ten years time, a spacious and most beautiful city had arose in the midst of war,[119] and proved the genius of a founder greater in civil than in military arts, tho' it must be owned he was indefatigable in the study of both.

The officers of the king of Sweden were entertained with the same elegance and good humour they had been the night before; and as they were now resolved to quit the city extremely early, the prince took leave of them that night, and in doing so put a purse of gold into the hands of every one to defray the expences of their travelling. This behaviour obliged them to own there was a possibility of sowing the seeds of humanity in Muscovy, and that the czar had made some progress in influencing those about him with the manners he had himself learned in the politer courts.

---

[119] *from a wild waste, in ten years time, a spacious and most beautiful city had arose in the midst of war*: St Petersburg was not created from nothing, although the idea that it had been became part of the myth of the city's foundation. The city began as a fortified port, and contained a Swedish fort and several small settlements. Tsar Peter only gave his full attention to developing the city some years after the Battle of Poltava. (See P. Keenan, *St Petersburg and the Russian Court, 1703–1761* (Basingstoke: Palgrave Macmillan, 2013), pp. 14–15.)

CHAP. XXII.

What befel Louisa in the monastery: the stratagem she put in practice to get out of it: her travels thro' Italy, and arrival in Paris.

BUT while Horatio was thus experiencing the vicissitudes of fortune, his beautiful sister suffered little less from the caprice of that fickle goddess. Placed as she was, one would have thought she had been secure from all the temptations, hurries, and dangers of the world, and that nothing but the death or inconstancy of monsieur du Plessis could have again involved her in them. These, indeed, were the sole evils she trembled at, and which she chiefly prayed might not befal her. Yet as it often happens that those disasters which seem most remote are nearest to us, so did the disappointments she was ordained to suffer, rise from a quarter she had the least reason to apprehend.

The abbess and nuns, with whom she was, being all Italians, she set herself to attain to the knowledge of their language, in which she soon became a very great proficient, and capable of entertaining them, and being entertained by them in the most agreeable manner. — The sweetness of her temper, as well as her good sense, rendering her always ambitious of acquiring the affection of those she conversed with, she had the secret to ingratiate herself not only to the youngest nuns, but also to the elder and most austere, that the one were never pleased but when in her company, and the others proposed her as an example of piety and sweetness to the rest.

She had a very pretty genius to poetry, and great skill in music, both which talents she now exercised in such works as suited the place and company she was in. — The hymns and anthems she composed were not only the admiration of that convent, but also of several others to whom they were shewn, and she was spoke of as a prodigy of wit and devotion.

In fine, her behaviour rendered her extremely dear to the superior; and that affection, joined to a spiritual pride, which those sanctified devotees are seldom wholly free from, made her very desirous of retaining her always in the convent: — she was therefore continually preaching up to her the uncertainty of those felicities which are to be found in the world, and magnifying that happy serenity which a total renunciation from it afforded; — nay, sometimes went so far, as to insinuate there was scarce a possibility for any one encumbered with the cares, and surrounded with the temptations of a public life, to have those dispositions which are requisite to enjoy the blessings of futurity. — Ah my dear daughter, would she say frequently to her, how much should I rejoice to find in you a desire to forgo all the transitory fleeting pleasures of the world, and devote yourself entirely to heaven! — what raptures would not your innocent soul partake, when wholly devoid of all thought of sensual objects! you would be, even while on earth, a companion for angels and blessed spirits, and borne on the wings of heavenly contemplation, have your dwelling above, and be worshipped as a saint below.

All the old nuns, and some of the young ones, assisted their abbess in endeavouring to prevail on Louisa to take the veil; but all that they said made no impression on her mind, not but she had more real piety than perhaps some of those who made so great a shew of it, but she was of a different way of thinking; and tho' she knew the world had its temptations, having experienced them in a very great degree, yet she was convinced within herself, that a person of virtuous principles might be no less innocent out of a cloyster than in one. — She saw also among this sisterhood a great deal of envy to each other, and perceived easily that the flaming zeal professed among them, was in some hypocrisy, and enthusiasm in others; so that had she had no prepossession in favour of du Plessis, or any engagement with him, the life of a nun was what she never should have made choice of.

She kept her sentiments on this occasion entirely to herself however, and made no shew of any repugnance to do as they would have her; but whenever they became strenuous in their pressures, told them, she doubted not but such a life as they described must be very angelic, but having already disposed of her vows, it was not in her power to withdraw them, nor would heaven accept so violated an offering. This, they told her, was only a suggestion of some evil spirit, and that all engagements to an earthly object, both might and ought to be dispensed with for a divine vocation. The arguments they made use of for this purpose were artful enough to have imposed on some minds, but Louisa had too much penetration not to see thro' them; and being unwilling to disoblige them by shewing that she did so, made use, in her turn, of evasions which the circumstances of the case rendered very excusable. But fully persuaded in their minds that it was solely her engagements with du Plessis that rendered her so refractory to their desires, they resolved to break it off, if possible, and to that end now intercepted his letters; two of which giving an account that he was very much wounded and unable to travel, they renewed their pressures, in order to prevail on her to take the habit before he should be in a condition to come to Bolognia.

These sollicitations, however, had no other effect but to embitter the satisfaction she would otherwise have enjoyed during her stay among them; — the time of which began now to seem tedious, and she impatiently longed for the end of the campaign, which she expected would return her dear du Plessis to her, and she should be removed from a place where dissimulation, a vice she detested, was in a manner necessary. She had received several letters from him before the abbess took it into her head to stop them, each more endearing than the former; and the last had flattered her with the hope of seeing him in a very short time.

Days, weeks, and months passed over, after an assurance so pleasing to her wishes, without any confirmation of the repeated vows he had made; and receiving from him no account of the reasons that delayed him, she began to reproach herself for having placed too much confidence in him: — the more time elapsed, the more cause she had to doubt his sincerity, and believe her misfortune real: — in fine, it was near half a year that she languished under a vain expectation of seeing, or at least hearing from him. — Sometimes she imagined a new object had deprived her of his heart; but when she called to mind the many proofs he had given her of the most unparalleled generosity that ever was, she could not think that if he even ceased to love her, he could be capable of leaving her in so cruel a suspence: — no, said she to herself, he would have let me know I had no more to depend on from him: — paper cannot blush, and as he is out of reach of my upbraidings, he would certainly have acquainted me with my fate, confessed the inconstancy of his sex, and exerted that wit, of which he has sufficient, to have excused his change: — I will not therefore injure a man whom I have found so truly noble: — death, perhaps, has deprived me of him; the unrelenting sword makes no distinction between the worthy and the unworthy; — and the brave, the virtuous du Plessis, may have fallen a victim with the most vulgar.

These apprehensions had no sooner gained ground in her imagination, than she became the most disconsolate creature in the world. The abbess took advantage of her melancholy, as knowing the occasion of it, and began to represent, in the strongest terms, the instability of all human expectations: — you may easily see, my dear child, said she, that monsieur either no longer lives, or ceases to live for you: — young men are wavering, every new object attracts their wishes; — they are impatient for a time, but soon grow cool; — absence renders them forgetful of their vows and promises; — there is no real dependance on them; — fly therefore to that divine love which never can deceive you; — give yourself up to heaven, and you will soon be enabled to despise the fickle hopes of earth.

Instead of saying any thing to comfort her, in this manner was she continually persecuted; and tho' it is impossible for any one to have less inclination to a monastic life than she had, yet the depression of her spirits, the firm belief she now should never see du Plessis more, the misfortune of her circumstances, joined to the artifices they made use of, and the repeated offers of accepting her without the usual sum paid on such occasions, might possibly at last have prevailed on her. — She was half convinced in her mind that it was the only asylum left to shield her from the wants and insults of the world; and the more she reflected on the changes, the perplexities, and vexations of different kinds, the few years she yet had lived presented her with, the more reason she found to acquiesce with the persuasions of the abbess. But heaven would not suffer the deceit practised on her to be crowned with success, and discovered it to her timely enough to prevent her from giving too much way to that despair, which alone could have prevailed with her to yield to their importunities.

There was among the sisterhood a young lady called donna Leonora, who being one of many daughters of a family, more eminent for birth than riches, was compelled, as too many are, to become a nun, in order to prevent her marrying beneath her father's dignity. She had taken a great liking to Louisa from the moment she came into the convent, and a farther acquaintance ripened it into a sincere friendship. Tho' secluded from the world, the austere air of a monastery had no effect upon her, she still retained her former vivacity; and it was only in the conversations these two had together whenever they could separate from the others, that Louisa found any cordial to revive her now almost sinking spirits.

One day as she was ruminating on her melancholy affairs, this young nun came hastily into her chamber, and with a countenance that, before she spoke, denoted she had something very extraordinary to acquaint her with, — dear sister, cried she, I bring you the most surprizing news, but such as will be my ruin if you take the least notice of receiving it from me; and perhaps your own, if you seem to be acquainted with it at all.

It is not to be doubted but Louisa gave her all the assurances she could desire of an inviolable secrecy; after which, know then, resumed this sweet-condition'd lady, that your lover, monsieur du Plessis, is not only living, but as faithful as your soul can wish, or as you once believed: — the cruelty of the abbess, and some of the sisterhood in the plot with her, have concealed the letters he has sent to you, in order to persuade you to become a nun: — I tremble to think of their hypocrisy and deceit: — but what, continued she, is not to be expected from bigotry and enthusiasm! — To increase the number of devotees they scruple nothing, and vainly imagine the means is sanctioned by the end.

Little is it in the power of words to express the astonishment Louisa was in to hear her speak in this manner; but as she had no room to doubt her sincerity, only asked by what means she had attained the knowledge of what the persons concerned, no doubt, intended to keep as much a secret as possible; on which the other satisfied her curiosity in these terms:

To confess the truth to you, said she, I stole this afternoon into the chapel, in order to read a little book brought me the other day by one of my friends; as it treated on a subject not allowable in a convent, I thought that the most proper place to entertain myself with it; and was sitting down in one of the confessionals, when hearing the little door open from the gallery, I saw the abbess and sister Clara, who, you know, is her favourite and confidant, come in together, and as soon as they were entered, shut the door after them. I cannot say I had any curiosity to hear their discourse; but fearing to be suspected by them in my amusement, and not knowing what excuse to make for being there, if I were seen, I slid down, and lay close to the bottom of the confessional. They happened to place themselves very near me; and the abbess taking a letter out of her pocket, bad Clara read it, and tell her the substance of it as well as she could. I found it was in French, by some words which she was obliged to repeat over and over, before, not perfectly understanding the language, she could be able to find a proper interpretation of. The abbess, who has a little smattering of it herself, sometimes helped her out, and between them both I soon found it came from monsieur du Plessis, and contained the most tender and compassionate complaint of your unkindness in not answering his letter; — that the symptoms he had of approaching death were not half so severe to him as your refusing him a consolation he stood so much in need of; — that if you found him unworthy of your love, he was certainly so of your compassion; and concluded with the most earnest entreaty, you would suffer him to continue no longer in a suspence more cruel than a thousand deaths could be.

Oh heaven! cried Louisa, bursting into tears, how ungrateful must he think me, and how can I return, as he deserves, so unexampled a constancy, after such seeming proofs of my infidelity! — Cruel, cruel, treacherous abbess! pursued she; Is this the fruits of all your boasted sanctity! — This the return to the confidence the generous du Plessis reposed in you! — This your love and friendship to me! — Does heaven, to increase the number of its votaries, require you to be false, perfidious, and injurious to the world!

She was proceeding in giving vent to the anguish of her soul in exclamations such as these; but Leonora begged she would moderate her grief, and for her sake, as much as possible, conceal the reasons she had for resentment. Louisa again promised she would do her utmost to keep them from thinking she even suspected they had played her false; — then cried, But tell me, my dear Leonora, were they not a little moved at the tender melancholy which, I perceive, ran thro' this Epistle? Alas, my dear, replied the other, they have long since forgot those soft emotions which make us simpathize in the woes of love: — inflexible by the rigid rules of this place, and more by their own age, they rather looked with horror than pity on a tender inclination: — they had a long conversation together, the result of which was to spare nothing that might either persuade, or if that failed, compel you to take the order.

It is not in their power to do the latter, interrupted Louisa, and this discovery of their baseness, more than ever, confirms me in the resolution never to consent.

You know not what is in their power, said Leonora; they may make pretences for confining you here, which, as they are under no jurisdiction but the church, the church will allow justifiable: — indeed, Louisa, continued she, I should be loth to see you have recourse to force to get out of their hands, which would only occasion you ill treatment: — to whom, alas, can you complain! — you are a stranger in this country, without any one friend to espouse your cause: — were even du Plessis here in person, I know not, as they have taken it into their heads to keep you here, if all he could urge, either to the pope or the consistory, would have any weight to oblige them to relinquish you. A convent is the securest prison in the world; and whenever any one comes into it, who by any particular endowment promises to be an ornament to the order, cannot, without great difficulty, disentangle themselves from the snares laid for them. — It is for this reason I have feared for you ever since your entrance; for tho' I should rejoice in so agreeable a companion, I know too well the miseries of an enforced attachment to wish you to be partaker of it.

Louisa found too much reason in what she said, to doubt the misery of her condition; — she knew the power of the church in all these countries where the roman catholic religion is established, more especially in those places under the papal jurisdiction, and saw no way to avoid what was now more terrible to her than ever. These reflections threw her into such agonies, that Leonora had much ado to keep her from falling into fits: — she conjured her again and again, never to betray what she had entrusted her with; assuring her, that if it were so much as guessed at, she should be exposed to the worst treatment, and punished as an enemy to the order of which she was a member. Louisa as often assured her that nothing should either tempt or provoke her to abuse that generous friendship she had testified for her; but as she was not able to command her countenance, tho' she could her words, she resolved to pretend herself indisposed and keep her bed, that she might be the less observed, or the change in her should seem rather the effects of ill health than any secret discontent.

It was no sooner mentioned in the convent that she was out of order, than the abbess herself, as well as the whole sisterhood, came to her chamber, and shewed the greatest concern: the tender care they took of her would have made her think herself infinitely obliged to them, and perhaps gone a great way in engaging her continuance among them, had she not been apprized of their falshood in a point so little to be forgiven.

So great an enemy was she to all deceit herself, that it was difficult for her to return the civilities they treated her with, as they might seem to deserve; but whatever omissions she was guilty of in this particular, were imputed to her disposition; and the whole convent continued to be extremely assiduous to recover her.

During the time of her feigned illness, her thoughts were always employed on the means of getting away. Whenever Leonora and she were together, a hundred contrivances were formed, which seemed alike equally impracticable; but at length they hit upon one which had a promising aspect, and Louisa, after some scruples, resolved to make trial of. It was this:

As hypocrisy was made use of to detain her, hypocrisy was the only method by which she could hope to get her liberty: — pretending, therefore, to be all at once restored to her former health, she sent to entreat the abbess, and some other of the most zealous of the sisterhood to come into her chamber, where, as soon as they entered, they found her on her knees before the picture of the virgin, and seeming in an extacy of devotion: Yes, holy virgin, cried she, as if too much taken up to see who entered, I will obey your commands; — I will devote myself entirely to thee; — I will follow where thou callest me: thou, who hast restored me, shalt have the first fruits of my strength: — and oh that Lorretto[120] were at a greater distance, — to the utmost extent of land and sea would I go to seek thee! — In uttering these ejaculations she prostrated herself on the floor; — then rising again, as transported in a manner out of herself, — I come, — I come, cried she; — still do I hear thy heavenly voice!

In this fit of enthusiasm did she remain for above half an hour, and so well acted her part, that the abbess, who would not offer to interrupt her, believed it real, and was in little less agitation of spirit than Louisa pretended to be.

At length seeming to come to herself, she turned towards the company, as tho' she but just then discovered they were in the room; Oh, madam, said she to the abbess, how highly favoured I have been this blessed night! — The virgin has herself appeared to me, whether in a vision, or to my waking eyes, I cannot well determine; but sure I have been in such extacies, have felt such divine raptures, as no words can express!

Oh my dear daughter! cried the abbess, how my soul kindles to behold this change in thee! — but tell me what said the holy virgin!

She bad me wait on her at Lorretto, answered she, and gave me hopes of doing something wonderful in my favour: — I will therefore, with your permission, undertake a pilgrimage, and at her shrine expiate the offences of my past life in tears of true contrition, and then return a pure and spotless partaker of the happiness you enjoy in an uninterrupted course of devotion: — oh! continued she, exalting her voice, how do I detest and despise the vanities and follies of the world! — how hate myself for having been too much attached to them, and so long been cold and negligent of my only happiness!

The abbess, and, after her, all the nuns that were present, embraced Louisa,

---

[120] *Lorretto*: Loreto, near Ancona on the Adriatic coast of Italy. The Holy House at Loreto was believed to be the same house at Nazareth where the Virgin Mary was born and Jesus Christ was conceived. A host of angels were said to have transported the house first to Dalmatia and then to Loreto. It has been a site of Marian pilgrimage since the fourteenth century.

— praised to the skies this miraculous conversion, as they termed it, and spared nothing to confirm the pious resolution she had taken.

In fine, they consented to her pilgrimage with a satisfaction equal to what she felt in undertaking it, — they not in the least doubting but she would return to them as soon as she had fulfilled her devotions, and flattering themselves that the report of this miracle would do the greatest honour to their convent that it could possibly receive; and she, delighted with the thoughts of being at liberty to enquire after her dear du Plessis, and being freed from a dissimulation so irksome to her nature.

Her pilgrim's habit, and a great crucifix to carry between her hands, with another at her girdle, and all the formalities of that garb being prepared, she set forward with the prayers and benedictions of the whole sisterhood, who told her, that they should be impatient till they saw her again, and expected great things from her at her return, which, in reality, they all did, except Leonora, who laughed heartily at the deception she had put upon them, and whispered in her ear as she gave her the last embrace, that she wished her a happy meeting with that saint she went in search of.

To prevent all suspicion of her intention she left her cloaths, and every thing she had brought into the convent, under the care of the abbess, saying, that, at her return, she would have them disposed of, and the money given to the poor: but, unknown to any one except Leonora, she quilted some pieces of gold and valuable trinkets into her under garment, as not doubting but she should have occasion for much more than, in effect, she was mistress of.

When on her journey, the pleasure she felt at seeing herself out of the walls of the monastery, was very much abated by the uncertainty how she should proceed, or where direct her way: and indeed, let any one figure to themselves the condition she was in, and they will rather wonder she had courage to go on, than that she was sometimes daunted even to despair. — A young creature of little more than eighteen years old, — wholly unacquainted with fatigue, — delicate in her frame, — wandering alone on foot in the midst of a strange country, — ignorant of the road, or had she been acquainted with it, as a loss where to go to get any intelligence of what she sought, and even doubtful if the person she ran such risques to hear of, yet were in the world or not. The letter Leonora had informed her of, gave no account, at least that she could learn, either where he was, or whether there were any hopes of his recovery from that illness it mentioned; she had therefore everything to dread, and little, very little to hope: yet did she not repent her having quitted the convent; and the desire of getting still farther from it, made her prosecute her journey with greater strength and vigour than could have been expected: her pilgrim's habit was not only a defence against any insults from persons she met on the road, but also attracted the respect, and engaged the civilities of every one. — As that country abounds with religious houses, she was not only lodged and fed without any expence, but received a piece of money at each of them she went to, so that her little stock, instead of being diminished, was considerably increased when she came to Lorretto, for thither, not to be false in every thing, she went; and being truly sorry for the hypocrisy which a sad necessity alone could have made her guilty of, paid her devotion with a sincere heart, tho' free from that enthusiasm and bigotry which is too much practised in convents.

From Lorretto she crossed the country to Florence, every one being ready to direct a holy pilgrim on her way, and assist her with all things necessary. As she went very easy journeys, never exceeding four or five miles a day, she easily supported the fatigue; and had she been certain at last of seeing du Plessis, it would have been rather a pleasure to her; but her mind suffered much more than her body during this pilgrimage, which she continued in the same manner she had begun till she reached Leghorn, where a ship lying at anchor, and expecting to sail in a few days for Marseilles, she agreed to give a small matter for her passage, the sea-faring-men not paying altogether so much regard to her habit, as the land ones had done.

No ill accident intervening, the vessel came safely into her desired port, and Louisa now found herself in the native country of the only person who engrossed her thoughts: as she had heard him say he was of Paris, she supposed that the most likely place to hear news of him, but was in some debate within herself whether she should continue to wear her pilgrim's habit, or provide herself with other cloaths at Marseilles. She was weary of this mendicant way of travelling, and could have been glad to have exchanged it for one more agreeable to the manner in which she had been accustomed; but then, when she considered how great a protection the appearance she made, had been from all those insults, to which a person of her sex and age must otherwise infallibly have been exposed in travelling alone, she resolved not to throw it off till she came to the place where she intended to take up her abode, at least for some time. Young as she was, she had well weighed what course to take in case du Plessis should either be dead, or, by some accident, removed where she could hear nothing more of him; and all countries and parts being now equal to her, as she must then be reduced once more to get her bread by her labour, she doubted not but to find encouragement for her industry as well in Paris as elsewhere.

With this resolution, therefore, after laying one night at Marseilles, she proceeded on her way in the same fashion as she had done ever since she left Bolognia, and in about six weeks got safely to that great and opulent city, where she took up her lodging at a hotel, extremely fatigued, as it is easy to believe, having never even for one day ceased walking, but while she was on board the ship which brought her to Marseilles, for the space of eight months; a thing almost incredible, and what perhaps no woman, but herself, would have had courage to undertake, or resolution to perform, but was, in her circumstances, infinitely the most safe and expedient that prudence could suggest.

CHAP. XXIII.

Shews by what means Louisa came to the knowledge of her parents, with other occurrences.

THE first thing she did on her arrival, was to send for proper persons to equip her in a manner that she might once more appear herself, resolving that till she could do so, not to be seen in the streets.

While these things were preparing, she sent a person, whom the people of the house recommended to her, to the palace of the prince of Conti, not doubting but that some of the gentlemen belonging to his highness might give some intelligence where monsieur du Plessis was to be found; but the messenger returned without any other information, than that they knew him very well, but could give no directions in what part he was at present, he not having been seen in Paris for a long time.

It is hard to say whether she most rejoiced or grieved at this account: she imagined that had he been dead they would not have been ignorant of it, therefore concluded him living to her infinite satisfaction; but then his absenting himself from the capital of the kingdom, and from the presence of a prince who had so much loved him, filled her with an adequate disquiet, as believing some very ill accident must have been the occasion: — she dispatched the same person afterwards to all the public places she heard gentlemen frequented, but met not with the least success in her enquiries. It would prolong this narrative to a tedious length, should I attempt any description of what she felt in this situation, or the reflections she made on the odd circumstances of her life: — the greatness of her spirit, and the most perfect resignation to the divine will, however, made her support even this last and severest trial with fortitude and patience; and as soon as she had put herself into a convenient neat garb, but plain, befitting her condition, she went out with a design to take a private lodging, where she might live more cheaply than she could at the hotel, till providence should throw some person in the way that might recommend her either to work, or to teach young ladies music.

She was wandering thro' several of the streets of Paris, without being able, as yet, to find such a chamber as she wanted, when a great shower of rain happening to fall, she stood up under the porch of a large house for shelter till it should be over, which it was not for a considerable time; and the street being very dirty, she returned to the hotel, intending to renew her search the next day: she had not been come in above half an hour, before the man of the house told her that a servant, in a very rich livery, who, he perceived, had followed her, and had asked many questions concerning her, was now returned, and desired to speak with her.

As du Plessis was ever in her thoughts, a sudden rush of joy overflowed her heart, which seemed to her the presage of seeing him, tho' how he should imagine she was in Paris was a mystery: — but she gave herself not much time for reflection, before she ordered the man to be admitted.

The manner of his approaching her was very respectful; but the message he had to deliver seemed of a contrary nature. — After having asked if her name was Louisa, and she answering that it was, I come, madam, said he, from a gentleman who saw you stand just now at the gate of a house in the Fauxbourg St Germains, he commands me to tell you, that he has something of moment to acquaint you with, and desires you will permit me to call a chair, and attend you to his house, where he is impatient to receive you.

What, indeed, could Louisa think of a person who should send for her in this manner? — all the late transport she was in, was immediately converted into disdain and vexation at being taken, as she had all the reason in the world to suppose, for one of those common creatures who prostitute their charms for bread. —

Tell your master, said she, that by whatever accident he has learned my name, he is wholly ignorant of the character of the person he has sent you to: — that I am an entire stranger at Paris, and he must have mistaken me for some other, who, perhaps, I may have the misfortune to resemble, and may be also called as I am; — at least I am willing to think so, as the only excuse can be made for offering this insult: — but go, continued she, with that pride which is natural to affronted virtue; — go, and convince him of his error; — and let me hear no more of it.

It was in vain he assured her that his master was a person of the strictest honour, and that he was not unknown to her. All he could say had not the least effect unless to enflame her more; when, after asking his name, the fellow told her he was forbid to reveal it, but that he was confident she would not deny having been acquainted with him once she saw him.

I shall neither own the one, cried she, nor consent to the other; then bid him a second time be gone, with an air which shewed she was not to be prevailed upon to listen to his arguments.

This man had no sooner left her than she fell into a deep study, from which a sudden thought made her immediately start: — the count de Bellfleur came into her head; and she was certain it could be no other than that cruel persecutor of her virtue, that her ill fate had once more thrown in her way. — As she knew very well, by what he had done, that he was of a disposition to scruple nothing for the attainment of his wishes, she trembled for the consequences of his discovering where she was. — The only way she could think on to avoid the dangers she might be exposed to on his account, was to draw up a petition to the prince of Conti, acquainting him that she was the person who was near suffering so much from the ill designs he had on her at Padua, when so generously rescued by monsieur du Plessis, and to entreat his highness's protection against any attempts he might be base enough to make.

She was just sitting down, in order to form a remonstrance of this kind, when a chariot and six stopping at the door, she was informed the gentleman who sent to her was come in person, and that they knew it was the same by the livery. — Louisa run hastily to the window and saw a person alight, whom, by the bulk and stature, she knew could not be the count she so much dreaded, this having much the advantage of the other in both. Somewhat reassured by this sight, she ordered the master of the hotel to desire him to walk into a parlour, and let him know she would attend him there.

As she saw not the face of this visitor, she could not be certain whether it were not some of those she had been acquainted with at Venice, who having, by accident, seen her at Paris, might, according to the freedom of the French nation, take the liberty of visiting her; — but whoever it were, or on what score soever brought, she thought it best to receive him in a place where, in case of any ill usage, she might readily have assistance.

The master of the hotel perceiving her scruples, readily did as he was ordered, and Louisa having desired that he, or some of his people, would be within call, went down to receive this unknown guest, tho' not without emotions, which at that moment she knew not how to account for.

But soon after she was seized with infinitely greater, when, entering the parlour, she found it was no other than Dorilaus who had given her this anxiety. — Surprize at the sight of a person whom, of all the world, she could least have expected in that place, made her at first start back; and conscious shame for having, as she thought, so ill rewarded his goodness, mixed with a certain awe which she had for no other person but himself, occasioned such a trembling, as rendered her unable either to retire or move forward to salute him, as she otherwise would have done.

He saw the confusion she was in, and willing to give it an immediate relief, ran to her, and taking her in his arms, — My dear, dear child, said he, am I so happy to see thee once more! — Oh! sir, returned she, disengaging herself from his embrace, and falling at his feet! — How can I look upon you after having flown from your protection, and given you such cause to think me the most ungrateful creature in the world!

It was heaven, answered he, that inspired you with that abhorrence of my offers, which, had you accepted, we must both have been eternally undone! — You are my daughter, Louisa! pursued he, my own natural daughter! — Rise then, and take a father's blessing.

All that can be said of astonishment would be far short of what she felt at these words: — the happiness seemed so great she could not think it real, tho' uttered from a mouth she knew unaccustomed to deceit: — a hundred times, without giving him leave to satisfy her doubts, did she cry out, My father! — my father! — my real father! — How can it be! — Is there a possibility that Louisa owes her being to Dorilaus!

Yes, my Louisa, answered he, and flatter myself, by what I have observed of your disposition, you have done nothing, since our parting, that might prevent my glorying in being the parent of such a child.

The hurry of spirit she was in, prevented her from taking notice of these last words, or at least from making any answer to them, and she still continued crying out, — Dorilaus, my father! — Good heaven! may I believe I am so blessed! — Who then is my mother! — Wherefore have I been so long ignorant of what I was! — And how is the joyful secret at last revealed!

All these things you shall be fully informed of, answered he; in the mean time be satisfied I do not deceive you, and am indeed your father: transported to find my long lost child, whom I myself knew not was so till I believed her gone for ever; — a thousand times I have wished both you and Horatio were my children, but little suspected you were so, till after his too eager ambition deprived me of him, and my mistaken love drove you to seek a refuge among strangers.

Tears of joy and tenderness now bedewed the faces of both father and daughter: — silence for some moments succeeded the late acclamations; but Dorilaus at length finding her fully convinced she was as happy as he said she was, and entirely freed from all those apprehensions which had occasioned her flying from him, told her he was settled in Paris; that he lived just opposite to the house where she had stood up on account of the shower, and happening to be at one of his windows, immediately knew her; that he sent a servant after her, who had enquired how long she had been arrived, and in what manner she came; that he had sent for her with no other intent than to make trial how she would resent it, and was transported to find her answer such as he hoped and had expected from her: he added, that he had all the anxiety of a father to hear by what means she had been supported, and the motive which induced her to travel in the habit of a pilgrim, as the master had informed his servant; but that he would defer his satisfaction till she should be in a place more becoming his daughter.

On concluding these words he called for the master of the hotel, and having defrayed what little expences she had been at since her coming there, took her by the hand and led her to his chariot, which soon brought them to a magnificent house, and furnished in a manner answerable to the birth and fortune of the owner.

Louisa had all this time seemed like one in a dream: — she had ever loved Dorilaus with a filial affection; and to find herself really his daughter, to be snatched at once from all those cares which attend penury, when accompanied with virtue, and an abhorrence of entering into measures inconsistent with the strictest honour, to be relieved from every want, and in a station which commanded respect and homage, was such a surcharge of felicity, that she was less able to support than all the fatigues she had gone thro': — surprize and joy made her appear more dull and stupid than she had ever been in her whole life before; and Dorilaus was obliged to repeat all he had said over and over again, to bring her into her usual composedness, and enable her to give him the satisfaction he required.

But as soon as she had, by degrees, recollected herself, she modestly related all that had happened to her from the time she left him; — the methods by which she endeavoured to earn her bread; — the insults she was exposed to at Mrs C — — ge's; — the way she came acquainted with Melanthe; — the kindness shewn her by that lady; — their travels together; — the base stratagems made use of by count de Bellfleur to ruin her with that lady; — the honourable passion monsieur du Plessis had professed for her; — the seasonable assistance he had given her, in that imminent danger she was in from the count's unlawful designs upon her; — his placing her afterwards in the monastery; — the treachery of the abbess; — the artifice she had been obliged to make use of to get out of the nunnery; — her pilgrimage; — in fine, concealed no part of her adventures, only that which related to the passion she had for du Plessis, which she endeavoured, as much as she could, to disguise, under the names of gratitude for the obligations he had conferred upon her, and admiration of his virtue, so different from what she had found in others who had addressed her.

Dorilaus, however, easily perceived the tenderness with which she was agitated on the account of that young gentleman, but he would not excite her blushes by taking any notice of it, especially as he found nothing to condemn in it, and had observed, throughout the course of her whole narrative, she had behaved on other occasions with a discretion far above her years, he was far from wronging her, by suspecting she had swerved from it in this.

But when he heard the vast journey she had come on foot, he was in the utmost amazement at her fortitude, and told her he was resolved to keep her pilgrim's habit as a relique, to preserve to after-ages the memory of an adventure, which had really something more marvellous in it than many set down as miracles.

And now having fully gratified his own curiosity in all he wanted to be informed of, he thought proper to ease the impatience she was in to know the history of her birth, and on what occasion it had been so long concealed, which he did in these or the like words:

CHAP. XXIV.

The history of Dorilaus and Matilda, with other circumstances very important to Louisa.

YOU know, said he, that I am descended of one of the most illustrious families in England, tho', by some imprudencies on the one side, and injustice on the other, my claim was set aside, and I deprived of that title which my ancestors for a long succession of years had enjoyed, so that the estate I am in possession of, was derived to me in right of my mother, who was an heiress. It is indeed sufficient to have given me a pretence to any lady I should have made choice on, and to provide for what children I might have had by her: but the pride of blood being not abated in me by being cut off from my birthright, inspired me with an unconquerable aversion to marriage, since I could not bequeath to my posterity that dignity I ought to have enjoyed myself: — I resolved therefore to live single, and that the misfortune of my family should dye with myself.

In my younger years I went to travel, as well for improvement, as to alleviate that discontent which was occasioned by the sight of another in possession of what I thought was my due. — Having made the tour of Europe, I took France again in my way home: — the gallantry and good breeding of these people very much attached me to them; but what chiefly engaged my continuance here much longer than I had done in any other part, was an acquaintance I had made with a lady called Matilda: she was of a very good family in England, was sent to a monastery merely for the sake of well-grounding her in a religion, the free exercise of which is not allowed at home, and to seclude her from settling her affections on any other than the person she was destined to by the will of her parents, and to whom she had been contracted in her infancy: — she was extremely young, and beautiful as an angel; and the knowledge she was pre-engaged, could not hinder me from loving her, any more than the declarations I made in her hearing against marriage, could the grateful returns she was pleased to make me: — in fine, the mutual inclination we had for each other, as it rendered us deaf to all suggestions but that of gratifying it, so it also inspired us with ingenuity to surmount all the difficulties that were between our wishes and the end of them. — Tho' a pensioner in a monastery, and very closely observed, by the help of a confidant she frequently got out, and many nights we passed together; — till some business relating to my estate at length calling me away, we were obliged to part, which we could not do without testifying a great deal of concern on both sides: — mine was truly sincere at that time, and I have reason to believe her's was no less so; but absence easily wears out the impressions of youth: as I never expected to see her any more, I endeavoured not to preserve a remembrance which would only have given me disquiet, and, to confess the truth, soon forgot both the pleasure and the pain I had experienced in this, as well as some other little sallies of my unthinking youth.

Many years passed over without my ever hearing any thing of her; and it was some months after I received your letter from Aix-la-Chapelle, that the post brought me one from Ireland: having no correspondence in that country, I was a little surprized, but much more when I opened it and found it contained these words:

To DORILAUS.

SIR,

THIS comes to make a request, which I know not if the acquaintance we had together in the early part of both our lives, would be sufficient to apologize for the trouble you must take in complying with it: — permit me therefore to acquaint you, that I have long laboured under an indisposition which my physicians assure me is incurable, and under which I must inevitably sink in a short time; but whatever they say, I know it is impossible for me to leave the world without imparting to you a secret wholly improper to be entrusted in a letter, but it is of the utmost importance to those concerned in it, of whom yourself is the principal: — be assured it regards your honour, your conscience, your justice, as well as the eternal peace of her who conjures you, with the utmost earnestness, to come immediately on the receipt of this to the castle of M——e, in the north of Ireland, where, if you arrive time enough, you will be surprized, tho' I flatter myself not disagreeably so, with the unravelling a most mysterious Event.

Yours, once known by the name of MATILDA,

now

M——E.

I will not repeat to you, my dear Louisa, continued Dorilaus, the strange perplexity of ideas that run thro' my mind after having read this letter: — I was very far from guessing at the real motive of this invitation; which, however, as I once had a regard for that lady, I soon determined to obey; and having left the care of my house to a relation of mine by the mother's side, I went directly for Ireland; but when I came there, was a little embarrassed in my mind what excuse I should make to her husband for my visit. — Before I ventured to the castle, I made a thorough enquiry after the character of this young lady, and in what manner she lived with her lord. Never did I hear a person more universally spoke well of: — the poor adored her charity, affability, and condescending sweetness of disposition: — the rich admired her wit, her virtue, and good breeding: — her beauty, tho' allowed inferior to few of her sex, was the least qualification that seemed deserving praise: — to add to all this, they told me she was a pattern of conjugal affection, and the best of mothers to a numerous race of Children; — that her lord had all the value he ought to have for so amiable a wife, and that no wedded pair ever lived together in greater harmony; and it was with the utmost concern, whoever I spoke to on this affair concluded what they related of her with saying, that so excellent an example of all that was valuable in womankind would shortly be taken from them; — that she had long, with an unexampled patience, lingered under a severe illness which every day threatened dissolution.

These accounts made me hesitate no farther: — I went boldly to the castle, asked to speak with the lord M——e, who received me with a politeness befitting his quality: I told him that my curiosity of seeing foreign countries had brought me to Ireland, and being in my tour thro' those parts, I took the liberty of calling at his seat, having formerly had the honour of being known to his lady when at her father's house, and whom I now heard, to my great concern, was indisposed, otherwise should have been glad to pay my respects to her. The nobleman answered, with tears in his eyes, that she was indeed in a condition such as gave no hope of her recovery, but that she sometimes saw company, tho' obliged to receive them in bed, having lost the use of her limbs, and would perhaps be glad of the visit of a person she had known so long.

On this I told him my name, which he immediately sent in; and her woman not long after came from her to let me know she would admit me. My lord went in with me; and to countenance what I said, I accosted her with the freedom of a person who had been acquainted when children, spoke of her father as a person as of a gentleman who had favoured me with his good-will, tho', in reality, I had never seen him in my life, but remembered well enough what she had mentioned to me concerning him, and some others of her family, to talk as if I had been intimate among them. I could perceive she was very well pleased with the method I had taken of introducing myself; and, to prevent any suspicion that I had any other business with her than to pay my compliments, made my visit very short that day, not doubting but she would of herself contrive some means of entertaining me without witnesses, as she easily found her lord had desired I would make the castle my home while I stayed in that part of the country.

I was not deceived; the next morning having been told her lord was engaged with his steward, she sent for me, and making some pretence for getting rid of her woman, she plucked a paper from under her pillow, and putting it into my hand, — in that, said she, you will find the secret I mentioned in my letter; — suspect not the veracity of it, I conjure you, nor love the unfortunate Horatio and Louisa less for their being mine.

I cannot express the confusion I was in, continued Dorilaus, at her mentioning you and your brother, but I had no opportunity of asking any questions: — her woman that instant returned, after which I stayed but a short time, being impatient to examine the contents, which, as near as I can remember, were to this purpose:

> YOU were scarce out of France before I discovered our amour had produced such consequences as, had my too fond passion given me leave to think of, I never should have hazarded: — I will not repeat the distraction I was in; — you may easily judge of it: — I communicated the misfortune to my nurse, who you know I told you went from England with me, and has often brought you messages from the convent: — the faithful creature did her utmost to console me for an evil which was without a remedy: — to complete my confusion, my father commanded me home; my lord M——e was returned from his travels: — we were both of an age to marry; and it was resolved, by our parents, no longer to defer the completion of an affair long before agreed upon. — I was ready to lay violent hands on myself, since there seemed no way to conceal my shame; but my good nurse having set all her wits to work for me, found out an expedient which served me, when I could think of nothing for myself. — She bid me be of comfort; that she thought being sent for home was the luckiest thing that could have happened, since nothing could be so bad as to have my pregnancy discovered in the convent, as it infallibly must have been had I stayed a very little time longer: she also assured me she would contrive it so, as to keep the thing a secret from all the world. — I found afterwards she did not deceive me by vain promises. — We left Paris, according to my father's order, and came by easy journeys, befitting my condition, to Calais, and embarked on board the packet for Dover; but then, instead of taking coach for London, hired a chariot, and went cross the country to a little village, where a kinswoman of my nurse's lived. — With these people I remained till Horatio and Louisa came into the world: — I could have nursed them at that place, but I feared some discovery thro' the miscarriage of letters, which often happens, and which could not have been avoided being sent on such occasions; — so we contrived together that

my good confidant and adviser should carry them to your house, and commit the care of them to you, who, equal with myself, had a right to it: — she found means, by bribing a man that worked under your gardener, to convey them where I afterwards heard you found and received them as I could wish, and becoming the generosity of your nature. — I then took coach for London, pretending, at my arrival, that I had been delayed by sickness, and to excuse my nurse's absence, said she had caught the fever of me; — so no farther enquiry was made, and I soon after was married to a man whose worth is well deserving of a better wife, tho' I have endeavoured to attone for my unknown transgression by every act of duty in my power: — nurse stayed long enough in your part of the world to be able to bring me an account how the children were disposed of. — That I never gave you an account they were your own, was occasioned by two reasons, first, the danger of entrusting such things by the post, my nurse soon after dying; and secondly, because, as I was a wife, I thought it unbecoming of me to remind you of a passage I was willing to forget myself. — A long sickness has put other thoughts into my head, and inspired me with a tenderness for those unhappy babes, which the shame of being their mother hitherto deprived them of. — I hear, with pleasure, that you are not married, and are therefore at full liberty to make some provision for them, if they are yet living, that may alleviate the misfortune of their birth. Farewell; if I obtain this first and last request, I shall dye well satisfied.

P.S. Burn this paper, I conjure you, the moment you have read it; but lay the contents of it up in your heart never to be forgotten.

I now no longer wondered, pursued Dorilaus, at that impulse I had to love you; — I found it the simpathy of nature, and adored the divine power. — After having well fixed in my mind all the particulars of this amazing secret, I performed her injunction and committed it to the flames: I had opportunity enough to inform her in what manner Horatio had disposed of himself, and let her know you were gone with a lady on her travels: I concealed indeed the motive, fearing to give her any occasion of reproaching herself for having so long concealed what my ignorance of might have involved us all in guilt and ruin.

I stayed some few days at the castle, and then took my leave: she said many tender things at parting concerning you, and seemed well satisfied with the assurances I gave her of making the same provision for you, as I must have done had the ceremony of the church obliged me to it. This seemed indeed the only thing for which she lived, and, I was informed, died in a few days later.

At my return to England I renewed my endeavours to discover where you were, but could hear nothing since you wrote from Aix-la-Chapelle, and was equally troubled that I had received no letters from your brother. — I doubted not but he had fallen in the battle, and mourned him as lost; — till an old servant perceiving the melancholy I was in, acquainted me that several letters had been left at my house by the post during my absence, but that the kinsman I had left to take care of my affairs had secreted them, jealous, no doubt, of the fondness I have expressed for him. — This so much enraged me, when on examination I had too much reason to be assured of this treachery, that I turned my whole estate into ready money, and resolved to quit England for ever, and pass my life here, this being a country I always loved, and had many reasons to dislike my own.

Here I soon heard news of my Horatio, and such as filled me with a pleasure, which wanted nothing of being complete but the presence of my dear Louisa to partake of it.

Dorilaus then went on, and acquainted her with the particulars of Horatio's story, as he had learned it from the baron de Palfoy, with whom he now was very intimate; but as the reader is sufficiently informed of those transactions, it would be needless to repeat them; so I shall only say that Dorilaus arrived in France in a short time after Horatio had left it to enter into the service of the king of Sweden, and had wrote that letter, inserted in the eighteenth chapter, in order to engage that young warrior to return, some little time before his meeting with Louisa.

Nothing was now wanting to the contentment of this tender father but the presence of Horatio, which he was every day expecting, when, instead of himself, those letters from him arrived, which contained his resolution of remaining with Charles XII. till the conquests he was in pursuit of should be accomplished.

This was some matter of affliction to Dorilaus, tho' in his heart he could not but approve those principles of honour which detained him. — Neither the baron de Palfoy, nor Charlotta herself, could say he could well have acted otherwise, and used their utmost endeavours to comfort a father in his anxieties for the safety of so valuable a son.

Louisa was also very much troubled at being disappointed in her hope of embracing a brother whom she had ever dearly loved, and was now more precious to her than ever, by the proofs she had heard he had given of his courage and his virtue; but she had another secret and more poignant grief that preyed upon her soul, and could scarce receive any addition from ought beside: — she had been near two months in Paris, yet could hear nothing of monsieur du Plessis, but that, by the death of his father, a large estate had devolved upon him, which he had never come to claim, or had been at Paris for about eighteen months, so that she had all the reason in the world to believe he was no more. This threw her into a melancholy, which was so much the more severe as she endeavoured to conceal it: — she made use of all her efforts to support the loss of a person she so much loved, and who proved himself so deserving of that love: — she represented to herself that being relieved from all the snares and miseries of an indigent life, raised from an obscurity which had given her many bitter pangs, to a station equal to her wishes, and under the care of the most indulgent and best of fathers, she ought not to repine, but bless the bounty of heaven, who had bestowed on her so many blessings, and with-held only one she could have asked. — These, I say, were the dictates of reason and religion; but the tender passion was not always to be silenced by them, and whenever she was alone, the tears, in spight of herself, would flow, and she, without even knowing she did so, cry out, Oh du Plessis, wherefore do I live since thou art dead!

Among the many acquaintance she soon contracted at Paris, there was none she so much esteemed, both on the account of her own merit, and the regard she had for Horatio, as mademoiselle de Palfoy. In this young lady's society did she find more charms for her grief than in that of any other; and the other truly loving her, not only because she found nothing more worthy of being loved, but because she was the sister of Horatio, they were very seldom asunder.

Louisa was one day at the baron's, enjoying that satisfaction which the conversation of his beautiful daughter never failed to afford, when word was brought that madam, the countess d'Espargnes, was come to visit her. — Mademoiselle Charlotta ran to receive her with a great deal of joy, she being a lady she very much regarded, and who she had not seen of a long time.

She immediately returned, leading a lady in deep mourning, who seemed not to be above five-and-twenty, was extremely handsome, and had beside something in her air that attached Louisa at first sight. Mademoiselle Charlotta presented her to the countess, saying at the same time, see, madam, the only rival you have in my esteem.

You do well to give me one, replied the countess, who looks as if she would make me love her as well as you, and so I should be even with you. With these words she opened her arms to embrace Louisa, who returned the compliment with equal politeness.

When they were seated, mademoiselle Charlotta began to express the pleasure she had in seeing her in Paris; on which the countess told her, that the affair she came upon was so disagreeable, that nothing but the happiness of enjoying her company, while she stayed, could attone for it. You know, my dear, continued madam d'Espargnes, I was always an enemy to any thing that had the face of business, yet am I now, against my will, involved in it by as odd an adventure as perhaps you ever heard.

Charlotta testifying some desire to be informed of what nature, the other immediately satisfied her curiosity in this manner:

You know, said she, that on the late death of my father, his estate devolved on my brother, an officer in those troops in Italy commanded by the prince of Conti: — some wounds, which were looked upon as extremely dangerous, obliged him, when the campaign was over, to continue in his winter quarters; — on which he sent to monsieur the count to take possession in his name; this was done; but an intricate affair relating to certain sums lodged in a person's hand, and to be brought before the parliament of Paris, could not be decided without the presence either of him or myself, who had been witness of the transaction. — I was extremely loth to take so long a journey, being then in very ill health; and hearing he was recovered, delayed it, as we then expected him in person: — I sent a special messenger, however, in order to hasten his return; — but instead of complying with my desires, I received a letter from him, acquainting me that a business of more moment to him than any thing in my power to guess at, required his presence in another place, and insisted, by all the tenderness which had ever been between us, that I would take on myself the management of this affair: — to enable me the better to do it, he sent me a deed of trust to act as I should find it most expedient.

As he did not let me into the secret of what motives detained him at so critical a juncture, I was at first very much surprized; but on asking some questions of the messenger I had sent to him, I soon discovered what it was. He told me that on his arrival, he found my brother had left his quarters and was gone to Bolognia, on which he followed and overtook him there; — that he appeared in the utmost discontent, and was just preparing to proceed to Leghorn, but did not mention to him any more than he did in his letter to me, what inducement he had to this journey: — his servant, however, told him privately, that the mystery was this: — That being passionately in love with a young English lady, whom he had placed in a monastery at Bolognia, and expected to find there at his return, she had in his absence departed, without having acquainted him with her design; and that supposing she was gone for England, and unable to live without her, his intention was to take shipping for that country, and make use of his utmost efforts to find her out.

I must confess, pursued the beautiful countess, this piece of quixotism very much vexed me: — I thought his friends in France deserved more from him than to be neglected for one who fled from him, and who, as the man said, he knew not whether he should be able ever to see again. I resolved, however, to comply with his desires, and came immediately to Paris; but heaven has shewed me how little it approves his giving me this unnecessary trouble, for this morning I received a letter from him, that meeting with robbers in his way, they had taken from him all his money and bills of exchange, besides wounding him in several places, so that he cannot proceed on his journey till his hurts, which it seems are not dangerous, are cured, and he has fresh remittances from hence.

With what emotions the heart of Louisa was agitated during the latter part of this little narrative, a sensible reader may easily conceive: from the first mention of Bolognia, where there was no other English pensioner than herself, she knew it must be no other than her dear du Plessis who was in search for her abroad, while she was vainly hoping to find him at home: — every circumstance rendered this belief more certain; and surprize and joy worked so strongly in her, that fearing the effects would be visible, she rose up and withdrew to a window. Mademoiselle Charlotta, who knew she could not be capable of such an act of unpoliteness, without being compelled to it, asked if she were not well: — on which Louisa entreated pardon, but owned a sudden faintness had come over her spirits, so that she was obliged to be rude in order to prevent being troublesome.

As mademoiselle Charlotta knew nothing of her story, she had no farther thought about it than of some little qualm, which frequently happens when ladies are too closely laced, and she seeming perfectly recovered from, the conversation was renewed on the same subject it had turned upon before this interruption; and the name of monsieur du Plessis being often mentioned, confirmed Louisa, if before she could have had the least remains of doubt, that it was her lover who, neglectful of his own affairs, and the remonstrances of his expecting friends, was about to range in search of one who, he imagined, was ungrateful both to his love and friendship.

After having listened, with the utmost attention, to all the countess said of him, and other matters becoming the topic of discourse, she took her leave, in order to reflect alone what she ought to do in this affair.

She debated not long within herself before she resolved to write to him, and prevent the unprofitable journey he was about to take; and having heard, by madam d'Espargnes, the name of the village where he was obliged to wait, both for the recovery of his wounds and for remittances for his expences, she wrote to him in the following terms:

To monsieur DU PLESSIS.

I SHOULD ill return the proofs I have received of your generous disinterested friendship, to delay one moment that I had it in my power, in endeavouring to convince you that it was a quite contrary motive than ingratitude to you, that carried me from Bolognia: — but the story is too long for the compass of a letter; when you know it, you will, perhaps, own this action, whatever you may now think of it, merits more, than any thing I could have done, your approbation: — this seeming riddle will be easily expounded, if, on the recovery of your wounds, you repair immediately to Paris, where you will find

Your much obliged

LOUISA.

Having finished this little billet, a scruple rose in her head, that being now under the care of a father, she ought not to do any thing of this nature without his permission: — she had already told him how greatly she had been indebted to du Plessis for his honourable passion, but had not mentioned the least tittle of the tender impressions it had made on her; and she so lately knew him to be her father, that she was ashamed to make him the confidant of an affair of this nature; but then, when she considered the quality of du Plessis, which she was now confirmed of, and the sense Dorilaus testified he had of his behaviour to her while he believed her so infinitely his inferior, made her resolve to strain her modesty so far as to inform him all.

She began by relating her accidental meeting with madam, the countess d'Espargnes, and the conversation that passed at mademoiselle de Palfoy's, and then, not without immoderate blushes, shewed him what she had wrote, and beseeched him to let her know whether it would be consistent with a virgin's modesty, and also agreeable to his pleasure, that she gave this demonstration of her gratitude for the favours she had received from this young gentleman.

Dorilaus was charmed with this proof of her duty and respect, and told her, that he was so far from disapproving what she had wrote, that had she omitted it, or said less than she did, he should have looked upon her as unworthy of so perfect a passion as that which monsieur du Plessis had on all occasions testified for her: — that, in his opinion, she owed him more than she could ever pay; and that it should be his endeavour to shew he had not placed his affections on the daughter of one who knew not how to set a just value on merit such as his: — he made her also add a postscript to the letter, to give a direction in what part of Paris he might find her on his arrival; but Louisa would by no means give the least hint of the alteration in her circumstances, not that she wanted any farther proofs of his sincerity, but that she reserved the pleasure of so agreeable a surprize to their meeting. This letter was dispatched immediately, to the end he might receive it, at least, as soon as that from his sister with the expected remittances.

CHAP. XXV.

Monsieur du Plessis arrives at Paris: his reception from Dorilaus and Louisa: the marriage of these lovers agreed upon.

THE innocent pleasure Louisa felt in picturing to herself the extacy which du Plessis would be in at the receipt of her letter, was not a flattering idea: — to know she was in Paris, where, in all probability, she had come to seek him, and to have the intelligence of it from herself, had all the effect on him that the most raptured fancy can invent.

His orders to madam d'Espargnes being punctually complied with, his bills of exchange also came soon after to hand; and the little hurts he had received from the robbers, as well as those of his mind, being perfectly healed, he set out with a lover's expedition, and arrived in Paris to the pleasing surprize of a sister who tenderly loved him, and expected not this satisfaction of a long time.

He took but one night's repose before he enquired concerning Dorilaus, and was told that he was a person of quality from England; but, on some disgust he had received in his native country, was come to settle in France. As Louisa was extremely admired, they told him also that he had a very beautiful daughter, of whom he was extremely fond. This last information gave not a little ease to the mind of him who heard it, and dissipated those apprehensions which the high character they gave of Dorilaus had, in spite of himself, excited in him: he now imagined that as they were English, his Louisa might possibly have been acquainted with the daughter of this gentleman in their own country, and meeting her at Paris, might have put herself under her protection.

Full of those impatiencies which are inseparable from a sincere passion, he borrowed his sister's chariot, and went to the Fauxbourg St Germains; and being told one of the best houses in the place was that of Dorilaus, he asked for mademoiselle Louisa, on which he was desired to alight, and shewed into a handsome parlour while a servant went in to inform her: after this, he was ushered upstairs into a room, the furniture of which shewed the elegance of the owner's taste; but accustomed to every thing that was great and magnificent, the gilded scenes, the rich tapestry, the pictures, had no effect on him, till casting his eyes on one that hung over the chimney, he found the exact resemblance of the dear object never absent from his heart. — It was indeed the picture of Louisa, which her father, soon after her arrival, had caused to be drawn by one of the best painters at that time in Paris. This sight gave him a double pleasure, because it, in some measure, anticipated that of the original, and also convinced him she was not indifferent to the person she was with.

He was fixed in contemplation on this delightful copy, when the original appeared in all the advantages that jewels and rich dress could give her. — Tho' he loved her only for herself, and nothing could add to the sincere respect his heart had always paid her, yet to see her so different from what he expected, filled him with a surprize and a kind of enforced awe, which hindered him from giving that loose to his transports, which, after so long an absence, might have been very excusable; — and he could only say — my dear adorable Louisa, am I so blessed to see you once more! — She met his embrace half way, and replied, monsieur du Plessis, heaven has given me all I had to wish in restoring to me so faithful a friend; — but come, continued she, permit me to lead you to a father, who longs to embrace the protector of his daughter's innocence. Your father, madam! cried he; yes, answered she; in seeking a lover at Paris I found a father; Dorilaus is my father: — I have acquainted him with all the particulars of our story, and I believe, the sincere affection I have for you will not be less pleasing for receiving his sanction to it.

With these words she took his hand and led him, all astonishment, into an inner room where Dorilaus was sitting, who rose to meet him with the greatest politeness, and which shewed that to be master of, it was not necessary to be born in France; and on Louisa's acquainting him with the name of the person she presented, embraced him with the tenderness of a father, and made him such obliging and affectionate compliments, as confirmed to the transported du Plessis the character had been given of him.

After the utmost testimonies of respect on both sides, Dorilaus told his daughter she ought to make her excuses to monsieur for having eloped from the monastery where he had been so good to place her, which, said he, I think you can do in no better a manner than by telling the truth; and as I am already sufficiently acquainted with the whole, will leave you to relate it, while I dispatch a little business that at present calls me hence. He went out of the room in speaking this, and Louisa had a more full opportunity of informing her lover of all she had suffered since their parting, till this happy change in her fortune, than she could have had in the presence of her father, tho' no stranger to her inmost thoughts on this occasion.

The pleasing story of her pilgrimage rehearsed, how did the charmed du Plessis pity and applaud, by turns, her sufferings and fortitude! — How exclaim against the treachery of the abbess, and those of the nuns who were in confederacy with her! But his curiosity satisfied in this point, another rose instantly in his mind, that being the daughter of such a person as Dorilaus, wherefore she had made so great a secret of it, and what reason had occasioned her being on the terms she was with Melanthe. He no sooner expressed his wonder on these heads, than, having before her father's permission to do so, she resolved to leave him in no suspence on any score relating to her affairs.

Tho', said she blushing, I cannot reveal the history of my birth without laying open the errors of those to whom I owe my being, yet I shall not think the sacrifice too great to recompence the obligations you have laid upon me; and proceeded to acquaint him with every thing relating to her parents, as well as to herself, from the first moment she was found in the garden of Dorilaus.

It is not to be doubted but that he listened to the story with the utmost attention, in which he found such matters of admiration, that he could not forbear interrupting her, by crying, Oh heaven! oh providence! how mysterious are thy ways! — How, in thy disposal of things, dost thou force us to acknowledge thy divine power and wisdom!

He was also extremely pleased to find she was the sister of Horatio, whom he had often been in company with both at the baron de la Valiere's and at St Germains, and had admired for the many extraordinary qualities he discovered in him: this led them into a conversation concerning that young gentleman, and the misfortunes which some late news-paper gave an account were beginning to fall upon the king of Sweden; after that, renewing the subject of their mutual affection, and du Plessis running over the particulars of their acquaintance in Italy, Louisa asked whether the count de Bellfleur had ever testified any remorse for the injury he would have offered her, and in what manner they lived together in the army? To which monsieur du Plessis replied, that the authority of the prince had prevented him from attempting any open acts of violence; but that by his manner of behaviour it was easy to see he had not forgiven the disappointment; and he verily believed wanted only a convenient opportunity to revenge it: but, continued he, whatever his designs were, heaven put a stop to the execution of them; for, in the first skirmish that happened between us and the forces of prince Eugene, this once gay, gallant courtier, had his head taken off by a cannon ball.

The gentle Louisa could not forbear expressing some concern for the sudden fate of this bad man, greatly as she had been affronted by him; but when she reflected that the same accident might have befallen her dear du Plessis, she was all dissolved in tears.

They were in this tender communication when Dorilaus returned leading the countess d'Espargnes in one hand, and mademoiselle de Palfoy in the other. Monsieur du Plessis was surprized to meet his sister in a place where he knew not she was acquainted, and she no less to find him there. The occasion of it was this:

Dorilaus, when he left the lovers together, went directly to the baron de Palfoy's, and related to him and to mademoiselle the whole history of monsieur du Plessis and Louisa; on which they contriv'd to make a pleasant scene, by engaging the countess d'Espargnes to go with them to Dorilaus's without letting her know on what account. — The event answered their wishes; madam d'Espargnes rallied her brother on finding him alone with so beautiful a young lady; and mademoiselle Charlotta, for his inconstancy to his mistress at Bolognia: but when the riddle was solved, and the countess came to know that the lady left in the monastery and Louisa were the same, she no longer condemned an attachment which before had given her so much pain.

Mademoiselle Charlotta chid her for the reserve she had maintained to her in this affair, especially, said she, as you were obliged to the conversation you had with madam d'Espargnes in my apartment, that you received any intelligence of monsieur du Plessis, or knew how to direct your commands to him to return.

That, madam, is an obligation lies wholly on me, said monsieur du Plessis; and I believe I shall find it very difficult to requite it, any more than I shall to deserve my sister's pardon, for so industriously endeavouring to conceal from her the secret of my passion and its object.

Louisa told the ladies that she now hoped they would excuse the disorder she had been in at the countess's discourse, since they knew the motive: — a good deal of pleasantry passed between this agreeable company; and as they were in the midst of it, the baron de Palfoy, who had been hindered from accompanying Dorilaus, when he conducted the ladies, now joined them; and tho' he was considerably older than any there, was no less entertaining and good-humoured than the youngest.

Dorilaus had privately ordered a very magnificent collation, which being served up, Louisa did the honours of the table with so good a grace, that madam d'Espargnes was charmed with her, and took an opportunity of asking Dorilaus when she might hope the happiness of calling so amiable a lady by the name of sister. Du Plessis thanked her for the interest she took in his affairs; and the baron de Palfoy added, that as the lovers wanted no farther proofs how worthy they were of each other, he would join in solliciting for a completion of their happiness. To which Dorilaus replied, that he was too well satisfied with his daughter's conduct, not to leave her entirely at her own disposal; and as to what related to fortune and settlement, he should be ready to enter into such articles as, he believed, monsieur du Plessis would have no reason to complain of.

The passionate lover at these words cried out, that it was Louisa's self alone he was ambitious of possessing; nor had either that lady or her father any room to look on what he said as a mere compliment, because his love had long since waved all the seeming disproportion between them.

In fine, not only at this time, but every day, almost every hour, was Louisa, as it now depended wholly on herself, importuned by her lover and the countess d'Espargnes to render his happiness complete; but she still delayed it, desiring to hear some news of Horatio, the baron de Palfoy having settled every thing with Dorilaus concerning his marriage with mademoiselle Charlotta, she was willing, she said, that as they were born on the same day, their nuptials should be also celebrated at the same time.

Monsieur du Plessis was obliged to content himself with this since he could obtain no more; and for a time every thing passed smoothly and agreeably on; but news after news continually arriving of the king of Sweden's ill success in Ukrania, rendered all the noble friends of Horatio extremely dissatisfied: — the public accounts were too deficient for their information of any particular officer; and as there were very few French in the Swedish army, they could hope for no intelligence of him but from himself; which, as he omitted giving, they at last concluded he was either killed or taken prisoner; which last misfortune they looked upon as equal with the former: — the Russian barbarity, and their manner of treating those whom the chance of war threw into their hands, was no secret thro' all Europe; and whichever of these accidents had happened, must be very grievous to a gentleman of Dorilaus's disposition, who, when unknowing he was his son, loved him with more tenderness than many fathers do their offspring, but now convinced not only that he was so, but also that he was possessed of such amiable qualities as might do honour to the most illustrious race, had fixed an idea in his mind of such a lasting happiness in having him near him, that the thoughts of being deprived of him for ever threw him into a melancholy, which not all the friends he had acquired in Paris, not all the gaieties of that place, nor the sweet society of the engaging and dutiful Louisa, had the power to console. So deep was his affliction, that monsieur du Plessis, amorous and impatient as he was, had not courage to urge a grant of his own happiness, while those who were to bestow it, were incapable of sharing any part of it.

Soon after there arrived a thunder-clap indeed: — certain intelligence that the once victorious Charles was totally overthrown, his whole army either cut to pieces or taken prisoners, and himself a fugitive in the grand seignior's dominions. — Dorilaus, now not doubting but the worst he feared had come to pass, shut himself from all company, and refused the unavailing comfort of all who came to offer it. — The fair eyes of Louisa were continually drowned in tears, and the generous du Plessis simpathized in all her griefs. But what became of mademoiselle Charlotta de Palfoy! her tender soul, so long accustomed to love Horatio, had not courage to support the shock of losing him; losing him at a time when she thought herself secure of being united to him for ever; — when his discovered birth had rendered her father's wishes conformable to her own, and there wanted nothing but his presence to render both their families completely blessed: — all that excess of love which modesty had hitherto restrained her from giving any public marks of, now shewed itself in the violence of her grief and her despair. — She made no secret of her softest inclinations, and gave a loose to all the impatience of a ruined love. Even the haughty baron was melted into tears of compassion, and so far from condemning, that he attempted all in his power to alleviate her sorrows.

CHAP. XXVI.

The Catastrophe of the whole.

POOR Horatio, released, as I have already said, from his worse than Turkish bondage, had now, with the companions of his misfortunes, left a country where they had suffered so much and had so little to hope, that their enlargement seemed even to themselves a miracle. — As they passed, miserable and forlorn, thro' those provinces where, about a year before, they had marched with so much pomp and force, as, together with the king of Sweden's name, inspired admiration and terror over all those parts of the world, it filled them with the most poignant anguish, and drew tears from those among them least sensible of any tender emotions.

All this disconsolate company, except Horatio, being Swedes, they made the best of their way, some to Stockholm, and others to Straelsund.[121] — Now left alone, a long journey before him, and altogether uncertain what reception he should find at Paris, either from Dorilaus or mademoiselle Charlotta, his condition was extremely pityable, and he stood in need of more fortitude than could be expected from his years, to enable him to go thro' it.

The nearer he approached Paris, the greater was his shock at the necessity of appearing there in the despicable figure he now made; but his courage still got the better, and surmounted all difficulties. If Dorilaus thinks my disobedience to his commands a crime too great to merit his forgiveness, would he say to himself, or Charlotta disdains, in his misfortunes, the faithful Horatio, I have no more to do than to return to Poland and seek an honourable death in the service of Stanislaus.

He made his entrance into that opulent city thro' the most bye-ways he could, and concealed himself till towards night in a little cabaret,[122] where having soon been informed where Dorilaus lived, he went when it was quite dark to his house, tho' how divided between hope and fear it is easy to imagine. He knocked at the gate, which being opened by the porter, and he desiring to speak with his master, was answered with many impertinent questions, as — who he came from, what his business was, and such like interrogatories which the sawciness of servants generally put to such persons as this fellow took Horatio to be by his appearance.

But he had no sooner desired he would tell Dorilaus he came from Russia,

---

[121] *Straelsund*: Stralsund, a Baltic port.
[122] *cabaret*: formerly, a drinking-house or pot-house (*OED*).

and brought intelligence of Horatio, than his tone of voice and behaviour was quite changed. — Our traveller was now carried into a parlour and entreated to sit down, and the late surly porter called hastily for one of the servants, bidding him, with the utmost joy, run in and inform his master that here was a person come from Russia that could give him news of colonel Horatio.

This a little raised the lately depressed spirits of Horatio, as it assured him his name was not unknown in that family, nor had been mentioned with indifference.

He attended but a very little time before he was shewed up into Dorilaus's apartment, who was just opening his mouth to enquire if Horatio were yet living, and in what condition, when he saw it was himself. Surprize and joy rendered him incapable either of speaking to him, or hearing the apologies he was beginning to make for having disobeyed his commands: — but he fell upon his neck and gave him an embrace, which dissipated all Horatio's fears, and left him no room to doubt if his peace was made.

No words were exchanged between them for a considerable time, but — oh my dear son, my ever loved Horatio, on the one side, my more than father, patron, on the other: — at length the tumultuous rapture of so unexpected a meeting and reception, giving way to a more peaceful calm, — Dorilaus made Horatio relate all the particulars had happened to him; and when he had ended, now, said he, I will reward the sincerity I easily perceive you have made use of in this narrative, by acquainting you, in my turn, with secrets you are far from having any notion of, and which, I believe, will compensate for all your sufferings, and make you own, that while you seemed to groan under the utmost severities of fortune, she was preparing for you all the blessings in her power to give, and even more than your ambition aimed at. But I have first a message to dispatch, continued he; at my return you shall know all.

With these words he went out of the room, but came back in a moment, and, after renewing his embraces to Horatio, revealed to him the whole secret of his birth, with all had happened to Louisa till the time of their happy meeting in Paris.

With what pleasing wonder the soul of Horatio was filled at this discovery, is much more easy to conceive than describe, so I shall leave it to the reader's imagination to guess what it was he felt and spoke on so extraordinary an occasion. While he was pouring out the transports it occasioned in the most grateful thanks to heaven, and his new found father, Louisa entered, Dorilaus having sent to the baron de Palfoy's, where he knew she was, to let her know a messenger from Russia was arrived with news of her brother: — they instantly knew each other, tho' it was upwards of four years since they were separated, and in that time the stature of both considerable increased: — nothing could exceed the joy of these amiable twins: — never was felicity more perfect, which yet received addition on Horatio's part, when Louisa told him, that it was as much as Charlotta could do to restrain herself from coming with her to hear what account the supposed messenger had brought.

Dorilaus on this immediately sent to let her know his son was well, and expected in Paris the next day, for he would not suffer him to appear before her, or the baron, till a habit was made for him more agreeable to his condition than that he arrived in. It is certain that the impatience of a lover would have made Horatio gladly wave this ceremony, but he would not a second time dispute the commands of such a father.

But wherefore should I delay the attention of my reader, who, I doubt not, but easily perceives by this time how things will end: so I shall only say that the meeting of Horatio and Charlotta was such, as might be expected from so arduous and constant an affection: that every thing having been settled between the two fathers at the time they sent their joint mandates to call him home, there now remained nothing but to celebrate the long desired nuptials, which was deferred no longer than was requisite for preparations to render the ceremony magnificent.

The generous du Plessis and his beloved Louisa were also united on the same day; and it would be hard to say which of these weddings afforded most satisfaction to the friends on both sides, or were attended with the most happy consequences to the persons concerned in them.

By these examples may we learn, that to sustain with fortitude and patience whatever ills we are preordained to suffer, entitles us to relief, while by impatient struggling we should but augment the score, and provoke fate to shew us the vanity of all attempts to frustrate its decrees.

FINIS.

PART II

A Letter from H— G—g, Esq.

NOTE ON THE TEXT

The first edition of *A Letter from H— G— g, Esq.*; was published in November 1749, though dated, as was usual, for the following year. This edition, BL 1203.a.15 (7), is the copy-text. A second edition of 1750 was a reissue of the first. Patrick Spedding judges another 'second edition' of 1750, where the number of pages has been reduced from 63 to 48, to be a piracy. Researchers may like to be aware that this is the edition reproduced on the JISC database. The spelling of proper names has been regularized, and the long 's' (f) replaced with 's'.

A
LETTER
FROM
H---- G----g, Esq.;

One of the Gentlemen of the Bed-Chamber to the Young
Chevalier, and the only Person of his own Retinue that
attended him from *Avignon*, in his late Journey through
Germany, and elsewhere;

CONTAINING

Many remarkable and affecting Occurrences which happened
to the P— , during the course of his mysterious Progress.

TO

A PARTICULAR FRIEND.

Victrix fortunæ sapientia.   JUVENAL.

LONDON

Printed, and sold at the *Royal-Exchange, Temple-Bar,*
Charing-Cross, and all the Pamphlet-shops of *London* and
Westminster. 1750.

(*Price* One SHILLING.)

Victrix fortunæ sapientia: 'Wisdom is the conqueror of fortune', Juvenal, *Satire* XIII, l.20.

THE
EDITOR's PREFACE
TO THE
READER.

*A*S it may seem strange to some People how a Letter of this Nature stole into
the World, I think proper to acquaint the Reader, that it never reached
the Hands of the Person for whom it was intended, and fell into mine by a meer
Accident, which was this.

Happening to be lodged in an Apartment which had been lately occupied by a
Gentleman of almost the same Name with myself, a single Consonant making all
the Difference, and whose Affairs, as I have since learnt, had obliged him to leave
the Kingdom, this extraordinary Packet was delivered to me instead of him, which
I accordingly opened, and soon perceived the Mistake.

Finding the Perusal presented a great Variety of surprizing and interesting
Occurrences that befel the young Chevalier[1] *since his absconding from* Avignon,[2]
I was tempted to publish it in order to gratify the Curiosity of the Town, which
I observe has been raised pretty high on account of that adventrous Wanderer.
But then, the whole Tenour plainly shewing it was wrote only to oblige a much
trusted and valued Friend, and never intended for the Press, I knew not how far
I should stand excused to the Author, (should a printed Copy ever reach him)
for making so bold with what was none of my own. This Punctilio kept me from
doing any Thing with it for some Days, and probably it had still lain dormant,
if on consulting some Friends, I had not been persuaded, that the Regard owing
to me from the Public *ought not to be overbalanced by the Fears of displeasing*
any particular Gentlemen, especially one who is known to me only by Name and
Character, and whom it is not likely I shall ever be better acquainted with.

This Consideration at last determined me; and I have nothing farther to say,
than that the Reader may assure himself I send it abroad exactly as I received
it, not a single Word being added or diminished, excepting three lines in one
Paragraph, which the Printer thought improper to be inserted, and were indeed
of little Consequence to the subject Matter.

---

[1] the *young Chevalier*: Charles Edward Stuart (1720–1788), eldest son of James Francis
Edward Stuart (1688–1766) and Maria Clementina, *née* Sobieska, princess of Poland (1702–
1735).

[2] absconding from *Avignon*: Prince Charles secretly left the Apostolic Palace at Avignon in
February 1749.

A
Letter from *H— G—g* , Esq;[3]

DEAR SIR,

It is now many Months since I had the Pleasure of writing to you: — What must your Thoughts have been of this seeming Neglect! Certainly the most favourable Construction you could put upon my Silence, while ignorant of the real Cause, must be, that I was no longer an Inhabitant of this earthly Globe: — I shall therefore esteem it as not the least of those unnumbered Obligations I owe to the Goodness of my R— and most dear Master, that I am now permitted to let you know you still have a Friend, who lives to love, and serve you.

You may remember my last, which I doubt not but came safe to you, as I sent it by Mr *L—* , informed you, that I was under some Apprehensions the P— would not reside for any Length of Time at *Avignon*, but I then little imagined he would quit it so suddenly, as I soon after found the Circumstances of his Affairs obliged him to do.

You must have heard, as I perceive all the foreign Papers were full of it, with what Privacy his R— H— departed from *Avignon*, but cannot have been acquainted with any Thing material concerning him since, the Precautions he took having been so effectual, that a very small Part, even of the Tour he has made, has been discovered; but, after passing through various Climates, crossing huge Tracts of Land, and some of Sea, he is at present where he has less Necessity of concealing himself, and I do not doubt but, before this reaches you, all *Europe* will be convinced *where he is*, though not *where he has been*, which, as well as the *Motives* of his Journey must be a Secret, till Time shall ripen those Things into *Maturity*, which as yet are but in *Embrio*. — But though I cannot, without rendering myself the most base of Men, give you that Account your Curiosity might wish, yet there are some Occurrences, that it will be no Breach either of my Faith, or my Duty, to acquaint you with, and which, I flatter myself, you will find interesting enough to content you, especially as you may

---

[3] H— G — g, *Esq.*: Henry Goring (d. ca. 1754), younger son of MP Sir Henry Goring (1679–1731), who was himself involved in the Atterbury Plot of 1721. The plot, centring on Francis Atterbury, Bishop of Rochester (1663–1732), aimed at the restoration of the Stuart king. The younger Henry Goring was noted in State Papers as having accompanied Charles Edward Stuart on his tour of Italy in 1737. A letter of March 1749 (N.S.) from Horace Mann to Horace Walpole describes him as the Prince's only companion after the departure from Avignon [see above, n. 2]. In April 1749, he was with Charles at Lunéville, in Lorraine, and in 1751 he was working on his behalf in Prussia. By June 1752, however, he and Charles exchanged angry letters about the Prince's affair with Clementine Walkinshaw (c. 1720–1802), and he finally resigned from Charles's service in May 1754. (See Andrew Lang, *Prince Charles Edward Stuart. The Young Chevalier* (London: Longmans, Green and Co., 1903), pp. 354–55; 374–87.)

be assured, that, though it does not become me to tell you the whole Truth; you shall hear nothing from me that is not Truth; but I think you have known me too long, and too well, not to render all Apologies superfluous, and that the Facts I have to present you with, ought not to be delayed by any Thing relating to myself.

About a fortnight before our Departure, a Gentleman, who called himself the Chevalier *La Luze*[4] arrived at *Avignon*. — He was received by the P— with such extraordinary Marks of Distinction, and was so often shut up with him in his Closet, as gave us all Reason to believe, the Business he came upon must be of a very important Nature; and also that he was employed in it by some Persons to whom his R— H— thought himself obliged to testify the highest Respect.

As Curiosity is in a more or less Degree inherent to all Mankind, especially in Things wherein we imagine our Interest concerned, we, about the P— , had too much Zeal for the Success of his Affairs, not to be desirous of fathoming the Mystery this Stranger's Visit seemed to have in it. We knew he was no Subject of *Great Britain*, because he understood not one Word of *English*, and though he spoke *French* and *Italian* perfectly well, yet it was easy to discover by his Accents neither of these Languages were natural to him. Few of us but had the Opportunity of entertaining him, whenever the P— happened to be otherwise engaged; but, though he conversed with us in a very free Manner, yet his Discourse turned always on ordinary Affairs, never dropping the least Hint that could give us any Light into the Matter we were so anxious to know something of. — Some of the Domesticks were ordered to sound a Lacquey who came with him, but the Fellow either was, or seemed to be, as ignorant as those who questioned him, and only said, that, being hired at *Lyons*, he knew nothing of his Master previous to that Time. — Could we have been able to have discovered of what Country he was, or of what Power a Subject, we might, perhaps, have formed some probable Guess on what Sort of Negotiation he was sent; but the former being an impenetrable Secret, the latter, of Course, must be so too.

Though no Man that ever lived could behave with more Courtesy and Affability to all beneath him; though his every Command is delivered with an Air with which others would entreat, there is notwithstanding a certain Dignity in the Looks, Voice, and whole Deportment of the P— , which renders it impossible, even for the most audacious to presume on the Familiarity he vouchsafes to treat them with. — As he never thought fit to mention any thing concerning the Chevalier *La Luze*, none of us about him durst do it in his Presence: Mr *Kelly*[5] was the only Person who presuming on his Age, the

---

[4] *Chevalier* La Luze: from the Spanish *luz*, meaning light.
[5] *Mr* Kelly: George Kelly (1688–1747?), a Jacobite agent who joined the service of Charles Edward Stuart in 1744, becoming his sole secretary in 1747. (See Roger Turner, 'Kelly, George (*b.* 1688, *d.* in or after 1747)', *Oxford Dictionary of National Biography*, Oxford University Press, 2004; online edn, May 2006.) [http://www.oxforddnb.com/view/article/15297, accessed 2 June 2017].)

Merit of his long Services, and the Post he held under him, had the Courage to discover any Inquisitiveness on this Head. Being one Day in the P—'s Closet, he said to his R— H—, that he hoped the Arrival of this Stranger boded some Good. — Whatever his Business with me is, reply'd the P— very gravely — *you find I have not imparted it, and may therefore infer it is not of a Nature to require the Advice of Counsel.* This Rebuff silenced him entirely, and he told Sir *J — s H— n*,[6] myself, and some others, that he would never more attempt to pry into any thing his R— H— did not communicate of himself.

As I have since had good Reason to be assured the whole Success of this Negotiation in a Measure depended on its Privacy, it has not seemed strange to me, that a P— so naturally prudent and sagacious, should be more than ordinarily reserved on a Matter of such high Importance; but, not to detain your Attention with any farther Particulars of the Suspence we were in, I must inform you that the Person who occasioned it having received some Dispatches by a Courier, the Contents of which he immediately imparted to the P— took his Leave, and we had as little notice of his Departure, as we had of his Coming.

The ensuing Day the P— seemed more contemplative than usual, but in the Evening some of the principal Nobility of *Avignon* coming to sup with him, on an Invitation before made to them, he behaved in their Company with an unaffected Gaiety and Sprightliness as I cannot remember without some Astonishment, when I reflect at the same Time what great Designs must then of Necessity be rolling in his Mind; yet this is but a slight Instance compared with some others I have to present you with, how great a Command this illustrious Person has over himself, and how easy even the most difficult and dangerous Enterprizes sit on his Thoughts.

These Guests were no sooner retired than he went into his Closet, where in a few Minutes I was ordered to attend him. — After having by his Command shut the Door, *G — g*, said he, *I have found that of late, not only what I do, but even the very words I speak, have been reported through all the Courts in* Europe, *to the great Detriment of my Affairs*; not, continued he, after a little Pause, *that I suspect any who are now about me, of Treachery, or wilfully injuring a Person whose Fortune they at present follow; but an excess of good Will and Zeal for the Cause to which they are attached, may make some People discover Things that for its real Service had better be concealed. — As a Matter of the most important Nature is now upon the Tapis,[7] I am determined not to be betrayed in it, or to know at least by whom I am so — I shall therefore confide but in one Person, and that one shall be You.*

His R— H— in speaking these Words had his Eyes fixed intently on my Face,

---

[6]   *Sir J — s H— n*: James Harrington (dates of birth and death unknown), member of Charles Edward Stuart's household and one of his chief confidants.

[7]   upon the Tapis: see *FF*, n. 3.

where doubtless he beheld Astonishment and Joy pictured in every Feature.

Indeed, my dear Friend, I was perfectly confounded at so unlooked for, so unhoped a Condescension — I threw myself at his Feet, I embraced his Knees, and kissed the Hand, which he graciously stretched out to raise me with most unfeigned and warmest Transports of a duteous Love, Loyalty and Gratitude; but could find no Words suitable to express my Thanks. — My Soul was too much overwhelmed, and yet I know not but in these disjointed Phrases I was alone capable of uttering, if he was not more fully convinced of the high Sense I had of his Goodness, than he could have been by the most eloquent Professions.

I have a great Opinion, said he, *of your Fidelity and Discretion; there is, however, no Occasion to inform you at present any farther than that I go hence to morrow — be ready to attend me by Break of Day, and be cautious that nothing escapes you, which may give the least Suspicion of my Departure.* — I then attempted to make some Protestations of an inviolable Secrecy in the Discharge of every Trust his R— H— should be pleased to honour me with, and asked if he had no other Commands preparatory to our Departure; to which he replied with his accustomed Sweetness, that every Thing would be taken Care of, and saying the Night was far spent, bad me to retire to take what Repose the Time permitted.

I was not so punctual in my Obedience to this last Injunction as to the others, for besides my Head being too full of what I had just heard to give Way to Drowsiness, it did not a little Puzzle me in what Manner I should prepare for this Journey, as I knew not the length of it, nor could form any Guess at the Time of our Return. — The Privacy with which it was to be taken, however, made me think there would be no Opportunity of conveying any great Store of Baggage; I therefore set about packing up in the smallest Compass I could such Things as Decency would not suffer me to be without. — I had but just finished when the P—'s first *Valet de Chambre* knocked at my Door, and on my opening it, asked if I was ready, — I told him I was, and took up my Portmanteau; but he would not suffer me to carry it, saying, he would see it safely stowed, and that his R— H— expected me in his Apartment. — I used no farther Ceremony, but immediately went where I was commanded.

I found the P— quite dress'd, and humming an *Italian* Air as he walked backward and forward in the Room — *Well, G — g,* said he, smiling, when he saw me enter, *we have a fine Morning, and I doubt not but shall have a pleasant Journey — I hope you leave nothing behind you that may make it seem otherwise — for I fancy we shan't see Avignon again in haste* — These Words put me in a little Confusion, as I perceived by them he had been told of a Lady for whom I had indeed some slight Regard, and which our Gentlemen had magnified into a real Passion. The change of my Countenance made his R— H— laugh heartily; and though I said all I could do to assure him, as I might do with a great deal of Truth, that no Attachment whatever could make me regret one Moment any Command his R— H— should be pleased to lay upon me, yet he continued his Pleasantry on that Subject with the greatest *Gaieté de Cœur*, as the *French* term it, till the *Valet* came in, and said every Thing was prepared. *'Tis well*, replied the P— , and went hastily down Stairs. I followed into the Court-Yard of the Palace, where a travelling Chaise, and three Horses for our *Escorte* waited. His R— H— obliged me to sit by him in the Chaise, the *Valet*, and two Domesticks out of Livery mounted on Horseback, and with this Equipage we set forward towards *Lyons*.

We passed for *French* Officers, who, on the Conclusion of the Peace[8] had obtained Leave to visit our Friends; and the Postilion having Orders to stop for Refreshment only at the most obscure Houses, we had gone through good Part of this Journey without falling in with any Company to whom the P— was known, till arriving at a small Village two Leagues short of *Lyons*. Just as we entered the Yard of the Inn another Chaise arrived with one Gentleman in it, who proved to be the Marquis de *Valere*. — The P— and he alighted at the same Time: — They immediately knew each other, and naturally advanced, but the P— fearing he would accost him with the same Ceremonies he had been accustomed to do at *Paris*, said to him in a low Voice, Monsieur le Marquis, *I rejoice at this Opportunity of embracing you; but I travel incognito, and you will oblige me to know me here only for the Count* D'Espoir.[9] The Marquis assured his R— H— that he would take care nothing should drop that might make any Discovery of his real Dignity: — He seemed not at all surprized, nor indeed had he any Room to be so, that a P— , while in the Territories of a Power who had treated him so unworthily,[10] and who was still labouring to get him removed to as great a Distance as possible, should desire to be concealed. This was, however, a Subject too ungrateful to be touched upon, and no Mention was made of it on either Side.

They supped together, and did not separate till it was very late. Their Conversation happened more through Accident than Design, to fall on the Principles of Government, and in what consisted the true Happiness both of those who ruled, and those who obeyed — Being entered on this Subject, which I soon perceived was a favourite on with the P— , he by Degrees became more

---

[8]   *the Conclusion of the Peace*: the Treaty of Aix-la-Chapelle, of October 1748, that ended the War of the Austrian Succession.

[9]   *the* Count *D'Espoir*: from the French *espoir*, meaning hope.

[10]   *the Territories of a Power who had treated him so unworthily*: Under the terms of the Treaty of Aix-la-Chapelle (1748), England would make peace if Charles Edward Stuart was expelled from France and its dominions. Prince Charles resisted all attempts to persuade him to leave the country, including orders from his father, James. He was finally arrested by the French authorities, bound hand and foot, and committed to a dungeon on 10 December 1748. Goring and Harrington were sent to the Bastille. McLynn describes the events as 'the scandal of the decade' (p. 350).

particular, and confined his Remarks to the Affairs of those Nations for whose Glory and Prosperity he is the most nearly concerned.

I thought I had heard and seen enough of my R— Master to be ignorant of none of those great Talents Heaven has so bounteously endued him with— he had given the most public Proofs of the Greatness of his Courage in the extremest Dangers — of his Fortitude under Hardships more severe than any P— , or perhaps than any Man, but himself ever sustained — of his unequalled Clemency even to those, who breathed nothing but Wishes for his Destruction, — These Virtues not even his worst of Enemies are able to deny him the Merit of; and all we who have the Honour to be near his Person have been Witness of innumerable Instances of the Kindness and Benevolence of his truly R— Mind; we knew also that he had read much, delighted in History, particularly in that of *England*, but were not sensible, at least I was not, till this happy Opportunity, how perfectly he had made himself Master of the Laws and Constitution of those Realms, which he is doubtless not without Hope, that he may one Day rule — How deeply he enters into the Interest of the People, and how just his Notions are of kingly Duties.

He maintained, among other Things, that the Glory of a Sovereign was the Opulence of his Subjects, not in amassing Treasures for the Use of himself and Family. — That Avarice disgraced a Throne; and added, that nothing was more surprising to him than that any crowned Head could be guilty of it. — *A private Person*, said he, has the Excuse *of providing for his Family*; but the Children *of a King are the Children of the* Public — *they have their Appointments and their Dowries from the* Public, *and he has only to procure such Alliances for them as promise to afford most Advantage to the* Public — *A King therefore*, continued he, can never be *too* liberal *of his own* Money, *nor too* frugal *of the* Public.

All Kings, said he, *in general, would do well to follow this Rule; but those who wear the Crown of* Great-Britain, *to which so large a Revenue has of late Years been annexed, ought more particularly to observe it — the* English *are naturally kind-hearted, loving, and ready to give even beyond their Abilities, when they are made to believe the Necessities of the Government require it — it would therefore be most ungenerous and cruel in a Prince to oppress them with exorbitant Taxations on pretended Exigencies.*

He farther said, that a King ought not to imagine the Sceptre was put into his Hand merely to enforce Obedience, but should rather consider, that the Doves upon it are Emblems of the Love he owes to the Nations under him, and should never be extended in any Act that has not a Tendency to their Welfare — As all *Honorary Titles*, and great *Offices of State* are solely in his Disposal, it should be his Care to make the *One* the *reward* of *Merit*, and to confer the Other on Persons, whose *Integrity* as well as Abilities, should render incapable of abusing the Trust reposed in them — That he should beware of giving an implicit

Credit to the Report of any Minister, or Ministers, but have his Ears open to the Complaints of all his Subjects.

It would certainly be a Digression you would readily forgive, if my Memory served me to repeat all that this admirable P— said on a Theme so important to every Friend of Liberty, and Lover of his Country — He set forth the Excellence of the Constitution in its native Purity, and condemned all the Encroachments had been made on it by Princes who impoliticly as well as ungenerously, had aimed at arbitrary Power in Terms too pathetic not to convince any one that his Heart was the Dictator of his Tongue.

The Marquis was charmed with hearing him, and, perceiving he had concluded what he intended to say, cried out in a Kind of Rapture, *How noble! how glorious are these Notions of Government! — Heavens, What Blindness! What Infatuation misleads the ********** reject a ********** Great* and *Happy.*

To this the P— modestly replied, that he but repeated the Maxims his R— l Father had inculcated in him from his most early Years, and the Truth of which his own Reason and Observation had since abundantly convinced him.

There are few Things at which the P— testifies more Uneasiness than to hear himself praised — the lavish, though just Encomiums, the Marquis would not be hindered from making on him, occasioned him, I believe, to take Leave and retire to his Chamber, sooner than otherwise he would have done, for he never was a Friend to much Sleep, and did not go to Bed in two Hours after: We set out, however, betimes the next Morning, and passing through *Lyons* without stopping, went to a small Town about two Leagues further, where the P— shut himself in his Chamber, and passed the greatest Part of the Night, as I afterwards found, in writing Letters. In the Morning, when every Thing was ready, as I imagined, for prosecuting our Journey, he gave Orders to the *Valet* to go back with the Chaise and little Train that attended it, as far as *Grenoble*, and wait there four Days, at the *Expiration of which*, said he, *if you do not see or hear from me, return directly to* Avignon, *and deliver this to Mr* Kelly, *and tell him I expect he will be punctual in obeying the Contents, part of which are, that all my People shall have the same Appointments, and Tables as if I were there in Person.* With these Words he put a large Packet into his Hands.

'Tis impossible to represent the mingled Surprize and Grief that appeared in the Face of this honest Domestic: — He had doubtless flattered himself with the Hope of attending his R— H— through the whole Course of his mysterious Progress, and he had not Presence of Mind to conceal the sudden Shock of this Disappointment; he threw himself at the P—'s Feet, and begged to know if he had any Way offended his R— H— ; the P— assured him that he had not, and that on his Return to *Avignon* he would shew that he had not, and permitted him to kiss his Hand, on which the poor Man appeared somewhat better satisfied.

After he was gone, and none but my self left with the P— ; well, *G — g*, said he, pleasantly, *I have now no body but you — how shall we order it? Can you play the Barber, and shave me?* I told his R— H— I had small Skill that Way, but I would do the best I could; *it shall not need — Servants are to be had in every Town in* France. *Speak to the Host, and he will easily procure a Post-Chaise, a Valet de Chambre and a Lacquey.*

I found it as his R— H— said, and in two Hours we were provided with a new Retinue, with which we set forward the same Day, and took the Route to *Dijon*, where we no sooner arrived than this Equipage was dismissed, and another taken, with whom we proceeded to *Nancy*, and thence to *Strasburg.* — Here, to my very great Astonishment, the P— was met by the Chevalier *la Luze* — it appears an Agreement had been made between them, and our Postilion had Orders to drive to that House, where he was to attend our coming, and he had taken Care to provide an Apartment for his R— H— , much less unworthy of receiving him than any he had lain in since his Departure from *Avignon*.

I now found, by Circumstances which could not be hid from me, that the Title of Chevalier *la Luze* was only assumed to conceal a Character of much greater Note; and that he, who was distinguished by it, was a Person whose extraordinary Talents had gained him the Confidence of one of the wisest Princes in *Europe.* — This Discovery of the real Name and Quality of the pretended *la Luze* enabled me to form some Conjectures, not only concerning the Place to which he was to conduct us, but also of the Motives which induced the P— to take this Journey; but as these Conjectures of mine came pretty near the Truth of an Affair, which my R— Master thinks it necessary to be kept an impenetrable Secret to all but those engaged in it, you will not wonder at, nor blame me for not acquainting you with them. To Time alone, my dear Friend, and certain Contingencies, must be left the unravelling this Mystery, and I must shortly be obliged to leave a Chasm in my Journal, which, though you may regret, I am satisfied you will forgive on the Score that occasions it. — I have not, however, yet done with *Strasburg*, where an Accident detained us a Day longer then the P— intended, and which I may relate without the least Breach of the Trust I am honoured with.

I cannot, in what I am about to say, be suspected of Flattery, because it is scarce possible the illustrious Person, of whom I speak, will ever come to the Knowledge of what, in the Fullness of my Soul, I cannot forbear imparting to you; but, upon my Honour, it seems to me, as if Heaven, foreknowing the P—'s Constancy of Mind, and the absolute Command he has over all his Passions, permitted the Seducer of Mankind to throw Temptations in his Way, in order to give him an Opportunity of proving those Virtues, which, though most admire, few are able to imitate.

Some People might think the Adventure I am going to relate deserved not so serious a Prelude, or, perhaps, that it was not of Importance enough to be inserted at all; but I know to whom I write, and should be under no Apprehension, that the minutest Circumstances, in which the P— has any Share, will be esteemed light or trifling. — But to the Business.

A Fire happening to break out in a House directly opposite to that where we were lodged, and was also an Inn, the P— , who either was not asleep, or was soon awaked, jumped out of Bed, and, without calling for any Body to assist him, got on his Cloaths and flew down Stairs. — Some of the Family, meeting him, told him he need not have disturbed himself, there was no Danger, as the Street was very broad, and the Wind drove the Flames the other Way: *What then*, cryed this truely Christian Hero; *Are we born to take Care only of ourselves?* With these Words he flew, as I was afterward informed, rather like an incorporeal Being than one composed of Flesh and Bones, to the Place where the Mischief seemed to rage with the greatest Violence. — The first Object that presented itself to him, amidst that Scene of Horror, was a Woman from a Window screaming for Help. — The Room behind her seemed all a Conflagration; the P— , seeing no other Remedy, called to her to jump out, which she instantly did, and he, stretching out his Arms, received her without any Hurt.

While the P— was thus employed, I, who likewise had been rouzed with the Cry of Fire, though somewhat less early than my Master, ran directly to his Chamber in order to give him Notice of the Danger, for I knew not but that the Accident might be in the same House, and, finding the Door open and the Bed empty, I was turning out of the Room to make some Enquiry, when I met him with the above-mentioned fair Burden in his Arms. — She was naked to her Shift, and Night-dress upon her Head; to prevent her therefore from taking Cold, the P— laid her into the Bed he had lately quitted, and wrapt her in the Coverlids. — She all this while knew not the tender Care he took of her. — The excessive Terror she had been in, on Account of the Fire, had so much overwhelmed her Spirits, and from the Time of her escaping the Danger, had been insensible of every Thing.   Yet far from taking Advantage of the Condition she was in, her generous Deliverer thought of nothing but the Means of recovering her from it. It is impossible to express his extreme Caution as he put her into the Bed, to avoid every Thing that might have shocked her Modesty, had she been capable of knowing what he did. — It is certain, that to act in this Manner, is no more than what a Man of Honour ought to do, though I know not whether every Man of Honour would be able to do it, especially if he was of the P—'s Years, had the same Vigour, and was of the same amorous Complection; and I believe you will own, that the Temptation was such as required a more than ordinary Virtue to withstand; you will find it, however, weak when compared to that, which this Adventure afterward was productive of; but of that in due Time. — I ran, by the P—'s Command, and fetched some

Water in a Bason, which he sprinkled on her Face; on this she opened her Eyes though very faintly, but spoke not a Word.

In this Instant the Chevalier *la Luze* came into the Chamber, and beheld a Scene, which was afterwards the Subject of much Pleasantry: A young, and, Spite of her present Disorders, a very beautiful Lady in the P—'s Bed: He, upon his Knees by the Side of it, supporting her as she lay with one Hand, and with the other chaffing her Temples, — I waiting behind, like the Apothecary on the Physician. — There was no Opportunity for Speech; the Mistress of the House, having heard what had happened, came with a Glass of rich Cordial, and desired the P— to force it into her Mouth, if she was not in a Condition to receive it willingly, and at the same Time to bend her gently forward; his R— H— obeyed the Orders he received with so much Success, that the fair Patient recovered her Speech in a few Minutes, though not her Senses perfectly. — *Good God!* cryed she, looking wildly round *where am I? — Where have I been? — Was I not going to be burned, and did not Heaven send an Angel to my Relief?* — These, and some other Expressions, which, though incoherent, were uttered with a good deal of Strength and Energy, shewed the P— the good Effects of the Pains he had been at; he therefore quitted his Post, and, after recommending the Care of her to the Mistress of the House, went out of the Chamber; the Chevalier *La Luze* and myself followed, and the P— , having ordered a Bed to be prepared for him in another Room, while it was getting ready, we all went to take a View of the Fire, which, they told us, burned with less Vehemence than it had done, and we saw totally extinguished without any farther Damage than consuming one Wing of the House where it began.

So much of the Night had been taken up with this Accident, that it was very late before any of us were stirring. — After the first Salutations were over, the Chevalier *La Luze*, all Politician as he is, could not forbear being very merry on the P—'s Assiduity to the naked Lady: *Well, well*, replied his R— H— , *all your Railery shall not hinder me from inquiring how she has past the Night, after an Accident, that might have shocked the most courageous of her Sex.*

He was just going to send a Servant on that Occasion, when the Mistress of the Hotel came in, and told the supposed Count *D'Espoir*, (for he continued to pass by that Name) that the Lady, he had so happily preserved, begged he would give her an Opportunity of making him those Acknowledgments which were due to the extraordinary Care he had taken of her. She had scarce ended what she was about to say, when the Chevalier *la Luze* cried out, *is she still a naked* Venus? — *No Sir*, answered the good Woman, *all her Baggage escaped the Flames, — she has sent for it, and is dressed, and looks like a* Venus *indeed*. The P— , to prevent any farther Discourse on this Head, said he would attend the Lady that Instant.

By his Command we accompanied him, and were received with a great deal of Politeness by the Lady; but being told to which of us she owed her Redemption, addressed herself to her Protector in a Manner that shewed she had the highest Sense of the Obligation he had conferred on her; the Answers he made were such as might be expected from one who is so justly esteemed by all who know him the most accomplished Prince on Earth. I will not therefore take up my Paper with any Repetition of them, and only tell you, that the great Complaisance with which he always treats the fair Sex, seemed to me to be heightened by the Air, which accompanied all he said to this Lady. I thought too, that he was less uneasy at the Praises she gave to the Gallantry of his Behaviour on her Score, than ever I had seen him before, when any Attempt was made to do Justice to his Merit, though it were even in those Things for which he was most desirous of Applause.

It is certain I have not seen many Women who could boast more Charms: Her Person was extremely lovely, her Air noble and majestic, and, though her Years could not exceed sixteen or seventeen, she had a certain Ease and Freedom, in her Conversation, which is very rarely attained at that Age. — It was easy to perceive the P— felt an extraordinary Satisfaction in reflecting on the Service he had done so amiable a Lady; and that also he took some Interest in her Affairs, or he would not have asked her any Thing concerning them at a Time when his Mind was so much engrossed by those of the highest Importance relating to himself. The Lady was very communicative; She told us she was the Daughter of an eminent Merchant at *Lyons*; that her eldest Sister being married to a Banker at *Heidelberg*, she had been to pass some Months with her, and was now returning home; that she had no other Company with her than an old Woman, who had nursed her in her Infancy, and ever since attended her, *and for whose Sake*, added she, *I shall be obliged to stay some Time at* Strasburg, *the poor Creature being bruised by a Fall she got in escaping from the Flames, that she is at present incapable of travelling.* The P— on this, expressed some Regret that the Necessity of his Affairs obliged him to prosecute his Journey the next Day, which he then told her had been delayed only by the Accident of the preceding Night. *I must be strangely insensible*, said she, not to wish the Continuance of a Protection I have so *happily* experienced, on which the P desired, that, to prove the Sincerity of her Words, she would permit him not to lose Sight of her the only Day in which he could hope to enjoy that Happiness.

She readily complying with this Request, Dinner was ordered to be served up in the next Room: the Conversation was extremely lively. I never saw his R— H— more gay and spirituous: But I perceived that as his Vivacity encreased, that of our fair Companion became less. — Her Countenance betrayed she had Emotions in her Mind which she vainly laboured to conceal. — To beguile the Hours till Supper, Cards were called for, *Quadrille*[11] was the Game, and the

---

[11] Quadrille: a trick-taking card game for four players.

P— and she held Hands together; but she seemed so absent to what she was about, and committed so many Mistakes, that she lost his R— H— every Game. Conscious of her Incapacity of playing, she pretended to have no Relish of that Diversion: After such a Declaration it would have been the utmost Unpoliteness to have continued it. — We left off, but her Confusion still remained, — never sure did a few Hours produce so total a Change in the Deportment of any one Person! — She seemed fearful of looking towards the P— , yet had not the Power of restraining her Regards: — She answered the fine Things he said to her with a Hesitation which was far from being natural to her. — Whether he saw into the Cause of this sudden Reverse I cannot pretend to say, but we who were less interested were at no Loss to guess at it. — All the Afternoon, and during the Time of Supper, she was still the same; the P— pleasantly reproached her with having repented the Condescension she had made him, and told her he fancied she had Ideas in her Mind, which the Company she was in deprived her of the Pleasure of indulging. I do not well remember what Answer she made, but know it was of a Piece with her late Behaviour. — I perceived however that she endeavoured all she could to assume a more cheerful and composed Air, but the Constraint she put upon herself in doing so, only served to discover more plainly the Secret of her Soul. — In fine, finding herself unable to conceal her Agitations, she rose, and withdrew to a Window, the Curtain of which was let down: The P— soon followed, but what he said to her, I know not, but imagine it was somewhat extremely tender, for the Curtain being half pulled back by his going behind it, we saw him kiss her two or three Times; it was not however half a Minute before he led her back to her Seat; — he sat next her, and now drew his Chair more close than before. — She blushed, she trembled, and gave all the Symptoms of a Passion too potent to be controlled; — the P— too by a certain Languishment in his Eyes, made me imagine he would not be displeased to have an Opportunity of a more particular Conversation with her. — The Chevalier *la Luze* was of my Opinion, and, starting up as if something of Moment had just then come into his Head, went out of the Room, beckoning me to follow. — I did so, and we took a walk in the Gallery, believing that if the P— desired our Return, he would either call, or send for us; but we had scarce Time to make any Reflections on this Head before we saw his R— H— coming towards us. *I thank you*, said he, *for reminding me, that it was Time to break up Company, since the more early we go to Bed, the more early we shall rise. I assure your R— H— ,* replied the Chevalier la Luze, *I had no such Thing in my Thoughts, on the contrary, the Night is not so far elapsed, but that some Hours might have been devoted to the Service of a Lady, who, 'tis very plain, would have omitted nothing on her Part to make the Time pass agreeably.* I know nothing of that, cried the P— , *but suppose she were inclined to carry her Gratitude for the Service I did her, even to the Pitch you hint at, would it not have been ungenerous in me to have accepted the Reward? — You talk*, cried the Chevalier, *as there were no Allowances to be made for Love and Inclination. I am no Stoic*, answered that P— , *but I have always been taught that Pleasures, how* pardonable *soever they may be in themselves, become* highly Criminal *when indulged to the Prejudice of another. — The Lady I have just parted from is young, beautiful, and I believe innocent: — She may make some deserving Man extremely happy. — It would then have been an Action unworthy of my real Character, under a feigned Name to rob her of her Innocence; — to ruin, and then to abandon her for ever, for you know it suits not with the Circumstances of my Condition to enter into any Engagements of that tender Nature she has a Right to expect from the Count* D'Espoir. — *I know not, indeed*, added he, *how far I might have been lost in the soft Infatuation, had not your leaving us rouzed in me a just Sense of what I owed to her and to myself, for which I again thank you, though you meant it otherwise.*

The Chevalier *la Luze* listened with the utmost Astonishment all the Time the P— was speaking, and perceiving he had done, cried out, *ah! how fit is he to govern others, who knows so well how to govern himself! The most irresistible Impulse of Nature yields to your superior* Virtue.

I believe, Sir, you will own this was an Act of Self-denial not very easy to be parallelled. — History, indeed, tells us of an *Alexander*, who withdrew from beholding the dangerous Beauties of the Wife and Daughters of *Darius*; and of a *Scipio*, whose Virtue got the better of his Inclination for the *Capuan* Fair;[12] but neither of those Heroes were tempted like my P— , they, for the Accomplishment of their Desires, must have had Recourse to that Power which the Fortune of War had given them: *He*, to gratify his Passion, had only to accept what the fond Charmer even languished to bestow.

If I have been a little more circumstantial than you may think was necessary in this Part of my Narrative, you must forgive me, as I was willing to give you as exact a Picture as I could of an Incident which I can never remember without Admiration. — But I have now done, and shall proceed to Matters of a far different Nature.

Some Time after our Arrival at *Avignon*, a Person, who had the Appearance of a Gentleman, tho' somewhat reduced, came to the Palace, and sollicited the Gentleman about the P— to intercede with his R— H— to give him some Employment, saying he was a Native of *England*, was born in *Lancashire*, where he had an Estate, his Name *Blarthwaite*, and that he had joined the Army at *Carlisle*. — He was told by as many as he addressed on this Score, that what

---

[12] *History, indeed, tells us of an* Alexander... *his Inclination for the* Capuan Fair: Alexander the Great's refusal to see the wife and daughters of Darius in case he should be tempted by them, and Publius Cornelius Scipio Africanus's mercy towards the women of New Carthage (not Capua), were both widely cited instances of clemency in time of war. The first appears in Plutarch's *Life of Alexander*, 21, and that of Scipio in Polybius's *Histories*, 10.18. 'The Continence of Scipio' is the subject of more than a dozen Renaissance paintings.

he sought was a Thing absolutely impossible to be granted, every Post in the little Court the P— kept at that Place, being already filled up with Persons who neither could, nor ought to be displaced; yet, notwithstanding this, he watched an Opportunity of speaking to the P— himself, who, remembering nothing of his Name, or Face, asked whether he had bore any Commission, or was a private Man, and to what Corps he had belonged? To which he answered, that being unwilling to be with the *Scots*, he had served only as a Volunteer, that on their coming to *Manchester*, he intended to have applied for a Lieutenancy, but was taken Prisoner by some of the Country People, who threw him into Prison, where, after having lain upwards of two Years, he found an Opportunity of making his Escape. — He added many bitter Complaints of the Hardships he sustained, and said he had no Resource but the Compassion of his R— H— . The P— I believe did not give much Credit to this Story, especially that Particular of his having been taken Prisoner in *Lancashire*, he never having heard of such an Accident happening to any of his People in that Part of the Country; but, however that might be, the Distress of the Man was a sufficient Claim to his Generosity; he gave him ten Pistoles, bid him come and eat at the Palace while he remained at *Avignon*, but wished him to seek out some Means of Support, as it was not in his Power to provide for him in his Houshold.

Sir *James H— n*, who, from the beginning fancied he saw something in the Looks of this Fellow which contradicted his Pretences, remonstrated to the P— , that as there was the highest Reason to believe him an Impostor, there was also Reason to believe he might be a Spy, and that therefore it was unfit he should be suffered to come about the Palace. *Such a Thing may be*, replied the P— , *but we are not certain of it, — we know only that he is in Want, and I had rather relieve an hundred Enemies, than deny to any one Friend whatever Assistance is in my Power to grant.*

After this no more that I heard was said on the Occasion, and the Man dined regularly every Day at one or other of the Tables of the P—'s Domesticks, till all at once he left off coming without taking Leave of any one.

You may, perhaps, think it strange that I have run back to *Avignon* to fetch thence a Circumstance of this Kind, but will soon change your Opinion when you shall know how far the Conjectures of Sir *James H— n* were verified, and the dreadful Consequence with which it had like to have been attended, had not the all-directing Hand of Providence interposed.

The Morning we left *Strasburg*, happening to be walking in the Court-yard of the Hotel, I was surprised with the Sight of this very Fellow, whom since his Disappearance at *Avignon* I had never thought on; he seemed earnest in Discourse with one of the Grooms belonging to the Stables; but having a Glimpse of me, turned hastily away, and was presently out of the Reach of my Eyes, though I made towards him as fast as I could.

I asked the Fellow if he had any Knowledge of the Person, that had just left him, on which he answering in the Negative, I further questioned him concerning what Discourse they had together, he told me it was about a Horse he wanted to hire; *but I believe, added* he, *the Man is mad, for before I could give him any Answer, he ran away as if he were frighted.*

I thought there was something very odd in this, and it was my Duty to acquaint the P— with it, but he seemed not to look upon it as a Matter of any Moment; only said he was sorry the Man had seen me, because it might be a Means of discovering he was there himself.

We crossed the *Rhine* that same Day, lay at a small Village in the Palatinate,[13] and arrived at *Dourlach*[14] the next Night: but I shall not enter into a Detail of our several Stages, nothing material happening till after we had passed the city of *Wirtzburg*,[15] when we were met by five Men masked, well mounted and armed, who, without speaking a Word, all at once discharged their Pistols into the P—'s Chaise, and certainly not all his miraculous Escapes in *Scotland* ever equalled this: One of the Bullets lodged in the back Part of the Chaise just above his Head, another went through his Hat, and a third grazed upon his Breast, without any other Mischief than taking off one of the Buttons of his Coat; the others were so ill directed, that they were lost in the Air; the Horses took fright at the firing, and were running away with the Chaise; but his R— H—, with a Presence of Mind, which few Men would have had on the like Occasion, immediately jumped out, and at the same Time plucking a Pair of Pistols out of his Pocket, as he never went without, discharged them at the Assassins with so much Success, that one of them fell dead that Instant, and another was wounded, — then drawing his Sword, he sprung forward and seized the Horse of a third by the Bridle, and with a Strength and Agility scarce to be credited, dismounted the Rider and threw him on the Earth. In this Action he was in Danger of being cleft down by the Sword of another, but the Chevalier *la Luze*, who, as well as myself, had followed the P—'s Example, and fought on Foot, had the good Fortune to wound that audacious Wretch in the Arm, lifted against a Life so dear to Heaven. I also at the same Instant reached the Heart of him the Prince had thrown as he was attempting to rise; as for our Servants, they afforded no other Assistance than to run in among the Enemy, and keep them from maintaining any regular Fight. — What the Issue would have been Heaven only knows, if a sudden Interruption had not happened, the Appearance of a Gentleman, attended by two Servants, who came galloping up with drawn Swords, on Sight of whom the Villains thought it best to betake

---

[13]   *the Palatinate*: the Palatinate of the Rhine, one of the territories of the Holy Roman Empire.
[14]   Dourlach: Durlach, now a borough of the city of Karlsruhe, on the French-German border.
[15]   Wirtzburg: Würzburg, a city in northern Bavaria.

themselves to Flight, those of them, I mean, who had the Power of doing so, for two of them were fallen; on plucking off their Vizards, we discovered, that one was not quite dead, and that he who was so was no other than that Monster, who had been relieved by the P—'s Bounty at *Avignon*, and whom I had seen since at *Strasburg.* — His R— H— demanded of him, who had Breath, what Motive had induced him, and his Company to seek the Lives of Travellers, who could no Way have provoked their Malice? To which the Fellow in broken Accents replied, that he, with two others, had been hired only as Assistant in this Enterprize; — that the Persons chiefly concerned were one of those that fled, and that Man who lay dead. — *They told us*, continued he, *that we were to kill a Gentleman, who had done them an Injury, described You, and ordered us to aim only at You.* — The Wretch closed this Confession with entreating Heaven's Forgiveness, and immediately expired.

The P— stood looking on the dead Bodies in a profound Reverie, till the Stranger rouzed him from it, by congratulating his happy Deliverance. — Though his R— H— had nothing in his Habit to distinguish him from us, whom, in order to avoid giving any Suspicion, he always treated as his Equals during this Journey, yet it was remarkable, that, in the whole Course of it, every one addressed him as the Principal, which shews, that native Dignity stands in no Need of exterior Ornaments to command Respect. — The Gentleman, to whose seasonable Interruption we were so much indebted, said little less on this Occasion, excepting the Title, than he would have done had he known the P— for what he is.

This Gentleman, who was perfectly polite himself, was so charmed with the P—'s Person and Behaviour, that he would needs go with us, though somewhat out of his Way, to the next Village, where we were obliged to put up, in Order to have those slight Hurts examined, which the Chevalier *la Luze*, and myself had received in the late Skirmish.

Mine was, indeed, so small a Scratch that it was scarce worth troubling the Surgeon for a Plaister, but that of *la Luze* was pretty deep; the P— , though the most exposed, and the only Person aimed at, had not the least Mark of Violence about him, which occasioned the Stranger to use some Expressions in regard to the peculiar Care Heaven took of him, which, as he was far from guessing who the Person was to whom he spoke, seemed the Effects of a Divine Inspiration.

As it is natural for Travellers, who fall into Conversation on the Road, to ask how far, and to what Place they are going, the Stranger put that Question to the P— , who made no Scruple of telling him we intended for *Leipsic*, but maintained the same Character and Name he had assumed at leaving *Avignon*, that of Count *D'Espoir*, a *French* Officer.

The other, in his Turn, informed us that he was a Major in the Army of the

Empress Queen;[16] that he, as well as the supposed Count *D'Espoir* pretended, had taken the Opportunity, given him by the Peace, to visit some Friends he had in different Parts of *Germany*, and was now going to *Hanover*, where he had an Uncle in the *Romish College founded by his late *Britannic* Majesty.[17] — Here he took the Opportunity to toast the Memory of that Monarch in a Bumper, which the Prince made no Scruple to pledge without the least Emotion; nor was it any Matter of Surprize to me to see him do so, because I had always observed, that far from having any Malignity to that Family which at present wears the *British* Crown, he had testified the highest Disapprobation of any Discourse or Writings which had a Tendency that Way. But the Chevalier *la Luze*, who was less acquainted with the Excellence of his Nature, could not forbear afterwards making the greatest Encomiums on it.

We all lay in the same Inn that Night, and early in the morning set out, the Major for *Hanover*, and we for *Leipsic*, where being arrived, the pretended Chevalier *la Luze* threw off that Name, and appeared in his own Character, but the P— was still known only by that of Count *D'Espoir*.

Hitherto, Sir, I have been pretty punctual in my Journal, as to the different Stages of this Part of our Progress, which, as you will find, were sometimes irregular, and out of the Road, which ordinary Travellers would take: I must acquaint you, that this was done to avoid passing through some Towns where the Chevalier *la Luze* would have been known, it appearing there was no less Reason for his being concealed than that the P— himself should be so.

And now, my dear Friend, I must have done for a Time with any further Particulars of the Tour we made, and content myself with relating such Passages, during the Course of it, as I think worthy your Attention, while I draw a Veil over the Places in which they happened, and the Persons concerned in them.

And first, I must inform you that we lost the agreeable Society of the Chevalier *la Luze*, who, having executed his Commission in conducting the P— to a certain Court, on his R— H—'s quitting it, which was after a Stay of ten Days, was obliged to take his Leave, but not without testifying the highest

---

[16] *the Empress Queen*: Maria Theresa (1717–1780), Holy Roman Empress by marriage, and ruler of the Habsburg dominions after the death of her father, Holy Roman Emperor Charles VI, in 1740.

* [Original note:] 'The Editor, who is no Traveller, thought it so strange that a *Protestant* Prince should build a College for *Romish* Priests in his own Dominions, that he would not suffer this Part of the Paragraph to be inserted till he had informed himself more fully of the Truth of it, and been assured by the Testimony of several Persons who have been at *Hanover*, that his late Majesty, soon after his Accession to the Throne of *Great Britain*, had in Reality erected a fine College for *Romish* Priests, which he has endowed with large Privileges.'

[17] *the* Romish *College founded by his late* Britannick *Majesty*: George I's father, Ernst August of Brunswick-Lüneburg (1629–1698), had sanctioned the founding of a Jesuit mission, but his son in fact closed it down in 1711. (See Colin Timms, *Polymath of the Baroque. Agostino Steffani and his Music* (Oxford: Oxford University Press, 2003), p. 102.)

Sense of the Honour and Happiness he had enjoyed in the Conversation of the P— , more dignified by his uncommon Virtues than by his illustrious Birth.

During our short Sojourn here, the P— was lodged at the House of this Nobleman, and passed on the Family as a Person of Condition, who travelled for his Amusement. — The Interviews he had with those he came to treat with were extremely private, and I have all imaginable Reason to believe no less satisfactory to each; and the Business then negotiating being compleated, or in such a Way as was tantamount to a Completion, the P— , attended only by myself and two Servants, set out on a second Journey, much longer than the first. After passing through the Territories of several Powers, some Friends, some Enemies, his R— H— , without shewing himself to the one, or being discovered by the other, at last embarked in a small trading Vessel bound for a Port, where he knew himself impatiently expected, having, some Time before, dispatched a Messenger to notify his Coming, and had been prevented from making that Expedition he intended by some cross Accidents in his Way, such as the Difficulty of procuring Passes in some Towns, and waiting for the Exchange of Bills in others, which lost us, in the whole of the Route, several Days.

But the Protractions we suffered by Land, were nothing, compared to those we were obliged to submit to by Sea. — An unclouded Sky, and favourable Gale flattered our Hopes on setting out, but, like the deceitful World, which often puts the fairest Colours on the most foul Intents, soon was the smiling Prospect changed into one all dark and gloomy. — We were not, according to the Sailors Computation, above four Leagues from Shore, before the Weather began to grow haizy, and by Degrees thickened into so intense a Fog, that we could make little or no Sail, and what we did had like to have been fatal to us, for the Compass being of no Use, the Ship lost her Course, and struck upon the Sands: — The Captain cryed out, in the utmost Consternation, that we were lost, if we did not immediately get off, for he now found where we had drove; and that there were so many Eddies, and Whirlpools, that it was impossible to escape. — The P— , who was upon Deck, never wanting Presence of Mind, especially in Time of Danger, called to them to shift the Ballast, and, seeing they made less Haste than he thought the Exigence required, ran down, and began the Work, and animated by his Example, they all laboured so strenuously, that the sinking Side of the Vessel presently righted by the whole Weight being thrown on the other. — As you have seen one Scale in a Balance fly up, on any Thing ponderous being thrown into the other. — And thus we were delivered from the most eminent Danger, the Captain assured us he had ever been in, though forty Years a Sailor.

The Fog dissipated, the Wind rose, but happened not to be in that Point of the Compass we wished. — We had, however, Time to replace our Ballast before it blew hard, which it soon after did, in so much that we were obliged to humour it and steer directly contrary to our intended Course, in order to have Sea-room, and get far enough from these dreadful Sands we had so lately escaped; but the Storm encreasing gave us Reason to apprehend we had only been reprieved, and were not yet secure from the many Perils of that uncertain Element.

I will not trouble you with any Description of the Danger we were in, which, indeed, was such as I cannot make you sensible without acquainting you in what Seas they overtook us, it shall therefore suffice to say, that the Vessel being utterly disabled from combating any longer with the Fury of the Winds, we were obliged to endeavour (as the Sailors phrase it) to make Land at any Rate, which at last we did, to the great Satisfaction of every one except the P— , who, having been the least alarmed at the Danger, shewed himself the least elated with the Deliverance.

It is certain his R— H— had more Reason than any one, except myself, apprehended, to damp the Joy he might otherwise have felt, seeing himself in Safety; for besides the Disappointment of his Voyage, I must inform you, that the Country we were thrown upon belonged to those whom he had good Cause to know were not well affected to him, and that if he should by any Accident be discovered, the Consequence could not but have proved the greatest of Misfortunes; — he was therefore obliged to put a Constraint on himself, which, considering his natural Disposition, was the most mortifying that could be, that of keeping always in his Chamber, and never stirring out either for the Benefit of the Air, or the Satisfaction of his Curiosity — Several of the Gentry of those Parts hearing, I suppose, from some of the Ship's Crew, that a *French* Count had put in there by Stress of Weather, came to pay their Compliments to him on that Occasion; and this unwelcome Politeness gave us a good Deal of Trouble; the P— had no other Way to avoid seeing them than to feign himself indisposed, which was a very severe Mortification, especially as it was necessary to carry on the Deception even to his own Servants, who might otherwise, not only have thought there was some Mystery in his hiding himself in this Manner, but also as he could not depend on their Taciturnity in this Point, which, if divulged, might have occasioned Speculation in wiser Heads.

I was every Day in the Port inquiring of the Workmen, who were refitting the Ship, concerning the Time in which they imagined she would be ready to put to Sea, and found, that though they laboured almost Night and Day, it would take up to a Month, or five Weeks, to render her in a Condition for sailing.

I cannot say but his R— H— expressed somewhat more Impatience on this Account than I had ever heard him on any other, yet it was no more than what the Necessity of his Affairs might well excuse. — He commanded me to seek out if there was no Vessel ready to sail, bound for the Port he wished; I did so, but there was not any, nor like to be in a much longer Time than our Captain assured his own would be refitted.

It is one of the distinguishing Characteristicks of his R— H— , that he is indefatigable in his Endeavours for the Removal of every Impediment to his Designs, and on finding those Endeavours fruitless, to content himself with having done all that human Prudence could suggest, and wait with Patience for a more favourable Juncture. — In this Event, which was cross enough, as it threatned the Ruin of an Affair, which I will venture to inform you was of the most Importance he had ever been engaged in, since his glorious, though unfortunate Expedition into *Scotland*,[18] he exerted the Philosopher, and, after the first Day, uttered not the least Murmur against Fortune, but amused himself either with drawing out with his Pencil little Sketches of the Prospects presented him from the Windows, or with reading some Books which I procured for him in the Town.

Among other I brought for his Perusal, was a Treatise, in *French*, called *l'Ecole des Roys*.[19] The Prince had no sooner cast his Eyes on the Title, than he cryed out, *Ah! G — g, that must be Adversity; and happy would it be for the World if all its Rulers had been brought up in that School, they then would know how to commiserate the Misfortunes themselves have experienced, and be convinced, that the Dignity they enjoy is not given them for their own Sakes, but that of others.*

I could not here forbear saying something on this Head, which occasioned his R— H— to reply in the following Terms.

I would not, said he, *presume too far on the Strength of my own Resolution, but I think it is not in my Nature either to do, or permit to be done, any Thing oppressive, or unjust, even to the meanest Subject; and, as Power must sometimes be delegated, I would frequently make a Tour through the Provinces I should govern, by which Means I should have the Opportunity of hearing, in Person, what Grievances were complained of, and the inexpressible Pleasure of redressing them: — I hope I should remember I was King of the* Peasant *as well as of the* Peer; *and that the one had an equal Right with the other to be protected by me.*

I must write you a Volume instead of a Letter, if I pretended to repeat half the fine Observations his R— H— made on every Thing he read. You have been sufficiently informed by much better Judges than myself of the Greatness of his Capacity, and want not to be told of his Merits, but the Fortune which is likely to attend them — I shall therefore proceed to give you such Satisfaction as I am able, or that is permitted me to reveal.

Instead of five Weeks, as the Captain at first flattered himself, and us, it was

---

[18] *his glorious, though unfortunate Expedition into* Scotland: The Jacobite Rebellion of 1745, in which Prince Charles landed at Eriskay in the Western Isles in July 1745, and reached as far south as Derby in December. His army was finally routed at Culloden in April 1746.

[19] l'Ecole des Roys: an invention of Haywood's: no such work existed in 1750.

seven abating two Days before we put to Sea. — Our Voyage, however, was now as prosperous as before it had been the reverse; the Reverse, I say, as we at that Time thought, though in Effect every Delay in the Prosecution of it was a Mark of the peculiar Care Heaven seems to take for the P—'s Preservation.

We had no sooner landed, and got into a House, whence after taking some Refreshment, his R— H— proposed to go up into the Town, than we were told a Gentleman desired to speak with the two Strangers, that had just entred. This a little surprised the P— , and on the Person's being admitted, he was not the less so, tho' far from being troubled at seeing Mr *Macdonald* of *Lochgary*,[20] whom he thought had been one of the Number of those that fell at *Culloden*. After the first Testimonies of the most gracious good Will on the one Side, and Duty on the other, his R— H— asked by what Miracle he had escaped, having, as he thought, seen him fall dead before his Face? To which he replied, that his supposed Death was the Preservation of his Life; for being buried, as it were, beneath a Heap of Slain, he avoided the real Fate, which would doubtless have otherwise been inflicted on him. — *I live*, continued this faithful honest Man, *and have double reason to thank Heaven for my Deliverance, since in coming hither to seek my Bread, I have had the inexpressible Blessing of doing my ever dear, and R— Master some little Service.*

He then proceeded to inform the P— that on hearing of some Regiments which were forming in that Kingdom, he had come thither with an Intention of entring into some one, or other of them, — that, on his Arrival, he happened to lodge in the same House with two Men, who pretended to be Merchants. As they dined together every Day at a common-Table, one of them taking Notice that he was a *Scotchman*, asked him several Questions concerning the P— , as to what Part of the World he was in, what occasioned his leaving *Avignon* so suddenly, and on what new Enterprize he was now embark'd? — to none of which he, *Macdonald*, had it in his Power to answer, though had he been never so well acquainted with all they desired to know, he should not have communicated it; besides, he said he thought there was somewhat more than meer Curiosity in their talking to him in this Manner, resuming the Conversation, and still repeating the same Questions, though he had told them over and over he was intirely ignorant of every thing relating to the Person they mentioned; therefore he sounded them in his Turn, and affected even to rail against a Cause which he said had been the total Ruin of his Country.

Poor Mr *Macdonald* could not come to this Part of his Narrative, without imploring the P—'s Pardon for the Injustice his Lips had been guilty of.

---

[20] *Mr* Macdonald *of* Lochgary: Lieutenant-Colonel Donald Macdonell of Lochgarry, effectively in command of MacDonell of Glengarry's regiment after Col. Angus MacDonell was killed at Culloden on 22 January 1746. (*Muster Roll of Prince Charles Edward Stuart's Army 1745–46*, ed. Alastair Livingstone of Bachuil, Christian W. H. Aikman and Betty Stuart Hart (Aberdeen: Aberdeen University Press, 1984), p. 149.)

Necessary as it then seemed to him, and afterwards proved to be so, but the P—
bid him go on and relate what Effects this Deception produced.

Much greater than I expected, replied he, *for I acted my Part so well, that they
believed my Principles the direct opposite of what I have profess'd, and what I think
it my Glory to maintain. — On this,* pursues he, *they grew very communicative,
— told me they had good reason to believe your R— H— was here, for they were
informed by one who knew you well, that you travelled under a feigned Name;
that you had lately been at* Hamburg, *had received a considerable Remittance
there, and was embarked for this Port. — This very much alarmed me, — I knew
not but that their Intelligence might be true, and, no longer doubting if they were
Spies, thought it my Duty to carry the Discovery I had made to ***.*
Here he mentioned a Name, which you must excuse me from repeating.

I had some Difficulty, went he on, *in executing this* Design, but, on assuring
the Secretary that I had an Affair of *the utmost Importance to impart, I was at
last admitted to his Presence. — I could perceive he was a good deal startled at
what I related, that he dissembled it as much as possible, probably suspecting I
was myself a Spy, but on my acquainting him with my Name, Country, and the
Post I once had the Honour to hold in your R— H— 's Army, he had the Goodness
to treat me very graciously. — By his Command I continued to behave to the
Men as I had done; and, as he said he knew not but you might soon visit those
Parts, ordered me to watch the coming in of every Vessel, and give you Notice,
and conduct you with all Privacy to a House he hired. — He added that to seize
these Fellows would make too great a Noise, and might be attended with bad
Consequences at this Time.*

I flatter myself, continued Mr Macdonald, *I need say nothing to convince your
R— H— with what Diligence I obeyed the *'s Commands; I was scarce ever out of
sight of the Harbour; the Men I found were no less busy in prying about the Town,
for they firmly believed you were here concealed, till after a Stay of six Weeks
from the Time of their landing, finding their Endeavours fruitless, they resolved to
depart, and it was but Yesterday they went on Board a Ship bound for* Hamburg.

The P— then ask'd Mr *Macdonald* of what Country the Men he spoke of
were? To which he answered, that the one he took to be a *Swiss,* the other a
Flemming; and that neither of them seemed to understand *English,* and that
the Conversation he had with them was in *French;* his R— H— appeared a
little pensive at first on the account, but he soon recovered himself; and Mr
Macdonald went to acquaint the * with his Arrival. On that Gentleman's Return
we all went on Foot for about a Mile, when on the turning of a Street a Coach
waited with the Door ready opened, we all went into it, and alighted at the
House prepared for his R— H— 's Reception.

During the Time of our Stay in that Kingdom, which was about three Weeks,
the P— was royally though very secretly entertained by the * and other Persons

of the highest Rank, who were interested in the great Affair depending.

The P— had the Satisfaction before his Departure to see the Fidelity of Mr *Macdonald* rewarded with a Captain's Commission in the Army. — We embarked at the same Port where we had landed, in a small Frigate, but well equip'd and manned, for *Coningsberg*;[21] and happily arriving there, he remained no longer than was necessary to send Dispatches acquainting some of his Friends in *Poland* how near he was, and then proceeded directly to the great Duchy of *Lithuania*. Here we were met by a *Palatine* nearly related to his R— H—[22] and several others of the highest Distinction among the *Polish* Nobility. — I shall give you no Description of the Particulars of the Reception they gave him, and only say it was suitable to his Merits, and the high Idea his Character had inspired in them. But that which most of all affected me was the Manner in which he was saluted by a very old Nobleman, who had served under the famous King *John Sobiesky* at raising the Siege of *Vienna* in the Year 1683[23] and, on hearing his R— H— was arrived, would needs in spite of his great Age accompany those, who came to testify their Love and Joy on that Occasion. He was scarce able to refrain pushing by those of a superior Rank, and be the first to pay his Compliments; and when his Turn came, with what Impatience in his Eyes, with what an incredible Vigour did the Transport of his Heart animate his long enfeebled Limbs! — Youth could not spring forward with more Fire, he rather flew than walk'd towards the P— , and, embracing him with the utmost Fervour, *How happy am I*, said he, *to hold once again in my Arms so worthy a Descendant of the greatest Hero that ever graced the* Christian *World!* — then pressing him again more closely than before to his Bosom, *dear P—* , cried he, *methinks I see in you a second* Sobiesky *rise, and now for the first Time regret, that I am old, because Death will too soon deprive me of the Pleasure of beholding you encircled with those Glories Heaven has certainly decreed for such exalted Virtues.*

The P— was greatly touch'd with that Warmth of Affection, which the Caresses of this old Lord convinced him were sincere, and made him such adequate Returns, as drew Tears of Satisfaction from the whole noble Company.

Among other Matters which furnished Table Conversation, they told the P— , That the foreign News Papers had carried his R— H— to *Bologna*, *Venice*, *Padua*, and several other Places in *Italy*; at which he laughed heartily, and said, *Aye, aye, my Enemies would fain send me on the other Side the* Alps, *but they will*

---

[21] Coningsberg: Königsberg, now the Russian city of Kaliningrad, a Baltic port.

[22] *a* Palatine *nearly related to his* R— H— : the Electors Palatine were related to the Stuart dynasty through Frederick V of Bohemia (1596–1632), who in 1613 married Elizabeth, daughter of James I of England and VI of Scotland.

[23] *had served under the famous King* John Sobiesky at raising the *Siege of* Vienna *in the Year 1683*: King John (or Jan) Sobieski III of Poland (1629–1696) successfully lifted the Ottoman siege of Vienna in September 1683.

find my Constitution will agree with Colder Climates.

The P— here reassumed that Gayety, great Part of which he had lost since his late unworthy Treatment by the Ministers of *France*: For besides the Society of Friends, who all endeavour to outvye each other in their Demonstration of Affection, here are fine Woods to hunt in, fine Gardens to walk in, and every thing that can amuse his less serious Moments.

But his R— H— here received an Addition to his Contentment, of a much more important Nature than any I have yet mentioned: He had an Interview with a more illustrious and firm Friend to his Person and Interest, and one of those most capable of doing him a real Service.

Their Meeting was at a fine Country Seat belonging to the noble Family of *Wizinsky*, about 10 Leagues from *Lithuania*. This Intercourse, as most others between them of late have been, was kept extremely private for many Reasons; but I am well assured, that in it an Affair that has long been depending was then finally determined; and which is of so high a Nature, as, when brought to Light, will astonish all *Europe*.

As I find there has been much Talk in the World concerning the P—'s Marriage,[24] you will doubtless expect some Information from me on that Head; I shall therefore venture to assure you, that all you have been told, or can be told for some Time, at least, concerning such a Thing, is wholly fictitious, and that you must hear many Things of him, before you can hear with any Certainty, that he is married. — Proposals have indeed been made, and Negotiations for that Purpose have been carried on by some of his Friends, but his R— H— has always declined making any Applications of that Nature. Himself — on the contrary, when any such Discourse came upon the Tapis, he has publicly declared, He never would seek to involve any Princess in the Misfortunes of his Family; and that it was his fixed Determination to beget no Royal Beggars.

This Resolution in his R— H— is variously spoken of; many applaud it as a Proof of his Magnanimity, and the Greatness of his Spirit; others again say, that how severe soever the Disappointments of his Family may have been, he ought not to deprive the World of a Race of future Heroes, who might possibly live to see more equitable Times, and not suffer a Name illustrious for several Hundred Years to be extinguished in himself; for his Brother is now out of the

---

[24] *there has been much Talk in the World concerning the P—'s Marriage*: Many possible marriages were considered by Prince Charles and his father James throughout the 1740s. In 1742–43 James explored the prospect of an alliance with a daughter of Louis XV. In exile, Charles suggested the Tsarina Elizabeth, daughter of Peter I. After losing French support Charles aimed for marriages that would raise his status or provide him with a Protestant alliance. Frederick the Great of Prussia was approached for the hand of his sister, and the landgrave of Hesse-Darmstadt for that of his daughter. At the same time Charles conducted adulterous affairs with Marie de le Tour d'Auvergne, by marriage Duchesse de Montbazon, and with Marie-Anne-Louise la Trémoille, by marriage the Princesse de Talmont. (See McLynn, pp. 323–24; 348–49.)

Question[25] — and some there are, who impute it either to a Disinclination to Marriage in general, or to a Want of Sensibility of the Merits of those Princesses, who may have been offered to him — But tho' I will not take upon me to decide which of the two former Opinions is most just, I can venture to aver from my own Knowledge, that those who maintain this last, are little acquainted with the P—'s Sentiments.

Believe me, Sir, he loves, and is beloved with an Affection rarely to be found between Persons of their exalted Station; and when ever his Affairs shall take a more favourable Turn, you will soon see it followed by a Union with a Princess of the highest, and most pure Descent, and who for personal Accomplishments, and every amiable Quality of the Mind, is equal'd but by few, and excelled by none in *Europe*. — In a Word, a Princess as worthy of him, as he of her.

I give you not this Character from common Fame alone, but from the Testimony of my own Eyes and Ears, having had the Honour to attend her twice with Dispatches from his R— H— . Consummate as is her Beauty, yet is that Beauty the least of her Perfections — . She has a Dignity, a certain Sanctity of Manners, as one of our best of our *English* Poets expresses it, that shines forth in every Thing she says, or does, and speaks at once the Greatness and the Goodness of her Mind — . Tho' the Commission, with which I was entrusted, gave me Reason to think myself entitled to a gracious Reception, that which I met with from this lovely young Princess was such, as exceeded all I could have hoped; and, while it shewed how very dear the Person, who sent me was esteemed by her, discovered at the same Time her own Sweetness, and Excellence of Nature to those beneath her— ; She accompanied the Answer she returned to my P—'s Letter with a Bracelet of her Hair, encompassed with Diamonds of great Value, and was pleased to make a Present of a Gold Snuff-Box, most curiously engraved.

It is certain that nothing can be a greater Matter of Astonishment to all those, who know the strict Union there is between the Hearts of these two incomparable Persons, than that any of the Considerations above named should be of Force to retard the Consummation of their mutual Wishes.

Since our Arrival here his R— H— has been strongly pressed on this score, by some, who perhaps think he would not be sorry to be over-persuaded in this Point; and by others, who are really of Opinion, that he ought not to wait the uncertain Issue of his Affairs for propagating his Name and Family.

I was one Morning in the P—'s Chamber, when in a full Levee the Conversation turn'd on no other Subject; but the P—'s Resolution appearing inflexible in spite of all that could be urged, the Palatine of * who is a near

---

[25] *his Brother is now out of the Question*: Prince Charles's younger brother, Henry Benedict Stuart (1725–1807), styled duke of York, ruled himself out of any possible Stuart succession by becoming a Cardinal in the Roman Catholic Church in 1747.

Relation to the P— started up, and said, with some Emotion, *His Majesty of Sardinia is much obliged to your R— H— ; he has after you, the first Claim to the Dominions of* Great Britain;[26] *he is ambitious, he is warlike, and doubtless would not be inactive in the Prosecution of his Pretensions. Nor would it be the Interest of* France, *or any other Power, who may envy the Glory of* Great Britain, *either by open Force, or underhand Contrivances to disappoint the Views of that Monarch.*

The Speech of the *Palatine* was seconded by another Nobleman of great Distinction, — *Manifestoes and Protests,* said that Lord, *have already been issued from that Quarter, on the first settling the Succession of those Kingdoms in the present reigning Family, and should your R— H— , which God forbid, dye without Issue, the Effects of those Representations would soon appear.*

I know nothing, replied his R— H— , *that would give me an Affliction adequate to that of imagining there was a Possibility that* Great Britain *should ever be reduc'd to the Condition of becoming a Province to* Sardinia; *but at present I can see no Room for any such Apprehensions — if the whole Line of the* Stuarts *were totally extinct, it seems to me a Thing impracticable that my Couzen of* Sardinia *should reap any Advantage from it — a War might indeed ensue — , a bloody one perhaps, and some Powers might interest themselves in the Cause, but I will never believe, that the People of* England, *who have so vigorously opposed all the Efforts, both of my* R— Father *and myself, in Support of the Family, they have made Choice of to reign over them, will be less warm in repelling an Invasion of any other Claimant whatsoever— . And if the Bulk of the Nation, that is the Nobility, and Gentry, whose Example influences the Nation, should grow desirous of a Change, and ready to repeal what they have done, I am not so old as to despair of enjoying in my own Person the Fruits of such a Change, to which the Success of my present Enterprize can be no Manner of Impediment — .*

Methinks I see the Surprise you are in at this latter Part of the P—'s Speech, because it serves to inform you, that the grand Affair, in which he is now engaged, is not of that Kind, which you, and many of his Friends have all along believed — , I do not tell you, that his R— H— has renounced all Thoughts of filling the Throne of his Ancestors; no — , on the contrary, I am certain, that to be seated thereon, with the Consent of the People, is the first, and dearest Wish of his Soul; but this may not hinder him from entertaining other Views in the mean Time, provided they are not inconsistent with it, nor beneath the Dignity of his Birth.

Though these Things may appear Ænigma's to you at present, yet a little Time, as I told you in the Beginning of this Letter, will sufficiently explain them.

---

[26] His Majesty of *Sardinia* ... has, after you, the first Claim to the Dominions of *Great-Britain*: Charles Emmanuel III of Sardinia, duke of Savoy (1701–1773) had a claim to the British throne through his great grandmother, Henrietta Anne (1644–1670), youngest daughter of Charles I.

And now, my dear Friend, I must hasten to a Conclusion of this long Epistle, which I could wish to have rendered more explicit; what I have said will however convince you that the P— took not such fatiguing Journies, and conducted them with the Secrecy he has done merely to amuse the World, or to drop any of those faithful Followers, who had risked their Lives, and lost their Fortunes in his Cause, or for any other of those mean and frivolous Views, which his Enemies would have believed, but for Ends truly noble and worthy of himself.

How long we shall continue here is so uncertain, as it depends upon Events, which are extremely so, that I dare not desire an Answer to this, lest I should give you a Trouble, without any Advantage to my self. — A little Time perhaps may make me more assured, and I shall then write again, in Hope of receiving what is one of the first Things in my Wishes, the News of your Health; and that there is like to be a Period to those Perplexities, which your Zeal in the Cause of Virtue alone has so long involved you in.

I am, *Dear Sir, Sincerely Yours*, &c.

H— G — g.

Lithuania, Sep. 13.

SILENT CORRECTIONS

The Fortunate Foundlings

p.29, l.24 he] she
p.37, l.4 of] off
p.39, l.22 affect] accept
p.58, l.17 randsom] ransom
p.66, l.6 she] She
p.76, l.18 madem] madam
p.88, l.39 Sweeden] Sweden
p.95, l.8 doubtless] doubtful
p.99, l.38, gaanted] granted
p.100, l.17 more than] more cause for concern than
p.126, l.32, instea] instead
p.127, l.9 incuring] incurring
p.135, l.31 satieted] satiated
p.137, l.1 heigtht] height
p.140, l.23 recempence] recompence
p.147, l.28 intelligance] intelligence
p.148, l.24 aud] and
p.155, l.28 neeessary] necessary
p.159, l.28 appartment] apartment
p.162, l.22 no were] no where
p.165, l.25 he] the
p.174, l.39 Charlotta's.] Charlotta's
p.180, l.23 woman] women
p.181, l.19 horsback] horseback
p.188, l.40 the mother] them other
p.191, l.4 greata] great a
p.191, l.10 to thought] to be thought
p.192, l.9 caanot] cannot
p.192, l.30 mustconfess] must confess
p.199, l.9 atempt] attempt
p.199, l.28 fastene don] fastened on
p.201, l.15 repliod] replied
p.207, l.15 toge] together
p.218, l.7 theo] thro'
p.218, l.19 iminent] imminent
p.222, l.2 said,] said she,

A Letter from H — G — g, Esq.

p.251, l.33, desired;] desired,
p.257, l.28, haveing] having
p.259, l.14, cerrtain] certain
p.260, l.35, Shall] I shall
p.261, l.35, Country,] Country.
p.266, l.17, *Adaantage*] *Advantage*

www.ingramcontent.com/pod-product-compliance
Lightning Source LLC
Chambersburg PA
CBHW070219030726

47505CB00006B/1730